Dawnthief

Dawnthief

CHRONICLES OF THE RAVEN

James Barclay

GOLLANCZ
LONDON

First published in Great Britain in 1999 by
Victor Gollancz
An imprint of Orion Books Ltd
Orion House, 5 Upper St Martin's Lane,
London WC2H 9EA

Second impression published in Great Britain in 2002 by
Gollancz
An imprint of the Orion Publishing Group

Distributed in the United States of America by
Sterling Publishing Co, Inc
387 Park Avenue South, New York, NY 10016-8810

A CIP catalogue record for this book is available
from the British Library

ISBN 1 85798 594 X

Printed in Great Britain by
Clays Ltd, St Ives plc

For Tara, who always believed
when sometimes even I did not.

No book is constructed in complete isolation and the path to this one contains many milestones, some way back in my youth. Here goes.

To my parents, who never once complained at the incessant tap of the typewriter throughout my school days and, well, for just being you. To Stuart Widd, an English teacher who encouraged imagination and expression. To Paul H, Carl B, Hazel G, Chris G, Robert N, and Ray C who unwittingly gave birth to The Raven many years ago, did any of us but know it at the time. To readers like Tara Falk and Dave Mutton who criticised and improved me at every turn. But most to Peter Robinson, John 'George' Cross and Simon Spanton (more Ravenites) for cajoling, bullying, ideas and encouragement all the way.

I thank you all for your love, help and support.

Cast List

THE RAVEN	*Hirad Coldheart* BARBARIAN WARRIOR *Ras* WARRIOR *Richmond* WARRIOR *Talan* WARRIOR *Sirendor Larn* WARRIOR *The Unknown Warrior* WARRIOR *Ilkar* JULATSAN MAGE
XETESK COLLEGE OF MAGIC	*Styliann* LORD OF THE MOUNT *Denser* SENIOR MAGE *Selyn* MAGE SPY *Nyer* MENTOR TO DENSER *Laryon* RESEARCH MASTER *Sol* A PROTECTOR
DORDOVER COLLEGE OF MAGIC	*Erienne* LORE MAGE *Alun* HUSBAND OF ERIENNE *Thraun* WARRIOR *Jandyr* ELVEN BOWMAN *Will Begman* THIEF *Vuldaroq* TOWER LORD
LYSTERN COLLEGE OF MAGIC	*Heryst* LORD ELDER MAGE *Ry Darrick* GENERAL OF THE ARMIES
JULATSA COLLEGE OF MAGIC	*Barras* CHIEF NEGOTIATOR
BARONS, LORDS AND SOLDIERS	*Blackthorne* SOUTHERN BARON *Gresse* SOUTH EASTERN BARON *Tessaya* WESMEN LORD *Travers* A CAPTAIN

North Bay
Sunara's Teeth
Sethe River
TERENETSA
Torn Wastes
PARVE
Baravale Valley
Arch-Temple of the Wrethsires
Eye Lake
LEIONU
Sky Lake
Garan Mountains
WESMEN HEARTLANDS
(Uncharted)
Southern Force
SOUTHERN OCEANS

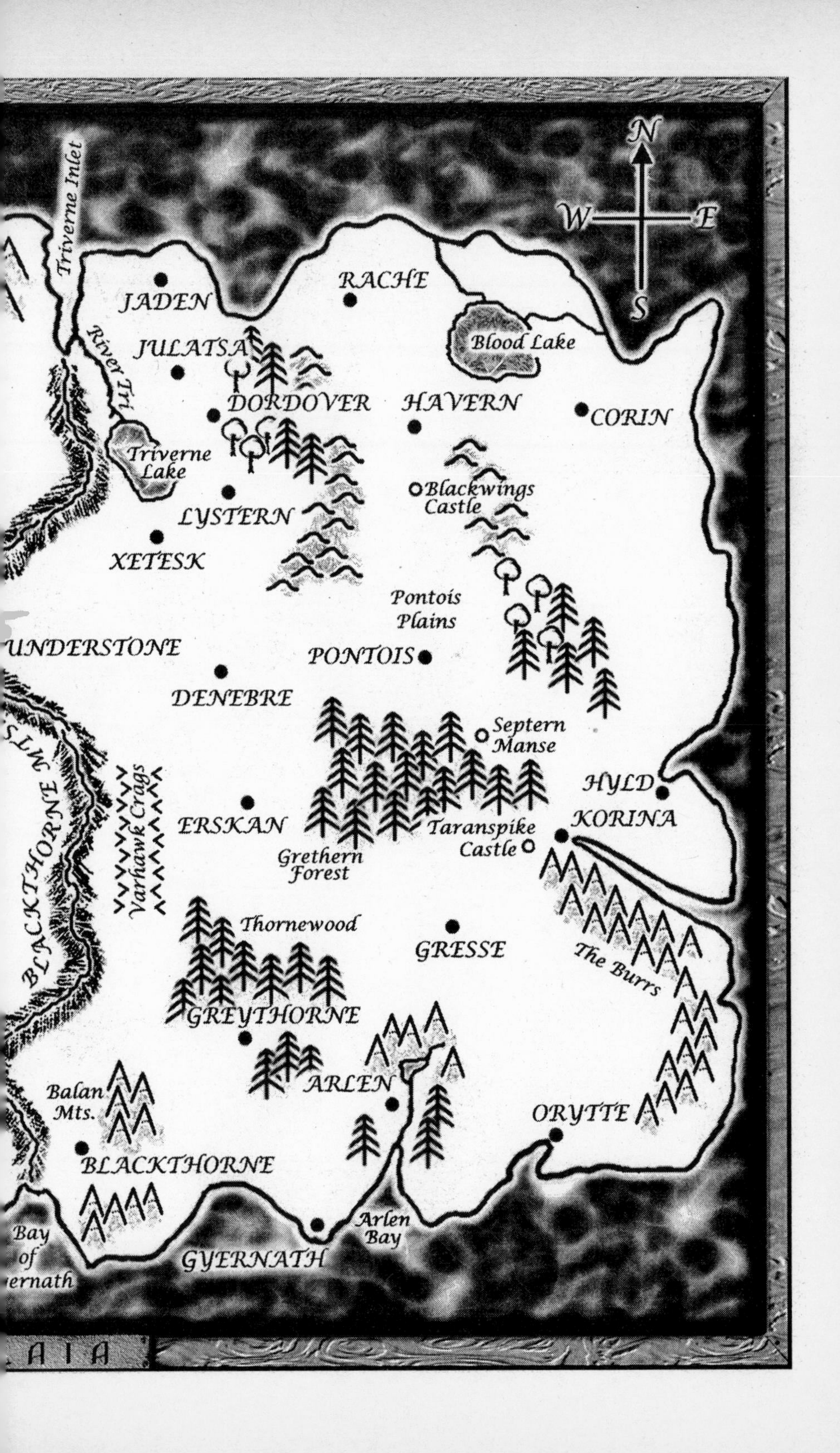

Triverne Inlet
N
W
E
S
JADEN
RACHE
River Tri
JULATSA
Blood Lake
DORDOVER
HAVERN
CORIN
Triverne Lake
Blackwings Castle
LYSTERN
XETESK
Pontois Plains
UNDERSTONE
PONTOIS
DENEBRE
Septern Manse
BLACKTHORNE MTS
Varhawk Crags
HYLD
ERSKAN
KORINA
Taranspike Castle
Grethern Forest
Thornewood
GRESSE
The Burrs
GREYTHORNE
ARLEN
Balan Mts.
ORYTTE
BLACKTHORNE
Arlen Bay
Bay of
ernath
GYERNATH
A I A

Prologue

The hand over her mouth stifled her screams as she awoke. Beside her in the bed, Alun was still. A face, shadowed by night, leaned into hers. She could make out his lean features and hard eyes. The hand pressed harder as her eyes bored into his.

'If you cast, your boys will die. If you struggle, your boys will die. If you don't co-operate, your boys will die. Your husband will remain as witness that we can take your kind from anywhere – even from the heart of a College City. Think on that while you sleep and curb your anger when you awake. We have a great deal to talk about.'

The thoughts crashed through her mind in time with the hammering of her heart. Her foolish determination to live a quiet life outside of the security of the College walls had put in jeopardy everything she loved. The man had mentioned her boys, her beautiful twin sons in whom she had so much faith and nurtured such great power. So young, so innocent. Her body quailed as she fought against the thought of what men such as these might do. They had no compassion. They saw what they believed to be evil and had vowed to destroy it. They didn't see the purity and the magic of what she was creating and their blindness made them so dangerous.

Voices struck notes of caution in her mind. The Masters of the College, who had sympathised with her desire for family life but had warned against the complacency of comfort in times when people could be open in their animosity towards the College and all for which it stood. Hers was an experiment, the Masters had reminded her, it was not a simple desire to settle down. Her children were children of the College, they had said, and their development was critical research.

But, as usual, she had had her way. After all, they were *her* sons and Alun had no wish to live in the College. She cursed herself for her stubborn stupidity and for her overconfidence in her ability to keep them all safe. Tears of frustration and anger welled up but they, like the voices of the Masters in her head, were echoes of warnings that were ignored too long and were heeded too late.

The man's other hand came across her vision. It was clutching a cloth which he pressed against her nose and mouth. The drug took swift effect and her struggle was that of an animal caught in a trap as the dogs close in. Futile, desperate, short. Brophane. The last thought through her mind was how ill she would feel when she opened her eyes.

Chapter 1

Blue light seared across the late afternoon sky, flaring against the broken low grey cloud and throwing the sheer opening of Taranspike Pass into sharp relief. A heavy explosion sounded. Men screamed.

The Raven made a calm assessment of the situation, looking out from the castle which controlled the pass, across the courtyard and on to the battlefield from their vantage point high up on the keep.

The left-hand end of the defensive line had been shattered. Bodies, burning and broken, were scattered across scorched grass and the enemy redoubled their efforts all along the battle front. They surged.

'Damn it,' said The Unknown Warrior. 'Trouble.' He raised a clenched fist above his head, spread his fingers then whirled his arm in a wide circle. Instantly, the flagmen in the turrets signalled the order. Five cavalrymen and a mage galloped out of a side gate.

'There. Look.' Hirad pointed towards the devastated line. Perhaps fifteen men were running through the gap, ignoring the battle as they rushed towards the castle walls. 'Are we in?' he asked.

'We're in,' said The Unknown.

'About time.' Hirad smiled.

'Raven!' roared The Unknown. 'Raven with me!' He swept his two-handed sword from the scabbard leaning against the ramparts and charged over to the steps, chest plate catching the dying rays of the sun, his massive frame moving with a speed and agility that remained a fatal surprise to many and his shaven head bobbing on his bull neck as he started down at a dead run.

The stairs led down from the ramparts along the inside of the wall before joining the roof of the keep. From there the way to the courtyard was through either one of the two turrets and down their spiral stairways.

The Unknown led the six leather- and chain-clad warriors and one mage who made up The Raven to the left-hand turret, threw the door open, barked the guard aside and took the stairs two at a time, leaning into the outside wall to steady himself.

Halfway down, a second, bigger explosion sounded, shaking the castle foundations.

'They're through the courtyard wall,' said Hirad.

'Almost there,' said The Unknown. The door at the base of the turret was open and Hirad doubted whether The Unknown would have paused had it been closed, such was his speed. The Raven sprinted out into the waning amber sunlight and headed for the left-hand corner of the courtyard where dust from the explosion filled the air.

From the fog of the dust, and picking their way through the rubble they'd created, came the enemy. The warriors, leather-armoured and cloth-masked, spread into the courtyard. Behind them, Hirad could see another making his way through the debris, seemingly at leisure. He too was wearing shining leather armour but also a black cloak that billowed behind him. A pipe smoked gently in his mouth and, if Hirad's eyes didn't deceive him, he was stroking a cat whose head poked out from the neck of the cloak.

Behind him, he heard Ilkar, the elven mage from Julatsa, curse and spit: 'Xetesk.' Hirad paused in his stride and glanced back. Ilkar waved him on.

'Get on and fight,' said the elf, his tall, athletically slim frame tense, his flat-oval hazel eyes narrowed beneath short dark hair. 'I'll keep an eye on him.'

The enemy fighting men began to move to The Raven's left at an even pace, trotting towards the bare rock wall along the base of which grain, tool and firewood sheds ran from outer defences to keep.

The Unknown Warrior immediately changed direction, cutting off the new approach. Hirad frowned, unable to take his eyes from the solitary black-cloaked figure behind the swordsmen.

The sounds of battle from outside the wall began to fade as Hirad focused on the task ahead. Seeing them, the enemy, who outnumbered The Raven by almost three to one, moved to intercept. Five warriors were ahead of the main group, running on, swords held high, shouts ringing from the walls as they came, confident in their numerical superiority.

'Form up!' shouted The Unknown, and The Raven switched seamlessly into their fighting line as they advanced. As always, The Unknown himself took the centre of a slight-angled and uneven chevron. To his left ranged Talan, Ras and Richmond and to his right, Sirendor and Hirad. Behind them, Ilkar prepared the defensive shield.

The Unknown tapped the point of his two-handed blade rhythmically on the ground with each pace and Hirad, searching for recognition in the eyes of their adversaries, bared his teeth as he found it, noting the ghost of a break in their stride.

'Shield up,' said Ilkar. It sent a shiver through Hirad even now, ten years on. And the reality was that he couldn't actually feel anything. But it was there; a net of security from magical attack, a momentary shimmering in the air. The Unknown ceased tapping his sword point, and a beat later, The Raven joined battle.

The Unknown brought his sword up in a right-to-left arc, making a nonsense of his opponent's defence. The man's blade was knocked aside and his face split from chin to forehead, blood spraying up from The Unknown's weapon as it exited.

The man was hurled backwards, crashing into two of his colleagues, not even raising a scream as he died.

To the right, Sirendor caught a blow on his kite shield before sweeping his sword through the enemy's ribcage and Hirad evaded a clumsy overhead with ease, swaying right then jabbing two-handed into the neck of his opponent. Others were hesitant to fill the gap. The barbarian fighting man grinned and stepped forward, beckoning them on with a hand.

To The Unknown's left, the going was less straightforward. Ras and Talan were trading blows with competent shield-bearing warriors while Richmond, distracted, was on the defensive, his quick, fluid strikes causing his enemy great difficulty nonetheless.

'Spellcaster moving. Our left,' he said. He parried a blow to his midriff and shoved his opponent back.

'I have him,' said Ilkar, his voice distant with the effort of maintaining the shield. 'He's casting.'

'Leave him to Ilkar,' ordered The Unknown. His blade thudded against the shield of an enemy. The man staggered.

'Still moving left,' said Richmond.

'Leave him.' The big man slashed open the stomach of the man in front of him as Talan, immediately adjacent, finished his first victim, taking a cut on his arm.

The enemy mage barked a command word. Heat scorched the air and in the moment's ensuing silence, both sides paused, falling back half a pace.

'Ward!' yelled the mage, and buildings along the back wall exploded, clouding the air with splinters and hurling broken planks to spin and tumble across the courtyard.

Chaos.

Half a plank thumped into Hirad's standing foot. His balance gone, he sprawled forwards, trying to turn on to his back even as he fell. To his left, The Unknown took the force of the explosion on his broad back with barely a flinch. Thundering his blade through waist high, he cut the man in front of him clear through to the spine.

'Shield down!' shouted Ilkar. The shock of the detonation had pitched him to the dirt, breaking his concentration. He was up on his feet immediately. 'I'll take the mage.'

'I've got him.' Richmond, who had all but fallen into his opponent's arms, recovered the quicker of the two and rammed his sword into the man's midriff. He turned from the battle.

'Stay in line!' roared The Unknown. 'Richmond, stay in line!'

Hirad was staring straight into the eyes of the man who was about to kill him. Hardly believing his luck, the man swung his sword towards the helpless barbarian but the blow never reached its target. Instead, it clattered against a kite shield. Legs straddled Hirad, and Sirendor's sword uppercut into the man's neck. Sirendor stooped and helped Hirad clear.

The half-dozen paces Richmond took away from the line before he realised his error were fatal. Ras, engaged with one man, was not aware that his left flank was totally exposed. Seizing his chance, the second enemy stepped quickly around his companion and buried his sword in the Raven warrior's side.

Ras grunted and collapsed, clutching at the wound as blood soaked through his armour, falling against Talan's legs with enough force to unbalance his friend. Talan just about defended one strike but was in no position to avoid the next.

'Shit!' rasped The Unknown. He set his blade horizontally across Talan's path, fielding two blows aimed at the struggling warrior, and kicked out straight with his right foot, connecting with his opponent's lower abdomen.

Richmond crashed back into the battle. At the same time, Talan recovered to stand across the stricken Raven man, skewering another enemy through the chest and wrenching his blade free, the man's screams turning to gurgles as he drowned in his own blood.

And behind the battle, Ilkar could only watch as the Xetesk mage, running towards the wall he'd exposed by destroying the wooden buildings, paused, turned to him, smiled, said one word and disappeared on his next pace forwards.

Ilkar gritted his teeth and switched his attention back to the fight.

Ras was lying curled and motionless. The Unknown hacked down another man, and to his right, Sirendor and Hirad killed with practised efficiency. Only Richmond's blade flailed, the whole set of his body giving away his feelings. Ilkar strode forwards, forming the mana shape for a holding spell. It was enough. The remains of the enemy unit saw him, disengaged and ran back the way they had come.

'Forget them,' said The Unknown as Hirad made to chase the fleeing enemy. The barbarian stopped and watched them go, hearing the jeers of the castle garrison help them on their way. Elsewhere, cheers rose from the ramparts as horns sounded retreat across the battle ground.

For The Raven, though, victory was hollow.

A pool of silence spread across the courtyard from where they stood, and as it reached out, others fell quiet, turning to see what few had ever seen. When Hirad looked around, all but Ilkar were crouched by Ras. Hirad joined them.

He opened his mouth to ask the question but swallowed his words hard. Ras, his hands still clamped to the horrible wound in his side, was not breathing.

'All day sitting around and now this,' said Hirad. 'We're never taking a reserve force job again.'

'I don't think this is the time or the place for this discussion,' said The Unknown softly. He was aware of a crowd beginning to gather.

'Why not?' Hirad rose, arm muscles bunching beneath his heavy padded leather armour, his braided russet hair bouncing as he jerked to his feet. He jammed his sword back into its scabbard. 'How much more evidence do we bloody well need? If you spend a day up on the ramparts you aren't sharp enough when it comes to the fight.'

'There's a few here that wouldn't agree with you,' snapped The Unknown, gesturing at the slain enemy.

'We've lost three men in ten years, all of them in contracts we shouldn't have taken on. We should be hired to fight, not to sit around watching others do it.'

'This was a good money contract,' said Ilkar.

'Do you think Ras cares?' shouted Hirad.

'I—' began Ilkar. He put a hand to his head, his eyes losing focus. He squeezed The Unknown's shoulder.

'This discussion and the Vigil will have to wait. The mage is still in here,' he said. The Raven were on their feet in a moment, each man ready.

'Where?' growled Hirad. 'He's a dead man.'

'I can't see him,' said Ilkar. 'He's under a CloakedWalk. He's close by, though. I can sense the mana shape.'

'Great,' said Sirendor. 'Sitting targets.' His grip tightened on the hilt of his blade.

'We're all right. He'll have to lose the Cloak before he casts again. I just want to know what he's doing here.' Ilkar's face was set, his frown deep.

Hirad switched his gaze up to the keep and round the ramparts. A closing of the cloud hastened the setting of the sun and the fading light washed grey across the castle. A light rain had begun to fall. All activity had ceased and a hundred eyes stared at The Raven and at the body they encircled. Taranspike Castle was quiet, and even as victorious soldiers walked back into the courtyard, their voices caught and faded when they saw the scene.

The Raven's circle moved gradually outwards, with Ilkar separate from it, always with one eye on the newly exposed wall.

'How could he miss us with that spell?' asked Talan, indicating the debris of wood and grain scattered about them. 'He was practically standing on top of us.'

'He couldn't,' replied Ilkar. 'That's why I'm—'

The mage was by the wall. He had blinked into view with both his hands on it. They probed briefly and a section of the wall moved back and left, revealing a dark passageway. The mage stepped into it and immediately the opening closed.

Ilkar ran to the wall and examined the section minutely, the others crowding around him.

'Open it, then,' said Hirad. The elf turned to stare at the barbarian, his leaf-shaped ears, pointed at the top, pricking in irritation.

'Can you open it?' asked Talan.

Ilkar nodded. 'I'll have to cast, though. I can't see the pressure points otherwise.' He switched his attention back to the wall and the rest of The Raven gave him space. Closing his eyes, Ilkar spoke a short incantation, moving his hands over the wall in front of him, feeling the mana trails sheath his fingers. Now he placed his fingertips on the stonework, searching. One after another, his fingers stopped moving, finding their marks.

'Got it,' he said. No more than half a minute had passed. The Unknown nodded.

'Good,' he said. 'But you' – he indicated the stocky figure of Talan, his short brown hair matted with sweat and the old scar on his left cheek burning bright through his tanned skin – 'stay and get that cut seen to, and *you*' – spitting the words at Richmond – 'start the Vigil and think on what you've done.'

There was a brief silence. Talan considered objecting but the blood dripping from his arm, and his drained face, told of a bad wound. Richmond walked over to Ras, sighting down his long thin nose, tears in his pinched blue eyes. He folded his tall frame to kneel by the body of the Raven warrior, his sword in front of him, its point in the dirt and his hands clasped about the hilt guard. He bowed his head and was motionless, his long blond ponytail playing gently in the breeze. It was he, along with Talan and Ras, who had joined The Raven as an already established and respected trio four years earlier, after the only other battle that had seen the death of a Raven warrior, in this case, two of them.

The Unknown Warrior came to Ilkar's shoulder.

'Let's do it,' he said.

'Right,' said Ilkar. He pushed. The wall moved back and left. 'It'll stay open. He must have closed it from the inside.'

There was light at the end of the passageway, wan and flickering. The Unknown trotted into the passage, Hirad and Sirendor right behind him and Ilkar bringing up the rear.

As The Unknown Warrior moved towards the light, a shout of terror, abruptly cut off, was followed by a voice, urgent and loud, and the scrabbling of feet. The Unknown increased his pace.

Rounding a sharp right-hand corner he found himself in a small room, bed to the right, desk opposite and firelight streaming in from a short passage to the left. Slumped by the desk, and in front of an opening, was a middle-aged man dressed in plain blue robes. A long cut on his creased forehead dripped blood into his long-fingered hands and he stared at the splashes, shuddering continuously.

With The Raven in the room behind him, The Unknown knelt by the man.

'Where did he go?' Nothing. Not even recognition he was there. 'The mage? In the black cloak?'

'Gods above!' Ilkar elbowed his way to the man. 'It's the castle mage.' The Unknown nodded. Ilkar picked up the man's face. The blood from his wound trickled over gaunt white features. His eyes flickered everywhere, taking in everything and seeing nothing.

'Seran, it's Ilkar. Do you hear me?' The eyes steadied for a second. It was enough. 'Seran, where did the Xeteskian go? We want him.' Seran managed to look half over his shoulder to the opening. He tried to speak but nothing came out except the letter 'd' stuttered over and over.

'Hold on,' said Sirendor. 'Shouldn't that wall let back on to—?'

'Come on,' said The Unknown. 'We're losing him the longer we wait.'

'Right,' said Hirad. He led The Raven through the opening, down a short corridor and into a small, bare chamber. In the dim light from Seran's study, he could see a door facing him.

He moved to the door and pulled it open on to another, longer passage, the end of which was illuminated by a flickering glow. He glanced behind him.

'Come on,' he said, and broke into a run down the passage. As he approached the end, he could see a large fire burning in a grate set into the wall opposite. Sprinting into the chamber, he glanced quickly left and right. There was a pair of doors in the right-hand wall perhaps twenty feet away, set either side of a second, unlit fireplace. One of them was swinging slowly shut.

'There!' he pointed and changed direction, not waiting to see if any were following. His prey was close.

Hirad skidded to a stop before the door and wrenched it open, stepping back to look before dashing in. It was a small antechamber, set with massive arched double doors opposite. They carried a crest, half on each side. The walls were covered in runic language; braziers lit the scene. Hirad ignored it all: one of the big doors was just ajar and a glittering light came from inside. The barbarian smiled.

'Come to Daddy,' he breathed as he ran through the gap and into the chamber beyond.

'Hirad, wait!' shouted Sirendor as he, Ilkar and The Unknown raced into the larger chamber.

'Get after that idiot, Sirendor,' ordered The Unknown. 'Time to take stock, I think.'

Above the fire hung a round metal plate, fully three feet across. On it was embossed the head and talons of a dragon. The mouth was wide, dripping fire, and the claws open and grasping. Otherwise, the room was bare of ornament. The Unknown moved towards it, half an eye on Sirendor as the warrior hurried towards the door through which Hirad had chased. He stopped suddenly, glanced behind him and frowned.

'What is it?' asked Ilkar.

'This isn't right,' said The Unknown. 'Unless I've gone badly wrong, this ought to be the kitchens and that end of this room' – he pointed right to the two doors flanking the unlit fire – 'should be in the courtyard.'

'Well, we must be under it,' said Ilkar.

'We haven't gone down,' said The Unknown. 'What do you think?' But Ilkar wasn't paying attention to him any more. He was staring at the crest over the fire, his face paling.

'That symbol. I know it.' Ilkar walked over to the fire, The Unknown trailing him.

'What is it?'

'It's the Dragonene crest. Heard of it?'

'A few rumours.' The Unknown shrugged. 'So what?'

'And you say we should be standing in the courtyard?'

'Well, yes, I think so but . . .?'

Ilkar swallowed hard. 'Gods, we'd better not have done what I think we've done.'

It was the size of the hall he entered that first slowed Hirad's advance, and the heat that assailed him the moment he was inside. Next it was the odour, very strong, of wood and oil. Pervasive and with a sharp quality. And finally, the huge pair of eyes regarding him from the opposite side of the room that brought him to a complete standstill.

'Gods, Hirad, calm down!' Sirendor yanked open the door to the right of the fireplace and ran inside, seeing the crested double doors in front of him. He pulled up sharply, the dark-cloaked mage appearing suddenly before him. He raised his sword reflexively and took a pace backwards, realising the mage's abrupt appearance was caused by the dispersal of a CloakedWalk spell. Probably in his late thirties, the mage would normally have been handsome beneath his tousled black hair and unkempt short beard, but now he looked pale and frightened. He held out his hands, palms outwards.

'Please,' he whispered. 'I couldn't stop him, but I can stop you.'

'You're responsible for the death of one of The Raven—'

'And I don't want another one to die, believe me. The barbarian—'

'Where is he?' demanded Sirendor.

'Don't raise your voice. Look, he's in trouble,' said the mage. There was movement in his cloak. A cat's head appeared briefly at its neck then disappeared once more. 'You're Sirendor, aren't you? Sirendor Larn.' Sirendor, standing still once again, nodded. The mage continued. 'And I am Denser. Look, I know what you're feeling but we can help each other right now and, believe me, your friend needs help.'

'What kind of trouble is he in?' Sirendor's voice was low too. He didn't know why, but something about the mage's attitude worried him. He should kill the man where he stood but he was obviously scared by something other than the prospect of death at a Raven warrior's hand.

'Bad. Very bad. See for yourself.' He put a finger to his lips and beckoned Sirendor to him. The warrior moved forwards, never taking his eyes from the mage nor the slightly shifting bulge on one side of his cloak. Denser motioned Sirendor to look through the doors.

'Great Gods above!' He made a move to go in but the mage restrained him with a hand on the shoulder. Sirendor turned sharply.

'Take your hand off me. Right now.' The mage did.

'You can't help him by rushing in.'

'Well, what can we do?' hissed Sirendor.

'I'm not sure.' Denser shrugged. 'I might be able to do something. You might as well get your friends. They won't find anything out there and they could prove useful in here.'

Sirendor paused in the act of heading for the door. 'Nothing stupid, you understand? If he dies because of you . . .'

Denser nodded. 'I'll wait.'

'See that you do.' Sirendor left the antechamber at a sprint, not realising he was about to confirm all of Ilkar's fears.

Hirad would have run only he'd come too far into the room, and anyway, he didn't think his legs would support him, they were shaking that badly. He just stood and stared.

The Dragon's head was resting on its front claws and the first coherent thought that entered Hirad's mind was that from the bottom of its lower jaw to the top of its head, it was getting on for as tall as he was. The mouth itself must have been more than three feet across, the whole muzzle probably five in depth. Those eyes sat atop, and at the base of, the muzzle. They were close set, rimmed with thick horn, and the pupils were narrow black slits, ringed in a startling blue. A pronounced ridge of bone ran away over the Dragon's head towards its spine, and Hirad could see the mound of its body behind it, huge and shining.

As he watched, it carefully unfurled its wings and the reason for the size of the room became all too obvious. With their roots at the top of the torso, above the front limbs, the wings stretched to what must have been forty feet on either side, and flapped lazily. With the balance afforded by them, the Dragon picked its head from the floor and stood upright.

Even with its slender, bone-edged neck arched so its eyes never left Hirad, it towered sixty feet into the hall. Its tail curled away to the left and was thicker than a man's body even at its tip. Stretched out, the Dragon would surely have been well in excess of one hundred and twenty feet in length, but now it rested on two massive rear limbs, each foot carrying a quartet of claws bigger than the barbarian's head. And it was gold, all over – skin glistening in the firelight and sparkling on the walls.

Hirad could hear its breathing, slow and deep. It opened its mouth wide, revealing long rows of fangs, and saliva dripped to the floor to evaporate on contact.

It raised a forelimb, single hooked claw extended. Hirad took an involuntary pace backwards. He swallowed hard, sweat suddenly covering his body. He was quaking from head to foot.

'Fuck me,' he breathed.

Hirad had always believed that he'd die with his sword in his hand but, in the moments before the huge claw dismembered him, it seemed such a futile gesture. A calmness replaced the instant's fury that had itself so quickly followed his fear, and he sheathed his blade and looked straight into the creature's eyes.

The blow never came. Instead, the Dragon retracted its claw, unarched its neck and moved its head down and forwards, coming to a stop no more than three paces from Hirad, hot, sour breath firing into his face.

'Interesting,' it said in a voice that echoed through Hirad's entire being. The barbarian's legs finally gave way and he sat heavily on the tiled floor. His mouth was wide, his jaws were moving but no sound came.

'Now,' said the Dragon. 'Let us talk about a few things.'

Chapter 2

'Who are these Dragonene, then?' hissed Sirendor.

Ilkar turned to him. 'All mages. They have, I don't know, an affinity, you know, with Dragons.' He gestured uselessly.

'No, I don't bloody know! Dragons don't exist. They are just rumour and myth.' Sirendor's voice was still barely more than a whisper.

'Oh yeah? Well that's one hell of a big myth I can see in there!' Ilkar's ears pricked.

'Does it really matter?' The Unknown's voice, though quiet, still carried all of its power. 'We only have one question that needs answering now.'

The Raven trio and Denser were all crowded around the partially open door to the Dragon's chamber, animosity forgotten for a while. Hirad sat with his back to them, his hands on the floor behind his back, and his legs drawn half up. The Dragon's head was scant feet from the barbarian's, the huge mound of its body resting on the ground, its wings folded. It was the scale of it all that Ilkar found so hard to take in.

Never mind that he had only half believed the books and the teaching. He had still imagined Dragons and he imagined they would be big; but Hirad looked *so* tiny in comparison that he had to look away and back before he decided that Sirendor was wrong and they weren't seeing an illusion. And he still didn't really believe it.

'He should be dead,' muttered The Unknown, his hands tightening and untightening around the hilt of his sword. 'Why hasn't it killed him?'

'We think they're talking,' said Denser.

'What?' Ilkar couldn't hear a thing. As far as he was concerned they were just staring at each other. But as Ilkar watched, his powerful eyes giving the scene complete clarity, Hirad shook his head and straightened his back so he could use his hands to make a gesture. He indicated behind him and said something but the mage couldn't pick out the words. The Dragon cocked its head to one side and opened its mouth, revealing the massed ranks of its fangs. Liquid dripped to the floor and Hirad started.

'What do you mean, "we"?' demanded Sirendor. Denser didn't reply.

'Later, Sirendor,' said The Unknown. 'We have to think of something to do. Quickly.'

'What the hell can they be talking about?' No one had an answer. Ilkar looked back to the unreal scene in the huge chamber and a glint caught his eye. For a moment he assumed it was a reflection off the Dragon's beautiful scales but it wasn't a golden colour, more a steel or a silver.

He stared hard, using all the range that his eyes afforded him, and there it was: a small disc, maybe a palm's width across and attached to a chain which seemed to be caught around one of the Dragon's large hind-foot claws. He pointed it out to Denser.

'Where?' asked the other mage.

'Its right foot, third talon along.' Ilkar pointed the way. Denser shook his head.

'Those are good eyes, aren't they? Hold on.' Denser mumbled a few words and rubbed a thumb on either eye. He looked again and tensed.

'What is it? Don't try to—'

'Just pray Hirad keeps it talking,' said Denser, and he began mumbling again.

'What are you talking about?' hissed Ilkar. 'What have you seen?'

'Trust me. I can save him,' said Denser. 'And just be ready to run.' He took a pace forwards and disappeared.

'Look, this is really hard for me to take in,' said Hirad. The Dragon put its head on one side and stretched its jaws a little. A line of saliva dripped from a fang and Hirad moved his leg reflexively to avoid it.

'Explain,' ordered the Dragon, the word bypassing the barbarian's ears on its way to thump through his skull.

'Well, you have to understand that never in my wildest drunken dreams did I ever imagine I'd be sitting and talking to a – a Dragon.' He gestured and raised his eyebrows. 'I mean I . . .' He trailed off. The Dragon flared its nostrils and Hirad felt his hair move in the breeze of its breath. He had to fight himself not to gag at the smell, rotten with that burned sourness.

'And now?' it asked.

'I'm absolutely terrified.' Hirad felt cold. He was still shivering intermittently and he felt as though his sweat was freezing on his body, yet the room was hot, very hot. Large fires crackled and snapped in ten grates set around the far half of the hall, surrounding the Dragon on three sides, and the beast himself was sitting in what looked like soft wet mud. He rested back on his hands once again.

'Fear is healthy. As is knowing when you are beaten. That is why you are still alive.' The Dragon twitched its left wing. 'So, tell me, what are you doing here?'

'We were chasing someone. He came in here.'

'Yes, I thought that you would not be by yourself. Who were you chasing?'

The barbarian couldn't help but smile; the whole situation was getting quite beyond him. Although he was, he was sure, talking to a beast he had only heard of in rumour, he couldn't dispel the idea that it was all some kind of illusion. Something with a sensible explanation, anyway.

'A mage. His men killed one of my friends. We want him . . . have you . . . seen anyone?' said Hirad. It was simply too much. 'Look, I'm sorry, but I'm having trouble even believing you exist.'

The Dragon laughed, or at least it was a sound that Hirad thought was laughter. It boomed around his skull like waves striking a cliff and he juddered and closed his eyes as the pain that followed smashed at his brain. And then those fangs were inches from his face and the nostrils blew gouts of hot air into his eyes. Hirad started violently but before he could experience the shock of the Dragon's speed of movement, it twitched its head up, catching him on the point of his jaw. He was hurled backwards to slide across the tiles, coming to rest, dazed. He sat up and massaged his chin, blood running from a deep graze.

'And now, little man, do you still have trouble believing I exist?'

'I . . . No, I don't think so . . .'

'And nor you should. Seran believes in me, although he has failed me now. And your friends beyond that door. I am sure they believe.' The Dragon's voice inside his head was louder now. Hirad got to his feet and walked towards the beast, shaking his head to clear his mind of the fog that encased it.

'Yes, I'm sorry. I didn't mean to offend.' Hirad's heart was pounding in his throat once more. Another sound from the Dragon. Perhaps another laugh, but this time it sounded dismissive, somehow.

'But you questioned my very existence,' said the Dragon. 'Perhaps you are lucky that I am slow to offend. Or perhaps that I am slow to question yours.' Hirad tried to slow his breathing and think, but there seemed no way out. The only question remaining was how long before the Dragon tired of the game and snuffed out his life.

'Yes.' Hirad shrugged and waited to die. 'But you must understand that you were the last thing I expected to find here.'

'Ah.' Feelings of amusement arose in Hirad's mind. 'Then I have disappointed you. Perhaps I should be apologising to you.' The Dragon laughed again. More quietly this time, more in thought than in mirth.

There was a faint rustling by Hirad's left ear, then a voice, just audible:

'Don't react to my voice and don't say anything. I am Denser, the man you are after, and I'm trying to help you.' He paused. 'So when I say run, run hard. Don't argue and don't look back.'

'Now, little man. Ask me a question.'

'What?' Hirad blinked and returned his attention to the Dragon, amazed that he could forget, however momentarily, that it was there.

'Ask. There must be something you want to know about me.' The Dragon withdrew its head somewhat, its neck arching high above the mound of its body.

'All right then. Why didn't you kill me?'

'Because your reaction in putting up your sword set you as different from other men I have encountered. It made you interesting, and very few humans are interesting.'

'If you say so. So what are you doing here?'

'Resting. Recovering. I am safe here.'

Hirad frowned. 'Safe from what?' The Dragon shifted. Moving its hind feet slightly further apart, it placed its head on the floor once more and stared deep into Hirad's eyes, blinking slowly.

'My world is at war. We are devastating our lands and there is no end in sight. When we need to recover our strength we use safe havens like this.'

'And where exactly is this?' Hirad's gaze took in the high roof and the scale of the chamber.

'At least you have the sense to know you are not in your own dimension.'

'I've no idea what you're talking about with dimensions. I'm sorry. All I know is that Taranspike Castle does not have a room this size.'

The Dragon chuckled again. 'So simple. If only you knew the effort it took for you to stand here.' It lifted its head slightly and shook it from side to side, closing its eyes. It spoke again without opening them. 'The moment you left Seran's chambers, you entered a robing room. That room is not placed in any one dimension, neither is this chamber or the prayer chamber you also must have seen. If you like, this is a corridor between dimensions, yours and mine. Its existence is reliant on the fabric of your dimension remaining intact.' Now the head raced in again, the Dragon's wings bracing slightly to compensate for the sudden movement. 'My Brood serve as protectors for your world, keeping you from the attentions of enemy Broods and withholding from you that which should never have been created.'

'Why do you bother?'

'Do not think it is for any liking of your insignificant peoples. Very few of you are worthy of our respect. It is simply that if we allowed you the means to destroy yourselves and you succeeded in so doing, we would lose our haven for ever. That is also why the door to your world is kept closed. Other Broods might otherwise choose to travel here to rule.'

Hirad thought on that for a moment. 'So what you're saying is that you hold the future for all of us.'

The Dragon raised the bone ridges that served as its eyebrows. 'That is certainly one conclusion you could reach. Now – what is your name?'

'Hirad Coldheart.'

'And I am Sha-Kaan. You are strong, Hirad Coldheart. I was right to spare you and speak to you and I will know you again. But now I must have rest. Take your companions and go. The entrance will be sealed behind you. You will never find me again, though I may find you. As for Seran, I will have to find another to serve me. I have no time for a Dragonene who cannot secure my sanctuary.'

It took the barbarian several heartbeats to take in what he had just heard and he still didn't believe it. 'You're letting me go?'

'Why not?'

'Run. Hirad. Run now.'

The Dragon's head swept from the floor at speed, eyes ablaze, searching for the source of the new sound. But Denser remained invisible. Hirad hesitated.

'Run!' Denser shouted, the voice some way to Hirad's left.

The barbarian looked up at Sha-Kaan and their eyes met for an instant. He saw raw fury. 'Oh, no,' he breathed. The Dragon broke eye-contact to look down at its right hind foot. Hirad turned and ran.

'NO!' Now Sha-Kaan's voice was there for all to hear, and it echoed from the walls. 'Give back what you have taken from me!'

'Over here!' shouted Denser, and as Hirad glanced right, the mage appeared briefly some thirty paces right along the wall from the double doors. The Dragon cocked its head and breathed in his direction, fire scorching a wall, rolling up to the ceiling and incinerating wood and tapestry, but Denser had already disappeared. An oppressive wave of heat washed over Hirad. He stumbled, crying out, gasping momentarily for breath, the roar of the flame and its detonation in the air shaking him to his core. The entire hall seemed to be ablaze; the sweat beaded on his face. Through the smoke and burning threads of tapestry he saw The Unknown appear at the door, holding it open for him. A shadow passed through it and then he heard the Dragon rise to its feet. The Unknown paled visibly.

'Run, Hirad. Run!' he screamed. The Dragon took a pace forward, and then another, Hirad feeling the ground shudder beneath its feet.

'Bring back what you have stolen!' it boomed. Hirad made the door.

'Close it!' shouted The Unknown. He and Sirendor leant their weights against it. 'Go, go!' They scrambled for the doors into the central chamber. Ilkar and Denser sprinted away with Sirendor in close pursuit. Sha-Kaan breathed again and the huge double doors exploded inwards, fragmenting, sending wood and metal against the walls to splinter, twist and smoulder. The shock sent Hirad sprawling and he crashed into the wall that backed the unlit fireplace, burning shards of wood covering the floor and his boots, the intense heat suffocating him. He lay confused for a second, seeing nothing but flame, then looked straight at Sha-Kaan as the Dragon drew more air into its lungs, its head thrust through the wreckage of the crested doors.

The barbarian closed his eyes, waiting for the end, but a hand reached round and grabbed his collar, hauling him to his feet and through the right hand of the two doors into the central chamber. The Unknown dragged him under the overhang of the fire grate as twin lances of flame seared through the openings, one to either side of them, disintegrating wood and howling away towards the opposite wall, melting the metal of the Dragonene crest above the fire to the right.

'Come on, Hirad. It's time to leave,' said the big warrior, and he pushed Hirad towards the exit passage after the rest of the retreating party.

'Bring back the amulet!' roared Sha-Kaan. 'Hirad Coldheart, bring back the amulet!' Hirad hesitated again, but The Unknown shoved him into the passage as another burst of flame lashed the large chamber, its pulse of heat stealing breath and singeing hair.

'Quickly!' shouted Sirendor from up ahead. 'The exit is closing. We can't hold it.'

The two men upped the pace, tearing down the passageway and into the robing room. Another roll of flame boiled into the prayer chamber, its tendrils lashing down the passage, licking at Hirad's back, the heat crinkling leather. Down the short entry tunnel Hirad could see Ilkar, arms outstretched, sweating in the light of a lantern as whatever spell he had cast kept the door at bay. But as he ran, he could see it inching closed. Ilkar sighed and closed his eyes.

'He's losing it!' yelled Denser. 'He's losing it. Run faster!' The door was sliding closed, the mage's bedroom disappearing with every step. Sha-Kaan's howls were loud in their ears. The Unknown and Hirad made it through, bowling Ilkar on to the floor as they did so. The door closed with a dull thud and the Dragon's voice was silenced.

Ilkar, Hirad and The Unknown picked themselves up and dusted themselves off. The barbarian nodded his thanks to the big man, who in turn nodded at the now closed entrance. There was nothing, no mark in the wall at all to suggest that there had ever been a door there.

'We were in another dimension. I knew the proportions were all wrong in there.'

'Not exactly another dimension,' corrected Ilkar. 'Between dimensions is more accurate, I think.' He kneeled by the prone mage. 'Well, well, well. Seran a Dragonene.' He felt for a pulse. 'Dead, I'm afraid.'

'And he won't be the only one.' Hirad turned on Denser. 'You should have run while you had the chance.' He advanced, sword in hand, but Denser merely shrugged and continued to stroke the cat in his arms.

'Hirad.' The Unknown's voice was quiet but commanding. The barbarian stopped, eyes still locked on Denser. 'The fight is over. If you kill him now, it's murder.'

'His little adventure killed Ras. It might have killed me, too. He—'

'Remember who you are, Hirad. We have a code.' The Unknown was standing at his shoulder now. 'We are The Raven.'

Eventually, Hirad nodded and put up his sword.

'Besides,' said Ilkar. 'He's got a lot of explaining to do.'

'I saved your life,' said Denser, frowning. Hirad was on him in a moment, pinning his head to the wall with a forearm under the chin. The cat hissed and scrambled to safety.

'Saved my life?' The barbarian's face was inches from Denser's. 'That's your phrase for having me all but burned to a crisp, is it? The Unknown saved my life after you risked it. You ought to die for that alone.'

'How—?' protested the mage. 'I got its attention to let you run!'

'But there was no need, was there?' Hirad grunted as he saw confusion in Denser's eyes. 'It was letting me go, Xetesk man.' Hirad stepped back a pace, releasing the mage, who felt his neck gingerly. 'You risked my life just to steal. I hope it was worth it.' He turned to the rest of The Raven.

'I don't know why I'm wasting my breath on this bastard. We have a Vigil to observe.'

Alun shoved the note across the table, his hands shaking. More hands covered his, they were strong and comforting.

'Try to be calm, Alun, at least we know they are alive, so we have a chance.'

Alun looked into the face of his friend, Thraun, whose powerful body was squeezed the other side of the table. Thraun was huge, better than six feet in height, with massively powerful shoulders and upper body. His heavy features sprang from a young face and his shining-clean blond hair was gathered in a ponytail which reached halfway to his waist. He was regarding Alun with his yellow-ringed deep green eyes, earnest and concerned.

He flicked his head, the ponytail swishing briefly into view, and looked around the inn. It was busy with lunchtime traffic and the noise of the patrons ebbed and flowed around them. Tables were scattered around the timbered floor, and here and there, booths like the one in which they sat gave an element of privacy.

'What does it say, Will?' Thraun's voice, as deep and gravelled as his barrel chest might suggest, cut through Alun's misery. He removed his hands from Alun's. Will sat next to him, a small man, wiry, bright-eyed and black-bearded, thinning on top. Will pulled at his nose with thumb and forefinger, his brows arrowing together as he read.

'Not a lot. "Your mage wife has been taken for questioning concerning the activities of the Dordovan College. She will be released unharmed assuming she co-operates. As will your sons. There will be no further communication." '

'So we know where she is, then,' said the third member of the trio whom Alun had enlisted. An elf, Jandyr was young, with a long and slender face, clear blue oval eyes and a short tidy blond beard that matched the colour of his cropped hair.

'Yes, we do,' agreed Thraun. 'And we know how far we can trust the words on that note.' He licked his lips and shovelled another forkful of meat into his mouth.

'You've got to help me!' Alun's eyes flicked desperately over them all, never coming to rest. Thraun looked right and across. Both Will and Jandyr inclined their heads.

'We'll do it,' said Thraun, through his chewing. 'And we'll have to be quick. The chances of him releasing them are very slim.' Alun nodded.

'You really think so?' asked Will.

'The boys are mage twins,' said Thraun. 'They will be powerful and they are Dordovan. Alun will tell you himself, when they've finished with Erienne, they will probably kill them. We have to get them out.' He looked back at Alun. 'It won't be cheap.'

'Whatever it costs, I don't care.'

'Of course, I'll work for nothing,' said Thraun.

'No, my friend, you won't.' A half-smile cracked Alun's face. Tears glinted in his eyes. 'I just want them home.'

'And home they will be. Now,' Thraun rose, 'I'm taking you home. You rest, we'll plan, and I'll be back later in the day.'

Thraun helped Alun from the bench and the two men walked slowly from the inn.

Richmond and Talan had moved Ras's body to a quiet chamber carved out of the mountain into which the castle was built. Candles burned next to him, one for each point of the compass. His face was clean and shaven, his armour sewn and washed, his arms lay by his sides and his sword in its scabbard was laid along his body from his chin to his thighs.

Richmond did not look up from his kneeling position as Hirad, Sirendor, The Unknown and Ilkar entered. Talan, standing by the door, inclined his head to each of them as they passed him.

Ranged around the central table on which Ras lay, The Raven, heads bowed, paid their respects to their fallen friend. Each man remembered. Each man grieved. But only two spoke.

As the candles burned low, Richmond stood and resheathed his sword.

'My soul I pledge to your memory. I am yours to command from beyond the veil of death. When you call I shall answer. While I breathe, these are my promises.' His last was a bitter whisper. 'I wasn't there. I am sorry.' He looked to The Unknown, who nodded and moved to the table, walking around it. Beginning at Ras's head, he snuffed the candles as he reached them.

'By north, by east, by south, by west. Though you are gone, you will always be Raven and we shall always remember. The Gods will smile on your soul. Fare well in whatever faces you now and ever.'

Again silence, but now in darkness.

Denser remained in Seran's chambers. The dead mage was lying on his bed under a sheet. For his part, Denser couldn't work out why he was still alive, but he was grateful. The whole of Balaia would be grateful, but no City would be breathing easier than Xetesk that the barbarian had been stopped.

The cat nuzzled his legs. Denser sagged down the wall and sat.

'I wonder if this really is it,' said Denser, turning the amulet over and over in his hands. 'I think it is but I have to know.' The cat gazed into his eyes. No clue there. 'The question is, do we have the strength to do it?' The cat jumped into his cloak, nestling into the warmth of Denser's body.

It fed.

'Yes,' said Denser. 'Yes, we do.' He closed his eyes and felt the mana form around him. This would be difficult but he had to know. A communion over such a distance was a strain on mind and body. Knowledge and glory would come at a price if they came at all.

They buried Ras outside the castle walls, branding the ground with The Raven mark; a simple profile of the bird's head, single eye enlarged and wing curved above the head.

All but Richmond left the graveside tired and hungry. For the lone warrior, kneeling in the cool damp of a windy, moonless night, the Vigil would last until dawn.

Sitting at a table in the huge kitchens, Ilkar described the events through the dimension door to Talan. It was only then that Hirad started to shake.

Picking up his mug of coffee from the table, he stared at it wobbling in his hands, liquid slopping out over his fingers.

'You all right?' asked Sirendor.

'I'm not sure,' said Hirad. 'I don't think so.' He raised the mug to his lips but couldn't close his mouth on it. The coffee dribbled down his chin. His heart slammed in his chest and his pulse thumped in his neck. Sweat began to prickle his forehead and dampen his armpits. Images of Sha-Kaan's head flooded his mind. That and the fire all around him, hemming him in. He could feel the heat again and it made his palms itch. He dropped the mug.

'Gods in the ground, Hirad, what's wrong?' Sirendor's voice betrayed alarm. The barbarian half smiled. He must look as terrified as he felt. 'You need to lie down.'

'Give me a moment,' said Hirad. 'I don't think my legs'll carry me anyway.' He glanced around the table. They were all staring at him, their food forgotten. He shrugged. 'I didn't even believe they existed,' he said in explanation. 'So big. So . . . so *huge*. And right here!' He put a quivering palm in front of his face. 'Too powerful. I can't—' He broke off, shuddering the length of his body. Plates and cutlery on the table rattled. Tears fogged his vision and he felt his heart trip-hammering. He swallowed hard.

'What did it talk about?' asked Ilkar.

'Loud. He thundered in my head,' said Hirad. 'He talked about dimensions and portals and he wanted to know what I was doing. Huh. Funny . . . that huge and he cared what I was doing. Me. I'm so small but he called me strong.' He shivered again. 'He said he'd know me. He had my life. He could have crushed me just like that. Snuffed me out. Why didn't he? I wish I could remember everything.'

'Hirad, you're mumbling,' said Sirendor. 'I think we should leave this for another time.'

'Sorry, I think I'll lie down now, if you'll help me.'

'Sure thing, old friend.' Sirendor smiled. He pushed back the bench and helped Hirad to shaky feet.

'Gods. I feel like I've been sick for a week.'

'You've been sick all your life.'

'Sod off, Larn.'

'I would, but you'd fall over.'

'Make sure he drinks plenty of hot, sweet liquid,' said The Unknown as the friends shambled past. 'Nothing alcoholic.'

'Is the Xetesk mage still here?' asked Hirad. The Unknown nodded.

'In Seran's chambers,' said Ilkar. 'Asleep. Hardly surprising after the casting he's done today. He won't be leaving until I've spoken to him.'

'You should have let me kill him.'

The Unknown smiled. 'You know I couldn't.'

'Yes. Come on, Larn, or I'll collapse where I'm standing.'

*

The two men sat in low chairs either side of a fire long dead. Night hurried to engulf the College City of Xetesk and, in response, lanterns glowed, keeping the dark at bay and lighting up the massed shelves of books that stood at every wall in the small study. On a desk kept meticulously tidy, a single candle burned above the ribboned and titled sheaves of papers.

Far below the study, the College quietened. Late lectures took place behind closed doors, spells were honed and adjusted in the armoured chambers of the catacombs, but the air outside was still.

Beyond the walls of the College, Xetesk still moved, but as full night fell, that movement would cease. The City existed to serve the College, and the College had in the past exacted a heavy price for its own existence. Inns would lock their doors, patrons staying until first light; shops and businesses feeding off those who fed off the College would shutter their windows. Houses would show no light or welcome.

No longer did Protectors issue from the College to snatch subjects for experiment. And no longer did Xetesk mages use their own people for sacrifice in mana-charge ceremonies. But old fears died hard and rumours would forever fly through the markets that bustled by day but echoed silence at night.

As darkness fell, a malevolent quiet still emanated from the College in a cloying cloud of apprehension and anxiety like fog rolling in from the sea. Countless years of blood ritual would never be forgotten and forever hearts would quicken at the sound of wood splintering in the distant dark, and cries would be stifled as footsteps were heard slowing by locked doors. Dread ran through the veins of Xetesk and the foreboding receded only with the lightening of the sky on a new morning.

It made the job of City Guard simple, as at dusk they closed the gates of the only fully walled City in Balaia and patrolled the empty streets. Fear stalked the alleyways as it had done for centuries. But now it was a legacy. It had no substance.

Change was so slow and the City was suffocating. Few native Xeteskians had left to enjoy the freedom granted them by the latest Lord of the Mount as his first action on assuming the mantle of the College's ruling mage. And in the twelve years since, Styliann had encountered nothing but reluctance to cast aside the old ways, as if his people drew perverse comfort from living in fear of everyone they met. Yet now, his failure to change the collective will and mind of his people could work to his advantage.

Styliann was an imposing figure, well in excess of six foot, with the body of a forty-year-old disguising his true age of somewhere over fifty. His hair, receding halfway across his skull, was long, dark and brushed hard into a ponytail that reached beyond his shoulders. He wore dark trousers and a shirt of deepest blue, and his cloak of office, gold-trimmed black, was draped about his shoulders. His nose was long and thin, his jaw set harsh and his cold green eyes scared all they looked upon.

'I take it she escaped Terenetsa unharmed?' asked his companion across the fireplace.

Styliann blinked several times and shook his head to clear his mind of his reverie. He regarded Nyer, a senior aide and archmage, for a few moments, remembering the old maxim concerning where to keep your friends and enemies. He thought he had Nyer, a wily political animal and sharp thinker, placed about right.

'Yes, she did. Just. And she's now well clear.' He shivered at the memory of his recent contact with Selyn, anxious for the mage spy's safety. Even under a CloakedWalk, she had been at risk from those she watched and the manner of her escape from Terenetsa, a small Wesmen farming community not far west of the Blackthorne Mountains, would trouble his dreams that night. He reached a slightly tremulous hand down to a low table and picked up his wine, a deep and heavy red that had not kept as well as he'd hoped. He felt tired. Communion over such a range sapped the strength and he knew he would need to visit the catacombs for prayer later that evening.

'But something is troubling you, my Lord.'

'Hmm.' Styliann pursed his lips, knowing any reluctance to speak would be taken by Nyer as a personal slight. He couldn't afford that. Not yet. 'She saw everything we have been fearing. The Wesmen are subjugating villages near the Blackthornes. She *heard* the Shaman offer them life for crops and obedience. The evidence is just overwhelming. They are massing armies, they are united and the Shaman magic is strong.'

Nyer nodded, pushing his hand through his long greying hair.

'And Parve?' he asked.

'I have asked her to travel there.'

'Selyn?'

'Yes. There is no one else and we must have answers.'

'But, my Lord—'

'I am well aware of the risks, Nyer!' snapped Styliann. His expression softened immediately. 'My apologies.'

'Not at all,' said Nyer. He placed a comforting hand briefly on Styliann's knee.

'We must be so careful now,' said Styliann after another sip of wine. 'Are our Watchers sure the Wytch Lords are still held?'

Nyer breathed out, a long, sighing sound. 'We believe so.'

'That isn't good enough.'

'Please, Styliann, let me explain.' Nyer's use of his Lord's name was against protocol but Styliann let it go. Nyer was an old mage who rarely followed etiquette. 'The spells to determine that the Wytch Lords are still in the mana cage are complex and are nearing completion for this quarter. Delays have been caused through unusually high activity in the interdimensional space in which the cage is located.'

'When will we have an answer?' Styliann pulled an embroidered cord next to the fireplace.

'In the next few hours. A day at most.' Nyer raised his eyebrows in apology.

'You know it's only a matter of time, don't you?'

'My Lord?'

'The evidence is all there.' Styliann sighed. 'The unification of the Wesmen tribes, Shamen at the head of war parties, armies building in the south-west . . .'

'Must it be the Wytch Lords?'

'You don't really need me to answer that question, do you?' Styliann smiled. Nyer shook his head. There was a knock at the door.

'Come!' barked Styliann. A young man entered, short red hair riding above a face taut with trepidation.

'My Lord?'

'Bring up a fire and another bottle of this rather average Denebre red.'

'At once, my Lord.' The young man left.

The two senior mages paused in their conversation, contemplating the future and not liking what they saw.

'Can we stop them this time?' asked Nyer.

'I fear that rather relies on your man,' replied Styliann. 'At least as much as the timing of the Wytch Lords' escape. He has reported, I take it?'

'He has, and we now hold the amulet.'

'Excellent!' Styliann slapped the arms of his chair with the palms of his hands and rose. He walked over to the window, hardly daring to ask his next question. 'And?'

'It is Septern's amulet. We can make progress now, assuming we get the right help.'

Styliann breathed deeply and smiled as he looked out of his Tower high above the College. The Tower dominated the College and its encircling balcony gave him unrivalled views of the City and its surrounds. The night was cool but dry. A thin cloud was bubbling up from the south-east, threatening to obscure the countless thousands of stars whose pale light pinpricked the dark. The smell of oil fires and the heat of the City wafted on a slight breeze, not unpleasant to the senses. Beyond the College walls, the quiet was growing.

Styliann's Tower was encircled by those of his six Mage Masters but stood far taller. Looking down, he saw lights burning in Laryon's Tower too. The most recently appointed Master, he was a man who would now have to join the inner circle, completing the seven-tower bond.

'This could mean everything to us,' he said.

'Laryon has worked hard,' said Nyer, coming to his side. 'He has earned the credit.'

'And your man. He'll see the necessary help is obtained?'

'I have every confidence.'

Styliann nodded and gazed out over Xetesk, at ease that his people would obey his every order without question. The first step had been successfully taken but now the way would become fraught and those who knew enough would have to be kept close.

'I think, Nyer, that when the wine arrives, we may permit ourselves a small celebration.'

Chapter 3

She lay back on the bed again, the pounding in her head bringing sweeping nausea through her body. She shuddered, prayed that she'd been sick for the last time but not really believing she had.

Every muscle ached, clotted with pain, every tendon strained. Her skin felt so tight across her chest it would split if she dared breathe in deep, and her shallow, gasping intakes drew whimpers as they stretched her tortured lungs. It would subside. However, having no idea how long she had been out, she had no idea when the symptoms would fade.

But the physical pain coursing her body was as nothing to the well in her heart and soul, opened by the loss of her sons. Her reason to live. For them, her body quaked and shivered. She reached out with her mind, striving to touch theirs but knowing she could not and cursing her decision to delay the teaching of communion.

Where were they? Were they together? Gods, she hoped so. Were they alive? The tears came as the drug eased its hold on her body just a little. Great heaving sobs tore through her being and her cries echoed around her prison. Eventually, exhausted, she slept again.

Dawn and a second waking brought no relief from the agony of her loss. Pale light came through a single window high up in her circular room. She was in a tower, that much was certain. The room contained a small pallet bed, a desk and chair, and a woven rug whose red and gold had long ago faded but whose weight gave welcome insulation from the stone-flagged floor. She was still wearing the nightgown they had taken her in. She had not been wearing any socks, let alone shoes, and the room was chill. Dust covered every surface, puffing into the air around her body as she shifted uncomfortably on the bed. She pulled the blanket up around her shoulders.

A single door commanded her attention. It was locked and bolted, its heavy wood flush in the stone frame of the tower wall. The tears came again, but this time she was strong enough to force them back, driving her mind to seek the mana and a way out of the tower. It was there, pulsing within her and flowing around her, never stopping, always shifting and changing, urgent and random in its direction. Escape was just an incantation away. The door would prove no barrier to her FlameOrb.

But even as she readied to cast, the words came back. *If you cast, your boys will die.* Her senses returned and she found she was standing. She sagged into the chair.

'Patience,' she said. 'Patience.' Anger in a mage could be so destructive, and while she didn't know the fate of her sons, she couldn't afford to lose the famously short Malanvai family temper.

While the yearning in her heart and the ache in her womb intensified with every passing second, her mind was beginning to see clearly at last. They had known she was a mage because they took her from Dordover for something specific. But they also wanted control. And controlling a conscious mage is difficult without restraint and violence. But they had found a way to chain her through her sons. It was for that reason she believed them alive. And not only that, close. Because whoever took her must know she wouldn't help them without seeing her boys first. Hope surged within her but the flicker of joy she felt at an imminent reunion died as she saw her locked door.

Her heart turned over at the thought of her boys, so young, so alone and so frightened. Snatched in the middle of the night and locked in a place they wouldn't recognise or comprehend. How must they feel? Betrayed. Abandoned by those who claimed to love them the most. Terrified by their solitude and helplessness. Traumatised by separation from their mother.

Fury bubbled beneath the hurt.

'Patience,' she murmured. 'Patience.' They would have to come soon. While a jug of water had been left on the desk, there was no food in the room.

She fixed her eyes on the door while the hatred for her captors seethed in her veins, the brophane dragged at her strength and her body pulsed mana and love to her children.

But when the key finally turned and the man she had dreaded seeing stood before her, she could do nothing but sob her thanks at his words.

'Welcome to my castle, Erienne Malanvai. I trust you are recovering. Now, I think we had better reunite you with your beautiful little boys.'

*

It was cold and he sat alone on cracked earth in a vast featureless empty space. There was no wind yet something was moving his hair and when he looked in front of him the Dragon was there. Its head was big, he couldn't see the rest of its body. It breathed on him and he just sat there as the skin was burnt from his face and his bones darkened and split. He opened his mouth to scream but nothing came out. He was flying above the land and it was black and smouldering. The sky above him was thick with Dragons but on the ground nothing was moving. He looked for his hands but they weren't there and he felt for his face but the flesh was gone. It was hot. He was running. His arms were pumping hard but his legs moved so slowly. It was catching him and there was nowhere to run. He fell and there it was in front of him again. It breathed and he just sat there as the skin was burnt from his face and his bones darkened and split. There was nowhere to run. Nowhere to hide and the heat scorched his eyes though he could not close them. He opened his mouth to scream.

Hands were about his face. He was sitting up but there was no Dragon, no blackened land. The fire was roaring in the grate. Ilkar put down the poker he'd been using to whip up the flames. Hirad thought it must be cold but he felt hot. Very hot. Talan and The Unknown were sitting up in their beds and it was Sirendor who was cupping his face.

'Calm down, Hirad. It's over. Just a dream.'

Hirad looked the room over again, breathing deeply, his heart beginning to slow.

'Sorry,' he said.

Sirendor patted his cheeks and rose to his feet. 'Scared the life out of me,' he said. 'I thought you were dying.'

'So did I,' replied Hirad.

'You and the rest of the castle,' said Ilkar, stretching and yawning.

'Loud, was I?' Hirad managed a smile.

Ilkar nodded. 'Very. Do you remember what you were dreaming about?'

'I'll never be able to forget. It was Dragons. Thousands of Dragons. And Sha-Kaan. But it wasn't here. Wherever it was was dead. Their world, I think. Sha-Kaan told me they were destroying it. It was black and burned. And Sha-Kaan burned me but I didn't die. I just sat and screamed but there was no sound. I don't understand. How can there be another world? Where is it?' He shivered.

'I don't know. All I do know is, I've never been so scared. Those things don't exist.'

'Yes they bloody do.'

'You know what I mean,' said Sirendor. 'You'll have to talk to Ilkar. But later. Maybe we all should. All this talk of dimensions and Dragons. I don't know.' He stopped. Hirad wasn't really listening.

'What time is it?'

'Dawn's about an hour away,' said The Unknown after hitching a drape aside.

'I think I'll pass on more sleep,' said Hirad. He got up and started pulling on his breeches and shirt. 'I'm going to the kitchens for some coffee.' A look passed between Sirendor and the other three. Hirad couldn't fathom it. 'No problem, is there?'

'No,' said Sirendor. 'No problem. I'll join you.'

'Thanks.' Hirad smiled. So did Sirendor, but it seemed an effort for him. They left the room.

The castle kitchens never closed and heat filled the cavernous rooms from six open fires. Work and eating tables covered much of the floor space, and on racks around the walls hung pots, pans and utensils, some of which defied understanding. Smoke poured up chimneys and steam through open windows high above. The heat of the fires gave the kitchens a consoling warmth, and the sounds of orders mixed with laughter and carried on the smells of roasting meat and the sweet aromas of freshly baked bread brought back memories of a home life long lost.

On one of the fires a huge pot of water was kept boiling. Mugs and coffee grounds sat on trays near by. Ensconced at a table away from the clatterings of cooks and servants, the two men talked across their drinks.

'You're looking glum, Sirendor.' The friends locked eyes. Sirendor's seemed sorrowful. His brow was furrowed and his whole face wore trouble like an ill-fitting shirt. Hirad wasn't used to it.

'We've been talking.'

'Who?'

'Who do you think? While you were asleep earlier.'

'I don't think I like the sound of this.' Whatever it was, it was serious. He hadn't seen Sirendor like this for years.

'We're not getting any younger.'

'You what?'

'You heard.'

'Larn, I am thirty-one! You're thirty and the big man's just thirty-three and he's the oldest! What are you talking about?'

'How many hired men do you know who are over thirty and still front-line quality?'

Hirad drew breath. 'Well, not many but, I mean . . . we're different. We are The Raven.'

'Yes, we are The Raven. And we're getting too old to fight.'

'You're kidding! We hammered that lot yesterday.'

'That's the way you saw it, is it?' Hirad nodded. Sirendor smiled. 'I somehow thought you might. The way I saw it is we didn't have our edge.'

'That's because we spend too much time standing and watching. Like I said, if we don't do it, we'll lose it.'

'Gods, Hirad, you're stubborn in the face of the facts. Do you think it's a coincidence that we've slowly taken fewer front-line contracts and more advisory and back-up jobs over the last couple of years?' Hirad said nothing. 'What we had, that edge, has gone. When we were called in yesterday, we almost weren't up to it.'

'Oh, come on, Larn . . .'

'Ras *died*!' Sirendor looked around, then lowered his voice. 'You could have died. Richmond made an unbelievable mistake and Ilkar lost the shield. If it hadn't been for The Unknown we could have been wiped out. Us. The Raven!'

'Yeah, but the explosion . . .'

'You know as well as I do that two years ago we'd have been through them and at the mage before he had time to cast that spell. We have to adapt . . .' Sirendor trailed off. He took a gulp of his coffee. Hirad just stared at him.

'Hirad, I want us to be able to look back on the good days in another ten years' time. If we try and keep The Raven going as it is, there won't be any ten years.'

'One dodgy fight and you want to give up.'

'It's not just about one fight. But yesterday was a warning of what could happen any time. We've seen the signs these past two years. We all have. It's just that you chose to ignore them.'

'You want to disband The Raven, the rest of you?' asked Hirad. He was only half surprised to find his eyes moistening. His world was dropping to pieces before him and he couldn't see a way out. Not yet.

'Not necessarily. Perhaps just a rest to take stock.' Sirendor leant back a little and spread his hands wide. 'God knows, none of us needs the money any more to be comfortable. I sometimes think we must own half of Korina between us.' He smiled briefly. 'Look, the reason

I'm bringing this up is that we want to have a meeting when we get back to the City. We need to talk it through, all of us, when we've had a little time to think.'

Hirad stared into his coffee, letting the steam warm his face. Silent again.

'If we go on pretending it's still like it was a few years ago, one day we won't be fast enough. Hirad?' The barbarian looked up. 'Hirad, I don't want to lose you the way we lost Ras.' Sirendor sucked his lip, then sighed. 'I don't want to see you die.'

'You won't.' Hirad's voice was gruff. He swigged back his coffee and stood up, having to push his lips together to be sure they wouldn't tremble. 'I'm going to see to the horses,' he said at length. 'We may as well make an early start.' He strode out of the kitchens and through the castle to the courtyard, where he stopped, staring at the place that might have witnessed The Raven's last fight. He wiped angrily at his eyes and headed for the stables.

Ilkar too decided against further rest and went instead to Seran's chambers. The mage from Lystern, smallest of the four College Cities, had been moved to a low table in his study, a sheet covering his body. Ilkar pulled the sheet back from Seran's face. He frowned.

The dead mage's skin was taut across his skull and his hair completely white. He hadn't looked that way the previous evening. And the cut on his forehead, now it was clean, looked as if it had been made with a small claw.

He heard movement behind him and turned to see Denser, the Xetesk mage, standing in the doorway to the bedroom. His pipe smoked gently in his mouth and the cat was in his cloak. Ilkar found the pipe incongruous. Denser was by no means an old man, though his exertions had given him an appearance well beyond his mid-thirties years.

'An unfortunate result, but inevitable,' said Denser. He looked terribly tired. His face was grey and his eyes dark and sunken. He leaned against the door frame.

'What happened to him?'

Denser shrugged. 'He was not a young man. We knew he might die.' He shrugged again. 'There was no other way. He wanted to stop us.'

'We.' In Ilkar's mind, the coin dropped. 'The cat.'

'Yes. He's a Familiar.'

Ilkar pulled the sheet back over Seran's head and moved towards

Denser. 'Come on, you'd better sit down before you fall down. There's questions I need answering.'

'I didn't think this was a social call.' Denser smiled.

'No.' Ilkar did not.

Once seated, Ilkar looked at Denser sprawled on Seran's bed and didn't have to ask his first question. The Xeteskian wouldn't have had the strength to try leaving the castle last night.

'Overdid it yesterday, did you?' asked the Julatsan.

'There was work to do once I had recovered this,' agreed Denser, pulling the amulet from his cloak, where it hung from its chain round his neck. 'I presume this is what you wish to talk about.'

Ilkar inclined his head. 'What sort of work?'

'I had to know whether it was the piece we were after.'

'And was it?'

'Yes.'

'Xetesk sent you?'

'Of course.'

'And this battle?' Ilkar waved a hand around vaguely.

'Well, let's just say it was fairly easy to place me in an attack force but it wasn't staged for my benefit, if that's what you mean.'

'So why didn't you just join the garrison defence?'

'With a Dragonene mage in residence? Hardly.' Denser chuckled. 'I'm afraid Seran and Xetesk didn't see eye to eye.'

'Surprise, surprise,' muttered Ilkar.

'Come now, Ilkar, we are none of us that different from each other.'

'Bloody hell! Is the conceit of Xetesk that great that your Masters really believe all mages are essentially alike? That is an insult to magic itself and a failing in your teaching.' Ilkar could feel the anger surging in him. His cheeks were hot and his eyes narrowed to slits. The blindness of Xetesk was sometimes staggering. 'You know where the power comes from to shape mana for the spells you were casting yesterday. There is no blood on my hands, Denser.'

Denser was quiet for a while. He relit his pipe and picked his cat out of his cloak, dropping it on to the bed. The animal stared at Ilkar while the Dark Mage ruffled its neck. Ilkar's temper frayed further but he held his tongue.

'I think, Ilkar,' said Denser at length, blowing out a series of smoke rings, 'that you shouldn't accuse my Masters of failings in their teaching until you are aware of the shortcomings in your own.'

'What are you talking about?'

Denser spread his palms. 'Do you see blood on my hands?'

'You know what I mean,' snapped Ilkar.

'Yes, I do. And you should also know that a Xeteskian mage has more than one source for his mana. As, no doubt, have you.'

There was silence between them, though around them the castle corridors were beginning to echo with the sounds of another day.

'I will not discuss College ethics with you, Denser.'

'A pity.'

'Pointless.'

'A shortcoming in your teaching, Ilkar?'

He ignored the jibe. 'I need to know two things. How did you know about Seran and that amulet, and what is it?'

Denser considered for a while. 'Well, I'm not about to divulge College secrets, but unlike you, apparently, Xetesk has always taken Dragonene lore seriously – patchy though it may be. Our work in dimensional research has led us to develop a spell that can detect the kind of disturbance caused by the opening of an interdimensional portal, like the one we went through yesterday. We suspected Seran – I won't tell you why – we targeted his chambers and got the desired result. I was sent to retrieve Dragonene artefacts and I got this.' He took the amulet from its chain and tossed it to Ilkar, who turned it over a couple of times, shrugged and threw it back.

'It has Dragonene lore on it, written in all four College lore scripts,' said Denser, rehanging it on its chain. A brief smile touched his lips. 'It will be incredibly useful to our research and, when we're done with it, we can simply name our price. You would not believe what collectors will pay for a piece like this.'

'And that's it?' asked Ilkar flatly.

Denser nodded. 'We all need money. You of all people should know that research is not cheap.'

Ilkar inclined his head. 'So what now?'

'I have to get this piece into the right hands, quickly,' said Denser.

'Xetesk?'

Denser shook his head. 'Too far and too dangerous. Korina. We can secure it there. You're going that way, I take it?'

'Yes.'

'I would like The Raven to bodyguard me. You will be well paid.'

Ilkar gaped at him, making sure he'd heard correctly. 'You have got to be bloody joking, Denser. After what happened yesterday? You've got some nerve, I'll give you that. Hirad still wants to kill you as far as I know. And even if the others didn't mind, do you really think that I would *ever* stoop to work for Xetesk?'

'I'm sorry you feel that way.'

'But you can't possibly be surprised.' Ilkar got up and dusted himself down. 'You'll have to find someone else. There are plenty still here looking for paid passage back to the City.'

'I would prefer The Raven. It seems the least I can do in recompense.'

'We don't want your money,' said Ilkar. 'I'll be making a report to Julatsa when I get back to Korina. You understand there will be a representation from the three Colleges to Xetesk over this whole incident.'

'We look forward to it.'

'I'll bet.' Ilkar turned as he reached the door. 'You hungry? I'll show you the way to the kitchens.'

'Thank you, brother.'

Ilkar's embryonic smile disappeared. 'I am not your brother.'

Chapter 4

Erienne sat on the double bed in the isolated tower room, a son cradled beneath each arm. Her body knew peace, however fleeting, and her children had ceased their crying.

But they had doubted her and the moment of their reunion would live with her for ever. Left alone at the top of the spiral stairway, she had grasped the handle and opened the door, half expecting to see them dead. Instead, they were sitting together on the edge of their bed, talking in whispers, food and drink ignored and cooling on the table that made up the only other furniture but for two chairs. Even the floor had no covering for its cold stone.

She'd taken them in in an instant, brown bobbed hair a little untidy, round faces, pale blue eyes, small noses, slightly jutting ears and long-fingered hands. Her boys. Her beautiful boys.

Their faces had turned to her in symphony and she'd held out her arms. It was then she knew hatred like she'd never felt before. Because for a moment they hadn't seen her, their mother and protector. They'd seen a betrayer, someone who had let them be taken, let them be afraid.

And as she'd stood in the doorway, dishevelled in her bare feet, her nightgown stained and torn, her face displaying the effects of the brophane and her hair tangled, the tears had flooded her eyes and smeared a clean track on her dust-darkened cheeks.

'I'm here. Mother's here.' They'd run into her arms, the three crying until nothing was left but to hold on in case they should ever be separated again. Now they sat, all three on the bed, the boys nuzzling her chest while her arms bound them and her hands stroked their sides.

'Where are we, Mummy?' asked Thom, sitting to her left.

'We're in a castle far from home, full of bad men,' said Erienne, gripping her boys closer and glaring at the closed door, outside which, she knew, Isman would now be standing. 'I've got to help them, answer some questions about magic, and then they'll let us go.'

'Who are they?' Aron looked up into his mother's eyes, lost and confused. She felt his hand grip at her back.

'When we get home, I'll tell you all about them. But they are men trying to understand magic and what men don't understand frightens them. It always has.'

'When will we go home?' Aron again.

Erienne sighed. 'I don't know, my loves. I don't know what they want to ask me.' She smiled to ease the tension. 'I'll tell you what. When we get home, I'll let you choose what you want to learn about next. What will it be?'

The boys leaned forward, shared a glance, nodded and chimed in concert:

'Communion!'

Erienne laughed. 'I knew you'd say that. Bad boys! Just so you can talk without me hearing you.' She tickled their stomachs, the boys giggling and squirming. 'Bad boys!' She fluffed their hair then held them close again.

'Now,' she said, eyeing their plates with distaste. 'I want you to eat the bread on those plates but nothing else, do you hear? I'm going to go and see about getting us home. I'll be back to teach you later, so I hope you haven't forgotten what I told you last week!' She made to rise but the boys clung on.

'Do you have to go, Mummy?' asked Aron.

'The sooner I do, the sooner we'll all be home with your father.' She hugged them again. 'Hey, I won't be gone long, I promise.' They both looked up at her. 'I promise,' she repeated.

She unlocked their arms and went to the door, pulling it open on a surprised-looking Isman. The rangy warrior lurched to a standing position from his slouch against the wall, the flaps of his leather tunic clapping together over his worn brown shirt.

'Finished so soon?' he asked.

'Just in a hurry,' said Erienne brusquely. 'I'll answer your questions now. My boys need their father and their own beds.'

'And we are just as anxious as you to see you are held here for as short a time as possible,' said Isman smoothly. 'The Captain will question you shortly. Until then—'

'Now,' said Erienne, closing the door at her back with one last smile at her boys, who waved at her.

'You are in no position to make demands of us,' sneered Ismam.

Erienne smiled and moved close to Isman. As she did so, her face hardened, the smile seeming to freeze on her cheeks.

'And what if I walk past you now?' she hissed, her face paling. 'What are you going to do?' Their faces were scant inches apart, his eyes flickering over her. 'Stop me? Kill me?' She laughed. 'You're scared of me because we both know I could kill you before your sword left your scabbard. And we're alone, so don't tempt me. Just take me to your Captain right now.'

Isman pursed his lips and nodded.

'He said you'd be trouble. We had you watched for months before we took you. He said your kind knew much but were arrogant.' He pushed past her and led the way down the spiral stairs. He turned at the bottom. 'He was right. He always is. Go ahead, kill me if you think you can. There are three men outside this door. You can't get far. We both know that too, don't we?'

'But I'd have the satisfaction of seeing you die,' said Erienne. 'And I'd see the fear in your eyes. Think on it. Unless you watch me all the time, you'll never know if I'm about to cast. Never know when you're about to die.'

'We have your children.' The sneer was back on Isman's face.

'Well, you'd better see you look after them, then, hadn't you? Don't turn your back, Isman.'

The warrior let out a contemptuous laugh, but as he turned to open the door, Erienne thought she saw him shudder.

Denser sat at the end of a bench table full of men who, not many hours before, would have killed him. The barbarian, Hirad Coldheart, was not there. Seeing to their horses, Sirendor Larn had said. Denser shivered inwardly, laid down his fork across his half-eaten breakfast of meat, gravy and bread, and sipped at his coffee. His cat purred as it lay on the bench beside him, luxuriating in the warmth cast by the range of fires in the kitchens.

They'd been prepared to die then, at the barbarian's sword. Their inner calm had been complete. And had they died, he in a crush of bone and his cat in a screaming mental explosion, the whole of Balaia might have died with them.

Denser looked up at The Unknown Warrior. They all still had a chance because of him. Him and the simple code The Raven had always followed. The reason why they above all other mercenary teams remained in demand, successful and so very effective. While killing was legal within the rules of battle, and in witnessed defence of self and others, outside of these boundaries it was murder. And The Raven, perhaps alone, had stood in battle lines for ten years with robbers, bandits, bounty hunters and other hired men little better than murderers, with their collective conscience clear.

There were plenty who said it was the total adherence to their code that made them strong and feared by opponents; and Denser had no doubt that the perpetuation of this myth helped them enormously. Mainly, though, he considered it was because while as individuals they were outstanding, if not brilliant, as a team they were simply awesome.

Yet it was the code that swung the balance when the cost of their hire was considered. It meant that their employers could expect the contract to be upheld and the battle to be fought by The Raven within the rules.

The Code: Kill But Never Murder.

So simple that many tried to live by it on taking up the career as a hired warrior or mage. But most lacked the discipline, intelligence, stamina or skill to keep true in the heat of battle, victory or retreat, and aftermath. And certainly none had done so for ten years without blemish.

It would be easy to cast them as heroes, but Denser had seen them fight more than once and what they were was, to him, obvious. They were a team of terribly efficient killers. Killers but not murderers.

But as Denser looked around the table at the men eating in silence, each walking the privacy of his own mind, he thought they looked tired, and a pang of fear flooded his gut lest they should ultimately refuse him.

Because he needed them. Xetesk needed them. Gods, all of Balaia would need them if the information the spies were sending back proved to be the prelude to the rising of the Wytch Lords. But could he convince them of what had to be done, and would Xetesk try to bring the Colleges together?

Despite the knowledge of what could be to come, Denser wondered whether he wasn't facing his most difficult challenge now.

The Raven.

Even if they heard the truth, he was pretty sure it wouldn't make any difference. They didn't take a contract because they believed in the cause. In fact the cause was largely irrelevant. The job had to be made worth their while, worth their reputation and worth their attendance. Worth the risk. That's why the truth was pointless, at least until he could hide it no longer. No compensation could possibly be worth the risks he would be asking them to face.

Denser took another mouthful of food. It was a great pity he hadn't met The Raven in Korina as planned. There he might have been able to conceal his College identity for long enough. Their being part of Taranspike Castle's defence hadn't figured in Xetesk's plans. Now he was truly up against it and right now he couldn't even persuade Ilkar to let him pay them to ride with him to Korina, the City they were headed for anyway.

He glanced up and caught The Unknown's eye. The warrior calmly held his gaze, swallowed his mouthful and pointed his knife at Denser.

'Tell me something,' he said. 'Ever see a Dragon before?'

'No,' said Denser.

'No. And what would you have done had Hirad not managed to distract it so effectively while you stole your prize?'

Denser smiled ever so slightly. 'That is a very good question. We hadn't planned on a Dragon being there.'

'Clearly. My guess is you would have died.'

'Possibly.' Denser half shrugged. Actually he thought he would have been fine but he could see where the line was leading and it gave him a chance.

'Definitely.' The Unknown smeared a chunk of bread around his plate and then placed it carefully in his mouth. 'There is an argument, therefore, that says we helped you take the amulet, however unwittingly.'

Denser inclined his head and refilled his mug from the copper pot on the table.

'What sort of percentage did you have in mind?'

'Five per cent of sale value.'

Denser blew out his cheeks. 'That'll be a lot of money.'

It was The Unknown's turn to shrug. 'Call it compensation for the death of a Raven man. Or for the countless nights we wake up shaking and sweating from the visions of what we saw in there. I don't mind telling you, it took all the control I had not to turn and run.'

'That would be a first ever,' said Ilkar eventually into the void. The Unknown inclined his head.

'He wouldn't have been the only one,' said Sirendor. More nods around the table mixed with the odd smile.

'And none of you know the half of it.' All heads turned to see Hirad standing in the doorway of the kitchen. He walked towards them slowly, his face drawn and pinched round the eyes.

'You all right, Hirad?' asked Sirendor.

'Not really. I was outside remembering what Sha-Kaan said, and if that doorway was still there I'd be taking the amulet back to him.'

'Why?' Sirendor again, and Denser held his breath.

'Something he said. About holding the portal from his world to ours and guarding something we shouldn't have made. Whatever it was, he is angry now, so what if he chooses not to hold the portal any longer?'

'I haven't got a clue what you're talking about, Hirad.' Sirendor for the third time.

'Neither have I really,' said Hirad. 'Just that if we ever see a Dragon in the skies of Balaia, it'll be the end for all of us.'

'What do you mean, exactly?' asked Denser.

'What do you *think* I mean?' snapped the barbarian. 'We'll all die. They are too powerful and there are too many of them. Trust me.' He moved to the cooking pots and ladled himself some meat into a bowl.

'Look. Going back a little.' Denser's attention was once again on The Unknown Warrior. 'I'll agree to the five per cent if you agree to bodyguard me back to Korina.'

Ilkar swung round from where he had been staring at Hirad as if he had been slapped in the face. 'I have already told you that we will not work for Xetesk.' His voice was low, steady and certain.

'Just exactly how much do you think that thing is worth, Xetesk man?' asked Hirad.

Denser raised his eyebrows. 'Well, though I can't guarantee it, I think we're talking in the region of five million truesilver.' There was a brief pause of slack-jawed disbelief.

'We'll take the job.'

'Hirad!' snapped Ilkar. 'You do not understand.'

'It's good money, Ilkar.'

'It's unbelievable, more like,' said Talan. 'That's a quarter of a million truesilver for taking a passenger down a road we're already travelling.' Hirad just mouthed the figure.

'You know something, Hirad, I just cannot believe that you of all people would agree to this. He all but had you killed.' Ilkar's tone bordered on contempt.

'Yeah, so he owes me.' Hirad kept his face away from the Xeteskian as he spoke. 'I don't have to like him. I don't even have to look at him. In fact I can go on hating him. All I have to do is put up with him riding near by on the way back to Korina. Then he pays us a great deal of money and we never see him again. I think I can handle it.'

'Anyway it's not that simple,' said Ilkar.

'Yes it is.'

'It isn't and I have a real problem with it,' began Ilkar, but the barbarian loomed over him.

'I know you don't agree with the Xetesk morality—'

'That's an understatement and a half—'

'—but considering what you lot have been about behind my back, I don't think it's the kind of money we should turn down, do you? It might be the last we ever make.' He straightened. Ilkar just scowled at him. 'Face it, Ilkar, you'll be outvoted. Don't make it difficult.' Ilkar's eyes narrowed to slits.

The Unknown reached a hand across to Denser. 'We have a contract. Talan will write it and you and I will sign it. No actual value will be mentioned but the percentage and intention to pay will be registered.'

'Excellent,' said Denser. The two men shook.

'Indeed it is.' The Unknown drained his mug. 'You know what, I can feel a Rookery party coming on.'

The door to the kitchens opened again.

'I hear you couldn't save my mage. A pity. He was a good man, Seran.'

The Raven turned to look at their employer, and Denser his erstwhile opponent for the first time. Baron Gresse was middle-aged with a powerful mind and a quartet of sons to make up for his own fading strength. Spurning rich man's clothes – and he was among the top five Barons in terms of wealth – he walked in wearing practical riding garb, cloak over one arm, leather jerkin, woollen shirt and leather in-thighed cloth trousers.

He dismissed his men at arms from the door and waved away the babbling kitchen folk as he made his way to The Raven's table. He studied them all through his large brown eyes, his balding grey head moving smoothly as he did so. He reached out a hand.

'The Unknown Warrior.'

'Baron Gresse.' The men shook.

'A pleasure to make your acquaintance.'

'Likewise.' The Unknown glanced along the table. 'Get the Baron some coffee, Talan.'

'Well, well, The Raven. Hardly a surprise we won the day. Seran always chose well.' Gresse chewed his lip. 'Where will I find another like him, eh?'

'Julatsa,' said Ilkar. 'At least we're consistent.'

Gresse chuckled. 'Do you mind if I sit down?' He gestured at the bench. Ilkar moved along and he sat. Talan placed coffee in front of him. He nodded his thanks.

An awkward silence fell around the table. Denser scratched his beard nervously. The Unknown gazed at the Baron, impassive as always. Ilkar's ears pricked.

'I shan't keep you in suspense,' said Gresse, sipping at his beverage, a smile playing about his lips. 'But I was hoping you might be able to back up something I've heard.'

'Of course,' said The Unknown. 'If we can.'

'Good. I'll be brief. I have been called to a meeting of the Korina Trade Alliance concerning deteriorating conditions to the west of the Blackthorne Mountains. There are rumours that the Wesmen have stepped up activity, broken the Understone Pass Right of Passage agreement, and there are fears of incursions into the east – although I should point out that the garrison at Understone itself has reported nothing out of the ordinary. I need to know whether you have picked up any rumours. I understand you were fighting with Baron Blackthorne himself not long ago, and he is unable to attend the meeting.' Gresse's eyes twinkled.

'We only fought with him so The Unknown could get a better deal on his wine.' Sirendor smiled.

'I feel sure you did not.'

'As it happened, that was part of the agreement,' said The Unknown. 'As regards rumours, we heard plenty while we were there, but this is six months ago we're talking about.'

'Anything you heard, even in passing, that I could bring to the table would be useful.'

'Put it this way,' said Ilkar. 'If you believed everything you heard, the Wytch Lords are back, Parve is a bustling city once again and the Wesmen are torching everything west of the Blackthorne Mountains.'

'And you give these rumours no credence,' said Gresse.

'Nothing a Wesmen war party might do would surprise me,' said Ilkar. 'But aside from that, no.'

'Hmmm.' Gresse was thoughtful. 'Interesting. Thank you for your help yesterday, by the way. I understand you lost a man. I'm sorry.'

'It's a risk, let's be honest,' said Hirad, though his tone was unconvincing.

'Nevertheless, to lose a friend cannot be easy. I am sorry and I am grateful. Yesterday's was a battle I couldn't afford to lose. Literally.'

'You make it sound as though you're on your uppers,' said Talan.

Gresse shrugged. 'Taranspike Castle is of major tactical importance. The owner negotiates rights of passage through one of the principal routes in and out of Korina. Had I lost it to Baron Pontois, he would have controlled both of my key transport routes to the capital as well as holding land on two sides of my estate. He could have chosen to deny me access or price it out of my reach, either way bankrupting me over time. My best alternative route takes days not hours.'

'Unless you chose to take one back by force,' said Hirad.

'That is always an option. Expensive but an option.' Gresse's face hardened.

'And yet you'll sit down with Pontois at the Korina Trade Alliance,' said Talan.

'Yes. Strange, I know, but reality. Such is the malaise of the KTA. The word "alliance" rings very hollow these days.' There was more than a hint of sadness in his tone.

The table fell silent for a time. The Unknown Warrior studied the Baron while he drank his coffee. The big warrior smiled, Gresse caught his expression and frowned in response.

'It seems to me that you omitted to tell us any rumours you might have heard,' said The Unknown.

'I did, and I have something rather more than rumour, I'm afraid. I have evidence that the Wesmen, far from burning, are subjugating, building and uniting again.'

'What do you mean, again?' asked Hirad.

'I'll teach you the history later,' said Ilkar with a shake of his head.

'How could you—' Denser bit his lip and closed his mouth.

'Something to say, Xetesk man?' Hirad growled.

'I was merely curious how he came by such information.' Denser's recovery was betrayed by a face that displayed his surprise.

'Everything has its price,' said Gresse, coolly. 'Might I ride to Korina with you this morning?'

'Be our guest,' said Hirad. 'Denser's paying, after all.'

'Good.' Gresse rose, shooting Hirad a quizzical look. 'My party will be ready in, shall we say, one hour?'

'It suits us petfectly,' said The Unknown. 'Gentlemen, The Rookery beckons.'

Erienne and the Captain met in the library. Warmed by two fires and lit by a dozen lanterns, the immaculately kept house of books was testament to his intelligence if not his morals.

Five shelves high, covering three sides of the room, perhaps fifteen by twenty-five feet, books loomed around her. A fire stood either side of the only door. Rugs covered the floor and a reading desk dominated the far end. She had been told to sit in a large green leather-upholstered chair near one of the fires, and when the Captain came in, followed by a warrior carrying a tray of wine and food, he said nothing before setting himself in a similar seat at right angles to her.

She had locked her gaze on the fire to stop her eyes catching sight of him, allowing the light of the flames to mesmerise her, only dimly hearing the clink of glasses, the glug of a pouring bottle and the metal sound of knife on carving tray.

'Once again, welcome, Erienne Malanvai,' said the Captain. 'You must be hungry.'

Erienne let her eyes travel over the tray that sat on a low table between them, surprised at the quality of its content.

'How dare you offer me that, when the muck you served up for my boys is hardly fit for a dog, let alone frightened young children?' she said. 'They will each have a plate of this now.'

She could sense the Captain's smile. 'You heard her. Fresh lamb and vegetables for the boys.'

'Yes, sir.' The door closed.

'I am not unreasonable,' said the Captain.

Erienne's face was pure disgust. 'You have taken two innocent children from their homes in the middle of the night and locked them terrified in a cold tower. You have kept me from them and fed them muck I wouldn't give to my pigs. Don't talk to me about reason.' Still refusing to look at him, she selected some meat and vegetables and ate in silence. She poured herself a glass of wine and drank staring at the fire. All the while, the Captain watched and waited.

'So ask,' she said, placing her empty plate on the table. 'I doubt I have any secrets from you.'

'That would certainly make things simpler,' said the Captain. 'I am glad you are being so co-operative.'

'Don't feel it's out of any fear of you or your band of lame monkeys,' Erienne said haughtily. 'I care for my sons and any way that I can help them that does not compromise the Dordovan College is fine by me.'

'Excellent.' The Captain refilled his glass. 'I do wish you'd look at me.'

'To do so would make me nauseous. To utter your name is an affront to my College and to speak with you is tantamount to heresy. Now get on with your questions. In an hour I want to see my sons again.' Erienne kept her face turned to the fire, drawing comfort from its warmth and colour.

'And so you shall, Erienne, so you shall.' The Captain stretched out his legs towards the fire; a pair of scuffed and age-cracked brown leather riding boots moved into Erienne's vision. 'Now then, I am becoming very disturbed by the extent to which so-called dimensional investigation and research is damaging the fabric of Balaia.'

'Well, you've clearly been very busy in here, haven't you?' said Erienne after a pause.

'Clever remarks will get you hurt,' said the Captain, his tone leaving her in no doubt that he meant it.

'I was trying to say that very few people have any knowledge of the existence of dimensional magics, never mind the potential for their danger.'

'No.' The Captain reached down and scratched his left leg, Erienne glimpsing his greying hair, thinning from the crown. 'Contrary to popular belief, I believe in the value of magic in the right place. But I also understand its dangers because I have taken the time to find out for myself. Meddling with dimensions could, I believe, destabilise the world balance that currently exists.'

'You're talking to the wrong College,' said Erienne.

'Well, Xetesk mages are just a little harder to come by,' said the Captain testily.

'I'd love to say I was sorry,' retorted Erienne. And at last, she looked at him. He kept his grey hair close-cropped and his beard, which still held flecks of brown, was similarly well trimmed. Skin was sagging under his eyes and his red-patched cheeks and nose were evidence of a reliance on the bottle. He was getting fat, too, as he breasted middle age, a fact which his leather coat and shirt failed to hide. He ignored her sudden attention.

'But Septern was a Dordovan mage.'

'We've already established that you've done your homework.' Erienne refilled her glass. 'It also no doubt told you that he's been presumed dead for about three hundred years.'

'And there the information ends?' said the Captain. 'I was rather hoping a Dordovan Lore Mage like yourself could fill in a few gaps.'

'And now the misunderstanding is yours,' said Erienne. 'Because you assume we have secret texts.'

'But Septern was a Dordovan mage,' repeated the Captain.

'Yes, he was. And a genius. And so far ahead of his time that we still haven't managed to re-create all of his work.' Erienne plucked some grapes from the fruit bowl and ate them, spitting the stones into her hand and throwing them into the fire.

The Captain leaned forwards, frowning. 'But surely he reported his findings. I understood that to be a requirement of every mage.'

'Septern didn't live by those rules.' Erienne sighed as the Captain's frown deepened. 'Look, you need to understand. Septern was a throwback to the days before the Colleges split.'

'So he wasn't just ahead of his time, he was behind it as well.' The Captain smiled, pleased at his own joke, revealing lines of brown, rotting teeth set in flame-red gums.

'Yes, I suppose so. The point is, his mind was able to accept lore at the very base level, and that let him read and understand Dordovan, Xeteskian and Julatsan lores with varying degrees of success. It made him brilliant but it also made him arrogant. He lived outside of the College, rarely reported on his work, made only cryptic logs of his research and not all of those logs are in our library. Xetesk has some, others are lost at his house – assuming he wrote anything at all about some of the things we know he was capable of.' Erienne took a sip of wine. 'Could I have some water, please?'

'Certainly.' The Captain rose and pulled the door open. The sound of a man dragging his feet to attention echoed in the corridor outside. 'Water and a glass. Now.' He returned to his seat. 'An interesting history. Of course, I am aware of his house. I have had men at the ruins on several occasions. So tell me, what is the state of your development of dimensional research, and what do you hope to achieve?'

Erienne opened her mouth to speak, then closed it, pondering her answer. It was all too easy. The Captain was nothing like she had been led to believe. That she would hate him for ever for the kidnap of her children was certain, but his behaviour was confusing. Here she sat in a warm room, where she had been fed with good food and asked gentle questions about her College activities. So far he had asked her nothing he couldn't have found out by knocking on the College's front door. There had to be more, it was just a question of when he dealt it to her. She had the uneasy feeling she was being softened up for a heavy blow. She determined to keep her mind sharp.

'What we know of Septern tells us that he achieved a great deal in terms of dimensional magics. He created a stable, self-sustaining portal for travelling between nominated dimensional spaces and we believe he travelled widely – some of his wilder writings suggest as much.

'Dordover is nowhere near his level of sophistication in dimension doors. We can't travel, we can't see in, all we can do is plot other dimensions and chart land and sea features. To progress more quickly, we need Septern's lost texts because we believe this magic mixes College lores.'

'And where do you hope this research will take you?'

'Into other dimensions. To explore, to chart, to meet other races. The possibilities are endless.' Erienne was enthused in spite of herself.

'To conquer, to subvert, to rule, to steal.' The Captain's tone was hard but not unpleasant.

'Is that the basis for your concern?'

He inclined his head. 'I believe we have no place interfering in other dimensions. We have our own and it is difficult enough to control without linking it to other places and times. I see nightmare scenarios where others might invade to avenge what we have done. No one will be safe anywhere because no one will ever know when or where a door might be opened.'

'All the more reason to complete our research and understanding,' said Erienne.

'Neither of us is naïve enough to believe that Dordover and Xetesk research this magic to benefit the population of Balaia, are we? I would hate to think you were opening doors which you were then powerless to close.' The Captain scratched an ear. 'Tell me, is Xetesk further advanced than Dordover?'

Erienne stared at him blankly. 'If and when the missing elements of Septern's dimensional texts are recovered, we may be forced to form a research group,' she said slowly. 'Until that time, communication remains minimal.'

'I understand.'

'It was a stupid question to ask a Dordovan.'

'Stupidity sometimes elicits the real gems.'

The door opened and a man entered carrying a jug of water and two glasses. He set them on the table and withdrew. Erienne filled a glass and drank it back in one.

'Anything else?'

'Oh, a good deal,' said the Captain. He drained and refilled his wine glass. 'I have hardly begun, although your information is gratefully received. I should let you get back to your children but think on this. Given that you appear to know all you can about dimensional magics already, I find it disturbing that there has been such a recent surge in interest surrounding Septern's research.

'Mastery of dimensional magic wasn't his only triumph, was it? There was one of even greater notoriety. He created a spell, didn't he? And I want to know why Xetesk has suddenly put all its muscle behind looking for it.'

Erienne's face became deathly white.

Chapter 5

The Raven and their charges rode from Taranspike Castle as the sun picked at the dew lying heavily on the grass of yesterday's battlefield. The rain of the previous night had blown away west across the central flatlands towards the dark line of the Blackthorne Mountains and a gentle breeze blew warmth through the dawn of the early spring day. Baron Pontois, his soldiers, mercenary warriors and mages were gone, disappeared north through the Grethern Forest from which they had come. All that was left of their encampment was flattened brush and a single, wood-picketed mound where the dead were buried.

At the head of the small horseback party were Hirad, Richmond and Ilkar, while much to his bodyguards' displeasure, Baron Gresse chose to ride flanked by Talan and The Unknown Warrior. Denser and Sirendor Larn rode behind the second trio, leaving Gresse's quartet of men bringing up the rear.

For the Baron, the ride was clearly a chance to shake off the shackles of an overprotective family and ride free. For The Unknown and Talan, the habit of gleaning information from whatever source came their way was impossible to break.

'Are you still allied with Blackthorne?' asked Talan.

Gresse nodded. 'We have a reciprocal passage arrangement but I wouldn't call it an alliance. He travels toll-free through this pass to Korina, I have similar rights through his lands to Gyernath.'

The Unknown frowned. 'Did he take the lands east of Gyernath? I heard he—'

'Six months ago. He's all but annexed Gyernath now, though the City Council has applied significant pressure on him to keep his passage levies low. Successfully so far.'

'So what happened to Lord Arlen?' asked The Unknown.

'He works for Blackthorne.'

'Ah—' Light dawned.

'Gods, no, there was no fighting. No more fighting, should I say. Arlen still nominally controls the lands east of Gyernath, though the truth is he's supported by Blackthorne's considerable muscle, furnished with metals from the southern mines and taking a rake off the levy on traffic from the south-east, including Korina.' Gresse chuckled and reached a hand out to pat The Unknown's thigh. 'If I were you, I'd cross Arlen off my list of potential employers. Blackthorne has all the finance around Gyernath now.'

'Anyone else we can strike off?' Talan asked.

'Not me,' said Gresse. 'Pontois hasn't finished yet, I'm sure. He's either already planning another strike on Taranspike or hoping I'll overfortify there and leave myself open to him further west.'

'Well, if you need us, get in early,' said The Unknown.

'Very early,' said Talan.

'Heard a rumour you lot might be hanging up your leather,' said Gresse, careful not to catch either man's eye.

'Believe it on seeing it,' advised Talan, raising his eyebrows.

'So much for a trade of information,' grumbled Gresse, a smile touching his eyes.

'You'll be the first to know if it happens, how's that?' said The Unknown.

'It'll have to do.' Gresse fell silent, shaking his head.

Taranspike Pass was sheer grey and no less than four hundred feet high all the way to Korina, its cool slate home to birds and tenacious vegetation. Either side of the walls of the pass, the land was precipitous, falling to black chasms, deep ravines and harsh, lifeless valleys where water ran beneath rock, its sound like the souls of the lost as it poured under the ground. In the pass itself, run-off from the previous night's rain puddled on the soft earth, making the way muddy. But with the sun lighting the pass throughout the day, that softness would be driven away and the cracks in a trail which varied between a dozen wagons and just three wagons wide were testament to the heat that sun on rock could generate in the hot season.

The sounds of birds, horses' hoofs and men's voices echoed from the walls, bringing with them an atmosphere that would have provoked discomfort in a lone rider but which a company, with the confidence of companionship, could ignore.

Sirendor Larn took another deep breath of the clean air of Taranspike Pass, revelling in the cool rush that filled his lungs and driving from his mind the smells and smoke of the castle and its surrounds. They would encounter no trouble along the pass. Gresse's men kept the way safe enough and, to Sirendor's knowledge, it wasn't particularly dangerous anyway. With Korina less than a day's ride away, his mood, never down, was lightening by the moment. The only cloud over him was the meeting, and he feared how Hirad would react.

He had kept up a light conversation with Denser for much of the ride, grinning at Ilkar's scowls when he caught the elf's eye. Denser seemed all right. It certainly wasn't the first time Sirendor had fought a man one day and ridden home with him the next. Such was the way of mercenaries. He was clearly a capable mage and, cut from the rules of war, was just another man wondering where the next job would take him. The only difference was that this mage seemed a lot more certain than most. Sirendor took that to be a function of his upbringing in Xetesk and he reminded himself to ask Ilkar more about the Dark College.

Looking across once again at Denser, he smiled. That pipe was clamped between his teeth, gently smouldering as always, and the cat was balancing on the front of his saddle. The mage had been very reticent when pushed for details about the cat, mumbling only that it was an ideal companion for what was, for him, a life largely consisting of solitude. Denser himself was, not for the first time, trying to drill holes with his eyes through The Unknown's back.

'He fascinates me, too,' said Sirendor. 'Always has.' Denser glanced around, his reverie broken.

'What?'

'The Unknown. I've known him ten years and I still don't even know where he was born.'

'Or his name?' Denser asked.

'No. Nor his name,' agreed Sirendor.

'I thought you lot were the only people he told.'

'Another rumour, I'm afraid. Not even Tomas knows.'

'Who's Tomas?' asked Denser.

'Landlord at The Rookery. Well, joint landlord with The Unknown. Tomas has known him more than twenty years. Looked after him at first when he turned up in Korina when he was thirteen.' Sirendor shook his head. 'You learn not to ask him certain questions.'

'So why do you call him The Unknown Warrior?'

Sirendor laughed. 'Our most popular question. Tell me what you've heard, first, then I'll tell you the truth.'

'All I've heard is that he didn't want to be found.' Denser shrugged. 'So he refused to tell anyone his name and took on the one he has now.'

'Common but fatally flawed,' said Sirendor. 'I mean, if he was trying to lose himself from someone, calling himself "The Unknown

Warrior" and fighting with The Raven is about the worst way he could have chosen, don't you think?' Denser nodded. 'No. When we first formed The Raven ten years ago in The Rookery, it was after we'd met on a contract we'd taken as individuals out by Gyernath. By we I mean him, me, Hirad and Ilkar. I remember us all riding back to Korina and how he said he was owner of an inn and we could have lodgings and food because there was something he wanted to discuss.

'The Raven name came up because of where we were drinking, then the code, and we all signed the parchment which Tomas keeps mounted in the back room. When it came to The Unknown's turn, he wouldn't sign, saying his name wasn't important, and it was only then that the rest of us realised that through the week of fighting, he'd not once told us who he was.'

'Why The Raven? Rooks live in rookeries.'

'Same family of birds, better name. Can you really imagine us being called "The Rook"?'

Denser chuckled, the sound dying on the rock in front of him where the pass opened out a little. Sirendor continued.

'Anyway, I remember what Hirad and Ilkar said like it was yesterday. The loudmouth said, "We don't want any mystery man in the team, so either sign up or bugger off."' Sirendor shook his head at the memory. So typical, so very, very Hirad. 'And Ilkar said, "Yeah, what are you, some kind of mystical unknown warrior or something?" That was the name that went on the parchment, under the code. And it stuck.' Sirendor shrugged. 'It's as simple as that.'

Denser chuckled. 'Well, well, well. Of such things are legends made.'

'We sincerely hope so,' said Sirendor.

'But doesn't it fascinate you to know what his name really is and why he won't tell you?' asked Denser, his tone serious again. 'I can't imagine why any man should claim his name wasn't important.'

Sirendor turned in his saddle and put a finger to his lips. He lowered his voice.

'Yes it did, and I suppose still does in moments when my mind wanders. And don't think we haven't asked him, got him drunk and tried to trick his name from him, refused to speak to his face, anything. But he won't let on, and if you press him, he gets angry. You learn to keep your fascination to yourself. He is our friend. If he wishes to be private about something, even his name, we respect it. He is Raven.'

'But he's hiding something from you,' pushed Denser. 'He's not telling you—'

'Enough,' said Sirendor. 'It is his decision. Let it rest.' But the look in Denser's eyes suggested he might not.

A flight of large grey-winged white gulls swept along the pass towards them, angling up away into the sunlight, their calls clattering into the clefts above. More birds, smaller, quicker, darker, rose in protest, their harsh calls scattering the flight, which re-formed high above to continue its journey west. With a loud fluttering of wings, the birds of prey returned to the cliffs, the nests and chicks protected from the marauding carrion gulls.

Gresse followed the exchange, straining his neck upwards before turning to The Unknown. 'Tell me, did Blackthorne show any concern about the Wesmen rumours?'

'I think you have an overblown view of our importance,' replied The Unknown. 'Mercenaries don't get to talk to Baron Blackthorne.'

Gresse turned in his saddle and fixed The Unknown Warrior with his bright eyes.

'Unknown, I am the oldest Baron and I have overblown views about very few things. The Raven's reputation and importance are not among them. I also speak to Blackthorne on occasion and know he enjoys your company.'

'So talk to him again.'

'He is two hundred and fifty miles south-west of here, so I am asking you,' said Gresse testily. 'You aren't telling me everything.'

The Unknown glanced across at Talan, who shrugged his shoulders. The party were moving at an easy trot and Denser was some way behind them, still chatting to Sirendor.

'Six months ago, when you say Arlen sold out to Blackthorne, we were in Eastern Balaia, assessing the Wesmen threat,' said The Unknown. Gresse punched the pommel of his saddle.

'I *knew* there was more. Sly bastard.'

'It just made good sense,' said Talan. 'Let's face it, if the Wesmen invade through Understone Pass and head south rather than north, Blackthorne will catch it rather than the Colleges, at least to begin with. The same goes for an invasion across the Bay of Gyernath, which would leave them only five days from the City itself and a couple of hours from Blackthorne Castle.'

'And what did you see?'

Ahead of them, Hirad called a halt and the party reined in and dismounted for rest and food. It was shortly past midday and the pass was heating up pleasantly. They had stopped in a natural bowl where the rock was scooped out on either side, focusing the strength of the sun.

'Nothing to back up anything you've heard.' Talan shrugged, dusted off a rock with a gauntleted hand and sat down. To his left, Gresse's bodyguards set about lighting a fire, gathering armfuls of the thick dry scrub that clung to the base of the pass the whole of its length. 'We went through the pass as guard to a Blackthorne wine convoy heading for Leionu. We went south after the pass and tracked the Blackthornes for four days, eventually crossing the Bay of Gyernath. We saw no burning villages, no war parties, nothing to suggest the Wesmen were even raiding.

'The Wesmen, if they are massing, are doing so in their Heartlands in the south-west peninsula. Sorry to disappoint you.'

'But that was six months ago.' Gresse sat beside him, choosing the softer grass and heather over a slab of stone.

'Granted, but Baron Blackthorne is not, to my knowledge, concerned about a Wesmen invasion,' said The Unknown. He sifted briefly through his pack and pulled out a small leather bag, stoppered at its neck. 'Hey, Sirendor, salt.' He tossed the bag at the warrior, who jumped to catch it one-handed. 'And use it this time. It makes your soup just about drinkable.' Hirad laughed. Sirendor swore.

'Then he should be concerned.' Gresse was thoughtful for a while. 'And what about the pass itself?'

'Well guarded. Tessaya is not a fool. He gets good revenue from the pass and isn't about to give it up to the KTA or a rival tribe.' The Unknown scratched his nose.

'The barracks?'

'Boarded and empty.' The Unknown shook his head slightly. 'He had a significant guardpost at either end of the pass but was not shoring up for siege.'

'Thank you,' said Gresse. 'Both of you. Sorry to press.'

Talan shrugged. 'No problem. You have other sources, I take it?'

'More recent and no less reliable. The pass is reportedly closed to the east, full of Wesmen, and war parties are emerging from the south-west. If it's true, we're in trouble. We have no organised defence and neither Blackthorne nor the Colleges are strong enough. Just keep your eyes and ears open is all I ask.' Gresse sighed. 'I haven't a hope in hell of persuading the Barons to ally at this meeting, not without Blackthorne. I only hope it's not all too late.'

Talan raised his eyebrows. 'It's that serious, you think? What about the Wytch Lords rumours?'

Gresse snorted. 'Yes, it is that serious. We could all be in a fight for our country very soon. As for the Wytch Lords, if by some appalling miracle they are returned, we can kiss Balaia goodbye.'

The fire crackled into life, flames casting pale shadow on the sunlit walls of the pass. The men lapsed into silence, each preferring his own thoughts on the exchange as he stared into the hypnotic flickering. It was a good time for a little quiet, and Sirendor's meat broth, when it arrived, tasted fine.

The Raven rode through Korina's East Gate as the sun began to be lost behind some of the City's few tall buildings. Where some were stopped and questioned, if not searched, The Raven were, as always, simply waved through to the crowded cobbled streets of Korina's late afternoon trading.

'Now that's an advantage of being us,' remarked Sirendor. 'And there aren't as many as you'd think.' Denser said nothing.

Shortly after their entry into the City, Gresse and his men made their goodbyes and headed south towards the offices of the Korina Trade Alliance and the tightly guarded apartments the Barons found it necessary to maintain.

Korina was the Capital City of Eastern Balaia, boasting a stable population of somewhere around two hundred and fifty thousand, which swelled to as many as three hundred thousand at festival and principal trading times. Most of the latter were dictated by the arrival of merchant fleets from the lands to the east and south of the Northern Continent. Korina sat at the head of the River Kour estuary and had developed safe deep-water ports that attracted southern traders away from the shorter but less profitable journey to Gyernath.

The City was characterised by its sturdy sprawling low buildings, a legacy of the high winds and hurricanes that periodically swept along the estuary as the season changed from winter to the warmer weather of spring. In three places, connected by streets packed with businesses and shops, inns and eating houses, brothels and gambling dens, markets bustled with life every day of the week.

Beyond the triangle, and closer to the port, heavy industry boomed, clanged, fired, sawed and moulded, producing goods for home and across the seas. And in every gap between the places of entertainment, trade, officialdom and work, people lived. Some in squalor, some in luxury undreamed of by those who saw nothing but the dirt on their hands, and most in a state of perpetual shift on a line between the two.

Slowing their horses to trotting pace, The Raven moved towards the western market on the north side of which sat The Rookery. The streets were full of people, carts and animals; and mixed with them, the fresh, foul and fetid smells blew with the noise of the City on a steady inshore breeze. Stalls, wagons, hand baskets and shoulder-slung trays offered everything from fine cloth shipped in from the distant elven southern lands; through pottery, iron and steel wares forged and cast in the foundries and kilns of Korina and Jaden; to meats, vegetables and pastries prepared in kitchens scattered all over the City, some clean, many squalid and filthy. The barrage of trade was held in the single language of hard currency, and everywhere, silver and bronze glinted in the reddening sunlight as it changed hands.

Mercifully, much of the traffic was moving in the opposite direction to their travel as the trading day waned. But the cobbled market square itself was packed with stalls between which The Raven had to pick. Speech was pointless and The Unknown led them in single file towards The Rookery and the quiet of the inn's back room that was their sanctuary after battle.

Tomas's son, Rhob, a youth forever in awe of the mercenaries, took their horses to the stables and the saddle-stiff companions went inside.

'Hello, boy!' Tomas's shout greeted The Unknown from behind the bar. It was what the innkeeper always called him, saying that 'Unknown' made him sound like a stranger. The Rookery was perhaps a quarter full, reflecting the time of day. It was a large inn, thirty tables spread widely around a low-roofed, oak-pillared room. The bar was directly opposite the door and ran in a quarter-circle from right to left, finishing by doors to kitchens, back room and the upstairs. On the right was The Rookery's open fire. Books ranged over the walls on three sides and reds and greys complemented the lanterns to give a warming atmosphere.

'Hello, Tomas.' There was a weariness in The Unknown's tone.

'Go straight through,' said Tomas, a tall, balding man in his late forties. 'I'll bring in some wine, ale and coffee. Maris is just firing the ovens. I—' He frowned, stopped speaking, his eyes flicking over The Raven, pausing briefly on Denser, then moving on. The Unknown nodded, walked to the bar and laid a hand on Tomas's arm.

'There'll be a party in here tonight. We have much to celebrate, much to remember and Ras to mourn.'

Nothing more was said and The Raven filed past Tomas on to the back room, each man nodding or smiling his greeting.

Three things characterised the back room: the Raven symbol and crossed short swords above the fireplace; its long banqueting table set with seven places which stood by large double doors in the far wall; and its exquisitely sewn soft chairs and sofas. It was into these that The Raven sank, their grateful sighs giving way to silence.

Denser hesitated. There were ten seats in all. Eventually he moved to a plainer, red-upholstered chair nearest the unlit fire.

'Not there.' Talan's voice stopped him in his tracks. 'Ras sat there. Sit on Tomas's sofa if you must. I expect he won't mind.'

Denser sat.

'Now then,' said The Unknown, turning to the Dark Mage. 'First things first. How long before we are likely to see payment?'

'Well, as I explained to Ilkar, the amulet is primarily a research tool and we won't be looking to sell it for some months. However, we will set a minimum price and I can advance you five per cent of that figure, say two hundred thousand truesilver?'

The Unknown glanced quickly around The Raven. There were no dissenters.

'Good enough. Our money is lodged in the Central Reserve. Your payment needs to be made there within a week.'

Denser stood. 'It'll be there tomorrow. Now, if you'll excuse me, I need a bath.' He made to leave, The Unknown stopped him.

'Where are you staying?'

'I hadn't given it any thought.'

'Get Tomas to make up a room. There'll be no charge.'

'That's very good of you. Thank you.' Denser seemed a little confused, though he smiled.

'And if you're up to it, come to the party. You financed it, after all. Main bar, dusk.' Denser nodded. 'Just one more thing. Ilkar? A ForeTell, please.'

Ilkar nodded, the ghost of good humour touching his face as he stood up and walked over to Denser.

'What do you need?' asked Denser.

'Not much,' said Ilkar. 'It's a very general spell, single trait only. I'm merely looking for honesty. When I touch you, just answer the question I ask yes or no.'

Ilkar closed his eyes and uttered a short incantation. His right hand made a pass in front of his eyes, mouth and heart before he placed it on Denser's shoulder.

'Will two hundred thousand truesilver be deposited in The Raven account at the Central Reserve within a week from today?'

'Yes.'

Ilkar opened his eyes and then the door. 'See you later.' Denser left.

Ilkar pushed the door shut and glared at The Unknown Warrior. 'Anything else you want us to give him? The freedom to use Julatsan blood to replenish his mana, perhaps?'

The Unknown said nothing.

'I don't trust him,' said Hirad.

'Why do you suppose he's staying here?' asked The Unknown.

'No, it's not the money,' said Hirad. 'The ForeTell says he'll pay that. There's much more. Like why he agreed to pay us so much so readily. Let's face it, we'd have done the job for two thousand each.'

'Why do you suppose he's staying here?' repeated The Unknown. 'If he's involved us in anything, I want to know where he is. That, Ilkar, is why I want him downstairs tonight.'

'You expecting trouble?' asked Talan.

'No.' The Unknown leaned back in his chair and stretched his legs. 'But even so, short swords should be worn, and not just out of respect for Ras.'

'It's only now, isn't it?' Ilkar had pulled the cork from a bottle of wine and poured himself a goblet.

'What is?' Sirendor motioned Ilkar to do the same for him. The mage passed over his goblet and filled another.

'Now you've stopped to think, now the glint of truesilver has faded, you're all getting twitchy, aren't you?' He sat down in his chair. 'Xetesk is dangerous. Nothing is ever what it seems. There's always a bigger story and I for one don't believe anything he said about that amulet.'

'Why didn't you say?'

'Oh, and you'd have listened, would you, Hirad?' snapped Ilkar. 'Two hundred and fifty thousand for a day's ride versus me. Don't shovel it my way.'

'I don't see the problem,' said Richmond. 'We're here, we're safe, the money will be paid. We've bought ourselves more choice.'

'If we live to enjoy it,' muttered Ilkar.

'You're over-reacting,' said Sirendor.

'You don't know them.' Ilkar spoke slowly. 'I do. If he's involved us in something, we're expendable. Xetesk doesn't have any code and they don't follow any rules.' He paused. 'Look, all I'm saying is, be careful around Denser. We may well have got away with this one but we'll just have to wait and see.'

'We don't have to work for Xetesk again,' said Hirad evenly.

'Too right we don't,' replied Ilkar.

'We don't have to work for anyone again.' Silence followed Talan's words. Hirad rose stiffly and walked to the table which carried the drinks. He poured himself wine and brought the bottle, another and more cups back to the fireplace. Those without helped themselves.

'We didn't have to work for anyone before but I know what Talan means,' said The Unknown. 'That two hundred and fifty thousand means we can do everything we talked of when we started and everything we never dared dream we could do. Just think of the possibilities.'

'I think you'd better start by telling me about last night and what you said.' Hirad drained his cup and refilled it.

'We tried to wake you. We had no desire to exclude you,' said Sirendor. 'We went out of the castle to join Richmond. I don't know about the others but looking down at Ras's grave I had my first fear that one day it could be me. Or Ilkar—' He gestured around The Raven, finally nodding at Hirad. 'Or you. I didn't want that. I want a future while I'm still young enough to enjoy it.'

'The decision's made, is it?' Hirad's voice was gruff.

Sirendor breathed deeply. 'While we were talking, it became obvious that we all felt the same. Gods, Hirad, even you've talked about packing it in during the last two years. We all want to live. Talan wants to travel, Ilkar's under pressure to go back to Julatsa. I . . . well, you know what I want.'

'Husband and father, eh?' Hirad smiled despite the thudding of his heart and the knot in his throat.

'All I have to do is stop fighting and the Mayor won't stop us marrying. You know how it is.' Sirendor shrugged.

'Yeah. Sirendor Larn tamed by the Mayor's daughter. It had to happen some time, I suppose.' Hirad wiped at the corner of his left eye. The atmosphere in the room was intense, focused on him. 'You know I won't stand in your way.'

'I know,' said Sirendor, but the look they shared spoke everything.

'You can see the sense in it,' said The Unknown. Hirad stared at him blankly. 'Gods, Hirad, I've been half-owner of this inn for a dozen years and if I've served behind the bar a dozen times I'm lucky.'

'And what about you?' The barbarian turned his attention to Richmond.

'Before yesterday I wasn't sure,' said the blond warrior. 'But I'm tired, Hirad. Even standing waiting for something to happen is tiring. I—' He stopped and rubbed his brow with three fingers. 'Yesterday, I made a mistake I'll have to carry to my grave. And right now, I'm not sure I trust myself to fight in line and I'd be surprised if you did. Any of you.'

Another silence. Long. Hirad stared around The Raven but no one said any more.

'It's unbelievable,' said Hirad. 'Ten years. Ten years and yet you've made the biggest decision of our lives . . . my life, while I was sleeping.' He was too angry even to shout and his voice held calm. But at the same time he knew it wasn't anger. It was a deep and bitter disappointment. The inevitable result of the formation of The Raven. The split. The funny thing was that, at the outset, Hirad never thought he'd survive this long. The future had been meaningless. Until now. Now it crashed over his head and he found he was frightened of it. Very frightened.

'Sorry, Hirad.'

'I just wanted someone to ask my opinion, Sirendor.'

'I know. But the decision wasn't taken last night, just confirmed.'

'You didn't ask me.' Hirad got up and moved to the door. He needed a few drinks and to laugh. 'Tell you what,' he said. 'You retired folk fund the party and I'll try to forgive you.'

Styliann's eyes blazed and his face reddened. In the holding chamber beneath his tower, the three mages cowered where they sat, too exhausted to stand in respect of their Lord.

'Tell me again.' Styliann spoke low and quiet, the power of his voice filling the small chamber.

'We were only sure three hours ago and even then we had to make our final fail-safe check. We didn't want to cause concern until we had absolute proof,' said one, an old mage whose life had been devoted to his single task.

'Concern?' echoed Styliann, voice cracking ever so slightly. 'The greatest evil in Balaia's history has gone missing. Causing me concern is the least of your worries, believe me.'

The three mages exchanged glances.

'Not just missing, my Lord. Not only are they not in the cage, we don't believe they reside in interdimensional space either.' The old mage swallowed. 'We believe that their essence and souls have returned to Balaia.'

The silence which followed dragged at the ears. Styliann's breath hissed between his teeth. He took in the small chamber, its sketches and maps of dimensional space and spell result equation covering every wall. Notebooks were scattered on the single pitted wooden desk. The chairs, arranged in a loose crescent, each contained a terrified mage looking up at him as he stood near the door, Nyer at one shoulder, Laryon at the other. He wouldn't look left or right; he didn't have to. The impact of what they had just heard sent ripples through the mana trails.

'How long have they been gone?' he asked. It was the question they were dreading.

'We can't – can't be sure,' managed the old mage.

Styliann pinned him with his eyes. 'I beg your pardon?' They looked from one to another. Eventually, a younger woman spoke.

'It has always been the way of the Watches, my Lord,' she said. 'The spells are cast and the calculations made every three months when certain alignments offer us more accuracy.'

Styliann didn't take his gaze from the old man. 'Are you telling me that the Wytch Lords could have been in Balaia up to three months ago?'

'They were in the cage last casting,' said the woman. 'They aren't there now.'

'Yes, or no.' Styliann almost believed he could hear their hearts pounding, then realised it was his own sounding in his ears and throat.

'Yes.' The old man looked away, tears in his eyes. Styliann nodded.

'Very well,' he said. 'Clear the room, your work is finished.' He turned to Nyer. 'We've no choice. Contact the Colleges but say nothing of events here or at Taranspike Castle. We must have a meeting at Triverne Lake. Now.'

'I wouldn't have believed it unless I'd smelled it with my own nose,' said Sirendor. He was standing close to Hirad at the bar of The Rookery, appraising the barbarian's clothes – leather trousers, a close-fitting dark shirt that showed off his upper body to good advantage, and a studded belt on which hung his scabbarded short sword. Ilkar was with them, dressed in a black-edged yellow shirt and leather trousers, and behind the bar stood The Unknown in a plain white shirt and similar leggings to his friends.

'What are you talking about?' asked Hirad.

'Well, my dear friend, in the hours that we have been apart, not only have you shed that revolting sweaty leather stuff you wear for talking to dragons, but you have obviously had a scented bath. This is truly a momentous occasion.' Sirendor leaped on to the nearest table, shouting, 'Ladies, gentlemen, Talan. The foul-smelling barbarian has had a bath!' There was laughter and the odd cheer. Hirad even saw Denser smile before the mage, dressed in voluminous black shirt and trousers, returned to stroking his cat and gazing into the fire as he sat in an armchair close to the flames.

'You can bloody talk, mighty mouth,' said Hirad, pointing a finger at Sirendor. 'Just look at yourself. Your clothes must beg questions about which sex you prefer to fiddle with your balls. Your future bride will be heartbroken.'

'Are you calling me a poof?' asked Sirendor.

'That's right.'

Sirendor pouted and looked down at himself. Embroidered knee-length moccasin boots, laced up the front, gave way to a pair of billowing gold-trimmed brown trousers into which was tucked a huge purple open-necked lace and silk shirt. On his belt was his short sword, and a gem necklace rested on a bed of chest hair.

'Maybe you're right.' Sirendor jumped lightly to the floor of the inn, which had filled quickly as word spread of The Raven's party, and swept his mug of ale into his hands.

Denser stood up from his seat, leaving the cat lounging by the fire, and weaved his way through a crowd towards the quartet. Ilkar picked up his drink, turned and walked away.

'I don't think those two are going to be friends,' said Sirendor.

'Not much gets past you, does it?' returned Hirad, a broad smile on his face as he watched the approaching Xeteskian.

'Denser.' The Unknown acknowledged the Dark Mage with a nod.

'Getting busy in here,' observed Denser, lighting his pipe.

'Is red wine all right?' Sirendor picked up a bottle.

'Fine.' Denser watched as Sirendor poured. 'Thank you.' He took a sip and raised his eyebrows. 'Not bad.'

'"Not bad"?' echoed The Unknown. 'That's a Blackthorne red, my friend. Expensive speciality of The Rookery.'

'I'm not much of an expert.' Denser shrugged.

'Clearly. You're on the cheap stuff then.' The Unknown turned and scanned briefly along the racks to his left, then picked out a bottle and stood it on the bar top, fishing in his pocket for a corkscrew.

He paused, looking out past his friends to the crowded bar. Here he was, the other side of the counter, and he felt comfortable. It was a simple feeling but he felt good. Very good. But behind all his comfort lurked an abyss he wouldn't let himself see into.

'This is the life, eh?' he said, stripping the cork from the bottle and gazing out over the thickening sea of goblets, faces, colours and smoke. He charged a fresh glass. 'This muck, Denser, from Baron Corin's yards, is your wine. Try not to choke.'

'I've got a proposition for you,' said Denser suddenly.

'Oh yeah? More opportunities to be burned alive, is it?'

Denser stared at Hirad. 'Not exactly. Will you hear me?'

'If you want, but you're wasting your time,' said The Unknown.

'Why?'

'Because we retired a couple of hours ago. I've taken a new job as a barman.' Hirad and Sirendor both laughed. Denser's face briefly betrayed both panic and confusion as he tried to work out whether they were serious or not.

'Even so . . .' he said.

'Go on, then.' Sirendor leant back against the bar, his elbows resting on it. Hirad did likewise, with The Unknown between them, resting on his arms on the wooden counter and fiddling with a corkscrew.

'The amulet we recovered is not the only one,' said Denser.

'Now there's a surprise.' Sirendor turned his head to his friends.

'Look, I'll be honest, we are developing a new attack spell that we want to be ready in the event of any Wesmen invasion. There are three more pieces we need to complete our research, and I, that is, Xetesk, want The Raven to help me get them.'

None of them said anything for a time as Denser studied their faces. Eventually, The Unknown straightened.

'We did wonder why you paid us so much for seeing you back here,' he said. 'We also agreed that we wouldn't work for Xetesk again. Take some Protectors.'

Denser shook his head. 'No. Protectors are just muscle. I need brain for this sort of recovery work.'

'And The Raven are – were – a fighting team. We've never done recovery work and we aren't about to start now,' said Sirendor.

'But it's not even a long-term commitment. And the pay will be on the same basis as today.'

The Unknown leant back on the bar top. 'Another set of five per cents, eh?'

'I can't promise it'll be as easy.' Denser half smiled at Hirad.

'Bugger me, but I'd like to see one of your tricky jobs.'

'Sorry, that came out wrong. I mean the bodyguarding was easy.'

Sirendor's face broke into a wide grin. He straightened and dusted himself down.

'Denser, a couple of years ago, we'd probably have bitten your hand off for that kind of money. But right now, I for one am no longer interested. I mean, we'd have trouble spending it. Sorry, old son, but retirement has one very clear advantage.' He turned and punched Hirad on the arm. 'See you later.' He strode off towards the main door, through which a stunning woman had walked with two men. She wore a shining blue cloak and pushed the hood back to loose a mass of curling red hair.

She saw Hirad first and waved. He and The Unknown returned the greeting. Then she began moving towards Sirendor. The two met, embraced and kissed, the warrior ushering her to a table on the right of the bar, close to the back room.

The Unknown placed a bottle of wine and two crystal glasses on a tray.

'Time for the barman bit, I think.'

'Yeah.' Hirad turned back to Denser. The Dark Mage's face was neutral but his eyes betrayed his disappointment and concern. 'Had it been up to me, I'd have taken your money. We should be taking bastards like you for every penny we can get.'

'I'm flattered. Was that the last word on the subject, do you think?'

Hirad breathed out. 'Well, The Unknown was interested, no doubt about it, and I'm pretty sure the boring brothers would tag along. Your problems are Sirendor, who is in love but can't marry till he stops fighting, and Ilkar, who hates everything you stand for.'

'Apart from that, no problem.' Denser lit his pipe.

'Tell you what, you work on Sirendor and play up the short time the job'll take and all the money he'll earn for his bride and all that. I'll try Ilkar. I reckon he might want to come along if he knows it's a spell you're developing. It'll be difficult, though.'

'And if you can't persuade him?'

'Then it's no go. The Raven never work apart.'

'I see.'

'Good. Right, where is he then?' Denser indicated the centre of the bar. Ilkar was talking to the cloth merchant, Brack, and a couple of decent-looking women. 'I could get my leg over if nothing else,' Hirad said, then shouted, 'Hey, Ilks! Need more drink?' Ilkar nodded. The barbarian picked up a jug and shouldered his way through the crowded inn.

'Hirad, good to see you.'

'You never were a good liar, Brack. Drink?' The merchant held up his goblet. Hirad filled it and Ilkar's. 'I need to borrow Ilkar for a moment, ladies, but I promise we'll be back very soon.' Ilkar looked askance at the barbarian but allowed himself to be led in the direction of the bar. Hirad saw Denser standing at Sirendor's table and was surprised to see Larn get up and follow the Dark Mage over to the fire. The man must have extraordinary powers of persuasion – he was not sure that he'd have been so lucky so soon after the two lovers had sat down.

'So what did Denser have to say?'

'Seven hundred and fifty thousand, Ilkar. Three jobs. Short term.'

Ilkar shook his head. 'You know something, Hirad, I'm surprised at you. And I'm disappointed that after ten years you don't know me well enough not to ask.'

'But—'

'I've said all I have to say. I will not work for or with Xetesk. They cannot be trusted. I don't care how much he is offering because it won't be enough.'

Hirad chewed his lip. 'Look, Ilkar, why not think of it as just taking even more money from them? Give it all to Julatsa if it bothers you, but I thought you'd want to keep your eye on what Xetesk is doing.'

Ilkar frowned. 'What exactly is Denser asking us to do?'

Hirad beckoned him close.

The Unknown Warrior leant against the bar, happy to watch the evening go by while he sipped his excellent Blackthorne red. He shifted slightly, moving the elbow of his white shirt out of a puddle of liquid on the bar top.

Surveying the bar, he could have stepped ten years back in time. Talan and Richmond – the boring brothers as Hirad liked to call them – were sitting together saying nothing to anyone and running their fingers around the rims of their goblets. Hirad and Ilkar were standing a few yards away. They were talking alone and intently. He smiled and shook his head, took another sip from his glass and refilled it from the bottle on the bar.

His eyes eventually came to rest on the fireplace and the pair sitting in armchairs either side of it, talking to each other. His smile faded. Denser. The mage's head was largely hidden by the wings of his chair but he could see the cat and the inevitable hand stroking its back. The sooner he was gone, the better. The Unknown hated feeling he was being lied to.

Sirendor, it appeared, was on good form. His eyes were bright in the firelight and his clothes made him a focus of attention for more than one of the women in the room. Indeed, The Unknown could see one eyeing him up now. She was standing near the door. Lucky bastard. He never had to work at it. They just fell at his feet then into his bed. He wondered if Sana knew just how envied she was. At the moment, though, she was looking a little irritated as she sat with her bodyguards at the table Sirendor had recently abandoned.

The woman by the door started moving towards the fireplace. She had long auburn hair pinned back away from her eyes but bouncing about her neck, one side of which carried a black mark. Her tall, slim figure was tied into cloth trousers, dark shirt and tight leather jerkin. A deep red cloak was fastened about her neck. The Unknown shook his head. The attraction of Sirendor was seemingly irresistible whether his betrothed was present or not, and he found himself feeling a little envious. No, very envious.

Turning past a knot of market tradesmen clashing their tankards together and roaring a toast, the woman's eyes crossed The Unknown's and the warrior's blood ran cold. Inside a pale face with full lips and an exquisite nose, those eyes were flat, dark and brimful of malice. His gaze switched automatically to her hands and he caught a glint of steel. There were two men sitting by the fireplace, and cool certainty told The Unknown the woman had no interest in Sirendor Larn.

'Oh, dear Gods,' he muttered. He loosened his short sword in its scabbard, ducked under the bar top and began pushing his way through the throng.

'Sirendor! Sirendor, guard yourself now!' he yelled. He flicked a gaze to the woman, who was breasting her way quickly towards the fireplace. 'Sirendor. To your left, dammit, your left.' Sirendor looked over at him frowning as someone moved in front of him. 'Out of my bloody way! Sirendor, woman, red cloak, red-brown hair, long, to your left.'

The Unknown's heart was racing. He sensed a change in the atmosphere in the bar, saw the woman, dagger now in hand, moving swiftly towards her quarry. She was close. She was too close, and Sirendor, looking about him with his hand straying to his sword hilt as he rose from his chair, hadn't seen her.

The Unknown wasn't going to make it. The assassin was almost on Sirendor. 'Stop her, Sirendor. For God's sake, let me through!'

And at the last, Sirendor, standing squarely in front of Denser, saw the assailant. As she attacked, he blocked the blow with his arm, the dagger slashing his sleeve and biting into his flesh. In the next instant, The Unknown's blade crashed through the woman's shoulder. She died instantly, dropping to the ground without a sound, blood spraying into the fire, where it hissed.

The room fell instantly silent. People moved aside as Hirad, Ilkar, Talan and Richmond hurried over to the fireplace. Sirendor was sitting down again, his hand up by his face and shirt rolled back to reveal the cut. It was deep and bleeding well.

'Thanks, Unknown, I didn't see her. I— What is it?'

The Unknown was kneeling by the woman's body and had picked up her dagger by its hilt, examining the blade.

'No! No no no, shit!' he said and rubbed his free hand across his head.

'Unknown?' asked Hirad.

The Unknown looked briefly at the barbarian. There were tears standing in his eyes. He shook his head and turned back to Sirendor.

'I'm sorry, Sirendor. I was too slow. I'm sorry.'

'Will you tell me what the hell you're talking about, Unknown?' Sirendor smiled, then gagged suddenly. 'Gods, I don't . . .' He turned aside and vomited into the fire. 'I'm cold,' he said. His voice was quiet, weak. His eyes, suddenly red, turned scared to Hirad, who pushed The Unknown away and crouched by his chair. 'Help me.'

'What's happening?' Hirad's heart was thumping in his chest. 'What is it?' He felt a hand on his shoulder.

'He's poisoned, Hirad. It's a nerve toxin,' said The Unknown.

'Get a healer, then!' Hirad shouted. 'Get one now!' The hand merely tightened its grip.

'It's too late. He's dying.'

'No he isn't,' grated Hirad.

Sirendor turned a sweat-covered face to his friend and smiled through the shivers coursing his body, tears falling on his cheeks.

'Don't let me die, Hirad. We're all going to live.'

'Keep calm, Sirendor. Breathe easy. You'll be all right.'

Sirendor nodded. 'It's so cold. I'll just . . .' His voice faded and his eyes slipped shut.

Hirad grabbed Sirendor's face with both hands. It was hot and slick with sweat.

'Stay with me, Larn. Don't you leave me!'

Sirendor's eyelids fluttered open and his hands covered Hirad's. They were so cold the barbarian flinched.

'Sorry, Hirad. I can't. Sorry, Hirad.' The hands slipped to his sides, his eyes closed and he died.

Chapter 6

'Who was she?' Sana's eyes bore into Hirad's, imploring him to help her understand. They were standing in the main bar just outside the back room; the Mayor and two bodyguards sat at a table near the door to The Rookery.

Sana was calm now but her red eyes and white face were the remnants of a tempest. The Raven had lain Sirendor on the table in the back room and covered him with a sheet. Sana had burst in and torn the sheet from him, screaming at him to wake up, to come back, to open his eyes, to breathe. She'd pumped at his heart, she'd raked the hair from his forehead, she'd kissed him long on his lips, she'd clung to his hands.

And all the while, Hirad had stood near by, half of him wanting to pull her away, the other half wanting to help her. To shake the life back into Sirendor, to see him smile. But all he did was stand there watching, fighting back his tears, his whole body quivering.

At last Sana had turned to him and buried her face in his shoulder, sobbing quietly. He'd stroked her hair and heard the silence of The Raven and could sense the passing of what they had been.

He'd moved her outside, and as she regained some composure, she drew back to ask her question. Hirad felt helpless. Useless.

'An assassin. A Witch Hunter.'

'Then why—?' Her voice caught.

'She wasn't after Sirendor. Sirendor just got in the way.' Hirad shrugged, a stupid gesture, he knew. 'He died saving another man.'

'So? He's still dead.'

Hirad took and held her hands. 'It was a risk he took every day.'

'Not today. Today he was retired.'

Hired said nothing for a moment. He smoothed away the tears rolling fresh down her cheeks.

'Yes. Yes, he was,' he said eventually. 'I'll get the man behind this.'

'That's your answer, is it?'

'It's the only answer I can give.' He shrugged again.

'Night has come, Hirad. Everything has gone.' And when he looked into her eyes, he knew it was true. She gave his hand the briefest squeeze, turned and walked to her father. Hirad looked after her for a second, pushed open the door to the back room and walked inside.

No one was talking. The fire crackled in the grate, they were all sitting holding drinks but no one was talking. Hirad moved to Sirendor's body. The sheet had been replaced. He looked at the outline of his face beneath the covering and laid a hand on one of his friend's, praying for the grasp of fingers he knew would never come. He turned.

'Why do they want you dead, Denser?'

'That's what we just asked him,' said Ilkar.

'And what did he say?'

'That he wanted you to hear it too.'

'Well, I'm here now, so he can start talking.'

'Come and sit down, Hirad,' said The Unknown. 'We poured you a drink. It won't help but we poured it anyway.'

Hirad nodded, walked to them and sat down in his chair. The Unknown pushed a goblet into his left hand, and with his right, Hirad reached out and felt the arm of Sirendor's chair though he wouldn't, couldn't, look at it.

'We're listening, Denser,' he said, his voice just holding together.

'I want you to know right away that what I am about to tell you was being kept from you in your best interests.'

'You are digging a deep hole,' said The Unknown slowly. '*We* decide what is in our best interests. The result of not being able to do that lies under a shroud for all to see. We want to know exactly what you have involved us in. Exactly. Then you will go and we will talk.'

Denser took a deep breath. 'Firstly, I make no apologies for being Xeteskian. It is simply a moral code, and much of what is said about us is fabrication. Our past, however, is not blameless.'

'You know something, Denser, you have a gift for understatement,' said Ilkar.

'We could have such fascinating discussions, Ilkar.'

'I doubt it.'

'Right,' said Denser after a pause. 'You heard what Gresse was saying, and his information is all too accurate. The Wesmen tribes are rising and uniting, the Shamen are running the organisation, the Elder Councils are working in concert and we are seeing subjugation of local populations practically in the shadow of the Blackthorne Mountains.'

The Unknown Warrior sat up straight. 'Just how far east are we talking about?'

'We've had an eyewitness account from a village called Terenetsa, three days' ride from Understone Pass,' said Denser.

'Gods, that's close,' breathed Talan. 'No wonder Gresse wanted Blackthorne warned.'

'I fail to see what this has to do with the death of my friend,' muttered Hirad.

'Please,' said Denser. 'This is relevant, believe me. We've had mage spies in the west for several months now and the picture is grim. We estimate that Wesmen armies approaching sixty thousand already armed and training are gathered in the Heartlands. An invasion of the east is surely imminent and we have no defence. There is no four-College alliance and the KTA has a tenth the armed strength it had three hundred years ago.'

'But what chance do they really have?' Ilkar was dismissive. 'A couple of thousand mages alone could stop their advance. They don't have the Wytch Lords for magical support this time.'

'I'm very much afraid that they do,' said Denser.

The fire crackling in the grate was suddenly the only sound. Talan's glass stopped halfway to his lips. Ilkar opened his mouth to speak but didn't.

Richmond shook his head. 'Hold on,' he said. 'I understood them to be destroyed.'

'You can't destroy them,' said Ilkar. 'We never knew how and we still don't. All Xetesk could do was trap them without a means to escape.' He switched his gaze to the Xetesk mage. 'What happened?'

Denser breathed in deeply and knocked the bowl of his pipe against the fire grate. He filled it as he spoke, his cat sleeping on his lap. 'When we destroyed Parve, it was to remove all vestiges of the Wytch Lords' power base from Balaia. It was never intended that that action would end the Wytch Lords themselves. While their bodies burned, their souls ran free and we trapped them inside a mana cage and launched it into interdimensional space.' The cat stirred. 'We've been watching it ever since.'

'Watching what?' asked Richmond.

'The cage. We and we alone have kept unfailing watch on the Wytch Lords' prison for three hundred years. As others refuse to accept us, so we refuse to accept the word of those who claim ultimate victory.' He shrugged.

'Clearly, you were right,' said Ilkar.

Denser nodded. 'We've noted increased dimensional transference, probably through Dragonene action, for some time. One particular move damaged the cage. We thought it was rectifiable.' He scratched his head, then lit his pipe from a flame produced on the tip of his thumb. 'We were wrong. Mana must have entered the cage because the Wytch Lords are no longer inside. We believe them to be back in Balaia. In Parve.'

Ilkar massaged his nose and pulled at his lips with his right hand. His eyes narrowed.

'How long have they been there?' he asked.

'Who cares?' said Hirad. 'I'm still waiting to—'

'Hold on, Hirad.'

'No, Ilkar, I will not bloody hold on.' Hirad raised his voice. He turned on Denser. 'You might as well have been talking tribal Wessen for all I've understood so far. You've got your stupid pipe stuck in your stupid mouth and you've balled on about dimensions, Dragonene and some old threat that's been gone hundreds of years like it was important. I haven't a clue what you're talking about and I'm no nearer knowing why that Witch Hunter bastard killed my friend.'

'I sympathise with your need to understand,' said Denser gently.

'You have absolutely no idea what I need, Xetesk man.' Hirad's voice was gruff. He drained his glass and passed it to The Unknown for a refill. 'You have no idea of the gulf that has opened up in my life and you are running in circles around the answer to the only question that could help me begin to grieve. Why did that assassin want you dead so badly?'

Denser paused before replying. 'I'm trying to make sure this all comes out the right way round,' he said. 'Can I explain a few other things first?'

'No, you can explain one. Why did that assassin want you dead?'

Denser sighed. 'Because of what I am carrying.'

'And what is that exactly?' asked Hirad.

'This.' He pulled the amulet stolen from Sha-Kaan from his shirt, where it had been hanging on a chain around his neck. 'It's the key to Septern's workshop.'

'Couldn't you just kick the door down?' Hirad's voice was layered with contempt. 'I mean, is that it? Is that trinket why Sirendor died?' He caught Ilkar's expression and stayed his next words. 'What is it, Ilkar?'

The elf snapped his gaze to Hirad and focused on him as if from a great distance.

'Dawnthief,' he breathed, his face white as death. 'He's going after Dawnthief.'

Erienne was settling Aron and Thom down to sleep when Isman walked into the room unannounced. She had been allowed the entire afternoon and evening with them and had chosen to tell them stories of old magic. Neither child strayed far from the comfort of her arms.

At her insistence, the fire had been lit and the single window opened all day, though her request for the boys to be allowed to play in the inner courtyard was refused.

She had spent some time calming their fears before they would listen to her words; and as usual, none were wasted in her pursuit of their detailed education in the ways of Dordovan magic. She spoke of the ancient days, when the Colleges were one and the first City of magic was built at Triverne Lake, and of the darker days of the sundering, when the City was raised and the Colleges split to build their own strongholds. And she talked of the lore which governed the lives of all mages and distanced one College's mages from the others, and of the mana with which they shaped their spells.

The boys tired as the light faded, and she built up the fire. They took a dinner of hot soup, potatoes and green leaves in near silence. She washed their faces and brushed their hair. The Captain had left flannels and a brush in the room, saying a man should always look neat and dignified. Erienne wished he'd take his own counsel.

Isman's intrusion came with her humming a tune to the boys as they nodded off, jerking them back to a startled, anxious wakefulness.

'Could you not have knocked?' Erienne didn't turn round at the sound of boots on the cold stone floor.

'The Captain will see you now,' said Isman.

'When my boys are asleep,' said Erienne, keeping her voice soft and stroking her sons' heads to soothe them. Their eyes played over her face, anxiety plain in the frowns they wore. Her anger stirred.

'The Captain feels you have spent enough time with them for now.'

'I will be the judge of that,' hissed Erienne.

'No,' said Isman. 'You will not.'

At last she turned to the door. Isman stood in the room with three other men behind him. She leaned into the boys and kissed each on the forehead.

'I have to go now,' she whispered. 'Be good and go to sleep. I'll be back to see you soon.' She smoothed hair from their faces.

Rising, she faced Isman and his henchmen, every fibre screaming at her to take them apart. And she could, all of them. But her boys would die as a direct consequence. They had no way to escape the castle grounds and the Captain had too many men. She bit back the spell, mana flow ceasing.

'You didn't need your muscle,' she said. 'I'm not going to cause trouble.'

'You and yours already have,' said Isman. He led the way to the library.

Despite the warmth cast by the fires still burning in the room, the air felt cool. The Captain was seated behind the reading desk, two soft lanterns illuminating the book he was studying. A half-empty bottle of spirits stood to his left and beside it, a freshly replenished glass. He didn't look up as she approached across the rugs as prompted by Isman, who withdrew, closing the door behind him.

'Sit.' The Captain waved his hand at a hard-backed chair the other side of the desk. 'Tell me,' he said, not looking up, 'why Xetesk might be after Dawnthief?'

'I should think that would be obvious,' said Erienne.

The Captain regarded her bleakly, his voice chill. 'Assume that it is not.'

'Ownership of Dawnthief guarantees domination for its owners. Why do you think they should want it?' She kept her face calm, but inside, her mind was in turmoil and her heart beat feverishly in her chest. She'd kept the thoughts from her mind while she was with Aron and Thom, but now the enormity of what the Captain had intimated earlier was scaring her.

'There isn't much written about it, you see,' he said. 'How much should I be worrying about it? Can Xetesk find it?'

'Gods, yes, we should all worry about it!'

'Can they find it?'

'I don't know.' Erienne bit her lip.

'That is a particularly unhelpful answer.' The Captain's voice rose a notch, his face flushing slightly.

'Well, it all depends on finding the way into Septern's workshop. If they have the information, they could go on to recover the complete spell, I suppose. It's all so much speculation.'

'You still aren't helping me,' said the Captain.

'I can help you best by reporting your concerns and information to Dordover. It would be the quickest way to stop them, or at least control them.'

The Captain drank deeply and refilled his glass. He smiled. 'Nice try, but I'm hardly going to let you take a report back to your elders merely to have both Colleges chasing the same prize, am I? And may I remind you that any attempt at communion would be most unwise. I have the ability to detect such a casting, and for your boys, I'm afraid it would be fatal.'

Erienne's jaw dropped. There was only one way he could do that.

'You have mages working for you?' Her tone was incredulous.

'Not every mage believes me a menace to magic,' said the Captain smoothly. 'For many I am the only source of control.' He smiled. 'And now you are working for me too, in a way.'

'As a slave,' snapped Erienne. She was badly shaken but it all made sense. How else could he gather his information so quickly? They had to be from Lystern, possibly Julatsa. Mages from Xetesk and Dordover would not entertain the thought of working for him. She tried again. 'You don't understand. Dawnthief is too big to play games with. If Xetesk controls it, they control everything, including you. If you make public what you know, the three Colleges will stop them; surely your pet mages have told you that.'

'No, indeed they have not,' said the Captain, all hint of mirth gone from his hard, reddening face. 'What they have told me is that this absolute power must be held by no mage or College and that the means to cast it must be destroyed or kept by a man who has the knowledge to hold it but not the ability to cast it. Should the spell be fully recovered, I will be its guardian.'

Erienne found herself stunned for the second time in so many minutes. But this time her surprise was edged with real fear. If the Captain truly believed he could act as guardian for Dawnthief, he was even more deluded and dangerous than she thought. He clearly had no conception of its power, or the length to which some mages would go to own it.

'Do you seriously think Xetesk, or Dordover for that matter, would agree to your holding the key to such power?' asked Erienne, keeping her voice as neutral as possible.

'They will have no choice when I control the players of the game,' replied the Captain.

Erienne frowned and shifted in her seat, a cold feeling creeping up her back. Just how much did this man know? 'I'm sorry, I'm not with you,' she offered.

'Oh, come now, Erienne, do you think you were chosen at random? Do you think my knowledge is so limited? You are Dordover's brightest lore mage and a known expert on the multi-lore nature of Dawnthief. I already control you.' He shrugged. 'All I need now is the man most capable of casting it.'

'You'll never take him. He is too well protected.' Erienne was dismissive.

'And there you are wrong. Again. Indeed, I almost succeeded in killing him very recently. In hindsight, a fortunate failure. Particularly for you.'

'Why?' But she already knew the answer.

'Because yesterday, I had the mind to destroy the means to cast it. And you know rather too much than is good for you. When I have you both, I will also have the respect I deserve to see my work through.'

'You know so little,' grated Erienne. 'We will not help you and you will not catch the Xeteskian.'

'Really? I would advise caution before making such statements.'

'He and I would both choose death over aiding you in your ridiculous scheme. Should your plan ever work, the walls of this castle would glow with the afterburn of so much destructive magic that they could be seen in Korina! You are not strong enough to hold such power.'

The Captain was silent for a time. He swirled the remaining liquid in his glass and downed it, immediately picking up the bottle to refill.

'Of course, death is an option you can choose,' he said, pulling at an ear. 'But it's not a choice you should be making for your children, is it?' He smiled. 'You need to give this matter some proper consideration. Your family depends on you giving the right answer. Isman will see you to your room. Isman!' The door opened.

'I want to return to my children,' said Erienne.

With startling speed, the Captain reached across the table and grabbed Erienne's chin and lower jaw, drawing her to him.

'You are here at my pleasure. Perhaps some time alone might help you remember that, eh?' He let her go. 'When you have come to the right decision, please come and see me. Until then, enjoy the peace and quiet. Isman, the audience is over.'

'Bastard,' whispered Erienne. 'Bastard.'

'I need to protect the innocents of Balaia from the march of dark magic. I expect you to help me.'

'I want to see my sons!' she cried.

'Then be of some use and stop telling me what a child could guess!'

The Captain's face softened. 'Until then, I don't think I can oblige.' He opened his book again and waved her away.

Everyone was speaking at once. Ilkar was shouting at Denser, whose hands were held palms outwards in an attempt to calm him. The Unknown was trying to get the Xetesk mage's attention, while Richmond and Talan merely exchanged confusion.

Hirad floated above it all, his eyes once more fixed on the shrouded form of Sirendor Larn, the noise like the sound of the sea heard from a distance. Ten years. Ten years as founder partners of the most successful mercenary team ever formed. They'd fought together in battles they should have lost but had won. They'd walked away unscathed when blood ran thick in the battlefield massacre. They'd saved each other's lives so many times it hardly warranted a nod of the head in thanks.

And now Sirendor lay dead. On the very night he'd sheathed his sword for love, he had been murdered by an assassin who struck out at the wrong man. And for what? Because the man now invading The Raven's space had stolen the key to a dead mage's workshop and the Witch Hunters didn't want him to have it.

He seethed, his voice deadening the hubbub like cloud over the sun. 'He died for a key you stole.' The room fell silent. 'That's it, is it? Satisfied with your day's work, are you?' His voice cracked. 'After all we survived, he died for a three-inch disc. For your sake, it'd better be unbelievably important.' He sat back in his chair, all pretence at bravado gone, a knuckle rammed into his mouth and tears welling behind his eyes.

'Oh, it's important all right, Hirad,' said Ilkar, the colour barely returned to his cheeks, his eyes narrow slits. 'If he succeeds in recovering Dawnthief, Sirendor's death could prove a mercy to him compared to what we'll be facing.'

'What the hell is this thing?' demanded Talan.

'Dawnthief is a spell. *The* spell, I think; and Septern is the mage credited with inventing it,' said The Unknown. He looked to Denser for support.

'Absolutely right, Unknown. The spell itself is very well known to all the Colleges of magic,' said Denser. 'Every magic-user knows of its power . . . its potential for catastrophe. Fortunately, although the words are common knowledge, Dawnthief will not work without three forms of catalyst, and no one has discovered what they are or even where to go to find out. That is, until now. This amulet will let us into Septern's workshop and we are expecting to find the information there.'

'You knew what you were looking for when we met you, right?' asked Talan.

'Yes,' agreed Denser. 'Look, I'm not about to go into detail on Xetesk's recent research but it led us to believe that Septern was a Dragonene mage—'

'What's a—'

'Later, Talan,' said The Unknown. 'Carry on, Denser.'

'There were many other pointers to this conclusion but the important fact was that it directed our search for Dawnthief in a new direction – other dimensions, to be exact. As I explained to Ilkar, we have developed a spell which can detect the mana movement and shape needed to open a dimension door. We've been through many in search of Dawnthief, all of which have been opened by Dragonene. This time we found what we were looking for.'

'And my friends are already dying because of it,' said Hirad.

'You do not know how sorry I am that that is the case,' returned Denser softly.

'I don't need your sympathy, Denser, I need to know why the Witch Hunters wanted to kill you.'

'Isn't it obvious?'

'No, it is not,' said Hirad. 'I asked you why my friend died in your place and you haven't told me.'

'Very well. To spell it out, they want me dead because of who I am and where I come from.'

'Why should it make a difference who you are?' asked Ilkar.

'I'm Xetesk's principal Dawnthief mage,' said Denser simply.

Ilkar's eyes widened. 'Oh, this just gets better and better,' he muttered.

'What—?' began Talan.

'Hold on,' said Ilkar. 'Are you saying that you *actually* plan to cast it?'

'It's the only way to destroy the Wytch Lords, Ilkar, we both know that.'

'Yes, but . . .'

'They are coming back, and if we don't find Dawnthief and use it on them as soon as we can, we will eventually be on the wrong end of it ourselves. Finding it and threatening them with it won't be enough.

They have to be destroyed or Balaia will be lost. There's going to be an invasion, and this time we don't have the strength to withstand the tide of Wesmen indefinitely. Not with the Wytch Lords backing them.'

'The light-stealer. This is it.' Ilkar's words sat heavy in the air, his anxiety evident in the way he was poised, tense in his chair as if about to leap from it.

'What is it, Ilkar?' asked Talan.

'You don't know what he's talking about, not really. I do,' said Ilkar. 'I've studied Dawnthief – it's a required text. Put in simple terms, technically, depending on quality and length of preparation, it can destroy everything – and by that I mean the world.' He shrugged. 'That's why it's called Dawnthief. It means the "stealer of light" because it can take the sun from the sky.'

'If it's so important that you find and cast this spell, shouldn't the Witch Hunters understand that?'

'You think they'd believe us?' Denser spread his hands wide. 'Don't be naïve, Richmond. All they know or care about is that I'm travelling, they don't want Dawnthief found, and killing me seems the simple solution.'

'So,' said The Unknown. He drained his glass, refilled it and passed the bottle around the circle. 'Now we've established that you are a marked and dangerous man we shouldn't even be speaking to, why don't you confirm what it is you are trying to hire us for?'

The atmosphere in the room cooled. Denser looked around at the angry faces.

'We have to recover the catalysts and I want you to help me.'

'Why us in particular?'

'Why does anyone hire The Raven?'

'A few more details wouldn't go amiss.'

Denser drew breath, finding the questioning from The Raven suddenly intense. He pulled the amulet out again.

'Assuming this works and we find information on the Dawnthief catalysts, we have to act to recover the catalysts themselves. I need protection plus fighting ability and defensive magical skills. I also need people who can be trusted completely. As far as Xetesk is concerned, The Raven is the only choice.'

There was a short silence.

'I'm not sure I'm getting this,' said Hirad. 'Why not just bring in a load of Protectors and Xetesk mages. Surely you can trust them?'

'It's not that simple, unfortunately,' said Denser. 'There are political issues to consider, and if Xetesk was seen to be mounting any kind of action, we'd have the agents of the Wytch Lords on to us straight away. This has to be a clandestine action as long as possible.'

'And that's not to mention the trouble it would cause in the College Cities,' said Ilkar.

'And the Witch Hunters,' added The Unknown.

'Bring them on,' growled Hirad.

'Oh, we'll be going to them, don't worry,' said Denser.

'So much the better.'

'Seriously,' continued Denser, 'they have to be silenced. What they know, or even think they know, could prove disastrous for the whole of Balaia if the wrong ears hear it.'

'Is it stupid of me to suggest a four-College alliance if this is really so critical?' asked Richmond.

'Not at all,' said Denser. 'In fact, a four-College meeting has been called, although it is to deal with the Wesmen threat, not the search for Dawnthief. We can't afford for the other Colleges to know about our search, not yet. Ilkar will tell you, they would interfere in the search and place impossible conditions on the spell's use. It must be kept quiet as long as possible.' He paused. 'Do you believe me, Ilkar?'

The elf gazed at him coolly. 'That's not a question I'm ready to answer. This has severe implications for my relationship with Julatsa. I'm honour bound to tell them everything. You know that.'

There was another silence. Richmond added a log to the fire.

'I know. And all I ask is that you give me time to prove my intentions. But I do need an answer,' said Denser at length.

'To which question?' muttered Hirad.

'Will you help us?'

'How much?' asked Talan.

'Five per cent of agreed value of each artefact, same idea as before.'

'I cannot believe you just asked that,' snapped Hirad. 'What does it matter how much? We already have a job to do.' Hirad indicated Sirendor's shrouded body.

'It always matters,' replied Talan. 'No decision will be made until all conditions are known. That's how it's always been.'

'We've retired, Talan, remember?'

'Balaia cannot afford for you to retire,' said Denser.

'Shut up, Xetesk man. This doesn't concern you.' Hirad didn't look round.

'Hirad, calm down,' said The Unknown. 'This is already difficult enough.'

'Is it? We find the Witch Hunters, we kill them. What's difficult about that?'

The Unknown ignored him. 'One more question, Denser. Assuming we recover the catalysts, what then?'

'You help me take them into the Torn Wastes and cast Dawnthief against the Wytch Lords in Parve. That is, if you want to.'

'Well, we aren't about to just hand them over to Xetesk,' said Ilkar.

'I didn't expect you would,' countered Denser.

'So has everyone heard enough?' asked The Unknown.

'Ages ago,' said Hirad.

'Right.' The Unknown rose and opened the door. 'Denser, it's time you left. We need to talk, and we have a Vigil to observe.'

'I need an answer,' repeated Denser.

'First light tomorrow,' said The Unknown. 'Please . . .' He gestured through the door.

Denser paused before leaving. 'You can't refuse,' he said. 'This means everything to all of us.'

The Unknown closed the door behind Denser and refilled all the glasses before returning to his seat.

'So, who wants to go first?' he asked.

'This is a nightmare,' said Ilkar. 'I'm not sure what to say.'

'Sirendor Larn is dead because of him, it's obvious that Ras's death had nothing to do with our last contract, and yet we're chatting about working for him!' Hirad was shouting. 'What are we debating this for?' He got up and strode to the fireplace. 'It's quite simple. We go and kill the Witch Hunters. Denser can stick his spell up his arse, and this' – he tore the code from its frame on the wall and ripped it in two – 'this is gone.'

They were all staring at him, or rather at the ruined parchment in his hands, eyes wide. He became very aware of his own quick breathing, the thudding of his heart and the sound of the fire behind him. He stared back, daring them to criticise or disagree.

'Sit down, Hirad,' said The Unknown quietly.

'Why, so you can—'

'I said sit down!' thundered the big man.

Hirad, still clutching the two pieces of the code, did so.

'We all know how much this is hurting you,' The Unknown's voice was calm once more, 'and we will deal with Sirendor's murderers, believe me. But what we've just heard, which you didn't seem to take in, has changed everything.'

'Really?' Hirad sighed.

'Really,' affirmed The Unknown. 'I expect Ilkar can explain it better than me. Ilkar?

The Julatsan raised his eyebrows. 'Putting it bluntly, the two worst things I can imagine have both happened at the same time. Or so Denser claims. The Wytch Lords are free and Xetesk has found the link to Dawnthief.'

'And?'

'Gods, Hirad, I wasn't joking earlier. Dawnthief can destroy everything. Literally. In theory at least. What that means is that if Denser succeeds in destroying the Wytch Lords – and we must pray that he does – the ultimate weapon will be firmly in the hands of the Dark College. And what do you think that'll mean for the rest of us?'

'So we kill him and take the spell after he's cast it.'

'Yes, but we have to be standing next to him to do that.'

'We could kill him now and take the amulet,' said Hirad evenly.

Silence. Richmond nodded.

'It could certainly save time,' he said.

'And what if he's right about the Wytch Lords?' asked Ilkar.

'Get somebody else to cast the spell,' said Hirad.

Ilkar snorted. 'Of course. I'll go and ask Tomas if he can spare us the time, shall I?'

'You know what I mean.'

'It's not that simple, Hirad. Denser will have been training all his life in the theory of Dawnthief casting. And if he is Xetesk's principal Dawnthief mage – and I have no reason to doubt that he is – then he is the man with the best and perhaps the only chance of casting it effectively.'

'So *do* you believe him, Ilkar?' Talan leaned forward in his chair, draining his glass and holding out a hand for the bottle that The Unknown proffered.

'Why would he lie about this? He's risking me making a report to Julatsa about Dawnthief, and he's right about the reaction he'd get if I did. Gods, what a mess.' Ilkar chewed his lip and sagged back to hunch in his chair.

'So, what are our options?' asked Talan.

'We don't have any,' said Ilkar. 'Not really. I mean, we could decide to refuse him and go after the Witch Hunters ourselves but what if he's telling the truth? We'd have turned our backs on the fight for Balaia, and worse still, we'd have left Xetesk and the Wytch Lords as the only competitors for Dawnthief. And Dawnthief means absolute domination, it really is that powerful, believe me. Make no mistake, if the Wytch Lords are coming back, they will be coming back to destroy us all.'

'Are they really that bad?' asked Richmond.

'Yes. Gods, yes,' replied Ilkar. 'You have to understand where they came from. They used to be part of the original single College but were banished across the Blackthornes for their beliefs. They spent centuries brewing their hate and developing ways of making themselves immortal. When they succeeded, they came back to take what they thought was theirs. That time, we won. This time, we won't, not without Dawnthief.' He paused, seeing they weren't quite with him. 'Look, the Wytch Lords won't want to conquer, they want to destroy, to wipe out everyone to the east of the mountains. It was the promise they made when they were pushed into the mana prison. In my view, we have to go with Denser . . . Put it this way, I'm going whether The Raven do or not, but I want the rest of you to do the same. We'll probably all die, but at least we'll have tried.'

'Martyrdom for my country is not something I've ever considered as an option,' said Talan.

'Still, it'll certainly be a new departure for The Raven,' said Richmond. 'Not just doing it for the money, I mean.'

'Retirement brings a new outlook to things.' Ilkar shrugged, but his smile was forced.

'It certainly did for Sirendor.' Hirad's voice was barely above a whisper.

'Yes, it did. And we must never forget the full circumstances of our accepting this job. Assuming, of course, we all accept?' The Unknown looked around.

'I need it written into the contract that I go to see Dawnthief properly used against the Wytch Lords only. I'm working for Balaia, not Xetesk,' said Ilkar, his tone uncompromising.

'And I want an undertaking on Denser's part that we will attack the Witch Hunters the first chance we get.' Hirad was looking over at Sirendor.

'Got all that, Talan?' asked The Unknown when no one ventured further thoughts. Talan nodded. 'Denser needs to sign the contract at first light, so you'd better draw it up now. Anything else from anyone?'

'Just one thing,' said Richmond. 'Shouldn't we be guarding Denser? Or the amulet he's holding, to be more accurate.'

'Don't worry. His cat'll see him safe,' said Ilkar.

Hirad looked askance at the elf, imagining the animal holding off several large armed men. 'Good with a sword, is it?'

Ilkar chuckled in spite of the mood. 'It's a Familiar, Hirad. It retains a part of his consciousness, for want of a better word, and I dare say it can take on more than one form.'

'Oh, I see,' said Hirad, not seeing.

'I'll explain another time. Just trust me for now, all right?'

'Right, gentlemen,' said The Unknown, standing. 'Back here in an hour for the Vigil. Until that time, I suggest we all leave Hirad to air his grief in private.'

Hirad smiled his thanks, tears already forming. When they were all gone, he allowed himself to weep.

Chapter 7

Selyn's escape from Terenetsa had an element of fortune to it, although she liked to think she was never in any real danger. She was certainly irritated that the Shaman had managed to see her so easily despite the spell she had used to conceal herself, and had ducked low as the arrows flew.

With the Wesmen advancing behind a hail of shafts, she had gathered together her concentration and cast another CloakedWalk before diving through an unshuttered opening at the side of the hut in which she had been hiding and watching.

Landing on hard-baked mud, she had scattered chickens as she rolled, the fowl looking on in blank confusion, sensing something but seeing nothing. She had come fluidly to her feet and had sprinted away into the forest, changing direction at the tree line and hearing the sounds of pursuit die away as she slipped unseen further and further into the forest.

Several hours later, as night fell, she had held communion with Styliann before sleeping deeply under a stand of low bushes she had hollowed out to accommodate her slender frame.

Selyn awoke the next morning with the sun dappling her face. The forest was quiet but for the sounds of nature, and the still air warmed quickly. She set and lit a fire before recovering the rabbit from the trap she'd laid the night before, then skinned it effortlessly and spitted it for breakfast. She was on the move in less than an hour.

The lands to the north-west, her direction of travel, were crawling with Wesmen raiding parties as the tribes sought local populations to subjugate and new areas for staging posts. As she moved quietly past encampment after encampment and saw the Wesmen building calmly and carefully, she wondered at their apparent lack of urgency. It was as if they were waiting for something. She feared finding out what.

As the first afternoon of her journey to the Torn Wastes began to pale towards dusk, she felt a sudden and involuntary spasm of fear. What she found in Parve would almost certainly herald chaos throughout Balaia and a war the scale of which hadn't been seen for over three hundred years – the last time the Wesmen invaded. She only hoped she could relay enough information back to Styliann before she was caught and killed. Because, if Styliann was right, she wouldn't be leaving the City of the Wytch Lords.

Her sense of fear was quickly quashed, replaced by one of loss, and for a time she struggled with her motivation. She knew it was best if she forgot all thoughts of a return to Xetesk. They might cloud her judgement, make her too careful. She substituted them with the cold desire to prove herself beyond all question Xetesk's greatest mage-spy. She had never doubted. Others had, simply because she was a woman in a male-dominated order.

And more than having her name exulted in her own ranks, she had the chance to achieve the ultimate sacrifice for the greater glory of Xetesk. She might even change the course of the war that was surely coming.

Desire rekindled, she focused very deliberately to build her inner strength. Supple but strong leather boots covered her feet and calves, their dark matt-brown colouring blending with the forest shades. Each boot carried a sheathed dagger. Mottled green trousers and jacket completed the camouflage picture.

On her hands, black gloves, skin tight, with fine grips sewn into palms and fingertips. Inside the sleeves of her jacket and under those of her brown woollen shirt, a spring mechanism attached to either wrist. Locked into each was a barbed bolt fatal in close combat but with no real range. Three more daggers hung from her waist belt in addition to a pick set, and on her back, beneath her jacket, hung a scabbarded short sword.

Her head and neck were wrapped in a long cloth scarf which, when tied for covert action, left open only the skin surrounding her large brown eyes. She kept her black hair cropped close to her head, her nails short but sharp and her feet in perfect condition. Her body, slim and athletic, long-legged and small-breasted, was built for agility and speed, attributes she used to the full.

She was fast and deadly because being clever enough to breach places undetected was only half the job. Being able to get out when the mana ran dry was the reason she survived. Styliann had quipped that she'd make a fine assassin, but personally she found the thought of killing to order abhorrent. Mind you, more than once her path had been sprinkled with the corpses of those who'd tried to stop her.

Selyn smiled. Maybe she would see Xetesk again after all. With care and belief, anything was possible. She was under pressure to reach Parve quickly. Knowing only one spell that would satisfy that pressure, she used it, moving off north-west through thinning trees towards increasingly mountainous and barren terrain that gave ample places to hide, but few in which to find any comfort. The western lands were characterised by sheer valleys and studded with ranges of mountains over which sudden and violent weather broke almost without warning. But for now, with the sun warming the earth, cold rock seemed a world away.

The sun was already past its zenith when The Raven rode out of Korina by the North Gate, heading for the ruins of Septern's mage house, three days' ride to the north-west. The morning had been taken up by Sirendor's funeral, an event to which Denser was not invited.

Now clear of the scene of sorrow, they rode in loose formation on the trail. Denser, drawn and sunken-eyed, was at the head with Talan and Richmond. The Unknown Warrior and Hirad Coldheart rode together some twenty strides behind. Ilkar was well adrift of them and had kept silent from the moment they saddled up.

It was an hour since their exit from Korina and Hirad had been half expecting an attack, particularly from the Witch Hunters. The idea that they had sent only one assassin after Denser made Hirad wonder what sort of organisation they were, and he found himself a little disappointed in them. He was relying on their determination to see Denser dead, and as he gazed at the Dark Mage's back, he had to smile. It was an odd situation for sure.

'Why is it Ilkar dislikes Xetesk so much?' he asked, still staring at Denser.

'Why don't you ask him yourself?' returned The Unknown. 'It's about time he joined up.' He turned in his saddle and beckoned the mage to join them, but it wasn't until Hirad turned too that Ilkar spurred his horse forwards.

As he moved closer, Hirad frowned. Ilkar displayed the import of Denser's revelations of the previous night in his face like a wound. He tried to smile as he joined his friends but couldn't muster any more than a raising of the eyebrows.

'Are you all right, Ilkar?' asked Hirad.

'That's a bloody stupid question,' replied Ilkar. 'What can I do for you two?' His voice was flat and shocked. Hirad knew how he felt.

'Hirad was wondering what you had against Xetesk, exactly,' said The Unknown.

'Everything,' said Ilkar. 'But putting it simply, in magic terms Julatsa and Xetesk disagree about all things magical. What it's for, how to research it, how to build mana stamina . . . everything. When we say stop, they say go. In Julatsa, it's a crime to work for the Masters of Xetesk. Do you understand?'

'No,' said Hirad.

Ilkar sighed. 'Look – and stop me if you know this – but the reason the Colleges split was largely moral, concerning the direction of research and the uses of magic that the research was leaning towards. It was also due to the methods used for gathering mana, and, not to put too fine a point on it, the faction that became Xetesk found a quick way to replenish their mana that was based on human sacrifice. Now I can forgive Xetesk many things, but not that.'

'Do they still practise sacrifice?' asked The Unknown.

'According to them, no, but the fact is that the method still works despite the fact that they have found other, hardly less reprehensible methods. Anyway, the point of it all is that two thousand years on, our lore – that is, our understanding of the physics of magic – is now so divorced from Xetesk's that we can understand very little of how they construct and use spells.'

'So could you cast Dawnthief?' asked Hirad. 'I mean, it's not a Xetesk spell, is it?'

'No it isn't, and no I can't,' said Ilkar. 'Well, in theory I can. I know the words and lore because Septern was careful to publish them to all Colleges. But in reality, having done no work on the mana shape or studied the intricacies of speaking the spell, I'd be certain to fail.'

'So we'd better keep Denser alive, then.' Hirad curled his lip.

'Until we discover whether he's telling the truth or not, at least.'

'Yeah. Until then,' muttered The Unknown.

They fell silent for a time. Hirad digested what Ilkar had told him and wished he'd paid more attention to what made mages beat. More important, though, was finding out what made Witch Hunters beat. The two, he reflected, would be linked.

'What do you know about these Witch Hunters, Unknown?' he asked.

'You didn't get much sleep last night, did you?' The Unknown turned up the corners of his mouth.

'Thinking was only part of it, big man. Well?'

'Not a great deal.' The Unknown shrugged. 'Their leader is a man called Travers. He was the commander of the garrison that finally lost control of Understone Pass while we were fighting for the Rache Lords up north in the early days of The Raven. He was a dangerous man but he must be getting old by now.' The Unknown paused. 'Ilkar's your man for this, I think.'

Now at least Ilkar smiled. His ears pricked and he kneaded his forehead between thumb and forefinger.

'I'm an elf, Unknown,' he said. 'It's not a great story, I'm afraid. Travers is either a shining hero waging a long war against the evils of magic, or a once great soldier who's blind to today's reality. It depends which side of the fence you're on.'

'And which side are you on?' Hirad leaned forward in his saddle, his hands on its raised pommel, stretching his back and breathing in the smell of leather mixed with the strong odour of his horse. He found it strangely comforting.

'The blind man,' said Ilkar. 'Look, it all started out as a grand scheme and there were many people who wanted him to succeed. I was one of them. After Understone Pass, he founded a group dedicated to creating a kind of moral code which was aimed primarily at restraining the destructive magics of Xetesk and, to a lesser extent, Dordover. Not outlawing, mind; he didn't believe they should be stopped, not then, just monitored and kept to quiet research.

'Anyway, at that time they were called the Winged Rose and had tattoos put on their necks of a red rose head in between a pair of white wings.' He stroked the left side of his neck in a circle as he spoke. 'It was supposed to signify passion and freedom, I think.'

'Does that make sense?' asked The Unknown.

'Sort of,' replied Ilkar. 'Initially their ideals were pure. It was all about their desire to see the country freed from the shadow of what they saw as dark magic, and they were going to pursue that aim without recourse to violence.'

'Bloody hell,' breathed Hirad.

'Yeah, I know what you mean,' said Ilkar. 'As you can gather, the ideals slipped by degrees, and what had been a plan for, I don't know, regulation, I suppose, became a witch hunt; and one aimed at any College's adepts Travers deemed dangerous. That, of course, now includes me, particularly since my unfortunate association with our glorious would-be leader up there.'

'Do they still wear this tattoo?' Hirad indicated his own neck.

'Not quite,' said The Unknown. 'They've recoloured it a rather unoriginal all-black now, although the motif itself is the same.'

'That's right,' agreed Ilkar. 'Black Wings, they call themselves. The rose must be an embarrassment or something.'

'That's how I knew the woman was trouble.' It was a beat before Hirad realised that The Unknown wasn't talking to either of them. 'Damn.'

'What are you talking about, Unknown?' asked Hirad.

'I recognised that tattoo, didn't I? If I'd acted sooner, I could have saved Sirendor. Maybe. The trouble was, for a moment when I knew she was after Denser, I had no desire to stop her. I couldn't have cared less if he lived or died, and in some ways I still can't.'

'Until Dawnthief came along,' remarked Ilkar.

'If you believe that,' said The Unknown.

'Still sceptical, are you, Unknown?'

'Still an elf, are you, Ilkar?'

The buildings of the Korina Trade Alliance retained the grandiose air of centuries gone by.

The halls, offices, kitchens and rooms of the once proud organisation were set in gardens still tended beautifully by the City's gardeners thanks to a legacy gifted by the third Earl Arlen in recognition of the KTA's sacrifices in the first Wesmen wars three hundred years before. How the Arlen family's fortunes had changed since then, swallowed up by the rising power of Baron Blackthorne on the back of the new rich trade in minerals.

The KTA put on a brave face for the public. A sweeping drive through ornate iron gates led to a pillared frontage whose double doors of ebony sat within a marble frame. The main building rose three storeys and was formed from quarried white stone brought from the Denebre Crags some seventy miles north and east.

It was inside that the cracks showed. The entrance hall was lined with standing armour, all dull and dusty. There was no money to employ the polisher any more. Paintwork peeled, damp and mould inhabited the corners of walls, and the air was musty in the nostrils.

The banqueting table was chipped, scarred and rutted, its chair fabrics torn, stuffing oozing from rents in the faded material. As for the rooms, no Lord or Baron would take one without a trusted bodyguard in attendance.

The whole atmosphere depressed Baron Gresse. His initial optimism that the meeting had been called at all disintegrated as the usual internecine bickering grew among the dozen delegates who could be bothered to attend.

Lord Denebre, who had called the meeting following losses he had suffered in a Wesmen raid on one of his convoys inside Understone

Pass itself, was the nominal Chairman of the KTA, and popular belief held that he would be the last. He had contested that Tessaya, the tribal leader holding the Understone Pass treaties, had broken the safe passage agreements and that military action was necessary to keep the trade route open.

But around the table, the dozen Barons and Lords, ranging from the white-haired, craggily old but still powerfully built Lord Rache, and the black-bearded, bloated obscenity that was Lord Eimot, to the young, hawk-featured and very tall Pontois, wore their cynicism like armour.

For three hours, futile arguments, speeches and discussions drove the delegates into two factions. Gresse, Denebre and the elder son of Lord Jaden, whose lands lay to the north of the College Cities, found themselves in an increasingly beleaguered position. Orchestrated by Pontois, Rache and Havern, resolution after resolution led to the systematic dismissal of Denebre's claims, accusations that he had triggered the skirmish, and calls for his words to be struck from the record. The culmination was a one-sided debate on how the KTA might best profit from any potential tribal unity, while the three excluded delegates sat in bewildered but furious silence.

Gresse, who had said little throughout, spoke only in response to a direct question from Pontois.

'Strangely silent, Gresse. Still wondering how to pay for the damage to your castle wall, or just keeping your thoughts to yourself?'

'My dear Pontois,' replied Gresse, 'I am rather of the opinion that you lost the little tiff that you began and that your wounds require significantly more licking than my own. Meanwhile, I am afraid that my thoughts do not tally with the decisions you are about to make. Particularly your move to begin again the selling of arms to the Wesmen.'

'Oh dear,' said Pontois. 'You are presumably in possession of harder facts than my Lords Rache and Havern?'

'Yes, I am,' said Gresse, and the respect in which he was held sobered the audience at least temporarily. 'The Wesmen, as Denebre has been trying to intimate, could invade Balaia at any time, given the numbers I believe are massed in the Heartlands even now. They are organised, strong and united, and I will be marching to the aid of Blackthorne at first light tomorrow.'

'Really?' Pontois held his smile. 'A costly venture.'

'Money is nothing,' said Gresse. 'Survival is everything.' There was a ripple of laughter around the table.

'Your fears are out of all proportion to the facts,' said Lord Rache. 'Perhaps your age is addling your mind.'

'For generations now, we – and I include my family in this – have lived off the ample fat of Balaia, its people and its rich resources. We have drunk in its beauty and basked in its security. Our disagreements blow away like chaff in the wind when set against the warfare that has so often torn the west apart. But no longer. There *is* unification and it is us to whom their attention is turned. We stand on the brink of a fight for our lives, all of our lives, and the enemy is stronger, fitter, more numerous and better trained than we are,' said Gresse. 'Don't you see it? Don't you hear what Denebre is telling you?' He turned to Pontois. 'I would weep tears of joy on my ramparts at the sight of your men trying to take Taranspike Castle again, I really would. But unless we deal with the threat that affects us right now, Taranspike Castle will be flying a Wesmen standard.'

'I would prefer to wait for these Wesmen while drinking wine from your cellars,' said Pontois. 'Balaia has such changeable weather this time of year.' His words found favour with others around the table. A chuckle echoed off the walls.

'Laugh now,' said Gresse, 'while you can. I pity you for your blindness, and I pity Balaia too. I love this country. I love being able to look out from my castle and see the distant Blackthorne Mountains shimmering in the morning sun, the dew lifting from the pasturelands below me, and smell the freshness of the air.'

'And I will be happy to reserve a place for your rocking chair on my ramparts,' replied Pontois.

'I sincerely hope you are dead long before I need my rocking chair,' spat Gresse. 'And I will curse every day the fact that I am protecting your sorry hide while I and those truly loyal to this country strive to save it.' He spun about and strode to the door, a tittering laugh in his ear. He paused, fingers on the handle. 'Think about the real reasons Blackthorne isn't here. Think about why the four Colleges are meeting at Triverne Lake right now. And think about why The Raven are working for Xetesk, something they swore never to do.

'They all want to save our country from the Wesmen and our women from mothering their bastard sons. And any of you who refuse to ride to Blackthorne, Understone or the Colleges to lay your lives before the Gods for Balaia will be cast down when the reckoning comes. And come it will.'

The banqueting hall was silent as Gresse departed the KTA for the last time.

As the day waned towards dusk, Denser took the party from the main path into an area of thick woodland. He stopped when they were well hidden from anyone riding on the trail. Once all had dismounted, Richmond set about a small fire.

Denser wandered over to his horse, put his mouth close to its ear and pointed deeper into the woods. The brown mare ambled away in the direction Denser's finger indicated, followed by all the others.

'Nice trick,' said Richmond.

'It was nothing.' Denser shrugged. He sat with his back to a tree and lit his pipe. The cat poked its head from his robes, darted to the ground and disappeared into the undergrowth.

'So what's the plan, Denser?' asked Talan, wiping at an eye smarting from the dust of the road.

'It's quite simple. We think the amulet gives the location of a dimension door that will let us into Septern's workshop. We are presuming it rests in interdimensional space. Given the lore on the amulet, Ilkar's going to have to cast the spell to open the door.'

'No problem, Denser,' muttered Ilkar. 'I cast dimensional spells all the time.'

'Right,' said Hirad. 'I've been hearing you talking about dimensions and portals for too long and I still have no idea what you're talking about. Any chance of an explanation I can understand?'

Ilkar and Denser looked at each other. The Xeteskian nodded to the Julatsan.

'Actually, the concept is simple but it takes quite a mind-leap to come to terms with it all,' said Ilkar. 'The fact is that there are a so far unknown number of other dimensions, worlds you'd call them, that co-exist with our own. We – that is, mages in general – have identified two, but there are clearly many more than that.'

'Oh, clearly,' said Hirad, pursing his lips.

'What's the problem?' asked Ilkar, his ears pricking.

'I know you saw a Dragon and you say it was in some other dimension, but now you're saying there are other worlds littering the place, that's what,' said Talan. 'Look, put it this way. We go outside, we see sky, ground and sea. Now you're asking us to believe there are other dimensions there with us, we can't see them and you gaily announce you even know what two of them are!'

'Sorry, Ilkar,' continued Richmond. 'But this has all come as rather a surprise.'

'Yeah.' Talan again. 'I mean, how the hell did anyone get the idea there could even *be* such things?'

'Denser?' prompted Ilkar. The cat reappeared from the undergrowth and curled up in Denser's lap, eyes on his master's face.

'We think Septern always knew, though probably no one will ever know how. He was the mage who first postulated the existence of other dimensions in addition to the one we'd long known about through mana research. It seems obvious now; but at the time, Septern was shunned by the greater mage community, though he is now regarded as a genius. It was the reason he left Dordover and built his own house.'

'I'm none the wiser,' said Hirad, deadpan.

'Our best guess is that something in Septern's mind made him open to the nuances of mana flow and flux that signify activity beyond our dimension. He could see and sense things no other mage ever could. He was unique,' said Denser. 'Sorry to be vague, but much is missing from Septern's early work. He understood the magic required, though, and developed lore that would base spells to create dimension portals of his own – or so we have to assume.'

'All right,' said The Unknown. 'So we accept Dragons have a world separate to ours, that they link to us to escape, whether we like it and can get our heads round it or not. That leaves me with two questions. What's stopping Dragons from any side of their war coming here to rule, and what's in the other dimension?' He rose and added a few branches to the fire.

'Denser, still yours.' Ilkar's tone was less than friendly.

'We know very little of the Dragon dimension. No one has ever travelled there, except perhaps Septern. The Dragon you met' – he nodded at Hirad – 'will, we think, have been one of a large Brood, or family, who have exclusive use of the corridor between our two dimensions. The corridor has many links to our world, one for each member of the Brood and their Dragonene mage. The Dragons defend the corridor against attack from other Broods – and what Sha-Kaan told you pretty much confirms that.' He drank deeply and chewed his lip, considering his answer to the next question carefully.

'No one,' he said slowly, 'has been able to replicate Septern's work. So there is no travel between dimensions. Finding the key to his workshop may well lead to our making great strides to change all that. In Xetesk, we know a good deal about interdimensional space based on Septern's writings, and it's where we launched the Wytch Lords' cage. We have also found evidence of other dimensions but we've only penetrated one.'

'But it was the only one you really needed, wasn't it, Denser?' Ilkar's face held an expression of deep distaste.

'We certainly found it to be useful, yes,' replied Denser testily.

'Please share this knowledge.' The Unknown's voice suggested it was not a request.

'In simple terms, it's a dimension inhabited by what you'd call demons, but don't get too excited,' said Denser. 'They can't live in this dimension without extensive, umm, modification and continuous help from a mage.' Denser's hand reached out and stroked his cat absently. The animal purred and stretched.

'Why not?' asked Richmond.

'Because they exist on mana. It is the air they breathe. And the concentration of mana here isn't even close to being enough. Likewise, we could not live there. What Xetesk does, I will freely admit, is tap this demon dimension for mana.'

'And that's bad, is it, Ilkar?' Richmond turned to the Julatsan.

'It's not so much the use of the mana, but the methods used to make the opening. There's no point going into them now, it's a moral thing.'

The group fell silent, each man taking in, or trying to, what he had heard so far. To Hirad, it was all so much bluster and babble. He'd asked the first question but he'd barely taken in that answer and he wasn't sure he understood, or cared if he didn't. He couldn't concentrate, his mind continually wandering to dreams and images of Sirendor while his heart tolled death in his chest.

'Have you heard enough?' asked Denser.

'One more question.' Richmond was frowning. 'Where are these other dimensions in relation to our own? I mean, I can see the stars, are those what you are talking about?'

'No,' said Denser, a half-smile touching his lips. 'Although it's not a bad analogy. Day to day, there is no hint or clue where other dimensions lie. The easiest way I can describe it is to ask you to consider a void more vast than you can possibly imagine and then populate it with bubbles, a possibly infinite number, each representing a single dimension.

'Then, and here's the tricky part, imagine the bubbles being everywhere and nowhere at the same time, so that no matter the number of bubbles, and the vastness of the void, there is no distance between each bubble, making travel between them theoretically instantaneous. subject to certain alignment criteria.' He paused. 'Does that sound right, Ilkar?'

'It tallies with my understanding, such as it is,' said Ilkar, though his face suggested he'd learned something new.

'So how come the Dragon had the amulet?' asked Talan.

'Good question,' said Denser. 'Shortly after Septern announced the text for Dawnthief, he disappeared. We're guessing he went through his Dragonene portal, or one of his own. We had to assume that Septern meant us to have his findings one day, and it made sense that, as a Dragonene, he would entrust the effective key to it all, this amulet, to the Dragons and let them decide when we were ready. We just got one step ahead, that's all. Anything else?' There was silence. 'Good. We'll set off at first light.'

Hirad glared at the Dark Mage, who was searching a pocket.

'Let me make something very clear, Denser,' said the barbarian evenly, fetching a dagger from his belt and testing its edge. He stared studiously at the short blade. 'You are not in charge here. If the members of The Raven agree, we will travel to this mage workshop of yours, and not before.'

Denser smiled. 'If that's the way you want to play it.'

'No, Denser,' said Hirad. 'That's the way it is. The moment you forget is the moment you're on your own. Or dead.'

'And Balaia would die with me,' said Denser.

'Yeah, well, we only have your word for that,' said The Unknown.

Hirad nodded. Denser looked confused.

'But I'm the only one who knows what we have to do,' he said.

'For now,' said The Unknown. 'But don't worry, when we understand, we'll have more to say about how we go about things. Be sure.'

There was quiet. Richmond's fire crackled and a breeze rustled the upper branches. Night was all but on them. Denser knocked the bowl of his pipe against the roots of the tree.

'If I might make a suggestion for discussion,' he said slowly. 'I think it's time we got some sleep.'

Chapter 8

Segregation. Distrust. Suspicion. Mana. The air crackled with it all.

Triverne Lake lay at the base of the Blackthorne Mountains as the great range began its slow descent to the seas of Triverne Inlet over one hundred miles to the north. Touched by magic, the lake waters were sheltered, giving perfect conditions for the vibrant green trees that bordered it on three sides, leaving only the eastern shore open. Lush vegetation thrown with bright-coloured flowers provided a spectacular matting between the trunks and the rich life clung far up into the foothills before the cooler air running off the mountains let only hardier scrub, moss and heather grow plentiful. A multitude of species of birds flocked to the shores, their song and flight in every colour of the rainbow a sight to gladden the most barren heart.

The rain which periodically crashed over the Blackthornes and ran from its peaks in magnificent waterfalls all along its length never seemed to ruffle Triverne's balance. Rivers ran beneath rock to feed the lake through every season and the waterfall which flowed in times of sustained rainfall splashed into a deep and glorious pool which overlapped the lake itself.

The surface of Triverne Lake on the day of the meeting was calm, an occasional breeze sending tiny surface ripples in every direction. The gentle lapping of the water on the shore should have completed the tableau of calm with the warm sun shining through a partly clouded sky.

But the Marquee ruined all that. Standing proud not fifty paces from the lake, it was the focal point of a tension so cloying it seemed to cling to clothes and deaden hair and skin.

The Marquee was a model of geometric perfection. It was exactly equal on each side, and had four entrances exactly equidistant from each other.

Awnings, each one coloured in a College livery, shaded the entrances, and protecting each awning was a phalanx of College Guards. A further phalanx stood inside each entrance.

Seated at identical square tables, immediately inside their respective entrances, sat the Masters and their delegations. For Lystern, Heryst, the Lord Elder. For Julatsa, Barras, Chief Negotiator and the College representative in Xetesk. For Dordover, Vuldaroq, the Tower Lord, and for Xetesk, Styliann, Lord of the Mount.

Each was flanked by two delegates, and as Styliann sat in his dark ermine chair, he gauged the mood of his – how would he describe them – contemporaries . . . or was it adversaries?

Barras, the Julatsan. An ancient elf he knew well. Impatient, irritable, intelligent. His clear blue eyes shone from his deeply lined face, his mane of white hair was tied back and draped across one shoulder, the fingers of his right hand, as always, drummed on the nearest surface, in this case the arm of his chair.

Heryst, the quiet man from Lystern. He sat back in his chair, his face darkened by the shadows cast by its wings. His long fingers were steepled and held just under his chin but otherwise he appeared relaxed and as at ease as was possible in this company. Styliann respected him for his careful counsel and for the fact that, at forty-five, he was the youngest Lord Elder Lystern had ever appointed. He saw parallels with himself, though his ascension had not been through such democratic means.

He sighed. Vuldaroq. Blubber and bluster. When riled, he fired with the speed of an elven arrow, but landed with the accuracy of a catapult round. Already red in the face, the Dordovan Tower Lord sat hunched forward, arms spread on the table in front of him, eyes squinting, his bulk squeezed into a chair that would surely have to be widened. And by the Gods, Styliann knew what that meant: a meeting of the College-appointed carpenters to assemble new chairs for them all. Damn the Dordovans and their petty equalities. Every time a stitch was added to a cloak it set debate back days.

But this time there could be no delays and no bickering or it would be the death of them all. And Styliann was determined that Xetesk, at least, would survive.

All eyes were upon Styliann. He checked his advisers were comfortable, sipped water from his glass and stood.

'From the one that we were, to the four we have become, I welcome you,' said Styliann. 'Gentlemen, I am much obliged that you were able to journey here at such short notice.' The standard form had no meaning. When a Triverne Lake meeting was called, it was attended at the expense of all else.

'None of you can have failed to notice the increase in activity to the west of the Blackthorne Mountains.' There was an uncomfortable shifting among the delegates. Styliann smiled. 'Come, come, gentlemen, I think we can dispose with the pious denials, don't you?'

'The intelligence-gathering activities of other Colleges are not as extensive as your own, you may be surprised to hear,' said Barras shortly, fingers ceasing their drumming momentarily.

'I don't doubt it,' said Styliann. 'But one worthwhile spy from each College will have gained enough information to make each one of us nervous, I'm sure.'

Vuldaroq mopped his face with a cloth. 'This is all terribly interesting, Styliann, but if you have merely come here to confirm our own spies' intelligence, then I have more important things to occupy my time.'

'My dear Vuldaroq,' replied Styliann with as great a degree of patronisation as protocol would allow, 'I am here to waste no one's time, least of all my own. However, I would be very interested in the scale of Wesmen activity your spies suggest is present.' He gave a small laugh and spread his hands deferentially. 'If, that is, you're willing to share such details.'

'Happy to.' It was Heryst from Lystern who spoke. 'We haven't had anyone in the west for some weeks but we saw evidence of a fledgling tribal unity. Frankly, though, without a binding force in the shape of an overlord, we don't see any concentrated or long-term threat.'

'I have to differ with your opinion,' said Vuldaroq. 'We are currently running spies in the Heartlands and mid-west. We estimate that armies in the region of thirty thousand are prepared, but inter-tribal conflict seems the most likely. There is no evidence of a mass movement of forces towards the Blackthorne Mountains.'

'Barras?' asked Styliann, aware of the beating of his heart. None of them had seen it. Perhaps the old elf . . .

'The point is that there is no real threat from the west no matter how large any Wesmen force might be. Without the magical backing of a power such as they enjoyed under the Wytch Lords, if enjoyed is the right word, they can never hope to gain dominion over us. Indeed, I doubt they would get a great deal further than Understone Pass.'

'After all, the Wrethsires are hardly an adequate substitute.' Heryst chuckled.

'Well, they could make the wind blow a little harder,' said Vuldaroq.

There was laughter around the table from all but the Xeteskian delegation. When they had quietened, Barras spoke.

'Presumably, Styliann, you have other information you wish us to hear, or is this just a social gathering?' He smiled, but it died on his face when he saw the Lord of the Mount's bleak expression.

'There has been a problem in interdimensional space.' Styliann's voice brought total quiet to the Marquee. Breaths half indrawn were stopped. Eyes widened. Styliann looked slowly around the tables. Vuldaroq's face was red and angry, Heryst looked as if he literally couldn't take in what he had heard, and Barras drummed his fingers with greater intensity. It was he who spoke.

'I take it the Wytch Lords' souls are no longer under your control.'

'No, they are not.' Styliann allowed his head to drop to his papers. A ripple of sound ran around the table. 'And that is why I have called this meeting. Xetesk believes the situation to be very grave.'

'Styliann, I think the floor is yours,' said Barras from a dry mouth.

Slyliann inclined his head. 'I'll be brief. At least sixty thousand Wesmen are armed and united and ready for invasion. Currently they are based in the Heartlands and therefore ten days on average from the Blackthornes, but farming communities less than three days' ride from Understone Pass are being primed as staging posts. Damage to the mana prison during Dragonene portal opening allowed the Wytch Lords enough mana leakage to gain the strength to break out. We believe them to have returned to Balaia, where they are presumably undergoing reconstitution in Parve. I have a spy travelling to Parve now to assess the situation. As far as I am aware, those are the bare and complete facts. We are facing catastrophe.'

Another pause for consideration followed. Scribbled notes were passed between delegates.

'A masterly failure for Xetesk and its incumbent Lord of the Mount,' said Vuldaroq. 'The mana cage was surely your greatest continuing triumph. Gone now.'

Styliann sighed and shook his head. 'Is that the sum total of your deliberations, Vuldaroq? We face a threat so severe that I am unsure of our chances of survival, let alone success; and yet your response is to snipe at three centuries of effort that we alone have made on behalf of all the peoples of Balaia. Unfortunately, that includes you.' He sat down.

'Let us not forget,' said Barras, taking up the cudgel, 'that only Xetesk had the means and the skill to imprison the Wytch Lords.

None of us in our Colleges were pushing to help them. I, for one, would like to register my thanks to Xetesk for their unstinting efforts, and indeed their instant reaction in the calling of this meeting.'

Vuldaroq's face reddened and he sat back, the cloth once again dabbing his forehead, fuming in the knowledge that he'd misjudged the mood of Julatsa and, as he was about to hear, Lystern too.

'I add my thanks to those of Barras,' said Heryst, rising to his feet. 'We have a critical list of questions to answer. These are they, as far as I can see. Can the Wytch Lords regain their former power and how long will their bodily reconstitution take? Does the Wesmen invasion rely on the Wytch Lords' reconstitution or will it take place in advance of this? Finally, of course, what is our response and can we expect help from other quarters? The floor is open.' He resumed his seat.

Styliann coughed. 'I am slightly embarrassed,' he said. 'There is one fact I neglected to mention.'

'Uh-huh,' said Vuldaroq, pursing his lips.

'Naturally, the assumption has been made that the mana cage has been breached recently, and this may well be the case. However, I must point out that the nature and frequency of the spell calculations means that our worst case is that they have been in Parve for three months.'

Another silence, this one angrier.

'So how long before they have reconstituted?' asked Heryst.

'I have no idea,' said Styliann. 'Their work is not a speciality of mine.'

'So they could already be up and walking.' Heryst's voice was dread.

'Steady, Heryst. I think that if they were, we would have heard about it by now.' Barras held out a hand to calm the Lysternan. 'Remember, they are merely collections of seared bones. I can't imagine any reconstitution being quick, can you?' He smiled.

'We've underestimated the Wytch Lords before,' said Heryst.

'And we will not do so again,' said Styliann. 'Hence this meeting.'

'This part of the discussion, at least, is pointless,' said Vuldaroq brusquely. 'Because we can only guess at a timetable. We have established a need for urgency and now we should move on to the shape that urgency should take.'

Styliann nodded. 'But we must still search for the information. I will report my spy's findings in Parve as soon as I have them. I advise any of you with active cells to see them into the Heartlands and towards the Torn Wastes immediately. We can't afford to be taken by surprise.'

Murmurs of assent ran around the table. Notes were made.

'Returning to Heryst's agenda of questions,' said Vuldaroq. 'I also believe his second to be vital but, as yet, unanswerable.' The obese Dordovan pulled at his nose.

'Why so?' asked Styliann.

'Because the answer will only become apparent when the Wesmen move. Whether it is before or after the reconstitution will give us our answer.'

'I disagree,' said Barras. 'We already have evidence that the Wesmen are acting under Shamen control, and that now points to Wytch Lord influence. We don't know the extent to which the Lords can dictate events before they are walking. I suspect their influence is great. Styliann's spy will no doubt confirm this. I think we can expect an invasion attempt before reconstitution is complete.'

'Don't forget that the Wesmen have clearly been massing for some time to develop such a large force,' said Heryst.

'Indeed,' said Barras. 'And they are not fighting each other so far as we can tell. Not yet. Again, that is surely down to outside influence. But, as Vuldaroq will no doubt point out, we don't know when they will move. All we can do is plug the gaps to the east, wait, and build as fast as we can.'

'And so, gentlemen, we reach the key to our meeting,' said Styliann. 'We need an army. And we need it now.'

'Thank the Gods we hate each other so well,' said Barras, 'or we'd never have kept up the level of our College Guards.' There was laughter. 'How many men can we muster?' The laughter ceased. 'Julatsa has perhaps six thousand regular soldiers, half of whom will guard my City. In a month, the reserve can offer maybe another eight thousand.'

'I have no accurate figures on our troop levels,' said Vuldaroq. 'The City Guard numbers in the region of two thousand and the College Guard must be three times that. I can confirm after communion.'

'Heryst?' asked Styliann.

'Eleven hundred regular soldiers, two hundred horse and no more than two thousand reservists, most of whom are part-time City guardsmen. We don't have the funds for a retained force any larger,' he explained.

'But including the best general in Balaia,' said Styliann.

Heryst bowed his head in acceptance of the praise. 'Indeed so.'

'And you, Styliann,' said Vuldaroq. 'I suppose you and your demon spawn are more numerous than the rest of us put together.'

'No, Vuldaroq,' said Styliann. 'Because we built walls to save manpower. The City Guard numbers seven hundred, the College Guard five thousand, and we currently retain a handful less than four hundred Protectors.'

Barras ran the calculations quickly in his head. 'We are outnumbered three to one even if we include all our reserve forces. What about the KTA?' Vuldaroq sighed and sniffed.

'I wish I could say they were mobilising, but the fact is their internecine squabbles drain them of money and keep them turned inwards,' said Styliann. 'I have fed all the information I care to to Baron Gresse, and he, at least, takes the threat seriously. The KTA are meeting but I hold no hope of a positive outcome. They make our suspicions about one another seem like playground rumours.'

'Can we expect anything from them?' asked Heryst.

'Gresse and Blackthorne will help us out with the Bay of Gyernath, but aside from that . . .' Styliann shook his head.

'Worthless parasites,' muttered Vuldaroq.

'I tend to agree,' said Barras. 'So, what's the next move?'

'We all agree how many men we are prepared to release, appoint ourselves a military commander and go home and review our offensive magics,' said Vuldaroq, drumming his fingers quickly on the arm of his chair.

'Heryst, is Darrick here?' asked Barras.

Heryst smiled. 'I thought it prudent to bring him,' he replied.

'Well, I think we can save ourselves the agony of choice over a commander. General Darrick has to be the only man with both the respect and the ability to do the job. I suggest we bring him in and ask him what he thinks he needs.'

There was a warmth around the table of a quality rarely experienced when the four-College delegation met. But it was a warmth Heryst dispelled.

'And while we are waiting, perhaps we could answer a question we seem to have overlooked. How by all the Gods are we going to stop the Wytch Lords this time?'

It had been coming. The tension had been growing since they left Dordover, but it didn't make the incident any less regrettable.

Now only at most two days' ride from the Castle, Thraun had taken his charges away from any known paths and deep into a region of typical Balaian wild countryside. Tumbledown crags and thick woodland shrouded small plateaux and sharp inclines which hid streams and bogland at their feet.

The going was difficult and slow, and more often than not, the riders were forced to dismount and lead their horses over treacherous terrain where a hoof out of place could mean disaster.

The pace preyed on Alun's faltering confidence. Thraun could sense it. And despite his reassurances, and the certain knowledge in himself that this was as safe a route as existed, Alun's impatience threatened to boil over into open dispute.

With the day disappearing behind the tree line and late afternoon cloud, Thraun brought them to a halt on an area of flat ground by a stream's edge. It was lush and green and hemmed in by sharp slopes from which scrub and tree clung precariously. A littering of large lichen-covered rocks told of falls in times long past.

Thraun dismounted and patted his horse's rump. The animal trotted away a couple of strides before bending its neck to the water, lapping gently. Cloud was building from the west and the scent of rain, though faint, was growing while the warmth of daylight was giving way to a cool evening.

'There's still daylight,' said Alun unhappily. 'We could go on.'

'Light'll fade quickly in these valleys,' said Thraun. 'And this is a safe site.' He laid a hand on Alun's shoulder. 'We'll get there in good time. Trust me.'

'How do you know?' Alun shook his hand off and walked away, his eyes flicking over the campsite.

'We'll be fine so long as it doesn't rain,' said Will, glancing in Alun's direction, a frown on his brow. 'Is he—?'

'No, not really,' replied Thraun. 'I think his nerves are going. Try to treat him gently. He needs all the reassurance we can give him.' He sniffed the air. A light breeze was rustling the foliage. 'And it won't rain, either.'

'Just keep him calm,' warned Will. 'We can't risk him buckling on us.'

Thraun nodded. 'You get the stove going, I think I ought to be explaining a few things to him.'

Will inclined his head. Thraun moved off towards his friend, his footfalls absolutely silent across the ground. Alun was sitting on a spit of gravelled stone on a right-hand bend in the stream. He had a handful of small stones and alternately rattled them in his fist or flicked one into the slow-moving water. Thraun sat beside him, startling him from his thoughts.

'Gods . . .'

'Sorry,' said Thraun. He flicked his ponytail absently.

'How can you be so quiet?' Alun's question was only half good-humoured.

'Practice,' said Thraun. 'Come on then, tell me what's on your mind and I'll tell you why you shouldn't be worrying.'

Alun's face reddened and he looked hard at Thraun, his eyes moist.

'Isn't it obvious?' he said, his voice overloud for the peace of the stream bank. 'We're travelling too slowly. By the time we get there, they'll be dead.'

'Alun, I know what I am doing. That's why you came to me, remember?' Thraun kept his voice deliberately calm and quiet, though its native gruffness was always evident. 'We know the motive for the kidnap wasn't murder or they wouldn't have taken them in the first place. We also know that Erienne will buy as much time as possible, and will be as co-operative as possible while she waits for rescue or release. I know how hard it is for you, I'd feel the same way, but you just have to be patient.'

'Patient.' Alun's voice was bitter. 'We're going to sit here, calmly eat and sleep, while my family are one step from death. How dare you be so calculating? You're playing with their lives!'

'Quiet down,' hissed Thraun, the yellow in his eyes gaining intensity. 'All your shouting will bring us is unwelcome attention. Now listen. I understand your pain and your desire to be on the move all the time, but I am playing with no one's life, believe me. We can't afford to flog ourselves in the rush to get there or we'll be serving ourselves up for slaughter. If we are to save your family, we have to be fresh and alert. Now please, come and eat.'

'I'm not hungry.'

'You need food. You're not helping yourself and you're not thinking clearly.'

'Well, I'm sorry, but I can't just sit here and do nothing!' Alun's voice put birds to flight.

From nowhere, Will appeared and clamped his hand over Alun's mouth. The little man's eyes were wild and his face was angry and contemptuous.

'Oh, you're doing something all right. You're risking my life with your bleating. Stop it, or I'll open your throat and the rest of us can get on with it.'

'Will, let him go!' growled Thraun. He half rose but the look in

Will's eye stopped him. Alun, his expression frozen, stared at Thraun demanding help his friend could not, or would not, give.

'We will get your family our way.' Will spoke into Alun's ear. 'We'll go slow and careful, because that way we'll all get out alive. Now whether you're with us or face-down in this water makes no odds to me because I'll get my pay. But I think your family would rather it was the former, so I suggest you keep your loud mouth firmly shut.' He thrust Alun away and stalked back past Thraun. 'Never let clients come along.'

From the other side of the stove, on which sat a pan of water, Jandyr paused and watched the exchange at the water's edge, a heaviness in his heart. For him it was easy to see why they would never get far as a recovery team although the ingredients were all there.

They had the master thief, the silent trailfinder and the hunter. All were quick, all could fight and all had good brains. But the personalities were wrong. Thraun, despite his size and presence, was too gentle, too easy to persuade. Witness that Alun was with them rather than keeping the lights burning at home. And Will was far too high-strung; his need for quiet and control spoke of his lack of inner calm, and it was at odds with his profession.

Looking at himself, Jandyr knew that his heart wasn't in it. He wasn't a mercenary, not really. Just an elf who could make money from his skill with a bow until he stumbled on his true vocation. He only hoped he'd find it before it was too late.

Tasting the angry atmosphere and seeing the three men sitting apart from one another, he thought it probably already was.

General Ry Darrick smoothed the map out over the table. The senior mages from the four Colleges grouped around him; the delegates had to be content with viewing from whatever angle they could. Only Vuldaroq remained seated.

Darrick was a tall man, well in excess of six foot, with a mass of light brown curly hair cut over the ears, across the forehead and above the nape of his neck. The untameable mane gave him a boyish look which his face, round, tanned and clean, did nothing to discourage despite his thirty-three years.

Few people mistook his youthful appearance for naïvety more than once, and as he bent over the map, the senior mages hung on his every word.

Darrick's reputation as a master tactician had been made in the years that culminated in the loss of Understone Pass to Tessaya and the Wesmen. He led raids deep into Wesmen lands to disrupt the build-up of men and provisions, extending eastern governance of the pass by probably four years.

Since then, Barons who could afford his and Lystern's fees, and who didn't already have The Raven, sought his advice in larger conflicts. That he would command the total respect of any four-College army was not in question.

'Well, the good news is that given our regular troop levels, we are defensible, but that does rely on your estimates of Wesmen numbers being accurate. I would also be happier if they attack without Wytch Lord support, because if they do breach our defences, I fear we will have little in reserve to halt their march to Korina, Gyernath and the Colleges.' He looked left and right. 'Can everyone see all right?' He gestured at the map of Balaia, the Northern Continent.

Dominating Balaia's geography were the Blackthorne Mountains, which ran like an untidy scar north to south, coast to coast, not quite dividing the land into two equal parts.

To the east, the marginally smaller area that its indigents liked to call civilisation. Rich farmland, dense forests, free-flowing water courses and natural harbours gave ideal conditions for people and trade to flourish.

To the west, rugged terrain, crag, thin windblown soils and shrubland predominated, with only small pockets suitable for settling to any profitable degree. South-west, the crowded Wesmen Heartlands; north-west, the Torn Wastes.

Popular myth held that East and West Balaia were once wholly separate lands drifting in the vast ocean waters before colliding with slow and cataclysmic result. The rockfalls that still blighted areas of the Blackthornes gave some credence to the story.

'Now, you don't have to be a general to know there are three points of potential entry into the east. To the south, the Bay of Gyernath, to the north, Triverne Inlet and, of course, Understone Pass a third of the way down the range. We can discount the three recognised overground passes here, here and here in terms of an invasion because they are long, dangerous and simply unsuited to mass troop movement. That doesn't mean, though, that I will be ignoring them completely.' He reached across the map and picked up a glass of water, standing straight while he drank.

'You don't think they'll attempt to sail further along the northern and southern coasts, I take it?' asked Barras.

Darrick shook his head. 'Not in great numbers, no,' he said. 'I fully expect them to send skirmish and raiding forces at least as far as Gyernath, but they don't have the ships for mass troop carriage. Going across the bays is easy, quick and any size of vessel will do.'

'So what will they do?' Vuldaroq's eyes traced the outline of the map and Balaia's uneven, pitted coastline.

'There are two linked agendas we have to consider, one subordinate to the other,' replied Darrick. 'The Wesmen have long vowed to rid the world of the four Colleges. The Wytch Lords want that too, but only as part of the plan to control the entire continent.

'The main thrust of an invasion is therefore likely to be concentrated on Understone Pass and Triverne Inlet. I'll take the two in turn.

'Understone Pass will take the majority of traffic. It's quick, heavy equipment movement is relatively simple and the Wesmen already control it at both ends. Fortunately, its width is not so great that overwhelming numbers can emerge at too fast a pace, but any army will have to be confronted right at its eastern entrance, so limiting our defensive options.

'I will station myself there with five hundred horse and five thousand foot as a matter of urgency. Understone itself is merely an early-warning station; its KTA garrison numbers fewer than one hundred and is pitifully trained and experienced. I will call for more magical support when I have assessed the defensive requirements first hand.

'I can't stress the importance of holding them at the pass. Understone is less than four days' ride from Xetesk, only five from where we are standing now, and there is precious little in between to halt an advance.'

He paused to gauge reaction. The senior mages were concentrating hard. Barras was biting the tips of his fingers, Vuldaroq's lips were pursed and Heryst was nodding, still scanning the map. Styliann frowned.

'You have a point to raise, my Lord?' Darrick asked of him.

'Could we not take the pass?' he suggested.

'It is not tactically necessary given my defensive brief, and I personally would consider it an act of monumental folly to try. The pass is undoubtedly being reinforced as we speak. The barracks inside can accommodate in excess of six thousand men.'

'But with significant offensive magic . . .' said Styliann.

'Hand to hand, we would lose men in a three-to-one ratio. We don't have the numbers to spare. Your magic would be required to improve those odds better than one to one for me to consider it as a serious option.' Darrick shrugged. 'I know of no such magics that can be brought to bear to that effect.'

Styliann smiled. 'No. But should taking the pass become a strategic necessity – after all, we will surely need to take on the Wytch Lords, and they can hardly be expected to come to us – is it possible?'

'Everything is possible, my Lord Styliann.' Darrick's response was cool.

'Do you have something in mind you'd like to share?' asked Vuldaroq.

'No,' said Styliann. 'I just do not wish to see us closing the door on any potential advantages.'

'I believe I can be trusted to ensure that doesn't happen.' Darrick's bow was almost imperceptible. 'Now, Triverne Inlet, open, hard to defend away from the beaches and less than four days' ride from Julatsa . . .'

But Styliann wasn't listening. Not to retake the pass risked ultimate victory. But he couldn't push the point without giving a clue to his aspirations. Something would have to give and, looking at Darrick, he knew he couldn't change the General's mind alone. Perhaps it was time to let the Colleges know of Xetesk's latest experiments. It would redefine the phrase 'significant offensive magic' for certain. He smiled inwardly and returned his attention to the military planning, suddenly desperate for a meeting with his best dimensional research mage, a man named Dystran.

Chapter 9

The Raven travelled for three days through countryside that changed by degrees from flat woodland to rough shrub and finally to barren hills, moors and valleys. The weather settled into a cycle of sunshine interspersed with cooling cloud blown up by occasionally strong winds, but throughout it all, the temperature had a warm evenness, even at night, and riding was comfortable.

They saw no one.

Approaching Septern's house across a high moor, the ground changed from heather-strewn hard soil to lifeless dusty earth. In the distance, the air shimmered, light shining through a thin film of what looked like dust whipped up by the wind. The horses moved easily over the flat ground, and all around them, as far as the eye could see, the terrain was largely featureless but for the odd stunted tree or plate of rock jutting from the cracked dead earth.

'What happened here?' asked Hirad. He looked back over his shoulder to where the vegetation sprang up in a line almost as if it had been planted deliberately.

The Dark Mage blew out his cheeks. 'I don't know. The after-effects of a spell battle, I should think. It's a little like the Torn Wastes, though not as blasted.'

'Could it be something to do with Septern's workshop?' asked Ilkar, peering into the dust-filled distance.

'Possibly.' Denser shrugged. 'Who knows what effects an unmaintained dimensional rip might have on its surroundings.'

'What in all the hells is a "dimensional rip"?' The Unknown's face was blank.

'Well, basically, it's a hole in the fabric of our dimension that leads to another one or simply into interdimensional space, although there's obviously far more to it than that.'

'Obviously,' muttered Hirad.

The Unknown glared at Hirad. 'And are we near enough to this dimensional thing to suffer some kind of interference?'

'Hard to say. I'm no expert on dimensional theory,' replied Denser. 'What Septern might have done is anyone's guess. Septern was a genius, but his records are incomplete.'

'He certainly was,' said Ilkar. He scanned the horizon in the direction in which they had been travelling. He narrowed his eyes and spurred his horse into a walk forwards. Hirad, dragging on the reins of his mare, fell into step by him.

'Can you see something, Ilks?'

'Nothing much,' replied Ilkar. 'That shimmering messes up my long sight, I'm afraid. All I can say is that there appear to be large dark shapes a little to our left. How far, I can't say.'

'Shapes?' Talan was the next to speak as the rest of The Raven began moving.

'Buildings, at a guess. It could be rocks but I don't think so.'

'Well, let's head for them,' said Hirad. 'They seem to be the only landmark we've got.' Hirad dug his heels into his horse's flanks and led the way across the plain with Ilkar at his side.

As they began to close, Ilkar added flesh to his earlier description. They were riding towards the ruin of a large mansion house and an outbuilding of some kind, probably a low barn.

'Ruined? Are you sure?' asked Denser.

''Fraid so,' said Ilkar.

'Is that bad?' asked Hirad.

'Not necessarily, though it certainly adds weight to the spell battle theory. Mage houses aren't known for being easy to knock down,' replied the Dark Mage.

'Except by other mages,' said Ilkar. 'Or Wytch Lords.'

Denser raised his eyebrows. 'Exactly.' Inside his cloak, his cat hissed loud enough for all to hear, poked its head out briefly then withdrew in a hurry.

'Oh dear,' said Denser.

'What is it?' The Unknown turned in his saddle.

'I think—' began Denser, but a chilling howl cut him off. 'That we are about to have company.'

'What the hell was that?' Hirad searched around him but could see nothing, though the single howl had been taken up by more throats.

'Wolves,' said Ilkar. 'Big ones.'

'No, they're Destranas.' The Unknown chewed his lip.

'Destranas? Then that means Wesmen,' said Talan, loosening his sword in its scabbard.

'Yes,' confirmed The Unknown. 'We've got to make cover. Where are they coming from?'

'The outbuilding.' Ilkar pointed, and now they could all see, through the swirling haze that made up the horizon, large moving shapes in front of the distant black barn.

'We're in trouble,' said Richmond.

'Well spotted,' muttered Hirad, staring around him for a way out. There was none.

'All right,' said The Unknown. 'Let's circle north and west and come to the buildings from another direction. We might lose them that way, and at least we'll have made up some ground.' He caught Hirad's eye and added, in a low voice, 'Although what good it'll do is open to debate.' He pushed his horse into a gallop, leaving the rest of the party temporarily trailing in his wake.

For a time it looked as though The Unknown's idea had paid off. Hirad could see the dogs heading away from them, their handlers following more leisurely on horseback. He spurred his horse on, glanced behind him again, and suddenly the beasts were so much nearer and closing with appalling speed. They were huge, four feet high at the shoulder, and their howls and barks tore at the air and stung the ear.

'Unknown!' called Hirad. 'We can't outrun them. Look.'

The big warrior turned, looked and immediately wheeled his horse to a stop. 'Everyone dismount!' he ordered.

'Ilkar, Denser, take the horses and let them loose if they are what the dogs want.'

'They won't be,' said Denser. 'If the Wesmen are here, we're in bigger trouble than I thought. I'm going to try something. Only disturb me if you have to.'

'What—?' began Ilkar.

'Don't ask,' said Denser, and he turned his eyes to the skies and spread his arms wide.

'We'll have to protect him,' said Hirad. The four fighting men formed a loose semicircle in front of Denser, the rhythmic tap of The Unknown's sword on the ground a metronome for Hirad's heartbeat. Behind them, Ilkar slapped at Denser's horse and it trotted away with the others. The elf took up station to Denser's rear, his sword ready, as the first of a dozen Destranas tore into the waiting quartet and the Wesmen, four of them, galloped up.

Fangs bared and flecked with foam, a huge dog leapt at Hirad's head. Surprised by the distance and speed of the jump, the barbarian swayed reflexively aside and put his sword arm across his face. The animal caught the side of his head and both tumbled to the ground.

The Unknown, his blade before him, took a squat stance and waited as a black Destrana, tongue lolling, sped towards him. As it closed, he shifted his weight forwards and, anticipating a jump, flicked his sword upwards and took the animal under the jaw, skewering its brain. He moved aside and dragged his weapon clear, the dead weight dropping to the floor.

Hirad had been lucky and had fallen on top of the dog. Reacting instantly, he clamped a hand on the dog's throat as it struggled to get its paws underneath itself. He dropped his sword, snatched a dagger from his belt and plunged it again and again into the exposed chest, blood jetting on to his armour. The next beast slammed straight into his back.

Talan and Richmond moved together as three animals slowed and paced towards their prey. Neither side seemed sure how to attack or defend, and in the ensuing pause, Denser's spell came to awesome fruition.

The Dark Mage brought his arms together and crossed them, fists clenched and held at either shoulder. He opened his eyes wide, saw six dogs waiting and circling, pointed the index finger of his left hand in their direction and said one quiet word.

'HellFire.'

Ilkar swore and flung himself to the ground.

Columns of fire screamed down from the sky, six of them, each striking a Destrana square on the top of the skull. Howls of animal terror and pain split the air as the beasts were transformed to flame, dying even as they stumbled and tripped. The three dogs circling Talan and Richmond turned and fled, but one ignored the mayhem behind it and grabbed Hirad's back, bowling him over in the dirt.

The barbarian's knife sprang from his hand. He was defenceless. He rolled over on to his back, shouting as the wound low down on his spine ground into the earth. The dog leapt forwards, lashing a claw across his chest, splitting the leather and drawing blood. Hirad scrabbled backwards but there was no escape. The Destrana loomed over him, saliva dripping in his face.

Grabbing a handful of dirt, Hirad flung it into the dog's eyes. Distracted for a moment, the animal shook its head to clear its vision and The Unknown split its neck with a downward strike, the blade exiting the body and plunging into the ground scant inches from Hirad.

Silence. The wind blew up dust and bent the sparse weed. In front of Ilkar, Denser slumped to his knees, breathing hard as sweat poured down his face and his limbs shook. Talan and Richmond ran over to where Hirad still lay on the ground. The Unknown cleaned his sword before walking over to retrieve the barbarian's weapons.

Ilkar got to his feet, brushed himself down and looked at the still burning carcasses of the dogs struck down by Denser's magic. He didn't know whether to congratulate the Dark Mage or rebuke him. HellFire. Gods above. No wonder he was on his knees. He did neither, trotting past Denser on his way over to Hirad. He could see the remaining dogs and their handlers still running away from them and the barn.

The barbarian was being helped to a sitting position by Richmond. He was pale and obviously shaken.

'How is he?' Ilkar asked Talan.

'He's been better,' replied Hirad. 'Can someone help me off with my shirt?'

'Not yet,' said The Unknown. 'We need to get to cover. Can you ride?'

Hirad nodded and raised an arm, which Richmond took, helping him to his feet. They moved to Denser, who had still not stood up. Behind him, the horses were ambling back in a group.

'You all right, Denser?' asked Richmond.

The Dark Mage looked up and nodded, a wry smile on his face. 'We have to stop the Wesmen,' he gasped. 'We can't let them contact the Wytch Lords.'

'We aren't in a position to stop them right now,' said Richmond. 'Hirad's hurt and we have to get to the barn.'

'Where did they come from?' asked Talan.

'They must be camped near by. Watching the house on the orders of the Wytch Lords, no doubt.' Richmond continued to scan the area into which the Wesmen had fled.

'You took a risk there,' said Ilkar, standing over the Dark Mage.

'Justified, I think,' said Denser, gesturing at the smouldering carcasses. 'I'm learning to control it.'

'So I see. Dangerous, though.' Something caught Ilkar's eye and he looked away.

'And exhausting,' said Denser. 'I'm not even sure I can walk.'

'Try,' said Ilkar. 'Try now.' He could feel them all looking at him as he stared into the middle distance. 'The dogs are coming back.'

'Richmond, get the horses,' ordered The Unknown. 'Ilkar, see to Denser. Hirad, with me.'

Ilkar pulled Denser to his feet, the Dark Mage having to cling on to the elf's cloak. With mounts spurred to a gallop, they began the race to the barn.

For Hirad, the ride was a blur of pain. He could feel the blood pouring from the wound in his back, soaking into his shirt and leather. With each stride, his energy ebbed as he thumped in his saddle, unable to maintain a riding rhythm. His eyes misted, his vision was ragged and he couldn't properly see the way ahead. He was dimly aware of The Unknown moving close to him to hold him in his saddle. He didn't even have the energy to indicate his thanks; it was all he could do to cling on to the reins.

Urgent orders were barked by The Unknown: the Destranas were catching them fast. They might just reach the barn before the animals overhauled them but it would be close. Richmond and Talan urged their mounts to greater effort towards the long low building. Hirad could feel his grip on consciousness slipping away. He dragged his head to one side to see Denser hunched over his horse with Ilkar shepherding him all the way. The Dark Mage looked for all the world as if he was dead.

Mustering the last of his strength, Hirad dug his heels into his mare's flanks. The horse responded. The barn was only a hundred yards away. Richmond and Talan, having just reached it, pushed open a large door and slapped their horses inside. Moments later, The Unknown and Hirad thundered in and reined to a halt. The Unknown leapt from his saddle and Hirad slumped from his, legs folding, body sliding down the heaving flank of his horse.

'Richmond, Talan, look after him,' barked The Unknown.

He ran to the door and looked out. Denser and Ilkar were just yards away, the dogs almost on their heels, and rode past him into the barn. The Unknown moved a pace outside, pushed the barn door closed and slid the heavy wooden bolt home to lock it.

'Unknown, what the hell are you doing?' shouted Ilkar from inside the bar, pulling on the door, which gave only slightly.

'Korina was the last time I fail to help my friends.' The Destranas would be on him in a few heartbeats.

'There's no need, Unknown. They won't hang around here for ever,' said Talan. The banging on the door increased.

'They will.' Denser's voice came laced with fatigue. 'You don't understand what they are. The door won't hold them.'

'He'll die, you stupid bastard!'

The Unknown could hear the shouts of the barbarian as he squared up to the dogs. 'We'll see, Hirad. We'll see.'

The huge dogs ate up the distance. One, a pale silver-grey, was slightly ahead of the other two, one of which was jet black, the other another shimmering shade of grey. The Unknown tapped the tip of his blade on the ground and breathed deep knowing his first strike was vital. With the front animal two paces away, he side-stepped and brought his sword through waist-high and rising, straight into the Destrana's mouth.

Its neck snapped and its jaws splintered but its momentum brought it crashing into The Unknown's shoulder. Man and beast fell against the door, the timbers groaned and The Unknown could hear someone kicking at the inside, then angry words.

Winded, the big warrior shovelled the dead animal from his legs and started to rise, but the others were on him so quickly. The grey one locked its jaws on to a shoulder plate, the other plucked at his helmet with a massive paw.

With a roar, The Unknown jabbed forwards one-handed and sliced into the grey's right hind leg. The limb collapsed but the mouth hung on, teeth crushing the metal plate ever further as hot breath fired into his face.

The unharmed dog clouted The Unknown's head again and he could feel himself weakening. His helmet was dashed from his skull, strap biting deep as it snapped. He choked and swung his blade in desperation, feeling only hilt and glove contact flesh. Snatching it back again, he felt the metal plate on his shoulder give a little more as the crippled beast shook its head from side to side. Waves of pain washed over The Unknown and the black Destrana howled, sensing victory. The noise cleared his head for a moment and he drove his blade deep into the beast's throat, its exultation drowning in a fountain of blood.

As the sound died away, the plate gave out and huge jaws closed on flesh and bone. The Unknown screamed in agony and his eyes dimmed. His blade was wrenched from his hand as the dog pulled him on to his back. He whipped his fist into its face time and again but the fangs held firm as his blood flowed into the dirt.

The dog pulled its head back and lashed in a claw. The Unknown's throat was torn out, and as his strength drained away, his head fell back. With a crack of breaking wood, the barn door opened inwards and a blade flashed across his fading vision. There was the thud of a body beside him.

It was enough.

'How dare you!' Erienne flew at the Captain as he entered her room. 'How dare you!' He caught her easily by the arms and pushed her back towards the desk chair.

'Calm yourself, Erienne. Everything is as it was,' he said.

'Three days,' she grated, her eyes ablaze beneath her tangled dirty hair. 'Three days you've denied me. How can you do it to them, never mind me?'

Since their last conversation, the Captain had been true to his word. She had spoken to no one but the guard who brought her food and water. At first it had been easy, her anger at his assumption that she would crumble burning in the pit of her stomach. She had occupied herself quoting lore, revising little-used spells – some of which she would dearly like to cast in the castle – and searching for weaknesses she could exploit to get free of the Captain. But he had her children, he'd threatened quick death for any magic use and she had no doubt he would do exactly as he said.

Unless she could be in a position while she was with them to cast effectively, she couldn't take the risk. But then there was the future, after he had no further need of her. Would he let them all go? Part of her wanted to believe that he wasn't a murderer of innocents, that his intellect had a compassionate side, but that part was small. Erienne knew in her heart that he had no intention of letting them leave the castle. He surely knew her sons had great potential power, and that power would scare him. And that left her having to prolong their lives in any way she knew how and hope that he would drop his guard even for a moment to give her the chance she wanted. Until he let the boys out of their room, that chance would never materialise.

As the hours went by, her anger faded, to be replaced by the dread feeling of longing over which she had no control. She stopped being able to concentrate and the lore lessons were forgotten. Her heart pounded painfully in her breast and the tears were regular and prolonged as her happy memories of the boys gave way to nightmare visions of them cold and alone in a dusty room without anyone to protect them.

She knew the answer was simple. To see them was to call the guard and agree to help the Captain. But to help him was abhorrent to her every belief. And not only that. She believed him to be deeply misguided, and to lend assistance would place Balaia in greater danger than it appeared to be in already.

After two days, she couldn't sleep, eat or wash, the longing was that great. All she could do was shuffle, head down, around the room, calling out their names and praying for their safe return to her. Her mind was full of them, her body racked with the need of them.

She called the Captain on the third day, when she feared she was losing her mind and when she was sure her boys would wither without her. Catching sight of herself in the mirror, she wept tears through the dirt on her face. Her hair was lank and greasy, knotted and straggling over her scalp. Great dark circles under her eyes told their own story about the state of her fatigue, and her nightdress was torn at one shoulder where she'd caught it on a loose nail.

'You have denied yourself,' said the Captain. 'The answer was forever in your grasp.'

She was too tired to defend herself, slumping instead into the chair. 'Let me see them,' she said.

The Captain ignored her plea. 'I assume you have some news for me.'

'What do you want from me?' she said, her voice thick with exhaustion.

'Good,' he said. 'Good. I knew you'd see sense. I'll tell you what we'll do. First, I want you to get some proper rest, and I'm going to make it easy for you by promising that you will see your sons very soon. And I never go back on my promises, as you are aware. Then we will talk about your role in saving Balaia from this appalling creation of Dawnthief.'

'I have to see them now,' said Erienne.

The Captain knelt beside her and held up her face. She looked at him, his smile softening his features into fatherly concern.

'Erienne, look at yourself. They will be frightened if they see you like this. You must sleep, then you must wash. Now come.' He rose and helped her out of the chair and across to the bed, moving the blankets over her as she lay down, unprotesting. 'I'll stay with you until you sleep. And dream happy, because when you awaken, you will see Thom and Aron and realise they are well.' He stroked her hair back from her face, and though she fought it, sleep took her in an iron grip and she slipped into a deep slumber.

The Captain turned to Isman and smiled broadly. 'You see, Isman?

Deprivation can get the results that violence does not.' He stood. 'Now, one more piece to the puzzle. Let's go and talk about how we might catch our most valuable prize.'

Ilkar just stared while he tried to compose himself. The quiet hurt his ears. Talan had kneeled and closed The Unknown's eyes, and now he, Richmond and Ilkar stood around the big man's body as the wind ruffled his bloodied hair and blew in through the open door of the barn. Hirad, having decapitated the last dog, had walked back two steps and collapsed. Denser was tending him.

Thoughts crashed through Ilkar's head in a confused barrage but one kept rising to the surface of his mind. It was the view in front of him. The Unknown lying dead was a sight he had never believed he would see. And the idea that he would no longer be there to say the right words or make the correct decision to save them all was one that Ilkar was unable to take.

'Why the hell did he do it?' he asked.

Richmond shook his head; tears stood in his eyes.

'I don't know,' he said. 'We could have helped him. If he hadn't locked the door, we . . . Why did he lock it?'

It was not a question Ilkar could answer. He dragged his attention to Hirad and caught Denser's eye. The Dark Mage was worried.

'Bad?'

Denser nodded. 'Do you know WarmHeal?'

'That bad, is it?'

'Yes,' said Denser. 'He's lost a great deal of blood. Well?'

'I've never used it,' said Ilkar.

'I'm not asking you to use it. All I need you to do is to shape the mana flow for me – I don't have the energy.'

'You want me to channel mana for you,' said Ilkar slowly. 'How can you ask that of me?'

Denser scratched his head beneath his skull cap. 'This isn't the time to discuss morals and College co-operation.'

'No?'

'No!' snapped Denser, standing and pointing down at the prostrate Hirad. 'I don't think you quite understand. If we don't do something now, he will die. Now you can either try it yourself, use your energy and probably screw up, or you can shape the mana for me and I'll make it work. I'm good at it.' He was standing very close to Ilkar, and the elf could feel the cat squirming in Denser's cloak. 'So which is it to be?'

Ilkar looked away, straight into the stern gazes of Talan and Richmond. He held out his hands.

'You don't understand,' he said.

'We understand that if you don't do something, Hirad will die,' said Richmond. 'And we've just lost one, so stop talking ethics and get on with it.'

Ilkar looked back to Denser and inclined his head. 'Let's get it over with.'

Denser removed Hirad's leather armour and shirt. The tear in his lower back was ugly, full of blood and over twelve inches long. Denser probed the area around the gash and Hirad moaned his pain through his unconsciousness.

'It'll be infected,' said Denser. 'Destranas are never clean. Are you ready?'

Ilkar nodded. Kneeling, he placed his hands on Denser's shoulders, index fingers on the base of his neck. He opened his mind to the mana, feeling a surge through his body before he began shaping the WarmHeal and channelling the energy through his hands. There was a jolt as Denser accepted the flow and something akin to pain as the two Colleges, Julatsa and Xetesk, met and melded. Focusing on the Dark Mage's hands, Ilkar blotted out the barn around him and the ache growing in his head, seeing Denser's gentle finger movements, hearing his quiet incantation and feeling the mana being dragged through him with greater force as the preparation climaxed.

He could feel himself beginning to weaken. Denser was hauling the stamina from him as he drew on the magical force with ever greater urgency. And then it was done, the flow shut off, the channel closed, and Denser's hands were encased in a red-tinged golden glow. For llkar, the colour would have been a pure green, soft and pulsating but he couldn't say that the feeling was any different than if the mage under his hands had been another Julatsan. Unable to move from his position, Ilkar watched as Denser moved his hands over the wound, his fingers kneading the skin and probing the torn flesh. Blood flowed briefly on to the floor of the barn, Denser breathed in slowly and, with his exhalation, the light dimmed and died.

Slowly, the rest of the world encroached once more on Ilkar's mind. His heart was hammering in his chest and his arms trembled as he took them from Denser's shoulders. The Dark Mage examined his work, then sat back on his haunches, turning to Ilkar and smiling.

'That was a very interesting experience. We should research it further,' he said.

Ilkar wiped his sweat-slick forehead. 'Don't get carried away, Denser. I only did it to save Hirad.'

'And save him we have,' said Denser. 'I'm sorry you feel the way you do. We should be learning from each other, not squabbling.'

Ilkar gave a short laugh. 'And there speaks a man who would have Dawnthief for himself and his College.'

Both stood up, brushing dust from their clothing.

'And you wouldn't?' Denser felt in a pocket for his pipe. 'Julatsa sets itself on a pedestal and asks to be knocked down. For one thing, you know you cannot cast Dawnthief with any hope of success, and for another, you refuse our constant hand of friendship and reason.'

Ilkar felt as if all the breath had been knocked from him. He could feel his ears redden and the blood flowed into his face with equal force.

'*Reason?* Xetesk? Denser, the last time I saw a Xetesk mage, she was fighting for Erskan's Merchant Lords and killing people using MindMelt. That's not reason.'

Denser merely tamped tobacco into his pipe bowl and lit the weed with a flame from his thumb.

'Of course,' he said. 'You have never killed anyone in your work with The Raven.'

'That is completely different.'

'Is it? Your killing spells stink of righteousness and that makes them all right, I suppose.' There was a sneer on Denser's face. 'You are a mercenary mage, Ilkar. Your moral is money and your code is that of The Raven. Forget my allegiance; my deeds are no worse than yours. In Julatsa you see yourselves as the white knights of magic, and yet, individually at least, you are no higher than any College's mage. We should have stayed talking to Lystern and Dordover.'

'You say that and yet you thrive on blood and the chaos in dimensional space. Your College has consistently ignored pleas to moderate and that's why Black Wings hunt you. And me. I—'

'For God's sake, will you two shut up? I'm trying to rest.' That voice drained the anger from Ilkar and he smiled. So did Denser.

'Ah, Hirad, you'll never know the angst that brought about your salvation,' said the Dark Mage.

Ilkar found it hard to suppress a chuckle. He looked down and the humour died on his face. Hirad's eyes were black-rimmed and sunken, and his expression spoke everything of recent events.

'I heard you,' said the barbarian. 'We'd better bury The Unknown.

I understand that a WarmHeal surge doesn't last for long.' He scrambled to his feet.

Denser nodded. 'You'll be asleep in less than an hour.'

Talan retrieved a shovel from his pack. 'I'll dig. Richmond can dress the body. We'll observe the Vigil in the morning.'

Ilkar nodded his thanks. He was more tired than he cared to admit. The exertion of the WarmHeal was weighing on his mind as much as on his body. In saving Hirad, he'd committed a crime against the Julatsan way that would see him shunned by his brothers. He shuddered. At least none of them was ever likely to find out.

Hirad squatted outside the barn by the mound of earth that covered The Unknown. His sword was drawn and held in his hands, point driven into the ground and hilt by his face. His sorrow wasn't as keen as that he had felt for the loss of Sirendor, but something lurked in the back of his mind that his exhausted body couldn't register. He felt empty and useless. Again. It was a feeling he was becoming too familiar with. His eyes smarted and he turned them to the darkening heavens, as the mist that had bothered their journey all day deepened and stole the stars from the sky.

They were all asleep. Richmond and Talan had taken the early watches and snored in unison, lying on their backs on either side of the barn. Ilkar, his energy gone, was stretched on a patch of loose earth, his hands thrust deep in the soil, replenishing his mana stamina slowly as he slept. Denser smiled. If only he knew how easy it was. All you needed was peace and a victim or a prayer and an opening.

Finally, his eyes came to rest on Hirad, sleeping so deeply his breath hardly registered. He had been lucky. For all his confidence, Denser had no idea whether Julatsan-shaped WarmHeal mana would mean anything to him, or whether Ilkar's reluctance to channel the mana would affect the flow. It was a sudden source of interest to Denser that, give or take the odd spike, the WarmHeal shapes of the two opposed Colleges were identical. Again the smile. He wondered if Ilkar would ever open his eyes to the truth his Masters had buried from him and all of his brothers.

One magic. One mage.

Denser was sitting close to the door, listening to the wind rattling the sparse brush against the base of the barn. He filled his pipe from his belt pouch, frowning as he felt around the dwindling supply.

'Hmm.' He lit the pipe, letting the flame he produced on his fingers warm his face for a moment. Within his cloak, his Familiar shifted, its head nestling against his stomach.

Outside, there was another sound; a whispering on the wind. Something gliding. It was a sound Denser knew very well, as did the Familiar, who poked its head from his cloak to look at him, nose and whiskers twitching, ears pricked.

The whispering came closer, the gliding changed to an idle flap and there was a landing just to the right of the barn door. Claws scrabbled briefly at the earth, the wings flapped again and the whispering became distant and was gone.

Denser and the cat stared deeply into each other's eyes.

'Well, well, well,' said the Dark Mage. 'That's why you did it. You knew they were coming.' He shook his head. 'And I never suspected a thing.'

Chapter 10

Hirad awoke to sounds of movement and organisation. As he opened his eyes, he could hear Ilkar demanding someone ready the horses, while the crackle and smell of a fire told of Richmond preparing a meal. Light streamed in through the barn's open door and any remaining shadows were criss-crossed with light that shone through gaps in the planking. Hirad shifted. He felt a dull ache in his back but the pain he remembered had gone.

'Good morning, Hirad.'

Hirad turned his head and pushed himself up on his elbows. 'Bugger me, Talan, but I pity the woman who wakes up staring at you.' He offered an arm and Talan hauled him to his feet. Once up, a look around the barn brought reality back with unpleasant force.

There weren't enough of them. No way. The gap left by The Unknown was enormous. Unbridgeable. Hirad feft his heart thumping in his throat, and his eyes swept the barn once more as if he'd somehow missed the big man, sitting on a bale of straw behind the horses perhaps. His eyes pricked and he set off for the door to give himself the confirmation he had to have.

Sure enough, the grave was there, and by it, Denser and the cat, the mage staring at the low mound of earth in a kind of sombre surprise. As Hirad watched, he shook his head slowly.

'I know how you feel,' said the barbarian.

Denser smiled thinly. 'Probably not.'

'What's causing all this?' Hirad waved an arm at the view in front of them. The air was no clearer than on the previous day. Despite the sun riding into the sky unchallenged by cloud, Septern's estate shimmered in a light mist, keeping anything further than thirty-odd yards away just out of plain focus. At least today there were no dark shapes moving against the horizon. Not yet, anyway.

'I think it's either another after-effect of all the spell casting around the house, or the rip is causing eddies in the atmosphere. We don't know how dimensions interact but it may be that they can't mix.' He glanced back down at The Unknown's grave. 'Perhaps we should talk.'

'Yes, I think we should. We're in trouble.'

Denser indicated they walk away from the barn, and the two men moved off together in the direction of the house.

'I'm not—'

'I think—'

A brief pause. Denser gestured for Hirad to speak.

'We've got to take stock,' he said. 'The Raven isn't used to its people dying. Not for years.'

'I appreciate that,' said Denser. 'And I know we didn't start off right—'

Hirad laughed, a contemptuous sound.

'I'll say we didn't.' His voice was low and cold. 'First of all, your damned secrecy about what you involved us in almost killed me and ended in the death of my best friend. Then, because of that, we end up in this nightmare country and the second of my friends dies. To save you.' Denser opened his mouth to speak but Hirad glared him down. 'Your life is forfeit and I want you to know that the only reason you aren't dead is that Ilkar seems to believe you are the only chance Balaia has got.'

The wind gusted, picking at Denser's cloak. The cat's ears appeared briefly at his neck line, twitched and withdrew. The mage pulled his pipe from a pocket, made to put it in his mouth and decided against it.

'That's all I really need to know. You of all The Raven have to believe in me even if you hate me for what has happened.'

'I didn't say I believed in you. I said Ilkar did, and that's good enough for me.' Hirad looked into Denser's face, seeing a frown developing as his words sank in. 'You just don't get it, do you? It really doesn't matter what I believe. Ilkar says this is important. The Unknown thought so too, and that means The Raven is with you. That's why we're so good. It's called trust.'

'And now there's a problem.'

'Well spotted, Denser. Yes, there is. Your lies and our haste led to The Raven's heart being torn out.' He took a pace forwards, threatening. Denser was unmoved. 'The centre of The Raven. Me, Ilkar, Sirendor and the big man. We've been fighting together for more than ten years. We meet you and in less than one week two of us are dead. Dead.' Hirad dropped his head and sucked his bottom lip as images of Sirendor crowded his mind.

'We can still do this without them,' said Denser. 'We have to.'

'Yeah? Did you somehow miss what happened yesterday? The Unknown took out five of those dogs on his own. Who do you think's going to do it next time?'

'Well, there's you standing in front of me and two other good swordsmen in the barn. The only reason we believed we had a chance of recovering Dawnthief was that The Raven would be involved.'

'And you've killed two of us already!' said Hirad. 'Gods, Denser, there just aren't enough of us now. And none of us who's left was ever as good as The Unknown. Or Sirendor.'

'But that doesn't—'

'Listen to me?' Hirad breathed deeply. 'We cannot face another attack like yesterday.'

Denser nodded. He filled the bowl of his pipe and tamped the tobacco down. A muttered word and a flame appeared around the mage's index finger. He lit the pipe.

'I've considered this, believe me. And like you say, we have to take stock. Depending on how wide our search is for the components will decide how it's going to go from here. That's all I ask right now – that we go to the house, find the information we need, assuming it's there, then all sit down and talk it through.' He paused. 'Now those Wesmen have got away from us, they'll report to Parve. The Gods knows what that will lead to.'

'Why were they here?'

'Because the Wytch Lords will have always assumed that here was the key to Dawnthief. You have to stay with me, Hirad, whatever you think of me. This is too important for the whole of Balaia.'

'So you keep saying,' said Hirad. 'But first we have a Vigil to observe. Then we'll sort out this house and see where we are.' He turned and walked back to the barn, Denser following a few paces behind.

The Dark Mage was invited to stay inside the barn while The Raven conducted a shorter Vigil than The Unknown deserved. It was a tradition as old as mercenary camaraderie, but this time reverence had to be tempered with the reality of the situation in which they found themselves; and it was for the same reason that they all left the barn and rode the short distance to the house soon after, instead of walking. Should the Wesmen come back, having the horses even as far away as the barn could prove fatal.

The once grand structure lay in almost complete ruin. Blackened stone and scorched wood were scattered around a central hub of collapsed walls, with the odd splash of colour from ancient furnishings somehow surviving.

The house was maybe two hundred feet on its longest side, and had a main entrance that was still just about discernible. Part of a stone archway leant at a crazy angle above a shattered stairway, and next to it the mangled remains of a window frame clung desperately to the vertical, a shred of material flapping in the breeze, stuck on a nail.

Hirad dismounted, the others following suit. Denser led the horses to a fallen tree some yards away, then returned to stand by Ilkar. Both stared at the destruction, concern plain on their faces.

'What's up?' asked Hirad. 'Someone burned his house down. So what?'

'That's the problem. You don't just burn down a mage's house,' said Ilkar. 'They're too well protected. The power needed to do this' – he gestured at the ruin – 'is enormous.'

'Is it?' Hirad turned to Denser. 'Still think we can do it?' The Dark Mage raised his eyebrows. 'So who did it? The Wytch Lords?'

'Almost certainly,' said Denser. 'They would have known the extent of Septern's research into Dawnthief just as we did. He obviously vanished before they got to him.'

'Not happy, were they?' Talan kicked at a piece of rubble.

'Nor would you be. If they'd got hold of Dawnthief, it would all be over by now.' It was Denser's turn to look at Hirad. 'That is why it's so important we succeed. We must believe we can, and we must do it.'

'Don't lecture me, Denser,' said Hirad. 'Let's get inside . . . well, you know, *in*.' He pointed through what was left of the arch.

'What are we looking for in there?' asked Richmond.

'If we've read the amulet correctly, the entrance to the workshop is through the floor, and Ilkar is going to have to divine the way through it,' said Denser.

'Why Ilkar?' Talan frowned.

'There's Julatsan code on the amulet. Septern wanted it to be as hard as possible for mages to find his workshop, it seems.'

'More than that,' said Ilkar. 'If it was going to be found, he wanted more than just Xetesk represented.'

'I'm sorry, I'm not getting this,' said Talan. 'What College was Septern?'

'Dordover,' replied Denser. 'And most of the code on there is Dordovan, but Xetesk could read that easily enough. What we couldn't read was a passage concerning the opening of the door to the workshop, because it was based in the lore of Julatsa.' Denser shrugged. 'We could never read it even if a Julatsan mage told us how.'

'So how did he write it?'

'That, Richmond, is a good question. And I don't know the answer. He may have worked with a Julatsan, but Ilkar'll tell you that's impossible.'

'Not impossible. Just extremely unlikely. Shall we?' Ilkar led the way over the crumbling rubble, leaping up the steps to the steadier ground on which the arch stood. He turned round. 'Aren't you coming in, Talan?'

'Not yet. I think someone should keep a look-out, don't you?'

'Good idea.' Ilkar moved gingerly into what was left of the mansion. Devastated stonework lay in chips, covering the cracked stone floor and making walking tricky. Nothing much else was left. The wall by a fireplace had survived to three feet, and beneath the flame marks, a pale blue was just visible. As for the furnishings, a few pieces of scattered wood and iron, the odd strip of deep green upholstery and the oval of a table top were all that remained.

Denser set about sweeping the stone dust and chips from the floor with his boot and gestured that he could do with some help. The floor itself was cracked in many places, particularly where it joined the walls. The central portion was scored and darkened but otherwise unscathed for an area covering maybe thirty square feet.

The Dark Mage fished out the amulet, his cat treading gingerly down his cloak as he did so. It padded about the floor, sniffing close, its ears and eyes alert. Denser clacked his tongue, took the amulet from its chain and walked into the middle of the cleared area.

'As obvious as this may seem, the way into the workshop is right in the centre here.' He knelt on the ground and brushed at it with his free hand. 'Ilkar, it's your turn.' He held the amulet up to the elf, who took it with reverential care and stared at it at length before turning it over in his hands to stare again at the other side.

'I should have looked at it closer the first time, shouldn't I?' he said.

'I was praying you wouldn't,' said Denser.

'Mean anything to you?' asked Hirad at his shoulder.

Ilkar glanced round. 'Not much of it, no. This bit, though' – he pointed with his little finger to an arc of symbols which ran around an inner ring near the hub of the amulet – 'that's Julatsan, although the lore is very old. The style, I mean.'

'Of course,' said Hirad.

Ilkar chuckled and patted Hirad on the shoulder. 'I'm sorry. Look, here's a very brief lesson. College lore is something that is passed down through the College over generations. It's not something you can learn like you can the words of a spell. You have to, I don't know, assimilate it over years, I suppose. That's why Xetesk couldn't read this. It's Julatsan lore code.' He stopped.

'Go on. I think I'm there,' said Hirad. 'What does this lore do, then?'

'Well, it doesn't do much in the sense you mean. It's a way of storing College memories. In simple terms, the lore I know teaches me how to shape mana for the spells I use, although it's actually much more complex than that. And if I can work out the code on this amulet, it'll tell me how to divine what it is that operates the entrance to Septern's workshop. Or at least, that's the theory.'

Hirad studied Ilkar's earnest face, the elf's sharply tapering eyebrows angled down between his eyes so that they almost met at his nose. He smiled.

'Thank you for that, Ilkar. I suppose you'd best get on with it.'

Ilkar nodded and walked to the centre of the room, sitting where Denser indicated he thought the entrance to be. Hirad moved to sit in the rubble, where he could watch Ilkar's face. It struck him again that for all the years they'd known each other, he'd never taken any interest in magic at all. How it worked, who was who, what you had to do. Nothing. Hardly surprising really, he reflected. Magic was Ilkar's job. Hirad could never perform it, so he'd never bothered to look into it.

Sitting cross-legged, Ilkar held the amulet on his open palms, examining it intently, occasionally mouthing words. He was breathing slowly and deeply, and when he closed his eyes, his chest continued to move, somewhat to Hirad's surprise.

Hirad glanced at Denser, who was also studying Ilkar, right hand absently scratching the cat's chin, unlit pipe clamped between his teeth. There was a half-smile on his face and fascination in his eyes.

Ilkar was searching for something, that much was apparent. His head was sweeping the area immediately in front of him, his eyes roving behind closed lids. Hirad frowned and shifted, his mouth turning up at one corner, dimpling his cheek. He found the sight unnerving.

Ilkar licked his lips and started probing the floor with his fingers, amulet now in his lap. Suddenly, his sightless eyes shifted to his right to where Denser was standing. The Dark Mage flinched reflexively. Ilkar kept staring, unmoving, for fully half a minute.

He opened his eyes. 'Got it,' he said.

'Excellent.' Denser's smile broadened.

Ilkar got to slightly unsteady feet and walked over to the Dark Mage. Hirad stepped over to examine the floor where Ilkar had been probing. To him it was just hard and cold.

'It's a control spell. Dordovan, I think. I'll try it, it should be simple enough.' Ilkar looked again at the amulet, turned it over and mouthed a few words. He glanced over his shoulder. 'Hirad, I would advise you to move a couple of paces backwards.' The barbarian shrugged and did so.

Ilkar placed a palm on either side of the amulet, closed his eyes and muttered a brief incantation. There was a momentary hiss of escaping air from a seal, and an entire slab of stone disappeared from where Hirad had been standing.

'All right, Ilkar, I'm impressed,' said Hirad.

'Thank you, Hirad.'

'Me too,' said Denser, moving to the hole Ilkar had made. 'Dimensional transference. No wonder the Wytch Lords never found the way in.'

He was joined by Hirad. 'They don't make doors like that nowadays, eh?'

'Hirad, nobody *ever* made them like that. Except Septern, it seems.'

They could see nothing down the hole. The first few steps of a flight led into the darkness, and there was an impression of size, but that was it. Hirad called to Talan to bring in two lanterns, and with them lit, he moved cautiously down the stairs, unsheathed sword in one hand, lantern in the other.

The air was musty and smelt of age, and Hirad could see he was descending into a chamber almost the same size as the room above it. All but covering the wall directly opposite him was a moving dark. Swirls of deep greys, flecked with brown, green and the odd flash of white, poured over each other, going nowhere. The dark roiled and swam within its frame, alien and menacing, its silence adding to its threat. The room held an air of expectancy and Hirad couldn't shift the sensation that the swirls would snatch out to grab him and pull him into nowhere. The thought made him shudder. He stopped and felt a hand on his shoulder.

'It's the dimensional rip. Nothing to worry about,' said Denser.

'Can't things come through, you know, from the other side?' Hirad wafted his sword in the direction of the rip.

'No. Septern stabilised it using his magic and lore. You have to start this side to get back to this side.'

Hirad nodded and moved on down, only half convinced by Denser's reply. The rip was compelling. It gave an aura of impenetrable depth but Hirad could see its edge and it seemed to hang on the wall like a picture, less than a hand's width thick.

All around was the debris of a life. To his left as he descended was a table covered in papers, and near it, another scattered with implements, flasks and powders. A chest was lodged against the right wall. A layer of dust faded sharp outlines and, at the bottom of the stairs, was the answer to a riddle.

'Septern,' said Hirad.

'Undoubtedly.' Denser moved past the barbarian to examine the body. 'Three hundred years and he could have died yesterday.'

The body, head forward, eyes closed, dark hair thinning and close-cropped, was crumpled against a wall in a half-slouch, hands partially covering a bloodied tear in an otherwise white shirt. As the lantern-light swept away the shadows, it revealed a large dark and dusty stain on the flagstones.

Denser looked up at Hirad. 'Think how close they came to ultimate victory. Septern escaping down here saved everyone. I wonder if he knew that?' He moved to the paper-strewn table, sat in a chair and began to leaf through the mass of documents.

Hirad moved off the stairs and was followed into the workshop by Ilkar, Talan and Richmond. The elf repeated his earlier spell and the hole closed above them.

'Ilkar?'

'Yes, Hirad?'

'If you've got the amulet there and you need it to open and close the door, how did he do it?'

The mage straightened. 'Good question. Any ideas, Denser?'

Denser, who had just uncovered a leather-bound book, turned. 'I don't know, what did you do?'

'It's similar to a FlamePalm but you have to be holding the amulet so that the flame is directed straight into it.'

'Whatever the amulet's made of will be the catalyst, then. Have you checked his neck?'

'His neck?' Ilkar's scowl was momentary. 'Oh, I see.' He bent to

Septern and put his hand inside the dead man's collar. Hirad could see the shudder from where he was standing.

'Feel good, Ilkar?'

'Clammy and cold, Hirad. Waxy too. Really, really unpleasant. He is wearing a chain, though.' Ilkar took the chain over Septern's head and nodded as he looked at the blood-stained copy amulet hanging from it. 'The faces are largely blank, it's just the edging that has the same design.'

'Good,' said Denser. 'I wouldn't like to think he'd made several copies of the way in here.' He went back to his reading.

Hirad turned his attention to Talan and Richmond who had been poking idly at the glassware on one of the tables but had now begun to examine the chest. Ilkar came to his side, wiping his hands down his armour.

'What do you think of this?' He pointed at the rip, its gentle swirling still slow and rhythmic.

'It gives me the shivers. I wonder what's on the other side.'

'Well,' said Ilkar, 'I have a strong feeling that you'll be finding out.'

'No question of it,' said Denser. 'There's some incredible stuff in here.' He tapped the book. 'It'll bring dimensional research on hundreds of years. And it answers a few other questions too.' He stood up and walked over to Ilkar, handing him the book and indicating a passage. 'Read it out, will you? I've got to try something. Have you got any rope, Talan?'

'Outside.' Talan was gazing at the rip, Richmond at his shoulder. Eventually he turned to find Denser looking at him. 'Do you want some?'

'No, I was just passing the time.'

'Well, I'm not a bloody mind-reader, Denser.'

'No, you'd need a mind for that,' muttered the Dark Mage. 'Just get the rope, will you?'

Talan strode towards him. 'In charge now, are you? Tell you what, go and get it yourself, or have you lost the power of movement?'

'I only want some rope, Talan,' said Denser. 'I'm not asking you to open the gates of hell or anything.'

'It's on my horse if you want it.' Talan turned and stalked to the other end of the rip and took up his gazing again.

'Gods alive,' said Denser. 'FlamePalm, you say?'

Ilkar nodded and tossed him the original amulet. 'Just leave out the command word and substitute whatever it is you say for manameld.'

Denser followed the Julatsan's instructions, and soon wan daylight appeared above them.

'I won't be long.' Denser trotted up the steps.

'Are you going to read that book, or keep it to yourself?' asked Hirad.

'Sorry,' said Ilkar. 'Do you two want to hear this?'

Richmond shrugged and walked over, Talan glowered at Ilkar then did likewise.

'It's a diary of sorts. A research log as well, though I won't go into that. Listen to this:

'It is only four days since I revealed my creation of Dawnthief and already the Wytch Lords are searching for me. I can feel the shock waves through the mana even here. I cannot leave this house and I am left hoping that the four Colleges will defeat the evil from the Torn Wastes, for the spell I created to destroy them myself I cannot unleash on Balaia. It was folly to tell the Colleges of my discovery. I have since found that Dawnthief is infinitely more powerful than I had imagined. While it would be an unstable spell to work, should it be cast with the right preparation, concentration and, of course, catalysts, it could plunge Balaia into eternal night. It would mean the end of everything.

'But I also find I cannot destroy the knowledge I have unearthed. Is that terrible when that knowledge could obliterate us all? I don't think so – you can never hope to unmake what has been made. So I have taken the information containing the names of the catalysts through the rip and into a place where those who guard it have sworn to do so though death take the breath from their bodies and the flesh from their bones.

'The key amulet has been left with the Brood Kaan in the Dragon dimension and they of all creatures know the price of Dawnthief falling into the wrong hands. Perhaps some day they will give the key back and this journal will be found and my actions understood. For myself, having hidden what had to be hidden, I must destroy the rip, closing the door for ever. To do so, I must remain on this side and will take my own life. No one must find Dawnthief. No one.'

The next page was blank.

Ilkar looked up from his reading, finding all eyes on him. Above them, Denser came back down the stairs, took the amulet from Ilkar and closed the slab once again.

'So what happened?' asked Hirad, indicating Septern's body. 'He didn't kill himself, that much is obvious. And he didn't destroy the rip either.'

Ilkar shrugged. 'Well, it looks to me as though the Wytch Lords got to him earlier than he expected. Like Denser said, he saved Balaia by getting down here before he died.'

'And we're about to do what he feared most,' said Denser. 'We're going to get that information. Now then.' Denser walked over to the closed chest, slapped open the clasps and opened the lid, finding clothes, boots and a pair of lanterns inside. He turned to the others. 'A going-away chest, if I'm not very much mistaken.'

'What is it you're going to do, Denser?' asked Hirad.

'A little test of what exactly is behind the rip, that's what.' He closed and clasped the chest again. Taking the coil of rope from his shoulder, he quickly bound the chest with it, leaving a length of perhaps twenty feet in his hands.

'Hirad, would you?' asked Denser, pointing at the chest.

Hirad frowned but walked over to the Dark Mage.

'What do you want?'

'Pick up the chest and throw it through the rip, if you don't mind.'

'Oh, I see. Good idea.' He knelt and wrapped his arms around the chest, picked it up and took a couple of paces backwards. 'Anywhere in particular?'

'In the centre, I think.'

Hirad nodded and moved to the middle of the rip. He hefted the trunk so that his hands were beneath it and it rested on his chest. A couple of bounces and he threw it straight into the rip, where it disappeared as if swallowed by thick mud.

All eyes switched to the rope as it moved gently through Denser's hands. After no more than ten seconds, the rope gathered speed briefly, dipped, fell to the bottom of the rip and went slack.

'I see,' said Denser.

'I wish I did,' muttered Hirad.

'It's quite easy. The rip itself is quite deep, maybe six feet, and travel through it is slow. Just beyond the rip is a short drop which we'll have to be ready for.' He paused. 'Now then, who's for a journey into the absolute unknown?'

Silence. And it had an odd quality about it. Hirad considered that they had always known they'd have to go through the dark swirling mass, but now the time had arrived, they were all thinking about what might actually be on the other side. Whatever it was, it was unlikely to be much like anything they had ever experienced.

'Well, we don't need to leave a guard, do we?' said Richmond.

'That we don't,' said Ilkar. 'What do you reckon, Hirad, The Raven's strangest ride?'

Hirad chuckled. 'Yeah. Let's do it.' He clapped his hands together and drew his sword. 'Lanterns, I think.'

'Definitely,' said Ilkar, picking up the one Denser had left on the table.

They lined up in front of the rip, each man staring deep into the gently moving picture in front of him. Hirad looked down the line one way then the other from his position in its centre. He breathed deeply, his heart rate leaping.

'Ready, everyone?' he asked. There were nods and murmurs of assent.

'Hirad, I think you have the honour of the cry,' said Talan.

'Thank you, Talan.'

'What's this?' asked Denser.

'Just listen,' said Ilkar.

Hirad drew in another huge breath. 'Raven!' he roared. 'Raven with me!'

They hit the rip at a dead run.

Chapter 11

Styliann warmed his feet by the fire in his study and took tea from the mug on the table by his right arm. There was a knock at the door.

'Come.'

Nyer and Dystran entered. He gestured them to the other chairs and poured them each a mug of tea. Nyer settled into his seat with the ease of one well used to such company. For Dystran, a man barely into his forties, the nervousness was apparent and he sat forwards in his chair, clutching his mug tight.

'Is Laryon on his way?'

'Regretfully not,' said Nyer. 'He has encountered a problem with certain of his staff.'

'I see.' Styliann's eyes narrowed. People didn't usually pass up one of his invitations. He made a note to speak with the Master presently. 'Now, Dystran, the DimensionConnect research, it is in an advanced state, I trust?'

Dystran looked to Nyer, who gestured him to speak.

'Yes, my Lord. We are testing in the catacombs.' He smiled before he could help himself.

'Something amuses you?'

'Sorry, my Lord.' Dystran's cheeks suddenly glowed red beneath his short brown hair. 'It is just that we had to improve drainage rather urgently after the initial, highly successful test.'

Styliann raised his eyebrows.

'Keep to the report,' said Nyer.

Dystran nodded. 'We have made three successful tests of the DimensionConnect spell, linking our dimension with that of another. Having made the correct calculations, we were able to steer a course of water between the two, unfortunately flooding one spell chamber.'

'Excellent,' said Styliann. 'How long before we are ready for a live test?'

'Any time,' said Dystran. 'The only question remaining is one of mage linkage. We assume that the more mages casting, the wider the channel. However, there are risks involved.' He paused. 'Finally, dimensions are not always in alignment, and although we can calculate when they will be, we have no control over exactly when it is possible to cast.'

Styliann frowned. 'What are the alignment windows?'

'Between several hours and several days. We are still searching for a pattern.'

The Lord of the Mount nodded. 'That will do. Dystran, I need you to bring your team of mages up to speed for a large-scale live test. How many do you have?'

'Thirty,' said the mage.

'Your view, my old friend?' asked Styliann.

'It is the ideal offensive weapon for the pass,' said Nyer.

'Naturally.' Styliann smiled. The door to victory opened once again.

Later, Styliann held communion with Laryon and what he heard took the smile from his face. It was sad when old friends began playing power games with him. It made him angry.

Flesh sucked from his bones. Blood pouring into the skin of his face. He could feel it swell until his cheeks burned with pain, and then swell yet more. Hirad's hands tightened reflexively, right hand attempting to crush the hilt of his sword. Eyes open, unclosable, seeing nothing but blackness mottled with grey. If he could have turned his head he was sure that he wouldn't have been able to see any of the others. Were they even there?

He could hear no sound but for the blood thrashing through his veins and his brain shouting at him to make sense of it all. Was he walking? He thought not, but he was certainly moving. Where didn't matter. He just wanted it to stop before the flesh was torn from his body and his blood surged into the void. Even then, he found himself thinking that he would still be moving. He felt a pulsing spread through his body. It began in the pit of his stomach and moved swiftly to enmesh his entire being. It was hot. Very hot. The blood felt as if it would boil his veins, melting them away.

Light.

The end of eternity.

A fall. Hard ground. A dimming of the light.

Hirad was sitting in an open space and it felt high up. No reason for that. It just felt that way. He looked left and right, counting the rest of The Raven off in his head. They were all there, all sitting, all looking at each other. Behind them, the rip hung in the air a couple of feet from the ground. The end of the rope that bound the chest hung in a slight bow. Hirad tracked it to the chest, which was lying on its side next to Ilkar. And behind the rip, a sheer drop into nothing.

Hirad stood up on juddering legs, quickly subsiding to calm, and drank in his first sight of another dimension. With the blood settling back to a normal pace through his veins, he felt the hairs all over his body stand as he breathed. He hadn't known what to expect, but it wasn't this. The air tasted different, dry and tinny, and the whole atmosphere was strange and cloying, slightly irritating to the skin and eyes.

The sky above them was dark, filled with cloud boiling across the sky, though he could feel only a light breeze on his face. He could see no break in the cover yet a half-light spread from the horizon where the black of the cloud met the black of the land.

And they *were* standing very high up. The feeling was confirmed by simply looking down a few feet behind and to his right. The rip was positioned at the very edge of the plateau on which they had landed and the drop was sheer immediately to both sides. Lightning, red and harsh, flared and sheeted across the land, illuminating nothing, only reinforcing the impenetrable dark. Almost as one, The Raven paced further from the edge, each man noting the small margin for error when they made to return to their own dimension.

But he knew what it lacked. Sound. Apart from the breeze sighing in his ears, he could hear nothing at all. No voices, no animals, no birds. No sound of any life whatever. Even the lightning behind them was silent. It made him uneasy. It was like standing in the land of the dead.

Hirad tracked the land to his left until his line was broken by a building. Of sorts, anyway. Gazing straight ahead across the open ground – and it was ground; soil and vegetation ruffling in the gentle wind – he saw a jumble of ramshackle structures. Broken timbers, crumbled stone and cracked slate littered the area and he could see the dereliction stretching away for what had to be five or six hundred yards until it stopped abruptly, presumably at the farther edge of the plateau.

Beyond that, another rip hung in space. And as his eyes adjusted to the light, he could see all around them, but scattered distantly, rough columns of rock which expanded at their heads to form more plateaux, disc- and oval-shaped. Clearly, they were on a similar structure and the realisation unbalanced him briefly. He thought he could just make out more buildings on the other discs, some towering like palaces. But no more light. Nothing moved but that under the sway of the breeze.

'Nice place,' muttered Talan, his voice sounding loud in the quiet.

Hirad started. 'Gods in the ground, what is this place?' The barbarian wished fervently The Unknown were there. It would have calmed him just a little.

'It doesn't make sense to my mind,' said Denser. 'How did they come to be up here, and how do they get from this platform to any of the others, and how do they get these buildings up here . . .?' His voice trailed away, his hand still pointing vaguely in the direction of the derelict village on the platform, if that was what it was.

'And who were *they*?' asked Ilkar.

'That's assuming they've all gone,' said Talan.

'You've all thought that far, have you?' asked Hirad. 'Personally, I'm still debating jumping straight back. This place makes my skin crawl.' He could feel his heart beating fast again.

'But isn't it fascinating?' said Denser. 'This is *another* dimension. Think what that means.'

'Yeah,' said Hirad. 'It's totally different, it makes me feel bad and I get the feeling we shouldn't be standing here.'

'Different but in so many respects the same,' said Ilkar. He bent down and grabbed a handful of earth. 'Look. Soil, grass, buildings . . . air.'

'But no noise. Do you think they're all dead, whoever they are?' Denser started walking towards the remains of the settlement. Reluctantly, Hirad followed with the rest of The Raven, chewing his lip, the sword in his hand providing no comfort whatever. The place was oppressive despite the lightness of the air, and the lack of noise made him dig repeatedly in his ears with the forefinger of his left hand, searching for the reason why he couldn't hear anything other than the sound of their feet and breathing.

'What is it we're looking for, Denser?' Richmond turned to the Dark Mage as they tramped across the dry earth, its crumbling texture crunching underfoot.

'I haven't a clue, to be honest. It's information we need, not pieces of this, that or the other, if you see what I mean.'

'So, some parchment, maybe?' suggested Richmond.

Denser shrugged. 'Maybe. Or another amulet. Perhaps even some sort of carved jewellery. Whatever, it ought to stand out amongst all the rubbish over there. It'll be Balaian, of that I'm sure.' He gestured again at the buildings. Collapsed though they largely were, it was plain that their design bore only nodding acquaintance to anything the races of Balaia might build. Many had openings that were probably doors. But they were oval and did not sit flush with the ground. And of those that were still partially roofed, all had a similar oval opening towards the apex of the domed structure.

In a way, they reminded Hirad of kilns, though they were wood and stone, not shaped stone like the Wesmen built. They were, or would have been, tall, each maybe twenty or more feet high. For a single-storey structure, that seemed high, although the absence of anything recognisable as a window meant he could be mistaken. There were other levels inside.

'I don't like this,' said Hirad. He shivered.

'So you've said, but I agree,' said Ilkar. 'It's not right. I feel as if I might fall any moment.'

'The less time I spend here the better.' Hirad shook his shoulders to relieve sudden tension. 'What the hell could Septern have wanted to come here for?'

A sheet of lightning flooded the night below the platform, illuminating everything it touched with a momentary mauve radiance. Shadows were plunged into even sharper relief and the after-effect lingered in Hirad's eyes for a few seconds. It was then that he saw the movement. The Raven moved as one, dipped sword points suddenly at the ready.

From inside and around the edges of the buildings, walking and half stumbling, came the inhabitants of the village. In a few moments they had filled the space in front of the buildings and had begun a ponderous move towards The Raven. Hirad tried to make a count, but at fifty their movement fooled his eyes, and surely there were many times more than that.

From this distance, they looked thin and pale, a confusion of limbs, but within a few strides, what they were became plain.

'Gods in the ground, I don't believe it,' whispered Hirad. The Raven, again as one, stopped.

'"Though death takes the breath from their bodies and the flesh from their faces",' quoted Denser, his voice a mutter.

There was something wrong with the way they balanced – or rather, didn't. Not that there should be a right way for a dead creature to balance, thought Hirad. He shuddered. He couldn't put his finger on it, but as the villagers continued their painfully slow approach, he thought he could see their backs twitching, almost with every stride.

One of the leaders stumbled over a rock and reflexively unfolded wings to steady itself. But they were nothing more than bone connected with shredded membrane and it fell. The others moved on, now only seventy paces away.

It was impossible to take in. A force of dead avian people, rotted cloth covering bones, oval heads centred with huge empty eye slits, and all walking at the same dull pace. They were moving to fill the space to either edge of the plateau. And they were closing remorselessly.

'Any suggestions?' asked the barbarian, a cool feeling of panic edging around his heart. The dead would be on them in a couple of minutes.

'They've got no weapons. What are they going to do?' asked Talan.

'Just walk on, I should think,' said Denser. 'After all, we've got nowhere to go except back through the rip and we can't hope to stand up to that number. They'll just keep on coming and eventually you won't have the room to use your swords. And if you aren't careful they'll push you straight off the edge.'

'But how can they be moving?' demanded Hirad. 'They're just bones, they're dead.'

'Is it some sort of spell?' asked Richmond.

'Perhaps something that tied their lives and deaths to that promise they made Septern,' said Ilkar.

'Let's worry about it later. We have to get behind them somehow,' said Hirad. 'Whatever it is we're looking for and they're defending has got to be in that village somewhere.'

'I've got an idea,' said Denser. 'Want to hear it?' Hirad nodded. 'Ilkar casts a ForceCone at them and punches a hole in the line. Me and you run through to search the village. Everyone else keeps them occupied as long as possible, then gets through the rip before they're pushed off the edge of the platform.'

'Why don't we all go?' asked Richmond.

'Because they'll just turn around. Or I think they will,' replied Denser. 'I'm hoping if there are people in front of them, they'll keep coming and you can delay them, give us time to look. It's worth a try, isn't it?'

There was a brief silence, punctuated by the ominous dry brushing noise of the approaching dead, now only a minute away, their density increasing as the plateau narrowed towards its edge, forcing them closer and closer together.

'It'll do,' said Ilkar.

'Make it a good one,' whispered Denser.

'It'll be nothing less,' Ilkar said coldly.

Hirad came to stand by Denser and just to Ilkar's left. 'Talan, Richmond, when Ilkar's cast the spell, make sure you all stand in front of the rip. At least when you get pushed back you'll have the best chance of falling into it instead of down there . . . wherever there is.'

Talan nodded. 'And what about you?'

Hirad shrugged. 'I don't know. Just keep your fingers crossed, all right?'

'Sure.'

'Just a couple of things,' said Ilkar. Hirad turned to him. 'I'm going to put a colour in the Cone so you can see it, and when I cast it, get down there quickly. When I can see you next to the villagers, I'll let it go. Then it's up to you.' Ilkar closed his eyes and began to shape the mana. An initial stab of alarm when he felt nothing was washed away by relief when a jolt shook his body as the base fuel of magic in Balaia breached the dimensional divide, drawing on the static power source that held the rip in place.

Ilkar wobbled on his legs, steadied and formed the ForceCone, adding speed and what he expected to be a swirling green to the spell's innate power. A short intonation followed, then Ilkar opened his eyes and chose an area close to the left-hand side of the platform.

Speaking the command word, he jabbed his hands forward and the Cone crashed into the advancing villagers, shattering three on impact, their bones hurled in all directions. It ploughed on, driving a wedge through the ranks of the dead, pushing bodies to either side and causing mayhem. Skeletons fell like dominoes left and right. Bone wings flapped uselessly as legs were swept away by falling comrades, and at the edge of the platform, some slipped over the edge and into oblivion.

The Cone held firm, Ilkar edging it back as the villagers slowly re-formed and advanced. Hirad turned to Talan and Richmond.

'Don't risk yourselves, don't come back and don't let him do anything stupid.' He jerked his thumb at Ilkar. The warriors said nothing, inclining their heads in tight-lipped acknowledgement.

Hirad placed a hand on Denser's shoulder. 'Let's go. Stay behind me.' The barbarian hefted his sword and trotted off down the clearly defined Cone. As he closed, the sight of the villagers was shocking. Collections of bones shambling forwards, some with hands missing, others with ribs, hips or shoulders smashed, all with black streaks discolouring the white of their bones. But it was the lifeless heads which never moved that caused Hirad to flinch as he looked deep into the black caverns that were eye sockets.

Inside was nothing. No light, no life, nothing. Yet still they moved. Still they had purpose. If one had spoken, the barbarian would have turned and fled.

Five paces from the front rank of the villagers, Ilkar cut the ForceCone, leaving them a gap through which to run. Hirad pulled his sword in front of his face and increased his pace to a sprint, hearing Denser right on his heels. The cat streaked through his legs, on past the skeletons and into the village. For a moment, the dead continued as they had with the Cone in place, but as Hirad moved through the first of them, the line started to close. He shuddered as he ran, crying out as bone hands snagged his leather and slashing in front of his face as a skull appeared right in front of him. His strike swept it from its neck and the body collapsed.

It was tight. Denser's breathing was loud in his ears, and he cursed under his breath. Hirad swung his sword through double-handed again and again at chest height, feeling it shatter bone and crunch into wing membrane, head and shoulder. And never once did a villager lift a hand to strike them.

They broke through the line, stumbling to a stop after a dozen or so paces and turning to see what they'd left behind. The gap was closed. The villagers walked on towards the rip, not looking back, advancing on The Raven trio who stood with their backs to the moving darkness that was the dimension gate, swords at the ready. Ilkar managed a wave and Hirad responded before turning a face running with sweat to Denser.

'We'd better be quick,' said the Dark Mage. 'Once those three are forced through the rip, the villagers will be coming back, only we don't have anywhere to fall except down or through the other rip.' Hirad raised his eyebrows, nodding nervously.

The two men trotted into the village, where they stopped again, staring at the derelict settlement. All around, they could see the crumbling remnants of a civilisation. Buildings, blasted and blackened, scorched and falling to rubble; large pots, jugs, and cauldrons lying over the ground. What was once furniture, tables, chairs and pedestals, could be seen in the ruins of the houses. Cloth had rotted to dust, pottery was cracked and chipped, wood was splintered and burned, and all that was left was chaos.

'How did they live up here?' asked Hirad, picking up the handle piece of a broken jug. 'I mean, it's so small.' He stared back the way they had come, looking afresh at the empty earth. From the settlement, he could see squares of darker ground meshed in a grid of lighter areas. Plots and paths. Gods, they had been farmers. Farmers who could fly. 'And what's down there?' He threw the jug towards the edge of the plateau. It shattered on the ground a long way from its intended destination.

'Nothing, at a guess,' said Denser. 'I expect that's why they came up here to live.'

'I don't get it,' said Hirad. 'Why would there be nothing down there?'

'You can't use Balaia as a reference to explain this. Hell, I'm just stabbing in the dark. All we know is, this is how they ended up. Draw your own conclusions.'

'But why did they die?'

Denser shrugged and turned away, scanning the village. 'I have no idea and we haven't the time to think it out just now. Start looking.'

Hirad peered inside one of the buildings, seeing a microcosm of the village itself reflected in its age-ridden remains. Bones littered the floor and a skull hung from the great oval hole in the roof. Black soot covered every surface.

'What are we looking for?'

'How many more times?' said Denser, moving away in a random direction. 'I don't know. Look, let's split up and see if anything is obvious. I don't know. I'm expecting it to be different from the rest of this bloody mess, something brought here, not made here.'

Hirad glanced behind him before setting off away from Denser. The villagers were still walking and The Raven were still standing. Still waiting. At that moment, he felt a wash of pride. Those men, his friends and companions, would never turn their backs.

He picked his way at a run past ruin after ruin and everywhere he looked it was the same. Broken buildings, rotten furnishings, smashed pottery. And scorched, as if some monstrous fire had swept the village aside like dust in the wind. He moved through the village, taking in what had been the far side of the platform and the other rip hanging in the sky. Even as he wondered what lay beyond it and considered that he wasn't in a hurry to find out, he heard Denser shout. Glancing to his left, he could see the Dark Mage running towards a building at the edge of the village on the way to the rip.

The barbarian scampered through the rubble and raced in through the opening of yet another half-fallen dwelling just a few paces behind the Xeteskian. And there, being circled slowly by the cat, sat a small child. A splash of light and colour and very much alive.

She wore a blue dress, and a matching scarf was tied around her long blond hair. Her eyes were large and blue, and below her tiny nose was a mouth which displayed no humour. She was staring at the cat, following its slow movements around her, clutching a small chest in her bare arms.

'Kill it, Hirad,' hissed Denser. 'Do it now and do it quickly.'

'What?' said Hirad. 'No! Just take the chest and let's get out of here.' He made a move towards the girl but was stopped by Denser's hand on his arm.

'It's not what it might seem,' said the Dark Mage. 'Open your eyes, Hirad. Do you really think she could live here as she is?'

The girl turned her gaze from the cat and to the two men at the doorway, noticing them for the first time.

'Keep your sword ready,' said Denser, drawing his own blade and taking a half-step to the side.

Hirad glanced at the mage's face. It was set, his eyes were on the girl and they were scared. The barbarian hefted his blade.

'Can't you cast a spell or something?'

A shake of the head. 'It won't wait that long.'

'Who is she?' asked Hirad.

'I'm not sure. Nothing ordinary. Septern must have created her. Just keep your eye on that chest. We mustn't lose it or damage it.'

'Whatever you say.'

The girl smiled. It was a gesture quite without feeling and it left her eyes cold. Hirad shivered. And when she spoke, though the sound of her voice was that of a nine-year-old, its weight and power set the back of his scalp crawling.

'You are the first,' she said. 'And you shall be the last and only.'

'And what are you?' asked Denser.

'I am your nightmare. I am your death.' She moved. Lunged forward at blurring speed. And as she moved, she transformed. Hirad screamed.

The villagers closed. Ilkar, Talan and Richmond had backed to within half a dozen paces of the rip. The flanks moved inwards, forcing a still greater pressure on the press of skeletons scant feet from them.

Behind the lines lay the sheared bones of perhaps forty of the walking dead, victims of the hacking and slashing swords of the Raven trio. And now, with sweat-slick faces and lungs heaving, they were staring at imminent defeat.

'We haven't slowed them at all,' rasped Talan, kicking the legs from under a skeleton and dashing its skull with the butt of his sword.

'No impression,' Ilkar agreed, and indeed there didn't seem to be. Their immediate vision was still crowded with jostling arms, legs and the remains of wings. And all they could hear was the hollow sound of fleshless feet on the hard-packed earth and the click of bone on bone, over and over.

'How many of them *are* there?' said Richmond, straightening from a strike which had shattered three spines.

'Hundreds.' Talan shrugged. 'Where the bastards come from, though, is another matter.'

They stepped back once more, feeling the edge of the rip at the backs of their thighs. They struck out again, sending slivers of bone flying and villagers crashing into one another. Still on came the dead. Never once raising their arms to attack, but then, it wasn't necessary. They pressed in from the sides and the front and the sheer weight of their numbers made the end inevitable.

'See you on the other side,' said Ilkar. He was pushed backwards into the rip, and even as he fell, followed moments later by Talan and Richmond, he saw the skeletons turn and head back to the village.

The girl's legs, suddenly brown, fur-covered and thick with muscle, thrust forwards, shooting her upright. Clawed feet scratched at the ground, a tail, spiked and leathery, sprouted from the small of her back, and as her dress melted away, it was replaced by a heaving bull chest with prominent ribs above a taut and hairless stomach. Her arms bulged to power, muscles bunched in her biceps and triceps, while those delicate hands swelled, grew and stretched, the fingers clawing to razor-sharp talons.

But the head. It was the head that drew the scream from Hirad's lips. The girl's face fell into itself like water down a hole but those eyes held, still blue until the last, when they too disappeared to be replaced by flat black slits. And out of the hole sprang forth fangs in a wide mouth, dripping saliva. The blond hair remained; the brow was heavy, chin pointed and jaws snapping. A thin tongue licked out of the creature's mouth and it hissed as it struck.

Reflexively, Hirad brought his sword in front of his face and the creature's claw skittered off it, nicking the flesh. It howled in pain and backed off a step, small chest still clutched in the other clawed hand.

'Fuck!' spat Hirad, shaking all over and moving to cover Denser.

'Careful, Hirad.'

'What else do you think I'm going to be?'

The creature flew forwards again, arms flailing, tail whipping in front of it. Hirad side-stepped and slashed downwards into the blur of the attack, praying he'd connect before one of those talons raked or skewered him. His blade connected with wood, then flesh as it hammered through its arc. There was a keening wail, a whiplash sound and a heavy crash. Splinters of wood flew in all directions.

Hirad straightened, trying to take it all in. Denser was lying prone, half in and half out of the door to the building. He wasn't moving. The creature had retreated to the back of the room, clutching at the stump of its left hand, trying in vain to stop the pulses of blood gouting from the wound. Its hand lay on the floor close to Hirad's feet, and in amongst the wooden debris of the broken chest lay a single sheet of parchment, folded, brown and dog-eared.

Even as he laid his eyes on it, the barbarian heard the whimpering stop. He looked up into the feral, now yellow eyes of the beast as it rose to its feet, new hand growing out of the healing end of its arm.

'Dear Gods,' muttered Hirad.

The creature staggered slightly and clutched at a shelf to balance itself. Hirad snatched a dagger from his belt and hurled it forwards as he launched himself at the creature. The gleaming metal blade whirred through the air, catching the creature's gaze. It traced the dagger's flight, eyes narrowing until they all but disappeared under its brow.

Hirad moved forwards across the few feet that separated them, slashing at the creature's neck as it switched its attention to him. The dagger, forgotten, slapped harmlessly into the wall of the building. The creature dodged the blow and whipped its tail into Hirad's legs, tripping him. He fell, rolled and sat up on his haunches. The beast came on, still unsteady. Hirad scrambled to his feet and the two faced each other.

The creature bellowed, blowing hot, stinking breath into the barbarian's face. Hirad stepped back a pace at the sound, so deep and powerful from so small a body. He switched his blade between his hands, three times; it finished in his left hand. He clamped his right hand above his left, stepped in again and brought the blade through in an upward left-to-right arc. The creature failed to follow the movement, its hands were too slow coming to its defence and the blade crashed into its pointed jaw, Hirad roaring as he forced the blade through its face to exit from its left eye. The split face sprayed blood and gore as its head snapped up and back on its neck, and the creature screeched and fell backwards, clutching at the sides of the gash.

Hirad stepped up, looked down on it, shuddered and drove his sword through its heart. Another screech and the creature jerked spasmodically and lay still.

'Burn it.'

Hirad spun round and saw Denser sitting up, leaning against the door frame, massaging his side, his cat nuzzling his face from a perch on his shoulder.

'Burn?'

'Now. It'll recover if you don't.'

The barbarian turned back to the creature and saw immediately that it had begun to breathe.

'I don't believe it,' he said. He sheathed his sword and scrabbled in his belt pouches for an oil flask. He pulled a tiny phial out along with his flint and steel.

'Here,' said Denser. A much larger flask rattled to the floor by Hirad's feet.

'This won't burn properly, it's lamp oil, isn't it?' said the barbarian, snatching it up.

'Trust me, it'll burn.'

Hirad shrugged and ran over to the creature. He sprinkled the oil over its furred body, spread some tinder on its chest by the wound in its heart, which was closing even now, and struck the flint and steel next to it. A sheet of flame instantly smothered the body. Hirad leaped back, wiping at the heat on his face.

The creature's eyes flickered and opened. An arm twitched.

Hirad shook his head. 'Too late.' He drew his sword and repeated the stab to the heart. The beast lay still. He walked backwards, watching the fire take hold. Wood crunched under his foot. He glanced down and saw he'd trodden on the large part of the shattered chest. His foot was right next to the parchment; he stooped and picked it up.

'Is it damaged?' asked Denser from behind him.

'No, I don't think so. How about you?'

'I'm all right, just winded.' He rubbed his side. 'We were lucky it was a parchment and not a crystal or something. That blow of yours would have finished our job rather abruptly, wouldn't it?'

Hirad raised his eyebrows, ambled over and handed the parchment to Denser, helping the Dark Mage to his feet. Denser looked over his shoulder and nodded.

'What was it?'

'Sentient conjuration,' said Denser. 'It takes so long to cast, I never really bothered with it. Obviously Septern did.' He turned his attention to the parchment.

'Why was it a girl to start with?'

Denser stopped reading. 'Well, a sentient conjuration is created for a specific purpose, in this case to protect this parchment. While they have no actual life, they can reason to a degree and that allows them to assess situations and react accordingly. I would guess the girl we saw was the image of a relative of Septern's, because if the mage has clear memories, the image requires much less mana to create and sustain.'

'But why—?'

'Hold on, I know what you're thinking. The girl would have been the "at rest" manifestation, the beast, something out of his nightmares by the look of it, would take too much mana to sustain, see?'

'Kind of, but even so, three hundred years. . .'

'Yes, quite. I can't believe that even Septern, powerful though he must have been, could create a sentient conjuration able to exist for anything more than forty years at the absolute outside. Presumably the rips provided it with enough static mana to keep it going.' Denser went back to the parchment, leaving Hirad to walk back towards the rip a few paces. All was quiet. He frowned and jogged further on.

'Ilkar?' he called. 'Ilkar!' Nothing. No answer, but no villagers either, and as he moved to the border of the village, he could see why. They had all dropped maybe eighty paces from the village, forming a carpet of bone. A line of cold ran up Hirad's spine. If The Raven *had* managed to kill them all, then where were they? And if they hadn't, then why had the skeletons fallen?

He turned a quick full circle, acutely aware of his isolation. Above him, the dark cloud boiled along, chased by an awesome wind he couldn't hear. Below, flash followed flash as lightning deluged the lands beneath, while dotted across the skyline, like sentinels of some ancient doom, the other plateaux loomed, their shapes dim against the blackness, their presence fraying his courage. Where were The Raven? He prayed that they had returned through the rip. The alternatives were unthinkable.

'Denser?' He half ran back to where the Dark Mage had been reading, but he wasn't there. A spear of panic stole his breath before he spotted the Xeteskian walking in the other direction, towards the rip at the opposite end of the platform.

'Denser!' The mage turned. Hirad could see his pipe smoking gently.

The cat was in his cloak, head alert, and Denser was stroking its head. Of the parchment there was no sign. 'Have you read it?'

Denser nodded.

'And?' Hirad was still walking.

'I couldn't read it all. Ilkar'll have to have a go too.'

Close to, Hirad could see something was amiss. Denser's gaze seemed unfocused and he glanced now and then over his shoulder at the rip.

'Are you all right? The Raven and the skeletons are all gone. Are you sure that thing didn't hit you on the head?'

Denser raised his eyebrows slightly. 'I'm sure they're fine.' He paused. 'Hirad, have you ever just *had* to do something. You know, something your curiosity just wouldn't let you forget?'

Hirad shrugged. 'Probably. I don't know. What are you on about?'

Denser turned and carried on towards the rip. For a moment, Hirad was confused. Just for a moment.

'You have got to be joking!' He set off after the mage.

'I have to know. It's just one of those things.' Denser's step quickened.

'What has got into you?' Hirad broke into a trot. 'You can't do it, Denser. You can't afford to. We've got—' He put a hand on Denser's shoulder. The cat slashed at it with a claw, missing as he snatched it back. The Dark Mage turned a hard-set face to him. His eyes were lost, adrift in his churning mind.

'Don't touch us, Hirad,' he said. 'And don't try to stop us.' He turned his face away, strode to the rip and jumped into it.

Seconds later the cat was back. It fell from the rip in an ungainly jumble of limbs, hit the ground and sprinted behind Hirad, scattering stones and grit.

The barbarian stared at it, its coat ruffled and flecked with dust, stomach heaving as it dragged air into its lungs. Its tail was coiled tightly under its hind legs and its eyes were fixed on the rip, waiting. It was shaking all over.

'Oh no,' Hirad breathed. He took half a pace towards the swirling brown mass before a shimmer in its surface stopped him. Denser plunged out and sprawled in the dirt. His face was sheet-white.

'Thank the Gods,' muttered the barbarian, but his lips tightened in anger. He helped Denser to a sitting position. feeling the mage quivering beneath his hands. He slapped some debris from his cloak.

'You satisfied now?'

'It was black,' said Denser, gesturing with his hands, not looking up. 'It was all black.'

'Make sense, Denser.' The mage locked eyes with him, his pupils huge.

'Burned and burning. It was all ruined, cracked and black. It made this place look alive. The ground was all black and the sky was full of Dragons.'

It was a line straight from Hirad's dream. The barbarian straightened and took an involuntary pace backwards. He swallowed hard and gazed at the rip. Beyond it, his nightmare lived.

The enormity of Denser's action hit him like a runaway horse. He switched his stare to the mage, who was on his feet.

'Feeling better?' he asked.

Denser nodded, half smiled. The barbarian's punch caught him square on the jaw, knocking him down hard.

'What the—?' he began.

Hirad leant over him and grabbed the neck of his cloak, pulling their faces close.

'What did you think you were doing?' the barbarian rasped, his anger burning, his brow a thundercloud. 'You could have thrown it all away.'

'I . . .' Denser looked blank.

Hirad shook him. 'Shut up! Shut up and listen to me. You took the parchment through there. What if you'd never come back? Your precious mission would have been over, and my friends' – he drew a deep breath – 'my friends who died for you would have died for *nothing*.' He dropped the mage back into the dirt and placed a foot on his chest. 'If you ever try anything like that again, I won't stop until your face is inside out. Understand?'

Hirad heard a whispering sound behind him. Denser looked past him, his eyes widened and he shook his head. Hirad turned, removing his foot from the supine mage. Denser's cat bored a stare of undisguised malevolence into him. He flinched, then grunted.

'Your cat going to sort me out, was it?'

'You're a fortunate man, Hirad.'

The barbarian swung round. 'No, Denser, you are. I should kill you. The trouble is, I'm beginning to believe you.' He stalked away through the village towards the first rip and, he hoped, The Raven. If there was anything left of it.

Chapter 12

Dropping to the ground in Septern's study, Hirad caught Ilkar's eye. The elf smiled. To his left, Talan stopped in the act of shouldering his pack. Hirad gathered his thoughts as his heart rate returned to something approaching normal.

'I said not to come back,' he said.

Talan shrugged. 'You're Raven.'

Hirad sucked his lip, nodded his thanks.

'Did you find anything?' asked Ilkar.

Hirad inclined his head.

'Where's Denser?' Richmond was frowning.

'Thinking hard, I hope,' replied Hirad.

'What about?'

'His responsibilities. And how he treats The Raven – alive or dead.'

'What are you talking about?'

Hirad didn't reply immediately. He dusted himself down and turned to the rip. Its surface shimmered.

'Perhaps you'd better ask the great explorer himself,' he said.

Denser emerged from the rip, his cat right behind him. He studiously avoided Hirad's cold gaze, choosing to examine the floor as he steadied himself. Presently, he rose to his feet. The cat jumped into his cloak. Denser rubbed his chin, pulled the parchment from a pocket and handed it to Ilkar. The elf examined the reddening area on the point of Denser's jaw. He pursed his lips and looked past the Dark Mage to Hirad as he took the parchment. Hirad flexed the fingers of his right hand.

'This is it, is it?' asked Ilkar. Denser nodded. 'Well?'

'Some of it's Julatsan lore, just like the amulet. I need you to help me understand it.'

'I see.'

The two men walked over to Septern's desk, where a lantern cast light enough to read by.

Hirad sat down. Talan and Richmond came over and squatted by him, wanting answers to questions. Hirad obliged and sketched in the events in the village, always with one eye on the mage pair, whose body language and hurried voices suggested problems. Hirad also had questions of his own, and The Raven warriors' shaken heads and dulled sword blades provided ample answers.

It wasn't too long before Denser and Ilkar had finished and moved back to the centre of the rip in front of the three fighting men. Ilkar held the parchment, his face troubled. Denser stared impassively at Hirad. The barbarian ignored him and addressed Ilkar.

'So, what's the plan, my friend?' he asked.

'Well, there's good news and really really bad news. The good is that we know what we have to do. The bad is that we have next to no chance of doing it.'

'He's always been good at making things sound attractive, hasn't he?' Talan raised his eyebrows.

'A master,' said Richmond drily.

'Spell it out then,' said Hirad. 'No pun intended.'

'Right,' the Julatsan began. He glanced at Denser, who motioned him to continue. 'Septern, as we keep saying, was very clever. When he constructed the spell and worked out how powerful it actually was, he wrote three catalysts into its lore without which it would not work. Catalysts can be any number and anything the mage chooses; Septern could have chosen a mug of beer if he'd wanted. The point is that once the lore is written, it can't be changed, and Septern chose three catalysts he knew it would be all but impossible to bring together in one place.

'This parchment is the complete spell, and while it doesn't tell how the catalysts underpin Dawnthief, it gives their names and locations as he knew them.' He paused. The room was silent. 'You ready for this?'

Richmond shrugged. 'I doubt it,' he said.

'So do I,' said Ilkar grimly. He referred to the parchment. 'The first is a Dordovan Ring of Authority. Now, all four Colleges have these. They are worn by Lore Masters and are signs of rank and seniority. All Rings of Authority are individually designed and cast and are only ever worn by the one Master. When he or she dies, the ring is buried with them. The particular ring Septern names belonged to the Lore Master Arteche, and so will be in his tomb in Dordover.'

Talan shifted. 'So we have to go into a College City, break into their Masters' mausoleum and take this ring, right?'

'That's about the size of it.' Ilkar had the grace to appear apologetic at least.

'Can't we just ask them to hand it over?' asked Richmond.

'Come on, man, think!' snapped Denser. 'We'd be asking a College to desecrate its tombs and we couldn't tell them why because they'd try to control the spell. It has to be a theft and they mustn't know until afterwards.'

'Going to give the ring back later on, are you?' Talan's laugh was dismissive.

'I expect I will be forced to, Talan, yes.'

'Too bloody right you will,' muttered Hirad.

'Can we discuss this later, do you think?' Ilkar waved the parchment. 'There's more, and it doesn't get any better.'

'I can't wait.' Talan stretched out his legs.

'The second catalyst is the Death's Eye Stone.'

'I've heard of that, haven't I?' Richmond aimed the question at Denser, who nodded.

'I expect you have,' replied the mage. 'It's the centrepiece of the Wrethsires' religion.'

'That's right. Death worshippers, aren't they?' His brow furrowed. 'Don't they have some magic?' He ground his teeth, thinking hard.

'Oh, yeah, "the fifth College".' Denser glanced across at Ilkar, his face all but dripping contempt. Ilkar huffed. 'They have no lore, no history and no mana ability. That they presume to liken themselves to the four Colleges is not only outrageous but a slur against magic itself.'

'But you're right, Richmond,' said Ilkar. 'They do worship Death in the belief it'll free them from eternal damnation, or something like that, and they do have some form of altered magic which they don't fully understand. It makes them dangerous.'

'They're going to love us, aren't they?' grumbled Hirad. 'Stealing their most important artefact.'

Ilkar shrugged. 'Denser never said we could pick the sodding things up from the market, did he?'

'No, he didn't,' said Hirad. 'He never wanted to tell us anything at all. I didn't choose to get involved in this and have my life totally screwed up, so if I want to moan about things I have to do that seem beyond my control; or about how he' – he stabbed a finger at Denser – 'has been responsible for the deaths of my friends, I will bloody well do so.'

Denser sighed. Hirad tensed but made no move.

'Have you got a problem with that, Xetesk man?'

'No, he hasn't,' said Ilkar quickly. 'Now then, the third catalyst.'

He scanned The Raven, daring anyone to speak further. 'Right. Now this one poses a problem of location, because it's the Badge of Office of the Understone Pass Guard Commander.' There was a contemplative silence.

'But the Korina Trade Alliance lost Understone Pass nine years ago. There isn't a commander any more,' said Talan at length. He took the parchment from Ilkar, frowning at the lore script it contained.

'Exactly,' said Ilkar. 'So where is the Badge?'

Another silence. Hirad tried hard to suppress a smile but failed. He gave a short laugh and stood up.

'And you buggers are always accusing *me* of not knowing my history!' he said.

Ilkar frowned at him. 'Explain.'

'When the pass was opened, the Badge of Office was given to Baranck, the first Commander, by the Baron Council which, as I'm sure you're all aware, was the forerunner of the Korina Trade Alliance. That must have been over five hundred years ago – before the Wytch Lords came to power the first time.

'It was a purely ceremonial pendant but the regulation stated that it was not to be removed from the pass unless it was lost. In that event, the Badge was to be taken by the defeated Commander and kept as a standard for the forces who would eventually retake the pass.' He stared around a row of blank faces.

'Must I spell it out?'

'I think so, Hirad, yes,' said Ilkar.

'Gods above, Ilkar, we were talking about him on the road the other day.'

'Were we?'

'Yes. And it looks as if I'll be getting my wish sooner than I thought.' Hirad bared his teeth. 'The last commander was Captain Travers.'

The loss of their Destranas would normally have led to harsh discipline, even death, but this time their information bought their lives. A day's ride from their encounter with The Raven near Septern's long barn, the Wesmen scouts stood in the centre of a clearing in dense woodland, speaking to their Shaman, who sat under canvas, drinking a colourless strength-giving spirit.

'It is as the Masters expected,' said the leader of the party. 'Easterners are searching the old house.'

The Shaman nodded and placed his cup on the ground. 'I must

relate the news immediately. Prepare to leave. I think war may be very close.'

There was no argument. It wasn't just that the Black Wings' castle was the nearest of the three catalyst locations. That wouldn't have figured as an issue. The fact was that Hirad was not interested in going anywhere else until Travers and all the Black Wings were dead.

With the day not far past its mid-point, The Raven ate a leisurely meal in the ruins of Septern's house before taking the horses back to the long barn. Hirad eventually agreed that they should not move on any further until the next morning; Ilkar's insistence that they give themselves the maximum daylight to escape the boundaries of the rip's influence was unshakeable. And the barbarian had to concede that a night spent in the total security afforded by Septern's sealed workshop, where no one had to stand guard, no one had to keep a fire tended and no one had to react to every sound, was a very attractive prospect.

The smoke from the camp fire continued to spiral calmly into the sky as the afternoon waned towards dusk. Richmond snapped a branch into three and added it to the small blaze, dry leaves crackling as they caught in the heat. Denser, having lost the toss earlier in the afternoon, was leaning against a wall, reading Septern's journal now that Ilkar had finished with it. His pipe was, as ever, clamped between his teeth, and his head never wavered, rapt in the information he was assimilating.

Faint sounds from the workshop below told that Denser's Familiar was still rooting around in Septern's other equipment and papers. The Dark Mage had cautioned them not to go down there. With Talan outside somewhere trying to make sense of the immediate area to give them some semblance of a route the following morning, Ilkar and Hirad were left to sit together in the wan sunlight.

'This Familiar,' said Hirad. 'What is it when it's not a cuddly cat?'

Ilkar looked askance. 'I don't think you could ever accuse it of being "cuddly", Hirad. You're lucky it missed you with those claws back in the village . . . Look, about that incident—'

'Oh, Gods, here we go.' Hirad placed his goblet on the ground and folded his arms. 'All right, let's have it, I shouldn't antagonise him, he's too powerful, right?'

Ilkar eyed Denser. The Dark Mage hadn't raised his head from the book. The elf cut his voice to barely more than a whisper.

'That's pretty much the size of it, yes. Now listen . . . and don't sigh like that, this is important. Not only is he too powerful, although I concede you won that last round, he's too central to this whole thing for you to pick fights with him.'

'I wasn't picking a fight,' hissed Hirad.

'Will you let me finish?' Ilkar's ears pricked in irritation. 'Officially, now that we have *all* the knowledge – you know, the words and the whereabouts of the catalysts – we could ditch Denser and try this out ourselves. But as I said the other day, he's the only one with the teaching to cast Dawnthief with any chance of success at all. Do you follow me?'

'What do you think?'

It was Ilkar's turn to sigh. He briefly put a hand over his face. 'Right. Umm, when you practise alone with a sword, it's with a dummy opponent, yes?'

'A hanging sack or maybe a mirror.' Hirad shrugged.

'But you don't know that the moves you're trying will work until a fight, do you?'

'I can't argue with that.'

'And if you didn't practise them at all, you'd have no control over them, would you?'

'What is this, a test?'

'Just answer the question,' said Ilkar. 'I'm trying to put it in terms you'll understand.'

'Fair enough.' Hirad shifted, took another gulp of his wine. 'No, Ilkar, I'd have no control over them, and what's more, I wouldn't even think of trying them in a fight. Satisfied?'

'Yes, and it's the same with spell-casting. Exactly the same.' Ilkar moved so that he was squatting in front of Hirad. 'If I try to cast a spell I haven't practised, it stands a good chance of not working, maybe even going wrong, and that can be fatal. Denser has trained all of his life in the casting of Dawnthief, so he knows in theory how to say the words, shape the mana and so forth. There's no guarantee it'll work in a live situation but, like you and your training, he'll be confident of success and he'll find out when push comes to shove. Do you understand now?'

'Yes. So I won't kill him.' Hirad leaned in close to Ilkar. 'But I will not have him risking himself that stupidly if he is so bloody crucial to all this. And I will not have him take chances with the memories of my friends!' Hirad's voice was audible all across the ruin. The noise in the workshop stopped, Denser looked up from his reading and Richmond paused in the act of hanging a pot of water over the now resurgent fire.

After a brief stare in which Hirad saw Denser smile thinly in Ilkar's direction, the Xeteskian buried his head once again.

'Anyway, so what about this Familiar, then?'

'Well, it's likely to be some kind of semi-intelligent winged demon, or so I've been taught.' Ilkar gave a slight shrug. 'That's the only reason I can think of for Denser being so anxious that we don't see it out of cat-form.' Hirad's face was completely blank. The elf closed his eyes. 'You may have learnt about Travers, Coldheart, but in all the years I've known you, you've clearly never listened to a word I've said, have you?'

'Well, most of the time you were talking about magic and all that rubbish.' Hirad grinned.

'You seem pretty keen to learn about it now,' returned the mage.

'It's important now.'

'It was important then!' snapped Ilkar.

'Could you two talk about who-knows-what later?' Richmond had joined them. 'I'm interested in this thing of Denser's.'

'Right.' Ilkar glanced over at Denser again. The Dark Mage was apparently paying them no attention whatsoever. 'Put simply, Denser's Familiar is a conjuration similar in construction to the girl you found through the rip. Where it differs is in what it can do and how it survives. As soon as it's created, a Familiar has to meld its mind with its master.'

'Has to what?' Hirad poured another goblet of wine and offered the skin to Ilkar and Richmond.

'You'd have to ask Denser, though I doubt he'd tell you. A Familiar is a very Xeteskian thing, it comes from their association with the demon dimension. Anyway, the result is that they share part of each other's consciousness. They are a pairing that can only be broken by the death of one or the other.' Ilkar paused to sip his wine. 'A Familiar has its own brain and can reason and act on its own initiative, but it will always be at the beck and call of its master and will never go against him. It's the kind of unswerving obedience you don't get anywhere else.'

'So what's the purpose of having one?' asked Richmond.

Ilkar blew out his cheeks. 'That rather depends on the individual mage. In Denser's case it clearly acts as a guard, a companion, a scout, a message-bearer and, I should think, a powerful offensive weapon.' He indicated the stairs to the workshop. 'Right now, it'll be looking for anything that's of interest, and no doubt it'll tell Denser all about it later.'

'They talk?' Richmond frowned.

'No, as far as I know, they don't talk. But close to, they can communicate. It's a kind of rudimentary telepathy,' said Ilkar. 'I mean, they can converse over a reasonable distance but it would be very draining.'

'So what does it actually look like?' Hirad nodded in the direction of the hole in the floor. The noise from below had stopped, at least temporarily.

'I can't say for certain, but they have an aura that can scare people rigid, almost literally. Imagine your own picture of a demon – you know, ugly with wings and a tail – and you probably won't be far wrong.'

'And what happens to it if Denser dies?' Richmond finished his wine and reached for the skin. Hirad prodded it towards him with a toe.

'It would die too. It can't survive without him.'

'Why not?'

'Something to do with how it lives, what it eats and the twinning of their minds, but I'm not clear on the details.'

'And what happens to Denser if the Familiar dies?' asked Hirad.

'Pain,' said Denser. The Dark Mage had put the book down and was standing up. He brushed himself down. 'Pain like someone reaching their hands inside your skull and squeezing your brain.' He walked towards them, acting out his words with a clenching of his fists. 'Luckily, they are very difficult to kill.' As he spoke, the cat appeared at the top of the stairs.

'I wonder if it knew we were talking about it,' mused Richmond.

'Oh yes,' confirmed Denser, his face bleak and serious. 'It knew very well.' The cat jumped into Denser's robe and snuggled against his chest.

On the fire, the pot of water was steaming away.

'Hot drink, anyone?' Richmond asked.

'Yes please,' said Ilkar. 'Tell me something else, Denser. What did you make of that place?'

'How do you mean?'

'Never mind that they walked, why were they all dead in the first place?'

'I'll tell you why,' said Hirad. 'You saw the searchings and burning. The Dragons got there and they came to rule. That's why.'

'Gods alive,' breathed Talan.

'And if you're right,' said Denser, 'just think of the consequences if the Dragons got here.'

'I told you,' said Hirad quietly. 'And you wouldn't listen.'

'It won't come to that,' said Denser.

'When this is over, that amulet goes back to Sha-Kaan,' said Hirad. 'Somehow we'll have to find him.'

'It's too late for that,' said Ilkar. 'Because we already have the knowledge. But it is down to us to prove that we can use that knowledge wisely.' He looked hard at Denser. 'If we don't, if we abuse what we now know, if it falls into the wrong hands, then we can expect nothing less than the removal of Sha-Kaan's protection.'

'I hope you're listening to this, Xetesk man,' said Hirad.

Denser nodded. 'Yes, I am. And I agree with everything he's saying. Now, please could I have a drink? I'm parched.'

Chapter 13

Thraun brought them to a halt off the track that led directly to the gates of the castle. They made camp about one hundred yards away, hidden from the track by bushes and trees. Rather than risk an open fire, Will unpacked his smokeless stove and set it going. Although very efficient for heating cooking pans, the wood-burning stove gave next to no light and channelled its heat upwards to the hot plate rather than outwards at those crowded around it. As a result, they chilled as a cloudless, breezy night fell.

The journey from the river valley had been made largely in a sullen and angry silence. Thraun had had to comfort Alun's tears on more than one occasion, and Will's snarling asides brought with them the threat of violence. Jandyr watched it all from the periphery, wondering how they would pull themselves together closely enough to have any chance of rescuing Erienne and the boys.

With the stove heating a pot of water and one of porridge oats, Thraun spoke.

'We are only an hour's walk from the castle,' he said. 'I will tolerate no raising of voices and no disappearing without my knowledge of where you are. Now, after we've eaten, Will and I will circle the castle, try to find a likely entry point and see if we can make any sort of guess as to the numbers we are facing. Meanwhile, Jandyr, you stay on guard, Alun, try to rest, you look exhausted. Any questions?'

'When will we make the rescue attempt?' asked Alun. He could hardly function any more, his anxiety making him jittery and keeping him from rest.

'Not tonight.' Thraun raised a hand to quell Alun's automatic protest. 'We've had a long day's ride, we're all tired, and after we've done the scouting there won't be time to plan and execute tonight. If all goes well, we'll go in tomorrow in the early hours of the morning when the guards will be at their most sluggish. Agreed?' Heads nodded. 'Good, now let's eat.'

*

It wasn't until after lunch the following day that Hirad voiced the fear that had nagged at him since Ilkar had read the parchment. The journey had been uneventful. Talan's wanderings of the previous afternoon had revealed a probable trail, and sure enough, they'd walked their horses into much more usual terrain and conditions well before the sun had reached its high point.

Relaxing slightly now the influence of the rip was behind them, The Raven and Denser had stopped in the lee of a hill they had descended. Richmond lit a small fire and the tendrils of smoke were picked away by a gusting breeze and blown into a sky half covered with slow-moving cloud. When the sun appeared, it was warm too, but a cool mood settled on them all as each had time to reflect on what they had lost and the enormity of what was still to come.

'We need more people,' said Hirad.

There was silence around the crackling fire. They were all looking at him, none willing to speak. Richmond pushed a ripple of thick soup around his plate with some soggy bread. Denser relit his pipe, blowing gouts of smoke from the corner of his mouth. Talan, eyes hooded from the sun, was absently sharpening his sword, the whetstone rasping on the metal while Ilkar chewed his lip thoughtfully before speaking.

'I'm glad to hear that from you. I expect we all are.'

There were nods and grunts of assent.

'So . . .' Talan led the train of thought.

'Exactly,' said Hirad. 'Where do we find people good enough that we can trust? Because of our need for secrecy, we'd have to take great care in town.'

'I'd go so far as to say we can't risk going into anywhere bigger than a village this side of the mountains and the College Cities,' said Denser. 'Too many tongues and too much greed.'

'That's all very well, but if we don't take the risk, we'll get nowhere.' Talan had pocketed his whetstone and was examining the edge he'd honed. He glanced up at Denser. 'You don't get groups of likely people loitering in the countryside waiting for the would-be saviours of Balaia to ride by.'

Ilkar laughed. 'It's an interesting image though, isn't it?'

'Ridiculous,' said Hirad. 'That anyone could ever see you as a saviour of Balaia, I mean.' Ilkar held up a middle finger. Hirad's face became serious once more. 'So what's the answer? We just aren't enough like this. Even with Sirendor and The Unknown, we'd have been pushing it.'

'I guess the first question is, do we try to recruit now or after the Black Wings' castle?' asked Talan.

'After,' said Hirad immediately. 'No one interferes with those bastards' deaths.'

Ilkar stared at him, tight-lipped. 'And there was me thinking you were about to be reasonable. Now you're asking us to storm a castle, just the five of us.'

'I'll do it alone if I have to,' said Hirad evenly.

'As it happens, it makes sense to do the castle first,' commented Richmond. He clacked his teeth. There was quiet for a moment.

'This must be some strange kind of sense I haven't encountered before.' Ilkar sniffed.

'No, I really think we can do it as we are,' said Richmond. 'As I understand it, although Travers himself rarely leaves the castle, most of the Black Wings are out doing their questionable deeds. There'll be twenty at most, I should think. Just enough to keep the castle running. Don't forget, they never have been a particularly numerous group. Just zealous.'

'And if you're wrong?'

'If he's wrong, Ilkar, we'll all die in one big bloodbath.'

Denser sighed. 'You know, Hirad, that really isn't the attitude we need to adopt if we're going to succeed.'

'Well, bugger me blind, is that right?' Hirad swung on the Dark Mage. 'I'd forgotten that correct procedure was to go rip-hopping while carrying the Dawnthief parchment.'

'All right, Hirad.' Ilkar raised his hands. 'But it doesn't change the fact that we'll be taking one hell of a risk going in there as we are.'

'God's sake,' muttered Hirad, getting to his feet. 'You're at it as well. Just when was it we all got careful? I must've blinked and missed it 'cos when he' – he jerked his thumb at Denser – 'jumped into the Dragon's bloody lair we weren't doing it, and we're not about to start now!' He turned and walked away to where the horses were quietly grazing, unconcerned by the troubles of men.

Denser made to rise but was restrained by Talan's hand on his ankle.

'Let it be,' said the warrior.

'He's right, Denser, you won't change his mind now.' Ilkar dipped his mug into the pot of coffee over the fire.

'So that's it, is it? We just go to the castle short-handed and take our chances because he's got some petty revenge to carry out?' Denser felt the surge of resentment as he spoke. His heart skipped a beat then began to race, his cat squirming uneasily in his cloak. When he looked round, Richmond, Talan and Ilkar were staring at him, expressions telling him he'd stepped badly astray. At least in that moment he had an inkling of what being a member of The Raven meant to these people. Ilkar's words reinforced his growing realisation.

'That is why you are an outsider,' said the elf carefully. 'You have to understand the bonds that hold The Raven together. Even in death they are unbreakable. It is the strength of Hirad's feelings, those that drive him to need Travers' blood, that is the reason we can trust him utterly.' He paused to eat some bread. Denser watched him, seeing the thoughts chase themselves across his face as he marshalled his next words.

'We're all alike,' he said at length, indicating himself and the two warriors. 'We're just not quite so outspoken about it. Never speak of petty revenge where The Raven is concerned and particularly where Sirendor Larn is concerned. You seem to forget that he died in your place, and when that happened, Hirad lost his closest friend. You're fortunate he didn't hear you.'

'I'm sorry,' said Denser. Ilkar nodded.

'While we're doing this,' said Richmond, his tone gruff but not unfriendly, 'perhaps we should clear up a couple of other things. Firstly, if anyone has the final say now The Unknown's gone, it's Hirad. It certainly isn't you, Denser. Second, while we all understand what we are doing, or trying to do, we are The Raven first and your hired hands second. So, if Hirad wants to take the castle first, that is what we will do.'

Denser gaped inwardly, confused by a conflict he couldn't untangle and was sure shouldn't have arisen. The destruction of the Wytch Lords had to be their only goal but they couldn't see it. Wrapped up in The Raven and its struggles, he was sure that they had no real conception of the disaster that would be visited on Balaia if they failed and the Wytch Lords won the ultimate battle. Xetesk would be gone, all realistic hope would go with them and The Raven would be blown away like so much chaff in the wind.

He drew in breath to speak but there was no point. Anyway, Talan got there first.

'We all want to succeed. But you have to keep in mind that until you joined us, only three people had died fighting for The Raven in more than ten years.' Talan glanced across at Richmond whose head was hung, eyes closed. 'We trust to our ways and our instincts because they are nearly always right. You know we wouldn't have taken this job if you'd been honest with us, but you involved us and two of us are dead in a week.

'See it from our perspective and don't try to comment on what you don't understand. We're alive because we're good and if you keep your nose out, we'll probably stay that way.'

'I'm sure we can agree a compromise,' said Denser evenly, beginning to see what he had taken on.

Talan's face softened and he smiled, rose and clapped the Dark Mage on the shoulder.

'That was quite a lecture, wasn't it? Maybe you could similarly enlighten us some time soon, eh?' He pulled down his jerkin where it had tucked up under his belt. 'Right now, I think we should be on our way. Hirad?' He walked off towards the barbarian. 'Hirad! Horses, please, we're leaving!'

Erienne felt awakened from a long nightmare. They were scared and a little dirty but her boys were fed and warm and had befriended one of their guards, a point she didn't fail to note. The relief she felt as she held them close and the love that flowed between all three of them re-energised her aching body. This time they had not regarded her with any doubt in their eyes. The guard had given them an explanation of why she couldn't see them that they had believed, and for that she was grateful.

The Captain had allowed her a full hour with them before coming in person to respectfully ask her to join him for some dinner, and so they had returned to the chairs by the fire in the library. This time, she allowed herself a glass of wine.

Now, as she regarded the slight smile that touched his otherwise serious face, she realised what it was she was about to do. She only hoped the Gods, or more accurately the Dordovan Masters, would forgive her for it. She didn't hold out much hope.

'Am I not a man of my word?' The Captain spread his hands wide.

'Don't expect me to rush into your arms just because you've let me see my own children.'

'Come now, Erienne, don't spoil the moment.'

'I am very happy they are alive and well and very unhappy that we are held here against our will. There is no moment to spoil,' she said coldly. 'Now tell me exactly how it is you want me to betray my own morals.'

'I don't want you to feel like that,' said the Captain. 'What I am doing is—'

'Save it for people who swallow your stories. Just tell me what you want, then let me get back to my children.'

The Captain looked at her, sucking in his cheeks. He nodded.

'Very well. It's quite simple. I need you to confirm the authenticity or otherwise of artefacts and information that might come into my possession concerning Dawnthief. If I am to control this spell for the protection of Balaia, I must be on solid ground.'

'You have no idea what you are dealing with,' said Erienne. 'This is a power far, far beyond your comprehension and if you are unfortunate enough to be successful, even in gaining key information, you and your monkeys will all be killed by those willing to do anything to get it.'

'Erienne, I am well aware of the dangers, but it is up to me to face them. Somebody has to.'

'Yes!' she said, leaning forwards, threatening to spill her wine. 'The four Colleges must guard this discovery, if such it is, collectively. It is the only way to ensure it is never used.'

The Captain laughed. 'I cannot believe you want me to leave this spell with the very people who are capable of using it. If I hold it, we are all safe.'

'If each of three Colleges holds a catalyst, it is safer still.'

'And you expect me to believe your curiosity won't lead you to experiment?' He was dismissive. 'I *know* mages. I know how they think, as do you. Only a non-mage can be charged with guarding Dawnthief. And that person will be me, with or without your help. Do you agree to do as I ask?'

She nodded, the fight leaving her. At least here she might exert some influence. She dropped her head. Control had nothing to do with it. She was helping him for one reason and one reason alone. And no magical moral was as important as the lives of her children.

The travelling was easy. Steering clear of the few hamlets spread thinly across the gently undulating forested and grassed terrain, The Raven stayed mainly under the cover of the often dense woodland, taking animal or seldom-used hunter and trade trails. Elsewhere, riding at the edge of the trees, Talan's eye for the sun's position and Richmond's ground knowledge kept them moving in the right direction.

Hirad found his mind wandering ever more away from the events through the rip as they rode and he was able to dispel the memories with a lungful of pure Balaian air. He had never before appreciated its beauty. Not until he had tasted that of another world. Conversation rolled easily around The Raven as the mood lightened under a warm sky, light wind and rich forest vegetation, and talk around the camp fire led to exaggerated tales of fight and victory. Only the great absence of The Unknown brought a cooling of the spirit. As yet, stories of the big man brought only sadness and loss and were followed by long silences.

It was at worst a three-day ride to the Black Wings' castle through the rolling hills and woodlands of Baron Pontois' lands. They were lands well known to The Raven, and as they travelled further north-east, where the hills gave way to cliffs and rock-strewn barren peaks, and the verdant growth of trees and grass to tough shrub, bracken and moss, they'd know when they were nearing their destination.

On the afternoon of the third day, a change in the weather brought The Raven to a stop beneath a deep overhang on the right-hand side of a valley they had been climbing south to north.

In something less than an hour, the sun was eclipsed by dense thundercloud blowing down the valley at them, whipped up by a wind made harsh and cold by the seas far to the north. The temperature plummeted and cloaks were thrown around shoulders, and then, as the deluge struck and the cloud obscured the apex of the valley, The Raven cantered to the shelter of the rock.

Dismounting, they moved as far back as they could, leaving the horses to gaze mournfully out on the dreary scene.

'Travers has sent us his welcome, then,' remarked Talan.

'Yes, I feel sure Hirad will find it in his heart to blame him for this as well,' said Ilkar.

'Too right I will.'

The rain fell yet harder, bouncing off exposed rock, gouging at close-packed earth and battering down vegetation which sprang back in mute defiance.

Talan poked his head out of the overhang and looked northwards.

'It's well set – it's got that feel to it,' he said, coming back inside and wiping a film of water from his hair.

He was right, thought Hirad. It was indefinable, but something about the smell of the air, the pace and weight of the rain and the feel of the wind told of a long soaking. Hours, probably.

'Well, we can't just stand here and watch it,' said Denser.

'Quite right,' agreed Richmond. shrugging off his backpack. 'We'll get cold. I'll get a fire going.' He pulled a tinder box from an outside pocket of his pack and unhitched a large roll of waxed leather from behind his saddle. He unravelled it and took wood from its centre.

'Tip for you, Denser,' he said. 'When the clouds come down, pick up dry sticks.' He waved the Dark Mage away from a space in the centre of the overhang amd started building the fire.

'So we're just going to sit it out, is that it?' asked Denser.

'That's about the size of it, yes,' replied Richmond.

'But the castle . . .'

Richmond shrugged. Finishing the pyramidal stick-structure, he pushed some tinder into a hole at its base. 'We're about half a day's ride away at a guess. Talan?' Talan nodded. Richmond continued. 'Yeah. So assuming the rain eases off towards dusk, we can rest up here, ride the rest of the way this evening and attack at night, which was, I presume, the original plan.' No one said otherwise.

Denser narrowed his eyes but made no further comment. Instead, he untied his bedroll, took the saddle from his horse and dumped both against the rock face at the southern end of the overhang.

'It'll be cramped,' he said.

'I wasn't suggesting we all laid down to sleep.' Richmond struck sparks with his flint and steel, blowing gently as a thin column of smoke rose from the tinder. 'Hey, Hirad. Make yourself useful and go and get some stream water and more wood we can dry out. Just in case.'

'Yes, Mother,' said the barbarian. 'Mind if I take this?' He pointed at Richmond's waxed leather. The warrior shook his head.

Hirad picked two waterskins from the nearest horse and put the leather over his head and shoulders, gathering it under his chin with one hand. He turned to Ilkar, who burst out laughing. Taking his lead, the others joined in.

'If I gave you a walking stick, you'd look just like my grandmother,' said the elf eventually, wiping his eyes.

'She must be spectacularly ugly, then,' said Talan.

Hirad tried to think of a witty reply, then a suitably obscene one, and failed. Instead he shrugged, smiled and left the shelter of the overhang.

He headed upstream for no other reason than to check out the route immediately ahead of them, though it fast became obvious that he'd gain little useful information from his walk.

Though the rain was easing a little, it was replaced by a cloying mist – the clouds sweeping off the hilltops to further obscure the valley and his visibility with every step. Still, at least the trail itself was solid, containing enough stone and gravel to limit the rain-driven erosion.

He trawled either side of him for likely-looking sticks, eventually finding a coarse, thick bush whose central branches were ideal. A few quick slashes and some shaving with a dagger and he had all the firewood he was prepared to carry.

Ambling back in the direction of the overhang, he diverted to his right to fill the skins from the stream, which was already running quickly as the rainwater poured off the hills to swell the flow. Squatting on a flat rock, he held the neck of the first skin under the water, listening to the complementary sounds of the water clattering by in the stream and the rain pattering off Richmond's leather.

But that was all he could hear, and when he turned to switch skins, the hilt of a sword thudded into his skull just below his left ear.

He sprawled over the rock, trying to gather his senses as the mist, the river, the rain and the roaring in his head took him towards unconsciousness. A shape loomed above him. A man in full helmet and chain mail. He leant in close.

'Go home, Coldheart, The Raven is finished. Go home.'

The pommel of the man's sword swung again. Sparks flew across Hirad's eyes then everything went quiet.

There was a look of thunder in Alun's eyes. And betrayal.

'You told me we were going in tonight.'

'The situation has changed,' said Thraun. 'Something's going on in the castle. You saw the riders who came past here earlier. There's too much activity. We have to wait.'

Will had returned to the castle, tracking after the riders, and had returned in the late afternoon, reporting an air of excitement around the castle. Someone had been taken there, presumably as a prisoner and presumably important. Thraun had decided to hold a watching brief for the night and make a decision the following morning. Alun, as he anticipated, had other ideas.

'Every second we wait brings my family closer to death, and yet we're going to sit around the stove and sing a few songs, is that it?'

Thraun massaged his nose with thumb and forefinger.

'This isn't a deliberate ploy to delay us,' he said, keeping his temper in check, his voice a low growl. 'I too am anxious to see your family safe but we cannot risk all our lives, because that will help no one.'

'We have to do something!' Alun's voice was desperate.

Will huffed, Thraun waved him silent.

'We *are*.' He gestured around him. 'We are out here, waiting for the right time to make our move. You must understand that that time isn't now. We have to keep watching and let the situation settle. I know it's hard but please try to be calm.'

Alun threw off the hand that Thraun placed on his shoulder but he nodded all the same, getting up and moving further away from the path.

'He'll be all right,' said Thraun to Will's scowl. 'Just leave him be.'

'He'll be the death of us,' warned the little man. There was a low whistle from the direction of the path and Jandyr trotted into the campsite.

'Someone's coming,' he said.

Thraun got to his feet. 'I've had enough of this. It's like a busy day in Dordover market. What do you say we stop them?'

'What do we really have to lose?' asked Will.

'Not a lot,' said Thraun, checking Alun was out of earshot. 'If we don't go in soon, we'll find nothing but corpses.'

Water. Lapping and bubbling, splashing off a stone. Wind, rain, water and cold. And pain. Thumping in his temple and howling in his ear.

Hirad moved, sending a wave of nausea through his body. His stomach lurched.

'Oh!' He opened his eyes. The mist was deep and disorienting. A light rain still fell.

He sat up gingerly, probing a swelling at the back of his jaw just under his left ear. He opened his mouth slowly and wide, feeling the dull ache in the bone but knowing at least that it wasn't broken.

There was a strange taste on his tongue. A taste that reminded him of a smell that he couldn't quite . . .

'Damn.' He'd been drugged. He slithered to his feet, firewood and water skins forgotten, swaying as his brain and stomach protested the sudden action. He put a hand to his temple. Another bruise, a big one, was forming. He felt groggy. Like a hangover but with none of the good memories. All he could remember was that helmet looming out of the mist and the force of the blows. And the voice. Familiar. Definitely familiar.

The path was slippery. Three times he fell painfully, retching the last time as his head connected with stone.

There were bodies outside the overhang. Inside, the fire guttered, almost dead.

'No,' he moaned through clenched teeth. He slid to a halt in front of a pile of gear, and relief flooded through him. The two bodies face up in the rain and mist were not Raven; and Richmond and Talan were both propped up by the fire. Talan's eyes were open, and while Richmond's were not, he was most certainly breathing.

Talan managed a limp smile. 'Hirad, thank the Gods. I thought you must be dead.'

'Where?' Hirad gestured to the empty spaces by the dying blaze. Talan raised a hand to silence him.

'The Black Wings attacked us. They just melted out of the mist. Denser must have sensed something, 'cos he smoked those two.' He paused, breathing heavily. Hirad noticed his eyes blackening, and a trail of blood was dried under his nose.

'They've taken them, Hirad. They've taken Ilkar and Denser.'

'Alive?'

'Yes, I think so. I was already down. Gods, that brophane is strong stuff. I feel awful.' Talan opened his eyes and mouth wide, stretching his face. Then he shook his head hard, smacking his lips together. 'That didn't help. So, what now?'

'We wake *him* up and get going.' Hirad shrugged. 'What else is there to do? Are you fit to ride?' Talan gave a short laugh. 'What?'

'Hirad, you're missing something.'

The barbarian's shoulders sagged. 'They took the horses.'

Talan nodded.

'Bugger it! Why didn't they just kill us? Have it done with?'

'Their fight isn't with us,' said Richmond, opening his eyes at last. 'It's with the Colleges.'

'Well, they got that wrong, didn't they?' said Hirad, feeling his anger gathering.

'Yeah, they did,' agreed Talan, levering himself to his feet.

'How far to the Black Wings' castle?' asked Hirad.

'Six hours on foot. Seven because it's getting dark and we aren't right just now.' Talan's face was pasty white in the gathering gloom.

'That's a long time,' said Hirad. 'Right. Ten minutes to chuck your guts up and be ready to leave. All right?'

'What're we going to do?' Richmond's mind was still confused. His legs wobbled as he pulled himself up the wall.

'We're going to get them back. Then we're going to torch that place and everyone in it.' Hirad's head was clearing with every passing moment, though he could feel that his body was still weakened by the drug clotting his muscles. 'If they didn't kill them, it's because they need them. It can only be for information, and you know how much mages hate talking.'

Richmond and Talan both looked at him, nodding their understanding.

A movement caught Hirad's eye. It came from beneath Richmond's cloak, which lay by the dead ash of the fire. As he watched, a black furred head poked out and tested the air. Denser's cat looked up at him, then jumped clean on to his shoulders, turning quickly so it could look into his face.

'A new friend, Hirad?' asked Talan, managing a smile.

'I don't think so.' The cat meowed loud and long. 'We're going, we're going, all right? We'll find him.'

The cat looked away past Hirad up the valley. The mist was a little clearer, though rain and approaching dusk kept visibility poor.

'Think he understood you?' asked Richmond.

'Probably.' Hirad shrugged. 'Come on, let's get out of here.'

Chapter 14

'Nasty spell, this. Planning a little surprise for someone, were you?' Travers had leaned in close to Denser's cut and bleeding face, dangling the amulet from its chain so it knocked gently into the mage's left ear. Denser could smell alcohol on Travers' breath.

He hoped the shock he'd just experienced didn't show on his face. Right at the time he thought things couldn't get any worse, he'd been betrayed by another mage. And one working for Travers. The Witch Hunter.

Ever since their capture at the overhang, Denser had been wondering why he was still alive. It wasn't Travers' way. The assassin was his way, but now he couldn't understand why one had been sent. Presumably they'd wanted him dead that night in The Rookery, so what had changed in the days following to make Travers so eager to question him?

He supposed it didn't matter much. At least while he was alive there was still a chance, however slim. It was obvious, though, that rescue was his only option; and that meant Hirad had to be alive, because if he was, he'd try to rescue Ilkar, no question about it.

But for now he was helpless, and it was clear the Black Wings were expert in keeping captured mages subdued. Their hands had been tied from the moment they'd been taken and the ride to the castle had been under the unending scrutiny of four men. At the castle they'd been pushed to the ground and walked straight through the gates, courtyard and main doors into a large hall, bare but for a few chairs, two low tables and a fireplace that was as cold as the room.

And then a beating, delivered professionally and, curiously, without malice. Its purpose was plain. Blows to the head, chest, stomach, upper arms and legs had left his body aching and throbbing and had sapped what little energy he had. Never mind that his arms were tied, he couldn't have cast a spell if his life depended on it and they knew it.

'Saying nothing, Denser?' Travers drew back. 'Plenty of time. And of course you don't know what we know, do you?' Travers stood up. Men stood to either side of him. There were eight of them in the hall. And Ilkar. He hadn't said one word since they'd been taken, not even to confirm his name. His beating had been more vicious. Denser wasn't sure why, but Travers looked at the elf with a mixture of disappointment and disdain. Tarred with the Xeteskian brush, perhaps.

Denser found himself wondering who had read the amulet and betrayed him. The fact was that it had to be a mage from either Xetesk or Dordover. Septern's name, the location of the rip and an allusion to what lay beyond it only appeared in Dordovan lore script.

He still couldn't quite believe it, and his feelings were swamped by disgust that a mage from either college would work for the Black Wings. It had to be a Dordovan. A Xeteskian would choose suicide first.

He breathed in and let his head fall forwards. There was a pain under his right arm and his mind turned to his missing Familiar. He presumed it was at the overhang. It was certainly alive, but unless it found him soon, it would weaken and die. Denser wasn't sure his brain could stand the pain right now.

A slap to his cheek brought him back to his grim here and now. He looked up into Travers' face.

'Let me tell you a little of what I know,' said the Captain. 'Please pay attention. I'd hate to think your mind was drifting.'

He pulled up a chair and sat down opposite Denser. One of his men brought over a small table, bottle and glass. The Captain poured himself a generous measure of what looked like a spirit, and took a long sip before leaning back and stretching his legs out in front of him.

'My sources tell me something big and very worrying is happening.'

'We agree there.'

A complete silence followed Denser's words. Travers locked eyes with Denser and drilled him with a baleful stare.

'Never interrupt me again or I will cut your tongue from your mouth and nail it to your forehead as a reminder.'

'Perhaps you should do it anyway, Captain,' said one of his men, a tall, rangy swordsman with a harsh face. 'Not much of a mage if he can't speak, eh?'

Denser and Travers both turned to him, the Xeteskian barely avoiding a smile. How wrong could a man be?

'Go and warm a kettle or something, Isman. Our friend might care for a hot drink. It is cold in here.' Isman left the room. 'Idiot.' Travers faced Denser once more. 'He is slow to learn. Now, where was I?' He drained his glass, then refilled it, picking it up to swirl the liquid around as he thought.

Denser watched him, his mouth firmly shut. Travers was well into middle age and it was beginning to show. Still, the sword at his side would be sharp and Denser had no doubt that he would carry out his threat. Travers did not have the reputation of a gratuitously cruel man, but he certainly had proved to be a man of his word.

'Now then, big and worrying. Dawnthief, I understand, is the most powerful spell in existence, and this' – he produced the amulet again – 'is the first step in recovering it. What I also know is that you need three catalysts to make it work. Apparently, this amulet doesn't list them.' He put the amulet away again, drained and refilled his glass. 'Well, that's enough of what I know. Now I want you to tell me a few things and so you are free to speak. Indeed, I insist that you make use of the privilege.'

Isman returned with a few mugs and a large copper pot. 'There's soup,' he said.

'Very good,' said Travers. 'Pour a mug for Denser and his rather quiet elven friend. Release one hand each and see that they hold their mugs steady and with all fingers.' Travers looked again at Denser. 'Now then, to work. Will you speak?'

'Don't count on it.'

'Maybe not immediately anyway.' Travers smiled, leaving Denser cold. Isman ambled over with two steaming mugs. At a nod, a man behind Denser and Ilkar released one hand.

'Thank you,' said Denser as he was handed his soup. It smelt strongly of onions and tomatoes. Ilkar said nothing, but accepted the drink anyway.

'Good,' said Travers. 'Now we're feeling more comfortable. Perhaps you'd like to tell me what Xetesk was planning to do with Dawnthief.'

'You won't believe me.'

'You could at least try.'

Denser shrugged and considered that the truth couldn't hurt the situation any further.

'The Wytch Lords are back. There are Wesmen armies massing on our borders even now, and with Shamen magic to support them, Balaia will be lost unless the Wytch Lords are destroyed. Dawnthief is the only way.'

Travers laughed out loud, causing Ilkar to start. He and Denser shared a look before he dropped his head and stared back into his soup.

'That's good. Very good,' said the Captain. 'But I do know my history very well, I am afraid. The Wytch Lords are long gone, and will never return.'

'I did say you wouldn't believe me.' Another shrug from Denser, another laugh from Travers.

'Of course, I'd forgotten how slavishly you believe your Xetesk Masters.' He continued chuckling. 'Yes, I can quite believe that is what they told you. And a grand reason on the face of it for one so eager to impress, eh?' Denser didn't reply. He sipped his soup and regarded Travers from over the rim of his mug, aware he was frowning.

'Let me ask you this, Denser. Do you seriously believe that the Wytch Lords are not already destroyed by the forces of Xetesk?'

'Your interpretation of history and mine differ, Travers,' replied Denser. 'We did not have the capability to destroy the Wytch Lords then. And they have now escaped their prison.'

'Oh, yes, the . . . what was it? Prison between worlds or something?' Travers shook his head. 'Nice story. Good for keeping the other Colleges in line, I'll grant you. You believe that as well, do you?'

Denser said nothing.

'Of course you do,' said Travers. 'Still, I can hardly expect you to turn against all your years of teaching and dogma, can I?'

'You misunderstand the motives of Xetesk,' said Denser. 'Our image is slow to change but our ideals and morals already have.'

Now Travers clapped slowly and Denser could feel his anger rising. He fought to keep it in check.

'Said with such feeling, but I am afraid you have been sadly misled. My knowledge of your researches paints a very different picture, and you must agree that Dawnthief is hardly a "moral" spell, eh?'

Another silence. Denser drained his mug and his hand was retied.

'So, have you discovered the identity of the catalysts?' asked Travers conversationally. He leaned forward, cradling his drink in both hands.

'No,' said Denser.

'I see. Very well. Never mind.' The Captain turned to Isman. 'You may as well show Denser to his room.' Isman nodded, untied the Xeteskian's hands and pulled the mage upright. Tall and rangy he might have been, but he was also very strong. 'You will find, Denser,'

Travers continued after topping up his glass, 'that your soup was somewhat drugged. Unfortunately for you Ilkar of The Raven, yours was not.'

The rain stopped slowly and the mist lifted from the hills to leave a dark layer of low cloud. Hirad felt as if he would never be dry again, or clear-headed for that matter. They'd been walking continually for over three hours and the damp clogged his every pore. Worse, the lasting effect of the brophane was a headache that grew to a steady pulsing pain that covered his entire skull. Glancing left and right, he could see that Talan and Richmond looked as bad as he felt.

Earlier, before the light had gone and the talking had given way to the sullen but determined sound of boots on rock and mud, Richmond and Talan had agreed that they wouldn't reach the Black Wings' castle until perhaps two hours before dawn. A combination of their physical condition, the difficult ground underfoot and the dark deepened by the thick clouds dictated a slow pace. Steep crags rose to either side of them and stunted trees, wind-blown heather and thick-stemmed grass were all that clung to the bleak landscape. The rock-strewn mountains ran away east and west as far as the eye could see, and the gentle slopes of Pontois' lands were already a distant memory.

As he trudged, head down, half a dozen paces behind his friends Hirad was hit by a wave of hopelessness and anger. Less than a week earlier, The Raven, seven strong and invincible, had stood on a castle's battlements and overseen another victory. He had been proud, vital and alive, continually buoyed by what they had achieved over ten great years.

Now they were reduced to three tired swordsmen crawling blearily towards what would probably be their deaths. And it was all down to one man. Denser. The Xetesk mage and his plans had already taken Sirendor and The Unknown from Hirad. And now it looked as if he had taken Ilkar too. All in the space of a few days. Hirad found it almost impossible to believe.

He shook his head and forced his mind into focus. The only thing that mattered right now was the attempt to rescue Ilkar. Denser could go to hell, and the fight for Balaia would have to be fought another way. They had no plan, though, and when they stopped another two hours later in a sheltered grove, they turned their thoughts to the attack.

'Has either of you seen the castle?' asked Hirad, shivering from the moment he stopped moving.

Both Talan and Richmond nodded.

'It was a Baronial seat before the fighting started,' said Richmond. 'It's actually a walled mansion. I'm sure that Travers has attended to the defence but it shouldn't prove too difficult to get in.'

'Any ideas?' Hirad himself had none. Try as he might, all he saw in his mind was the death of his friends, of The Raven, and of himself.

'Well, we had a chat a little earlier, and despite whoever it was telling you to go home, I suspect Travers at least will be expecting a rescue attempt,' said Talan. 'He will also know about how long it'll take us to reach him, that we'll be tired and his men won't. And we have no idea how many men he has, where Ilkar and Denser will be and what condition they're in.'

'Got any good news?'

'We should be free of magical attack or defence.' Talan half smiled.

Hirad brightened, seeing a glimmer of light.

'We can Rage then,' he said.

'Exactly,' said Richmond.

'Interesting. So?'

Richmond shrugged. 'So much depends on our getting into the house undetected, not just the grounds. If we do, a Rage might work. Neither of us has more than seen the place from a distance and it's set in open land, as you'd expect.

'If this cloud cover keeps low, we should be able to make the walls unseen. There is, or was, a stable block and a large kitchen garden at the back. Whatever, we're walking into the unknown, Hirad.'

'I only wish we were. Another blade, particularly his, and I'd be confident.'

'We'll do it, Hirad,' said Talan, rising and stretching. 'Or we'll take as many of those bastards with us as possible.'

Hirad nodded. 'Right,' he said. 'Right.' He too stood, a rush of energy hitting him. The cat moved in his cloak, making him start. He'd forgotten the animal was there. It poked its head into the open and Hirad scratched its ears, surprised to find that it was shivering and distinctly cool to the touch. They locked eyes but the cat's had lost their strength – dulled by distance from its Master.

'This thing isn't well,' said Hirad. 'We need to get it to Denser quickly. C'mon, let's not waste any more time.'

The pace for the next hour was high. Trade trails were well worn in the area and Richmond asserted that they were on a more or less straight line right through Travers' front door.

'Time?' asked Hirad. as they slackened speed to a gentle lope to save themselves a little.

'I'm guessing, but about four hours to dawn,' replied Talan.

'And the castle?'

'One and a half, maybe two hours. No more.'

'Excellent.'

They walked through terrain that eased noticeably; flattening and firming underfoot. The dark gave them little help, though their night-accustomed eyes allowed them to see the shapes of low hills, stands of trees and bushes mixing with shrubland and long grass.

The cat had ceased any movement in Hirad's cloak, and though he thought it still alive, he could all but feel it weakening with every passing minute.

Perhaps an hour from the castle, and on a wide track which only went to one place, Talan brought them to an abrupt halt. The cloud had lifted ever so slightly and a brighter patch above them betrayed the position of a moon.

'What's up?' asked Hirad, looking about him and loosening the sword in his scabbard. The wind was dying now, gusting and picking at his damp armour and clothes. He began to feel cold again.

'Something's not right. Spread left and right, you two, off to the sides, there are some odd marks on the path.'

Hirad nodded and motioned Richmond to the right. He took up station left, scouring the black and near-black outlines that made up their immediate position.

Behind him, Talan crouched to the ground, brushing a gloveless hand over it and putting his fingers to his nose. He edged forward, inch by inch, looking both immediately in front of him and perhaps two paces ahead.

'I think there's—' he began.

'Whatever it is, don't say it,' said a voice from the left, a good twenty paces distant by the sound. It was a man's voice, low and gruff, as if its owner spent a good deal of time whispering. The Raven froze but the cat, suddenly very much alive, dropped to the ground and darted away into the dark.

'Please don't move,' continued the voice. 'My friend here has an itchy nose and if he were to scratch it, his arrow would fly.'

Hirad couldn't believe it. His body tensed as he tried to decide what to do. Movement was out. If there was a bowman, he could take down two of them before they found his position. Calm and talk seemed the only option.

'What do you want?' he asked.

'You have something of ours and we want it back.'

'I doubt it,' said Hirad. 'And if it's money you're after. I'm afraid—'

'We don't want your money.' The voice betrayed disgust. 'You are holding my good friend's wife and we want her back. Now.'

'You're mistaken,' began Talan.

'Hardly,' said the voice. 'Your bastard Master, Travers, is interrogating her right now. And worse, I expect. Start moving over here and do it slowly.'

The Raven stayed put.

'Gods, Hirad, they think we're . . .' said Richmond.

'We are not Black Wings,' growled Hirad.

The man laughed, and there was another sound, higher-pitched, confirming that there were indeed two men away in the dark.

'Of course not,' said the voice. 'After all, all sorts walk this path in the early hours of the morning. Please move together and take your hands from your swords.'

The trio did as they were ordered.

'We are not Black Wings,' repeated Hirad.

'So you said—'

'We are The Raven.'

A short silence was ended by hurried whispering, then a snigger.

'Not many of you, are there?'

'No.' Hirad barely kept himself in check.

'Walk forward. There's someone here reckons he's seen you.'

The Raven looked at one another, raised eyebrows and walked forwards.

'Stop,' ordered the other voice. It had a gentler tone, less aggressive. There was another silence.

'It's been a lot of years, but you're Hirad Coldheart, no doubt about it.'

'That's right, now can we stop—'

'Where is Ilkar?'

'You know him?' returned Talan.

'I'm from Julatsa. Where is he?'

'Travers has got him,' said Hirad. 'He's in the Black Wings' castle, that's why we're going there. You're holding us up and it's pissing me off!'

The first man laughed, relieved.

'Come on in and join us. We have a stove and you look as if you could do with a hot drink.'

'Any reason we should?' asked Talan.

'Well, I happen to think we could be of great help to each other. Let's face it, it can't hurt to find out.'

Erienne was still shaking. She had no doubt that what the Captain had shown her was Septern's amulet. How could it be anything else? The lore in three College languages. The Dordovan code that revealed the location of Septern's workshop.

That the Captain held the amulet set her in the grip of fear, and she had been able to do nothing but confirm what he thought he already knew. That indeed there was a search for Dawnthief, that it was advanced and that he had, in all probability, managed to capture the Xeteskian mage, Denser.

Her skin crawled and for the first time she began to believe that the Captain was not just a man whose dreams matched her nightmares. There was now the possibility that he might actually be able to assemble the catalysts and control the spell. And if he could, the Colleges would tear each other apart to get it. There would be another war and she was very much afraid that Xetesk would win it.

'You see, I really am determined to find out all you know about Dawnthief, and I will hurt you if I have to.'

Ilkar raised his freshly bleeding face to Travers but said nothing. After Denser's departure, they had manacled his wrists to a wall and beaten his body with the flat of a shovel before leaving him on the wall for what had to be the best part of an hour. Then another, shorter beating, during which one wild swipe had caught his face, splitting his nose and lips. The pain was intense but he could handle that. What he was scared of was internal rupture. In his state, he didn't think he would be able to hold that type of wound at bay. Certainly not if he was drugged. Another thing he knew was that he couldn't buy any more time by keeping his silence.

'Come now, Ilkar,' said Travers. 'This is all so unnecessary.' The Captain had begun to slur his words just a little. 'It is Ilkar, isn't it?'

'You seem to think so,' said Ilkar.

'He speaks!' Travers clapped his hands. 'Bravo! I have to say, we were confident of your identity. After all, not too many elven Julatsans ride with The Raven, eh?'

'Not many,' agreed Ilkar.

'Indeed.' Travers smiled and laid a hand on Ilkar's shoulder. 'I expect you'd like to sit down now, eh?'

'Good guess.' Ilkar's manacles were removed and he was put back in his chair, arms once more tied behind him. The difference in comfort was enormous and the mage had to quash an unwanted smile at the thought that he could ever feel good battered, bruised and bound to a chair. A sense of perspective was going to be important.

The Captain sat himself down, poured another large drink and took a long sip. He had to be drunk, yet he seemed in complete control of his thoughts. In fact the only outward signs of any intoxication were his flushed face and slightly disabled speech.

'So, now we've begun at long last, Ilkar – and I do commend you on your resistance. But that must be over now, so please answer my questions and you can rest. I would hate to have to employ any further punitive measures but please understand that I will not shy from so doing should the need arise.'

Travers smiled again. Thinly this time. Ilkar gave no reaction.

'I assume we understand each other,' said Travers. He finished his glass and poured the last drops from his bottle. He waved the empty at a soldier, who took it away. Ilkar watched as he threw back the small measure.

'Think I might pass out?' This time, the smile was broader. 'You'll be disappointed, I'm afraid. What's my record, Isman?'

'Four bottles, Captain.'

'Four,' repeated Travers. 'Bottles.'

Ilkar just let him get on with it. Travers examined his empty glass but his frown turned to yet another smile as a full bottle was placed on his table. He unstoppered it immediately.

'Now, before we get on to Denser's delightful spell, I'd be terribly grateful if you told me why you, a Julatsan, were travelling with a Xeteskian.'

Ilkar looked up sharply, studying Travers' face for a moment.

'You really don't know?'

'Enlighten me.'

'You sent an assassin to kill Denser, yes?'

Travers nodded. 'Yes, she was evidently unsuccessful. Lucky, really, considering what I have to do now.'

'She wasn't entirely unsuccessful, your assassin.'

'Really?' Travers paused, mid-sip, and exchanged glances with Isman. The latter shrugged.

'She killed Sirendor Larn.'

'Oh.'

'Yes. Isman. Oh.' Ilkar turned to the tall swordsman. 'So Hirad wants all the Black Wings dead. And what Hirad wants, the Raven want.'

'Thank you for the warning,' said Travers. 'We really shall have to look out for ourselves, shan't we?' He leaned in close to Ilkar and patted his knee.

Ilkar turned up one corner of his mouth. 'If I were you, that's exactly what I would do,' he said quietly.

'Hmm.' Travers sucked his top lip and leaned back in his chair. 'Well . . . we'll return to that later, eh? Now while your friend's unfortunate demise explains why The Raven were on their way here, it doesn't begin to explain why Denser is with you.'

Ilkar allowed himself what he hoped was a wry smile. 'There will be precious few things on which we agree, Captain Travers, but I think our distrust of all things Xeteskian will be one of them.'

'Hmm.' Travers nodded. 'It is a shame you are with him, Ilkar. Your kind of mage I could tolerate, I think. Continue.'

'He owes The Raven money,' said Ilkar simply. Travers raised his eyebrows. 'Against my express wishes, we bodyguarded him to Korina. The plan was to watch him until the money went into our account. When you murdered Sirendor, that meant bringing him with us.'

Travers was quiet for a while. He took a mouthful of drink and sloshed it around the inside of his mouth before swallowing it.

'I am disappointed, Ilkar. You've had all this time and that is the best you can come up with? Are you seriously trying to tell me that you had no idea what Denser had in his possession?'

'No,' said Ilkar carefully. 'I knew it was valuable by the amount of money Denser offered us for the job. What I'm saying is that I had no idea what the amulet was. I can't read the inscriptions.'

Travers picked his bottle up by its neck, lunged and crashed it across the side of Ilkar's head. In trying to duck the blow, the mage succeeded only in toppling his chair over. His right side hit the floor hard, his arm beneath him flared in pain and all he could see were the shattered remains of the bottle, slightly out of focus, as his head warmed with trickling blood. He could smell the spirit strongly.

'Do not presume to insult my intelligence!' shouted Travers. 'Let me tell you what you were doing.' He paced backwards and forwards. grinding glass underfoot.

'You were after the Dawnthief catalysts. You know what they are. That amulet contains College lore in Julatsan as well as Xeteskian and

Dordovan. You and Denser both need each other and your pact of evil is threatening the whole of Balaia.'

Ilkar was silent. He was aware Travers was well versed in spell theory, but this latest speech really confirmed what he knew already but hadn't allowed himself to believe. There was a mage working for the Captain. At least one.

He was hauled upright, grunted as the pressure was lifted from his arm and was glad he couldn't move it; he thought it badly bruised if not broken.

'Isman, another bottle, please,' said Travers in a fatigued tone. He took his seat but said nothing until the swordsman had returned and his glass was refilled.

'You can't lie to me for ever,' he said.

No, but long enough, thought Ilkar.

'There's no one to save you. No one knows you're here.'

'They do, and they're coming.'

'Who, The Raven?' Isman spoke with a sneer.

Ilkar turned to him. 'It's a pity, you know, Isman. Hirad thought you were Raven material. It was only because we'd never seen you fight ourselves that you weren't invited to join.'

'I'd have refused.'

'No one ever refuses.'

'At least I'm still alive,' said Isman.

'Oh, yes, I neglected to mention,' said Travers. 'Isman did have to kill your friends. After all, we couldn't have them following us now, could we?'

But Ilkar wasn't really listening because, as Travers spoke, he leaned right forward and there, visible inside his part-open shirt, hung the Understone Pass Commander's Badge. He had one third of the key to unbelievable power around his neck and he didn't even know it. Ilkar smiled.

'Something funny?'

'There's humour in everything, Travers,' said Ilkar. 'You're telling me something I don't believe in order to get me to give you information I don't have. And when I fail to tell you, you'll try to extract it by force.'

Travers smiled too and poured himself another drink.

'And so we meet on either side of our disagreement,' he said. 'From where I sit, your friends are dead and you do indeed know the answer to my very simple question. But I will ask it again. Do you know the identity of the Dawnthief catalysts?'

'No.'

Travers stood up. 'I think it's time you were reminded of your predicament. Isman, put him back on the wall. Leave his head alone. I'll be back in a few minutes.' The Captain strode from the hall, his walk steady, unhindered by his consumption of alcohol.

'Oh, shit,' muttered Ilkar.

'Yes.' Isman smiled. 'Please don't struggle. It only makes things more difficult. For you, that is.'

Ilkar allowed himself to be hauled to the wall chains, his right arm thumping with a strength that made him nauseous. Bracing himself for the pain, he fought to keep in mind that Denser had not let out a mana scream. And while that was true, it meant the Familiar was still alive. And while that was true, help was on its way.

But as the first shovel blow caught him just below his ribs, making him gasp as the air was forced from his lungs, he also knew that the cat wouldn't last for ever without its master. If no help arrived by sun-up, none was coming.

'So how long has Travers had her?' Hirad remained dubious. The story he had just heard didn't make much sense. He cupped his mug of steaming coffee in his hands and was glad of it. At least their meeting would not be a complete waste.

'Just a few days,' said Alun, the man who had been doing most of the talking. He was, he said, the husband of the Dordovan mage, Erienne, whom Travers had kidnapped. He looked a quiet man, and though he carried a long sword, Hirad doubted whether he really knew how to use it. He didn't have the face of a swordsman.

'What for?'

'What does he ever take mages for? For questioning,' Alun said, his voice muted, desperate.

'Why don't the Colleges do something about him?' asked Talan.

'Because enough senior mages are in grudging agreement that his work may have some use in taming dark magic,' said the big man, Thraun.

'But we're talking about kidnap here,' said Hirad. 'Surely . . .'

'It's not that simple,' said Alun. 'Erienne is a maverick. She doesn't live by College rules and they are pig-headed enough to let her suffer for it. Maybe even die.' His voice was bitter, angry. 'Look, it isn't just her. They took our boys.'

Hirad caught Alun's eyes and felt a pang of sorrow for the man. It was the same expression he'd seen in Sana: knowing he'd lost something but not really believing it was gone.

'Boys?' prompted Talan.

'Twin sons. Four years old,' answered Jandyr, the Julatsan bowman. He was an elf and claimed a nodding acquaintance with Ilkar. For his part, Ilkar had never spoken of him.

'And you three are hired, I take it,' said Talan.

'You think we'd do this sort of thing for love?'

'We are,' snapped Hirad at the gruff-voiced man, Will. He was small, maybe five and a half feet, but he was wiry and well muscled, and his eyes were clever. He carried two short swords in a crossed back-mounted scabbard, wore dark-stained leather and had a small growth of stubble covering the jaw and neck of his thin face. Hirad didn't like him.

'I don't have to justify myself to you,' said Will. 'We're all hired men here. All but Alun. You choose to fight battles for the Barons; we recover things. And people.' He shrugged. Quiet fell. The stove hissed and smoked slightly, aside from which, nothing but a dim glow from the coals gave notice that they were sitting round a fire.

Hirad glanced at the other man, Thraun. He was huge, a man who could have given even The Unknown cause for thought. His long sword was at his side and he absently scratched at his brown-flecked blond beard as he stared into the night.

A rustling behind him caught Hirad's attention and he looked over his shoulder to see the cat entering the camp site. All was clearly far from well. It stumbled and swayed as if intoxicated as it moved towards the barbarian; and in the dim light from the coals, he could see its coat, as dull now as its eyes, ragged and unkempt.

'Gods, Hirad, look at it,' said Richmond.

Hirad nodded, scooped the stricken animal up and placed it inside his jerkin, against his skin, wincing as the cold of the cat touched the warmth of his flesh.

'Yours, is it?' asked Will.

'It belongs to Denser. It's dying.'

'Obviously,' said Will.

Hirad shot him a sharp glance. 'It can't be allowed to happen. We need Denser right now.' He glanced over to Richmond and Talan. 'It's time we sorted ourselves out.'

'So what was your plan?' asked Richmond of the others.

'Stealth,' said Jandyr. 'We've identified a way in through the back and were waiting for dead of night to go in when your friends were taken past. We'd just decided to wait further when you came along.'

'Hmm.' Hirad sucked his lip. 'I'm not sure that'll work now. They're going to be expecting some form of attack from us.'

'But not from seven people,' said Thraun. 'Only three.'

'Interesting,' murmured Talan. Then, louder, 'Your wife, what's her schooling?'

'Dordovan, I told you . . .' began Alun.

'No, no, sorry. I mean is she principally offensive or defensive?'

Alun looked blank for a moment. 'Well, neither, really. She's a research mage – a Lore Scribe. Or she will be.'

'But does she cast?' pushed Talan.

'Never to hurt others.' Alun was definite.

'Excellent,' said Talan. 'Even if Travers is controlling her, it makes a Rage all that much more likely to succeed.'

'A what?' Will frowned.

Hirad smiled. 'Perhaps we could interest you in The Raven's chaos tactic.'

They had broken three ribs and one, at the base of his rib cage, had cracked back to threaten his lungs. The blows had become more and more brutal, moving from his stomach to his chest and, finally, to his legs.

Then they had left him, hanging and bleeding from a dozen places outside and, when he went within, two inside. One of these, on his liver, felt serious. He ached. His battered legs shot pain into his back if he tried to stand; and his arm and broken ribs flared if he hung from his wrists.

Through the ill-fitting drapes in the hall, Ilkar thought he could see the first hint of dawn. His heart sank and he wondered if there was any point in keeping himself going. It was taking the last of his strength. Better to shut off and let himself die.

He tried to hate Denser then. Hate him for trapping The Raven into their futile and doomed action. Hate him for causing the deaths of his friends. Hate him for being Xeteskian and sleeping on, unaware of the agony Ilkar was enduring.

But he found he couldn't. Denser, for all his arrogance, had been telling the truth – the evidence was overwhelming. The discovery of the Dawnthief parchment, the fight with the Destranas, Gresse's word about the Wesman build-up. It all fitted with a return of the Wytch

Lords and a Xeteskian drive to recover the only spell capable of beating them.

He shuddered. At least in dying he'd be out of the battle for Balaia. A battle where there probably wouldn't be any winners. He breathed in hard and coughed up blood, gasping pain as his lung pushed against broken bone. He straightened his legs slowly, relieving pressure on his numb arms, wincing as the bruising in his hips pulsed agony right across his back.

They'd been away a few minutes now. Ilkar frowned. Would they bother to ask him any more questions? Gods, he hoped so. At least that would mean they'd put him back in the chair. Where had they gone? Travers had said he'd be back. Ilkar wondered if they were talking to Denser but presumed he would still be drugged asleep. He blew out his lips. More likely they were having breakfast or something.

The double doors at the end of the room opened and Travers walked in, flanked by two men. Bottle in one hand, glass in the other, the Captain had a pronounced stagger now.

'Fourth bottle!' he shouted, waving it at Ilkar. 'Maybe I'll beat the record today.'

'Or die trying, if we're lucky,' muttered the mage.

'Sorry, Ilkar, did you say something? You'll have to speak up.' Travers shambled towards his chair but another sight behind him caught Ilkar's attention. Stripped to the waist, head down and carried in between Isman and another was Denser. His feet were dragging across the floor and he looked for all the world as if he was dead.

They hauled him to a chair and set him in it, holding his shoulders to stop him falling to the ground. Travers laughed and Ilkar turned to find the Captain staring at him.

'That's the trouble with this drug of ours. A touch too much and you don't want to wake up. And we had so much we needed to ask Denser, and he needed such persuading to wake up and talk to us.' Travers' expression became one of mocking solemnity. 'I'm afraid he didn't agree with us for rather a long time.'

Ilkar could imagine the pain Denser was feeling. He could see harsh red marks on his upper body and, here and there, weals brought up by a whip or belt. He only hoped the Xeteskian was still numbed by the drug.

Travers drank directly from the bottle and stood up, swaying. He staggered back a step and would have fallen over his chair had not a soldier removed it smartly from his path. The Captain's face was bright red, his eyes hooded but wild and his chest heaving.

'And now we come to the first of two choices.' His speech, now slurred badly, would soon be unintelligible. He moved to stand between Ilkar and Denser, contriving to look at neither of them.

'One.' He held up a finger. 'Do you answer my questions honestly or do I have to carry on convincing you it is the only way? And you will bend to my will eventually.'

Travers looked from one to the other. Ilkar stared at Denser, who showed no reaction at all. The elf could see his chest moving though it juddered from some very imaginable pain.

'Nice try, Travers,' said Ilkar. 'Seems as though you'll have to carry on.'

'Two!' barked Travers, holding two fingers aloft. He drank from his bottle again, spirit dripping from his slack mouth, which he wiped with the back of a hand. 'In that case, which of you wants to see the other one die?'

Ilkar almost felt relieved. At least it would mean an end to the agony. He regretted not seeing Hirad again but he was beginning to believe the barbarian was indeed already dead. He would have volunteered to die but it was obvious that Travers had dragged Denser in here for one reason only. Ilkar doubted he could close his mind to Denser's torment.

He gazed over at the Dark Mage, feeling genuine sympathy for the first time.

'Goodbye, Denser,' he whispered.

Denser's body jerked violently and he clasped under his right arm with his left hand. He lifted his head and the sight made Ilkar flinch. He was all but unrecognisable. Blood matted his features, his nose skewed to the right, his mouth a swollen bubble of raw red and his eyes mere slits behind the swelling. He coughed and stared straight at Ilkar, and his mouth, incredibly, spread into a grin.

'They're here,' he croaked.

From beyond the hall, there was a shout of warning, then something more bestial, and mayhem moved to reign in the Black Wings' castle.

Chapter 15

Hirad was already having to concede, to himself, that Will could be useful. Useful enough to stay with The Raven after they'd dealt with the Black Wings, in fact. Fate was a curious thing, he concluded. He had to admit that he had thought of no one he'd want to recruit and yet now he'd literally bumped into three. Assuming they survived, of course. And then assuming he could persuade them to join The Raven. It wouldn't be as easy as it once was.

He could no longer offer people guaranteed work, well paid, and a reputation they could carry before them. Now the deal was almost certain death in pursuit of a cause of which only half the country seemed convinced and the other half looked to disrupt or destroy. And then maybe some reward. Hardly an enticing prospect.

Alun was not of the right calibre and Hirad doubted he'd care to travel with them anyway. But Thraun, with his solid muscle, and the elven bowman Jandyr would make ideal additions. It made Hirad wonder what The Raven would have been like with them as members in earlier times. Better times.

And then there was Will. Surly, sneering and ungrateful he seemed to be, talented he certainly was. It wasn't only his swift and accurate scouting of the area around the castle that impressed Hirad, but the way he had just climbed the wall behind the stable block as if it were a ladder. One end of the rope the wiry man had carried with him sailed back over the wall and dropped at the barbarian's feet. He glanced at it, then at Thraun, who smiled.

'Good, isn't he?' he said. Hirad nodded, hauled the rope taut and began climbing. In less than two minutes they were all in the grounds of the Black Wings' castle.

'Right,' whispered Will. 'The only guards outside the house are by the main gates. I couldn't see any signs of a roving watch but that's no reason to get careless. As you can see, the main building is about thirty paces away. We're in deep shadow here and safe from the house. I estimate the house to be a good one hundred and fifty feet on the longer side and maybe ninety feet on this side.' Will pointed behind him, then looked squarely at Hirad. 'And now it's up to you.'

'Nothing to it,' said the barbarian. 'I'll decide directions when we get inside, and the way in is through the nearest window.' He set off for the corner of the house. Reaching it, he looked left down the short side which led to the front before peering in through the darkened window before him. He shrugged and was about to speak when he felt Jandyr at his shoulder. The elf leaned in close and nodded.

'Empty,' he whispered. 'It's a study or something like that. Definitely small and definitely empty.'

'Excellent,' said Hirad. He drew back a fist.

'What are you doing?' hissed Will.

'Getting inside,' said Hirad.

'I've got a better way.' Will fetched a thin strip of metal from his belt and fed it between the windows. He foraged briefly, found the catch, jerked the metal up and popped it. The window swung gently open. 'After you,' he said, stepping back.

Hirad glared at him before climbing over the sill and padding towards the room's only door. He listened as the others made their way inside and could hear nothing. He turned back to the room.

'Right. When there's opportunity, Talan, Richmond, take Alun and Will and get upstairs. I'll stay down with the others.' He cracked the door a fraction, enough to know it was dark inside. He beckoned Jandyr over. The elf looked in briefly then withdrew and closed the door.

'It's small. A drawing room or something. There's a curtained opening ahead and right and a door at the top of the left wall.'

Hirad nodded and removed his cloak, the cat dropping to the ground and looking around itself, ears and nose gathering further information. 'Good. We'll split here. Talan, take the left.' He opened the door and moved inside. 'Anyone not sure, take a lead from a Raven man. Ready?' Murmurs of assent told him they were. He drew his sword from his scabbard and grinned at Richmond and Talan. 'RAVEN!' he roared. 'Raven and Rage!'

He strode to the opening and swept the curtain aside, allowing light to spill in from beyond. He howled, a sound immediately taken up by The Raven, and marched down a short passage, clashing his sword against the stone wall, feeling a high as Will and the others joined the discordant chorus.

The bestial screams and shouts, the sound of metal on stone, heavy boots on timber echoed about him. He could feel the blood surging in his veins, feel his muscles empowered, his ears ringing and his eyes wild. He broke from his walk, moving into the light at a dead run, only dimly aware that the cat had streaked away in front of him.

There were men in there, two of them. He laughed, his teeth bared, and rushed them. The first froze and Hirad barely paused in his stride, hacking the man down on his way to the second, whose token resistance was swept aside like a stray hair from his face. He roared again, deep in his throat, stopping to take stock.

It was a kitchen. He was by a double door. More doors were ahead of him. Jandyr and Thraun stood in front of a third.

'See how it works? See how it works? Now we split, one each way. Shout loud and keep moving or you'll die.' He turned, kicked open the doors by him and charged inside, another scream forming on his lips, the cat hard on his heels.

Talan hammered through the door in front of him and saw a windowed opening right and a door left. He pointed right, not pausing in his stride as he took the left route, yelling Will's name as he went. They burst into a large room with fireplaces and windows down the far wall. Double doors occupied the bottom right-hand corner and Talan ran at these, howling as he went, kicking over chairs and tables and clashing his sword on the stone-clad wall. Will did his best to keep up, initial self-consciousness lost in a wave of excitement.

On Talan's signal, Richmond crashed through the windowed opening, showering glass and wood into an enclosed quadrangle. Richmond exulted, crushing shrubs and plants underfoot and sparing a brief glance at the night sky above as he moved towards doors he could see in the glass-panelled wall to his left. Alun was hard on his heels. Halfway there, the doors opened, and a swordsman stepped into the quad. Richmond bellowed and increased his pace; the swordsman merely smiled and stood his ground. Battle was joined in a clash of sparks and the clamorous ring of metal.

Jandyr and Thraun exchanged a look of near disbelief as Hirad smashed his way through the double doors. The elf shrugged, drew in a huge breath and shuddered a guttural noise from deep within himself, his fists clenched about his bow. Thraun nodded, turned on his heel and ran for the doors in the far wall, his yell, truly animalistic, bouncing from the walls.

Jandyr nocked an arrow, kicked open the single panel next to him and looked on to a flight of stairs heading down. Now his hunter instincts cut in and, bow ready before him, he slipped soundlessly on to the first step, his eyes piercing the gloom easily, his nose twitching at a smell of stale sweat tinged with urine and blood.

There was a dim light below, coming from under a curtained opening. He took the stairs one at a time, absolutely silent as he progressed. There was at least one person behind the curtain, a stifled cough giving him away, and Jandyr moved to the right-hand edge of the curtain as he reached the bottom of the stairs. Satisfied that the man wasn't close to the opening, the elf swept the curtain aside with his bowstring hand, keeping the arrow primed with the other. The sight before him all but made him laugh.

Thraun slapped the doors aside, moving through with an animal fluidity. A single guard stood outside a set of double doors to the right; and when the man's bloodied corpse thumped to the floor he took in the rest of his situation. The entrance hall he found himself in was empty. In front of him, main doors. Left, more doors. He swung around, found stairs rising above him and, with a brief glance to the right from where he could hear fighting, climbed the flight three at a time.

The yell died on Hirad's lips as he saw the scene in front of him. It was a huge room, draped and cold, and halfway down it, Ilkar was chained to the wall by his wrists. His head, hanging on his chest, lifted.

'Hirad, thank the Gods.'

The barbarian sheathed his sword and ran over to the mage. 'You're alive at least,' he said, slapping aside the catch on Ilkar's right arm. The elf winced as he was released.

'Careful,' he said. 'My ribs aren't so good.'

'Anything else?' Hirad paused, looking into Ilkar's eyes. Ilkar managed to turn up the corners of his mouth.

'Legs, stomach, arms . . .'

Hirad nodded. 'Lean into me,' he said. He turned, back towards Ilkar, and felt the mage lean his head on his right shoulder. Reaching over his left, he slipped the catch on the other manacle. Ilkar had to cling on not to fall.

'All right?'

'No. But let me get my left arm round you and you can help me to one of those chairs over there.'

Hirad looked and saw Denser. He was lying flat on his back in front of the chairs, the cat burrowed under his right arm. His chest rose and fell, shuddering. The Raven pair edged over to the chairs, Hirad lowering Ilkar as gently as he could into one of them, turning his attention then to the Xeteskian.

Richmond fell back, breathing hard, clutching briefly at a cut in his sword arm just below the shoulder. He flapped behind him, hearing Alun move away.

'Not so big now, eh, Raven man?'

Richmond said nothing.

'You should have gone home. Nothing here but death.'

Richmond switched his sword to his other hand and squared up. His enemy raised his eyebrows, impressed in spite of himself. The Raven man edged to the right, hearing the whisper of sword from scabbard behind him.

'Keep away, Alun, this doesn't concern you.'

'Yes it does. It's my family they've got.'

'The doting father, eh? What are you doing here?' jibed the Black Wing. 'Come to collect the bodies?'

'Bastard,' grated Alun. 'Bastard!' He lunged forwards from Richmond's left. The Raven man reacted instantly, closing off the Black Wing's route to Alun, only his enemy wasn't there. Anticipating what Richmond would do, he moved the other way and plunged his sword into Richmond's chest.

Richmond breathed his pain and fell to his knees, the metal hot between his ribs. It was yanked clear and he collapsed on to his front, his blood soaking his clothes and hair. He heard a short laugh of triumph, the sound of running moving into the dim distance, and then the world went silent.

Talan burst into the hallway, Will right behind him. Opposite them, a body lay in front of a set of double doors. To their right, stairs led up. Talan paused to listen and could hear Thraun, who had evidently gained the upper level already. He frowned. There was not enough noise and he couldn't hear Richmond or Hirad.

'Let's go! Let's go!' he shouted and clattered up the stairs. Will joined his cry and chased after him.

Alun watched Richmond drop to the ground, then turned and fled back the way they had come. His heart quailed in his chest, sweat crawled over his body and he was quivering. He was alone in a castle full of steel and death. He paused back in the corridor, about to run out into the night. Not quite alone. His blood still pumped life somewhere in this place. He chose the route back into the house – he had to find Will.

Isman, a smile on his face, saw Alun run. He would have chased him but there were others more deserving of his attention. And before them, he thought he might attend to the mages.

Travers staggered along the upper level, hammering on doors as he went, yelling for wakefulness. The sounds of The Raven filled his castle, and his solitude and condition hastened his step. He didn't stop to check that his men had heard his cries, there was no time. Should the enemy reach the boys first and release them a blight would be unleashed on Balaia. Twin sons of a mage – there could be little more dangerous than that. And once they were dead, it would be time to terminate his association with their mother.

Denser lay back as the cat bit into him, feeling it draw power, knowing it regained its strength even as his ebbed still further. But there was a balance. There would always be balance. He was dimly aware of voices around him, one at least was directed at him, but he could not answer. Not yet. His right hand stroked the cat from memory as the animal sucked in his blood. There would be enough and the Badge would be his. Travers was doomed. He smiled.

The cat ceased its feeding and looked at him with eyes newly aflame. Their minds locked and he pushed an image of the Captain into their consciousness. *Seek and return*, he said. *Bring him to me. You know what you have to do.*

The cat blinked once, slowly.

I will live in your absence. Go.

The cat seemed satisfied, its purr almost a growl. It moved away from him and sized up the ways out of the room, but all the doors were closed.

'What is going on?' demanded Hirad. 'That thing was eating him. I saw it.'

'Hirad, please,' gasped Ilkar. He was collapsed in a chair, trying very hard to remain conscious. The pain in his chest and his legs had grown to a new intensity, the internal bleeding had begun again and he needed peace to heal himself. 'There are things you don't know, but they'll have to wait. I'm not feeling so good.'

'Tell me what to do, then. I can help.'

'By guarding us, letting us have peace and saving your questions. Where are the rest?'

Now Hirad drew breath and nodded. 'We met some others. They're here to rescue some woman. We're Raging. The castle will be ours in a few minutes.'

Ilkar pushed himself painfully to the floor and lay beside Denser. 'Good,' he said. 'Good.' He closed his eyes just as the far doors opened once again. Seeing its chance, the cat streaked through them and away. Hirad tensed and moved out of Ilkar's line of sight.

'Isman.'

'Hirad.'

And Jandyr would have laughed had the sight in front of him not been so pitiful. The man lay in the middle of a floor smeared with blood, his mouth open, unmoving. A weapon was clutched in one still hand and the wine he had been drinking dripped from the overturned goblet on to the ground.

'A man who will not face his own death is no man at all,' said Jandyr. There was no movement. 'Dead men do not cough, my friend. You might as well abandon your pathetic charade. At least face me.' Still no movement. 'I have no time . . .' Jandyr stretched his bow.

'Please!' The man jerked to a sitting position. 'I don't—'

'Like I said, I have no time.' He loosed the shaft, nocked another, turned and moved back up the stairs.

Travers rested on one wall of the narrow passage to the tower, frowning. The Raven were still moving through his castle. The shouts still echoed, though they were intermittent now. What worried him was that there were clearly more than three people attacking. He shrugged and moved on to and through the door to the guardroom. His two men stood to attention, swords drawn ready.

'Good,' he slurred. 'We can't leave this to chance. Those bastard sons cannot be allowed to leave the castle. Kill them.'

'Sir?' They exchanged a glance and hesitated.

'They are not mere boys. If the bitch takes them back they will be powerful beyond all our capacity to control. See to it.' One of the guards nodded and trotted up a spiral staircase in the corner of the room. There was the sound of young voices and then a door clanked shut.

*

Thraun sprinted along the top-level corridor. On his right, windows let on to an open quadrangle into which dim light spilled. He could hear the sounds of fighting from across the way. Ignoring a small opening to his left, he charged to a right-angle bend to the right, another roar ripping from his lungs. Double doors were ahead. They looked important. He kicked them open and ran inside.

Talan and Will split as they reached the top of the stairs. To their left, windows on to the quadrangle Richmond had taken. And right, an opening and two doors spaced further along the corridor. Will took the opening, saw a door in front of him and made towards it. Talan crashed through the first of the pair of doors and found himself in a large pillared room full of beds. Most were occupied, but some weren't. Perhaps enough.

He squared up, cleared his head with a shout and bared his teeth. 'Come on then, anyone think they can take me?'

Will heard Talan's shout and tumbled through the door he'd found, drawing his dual short swords as he came up in a crouch position. His eyes widened and his heart missed a beat. The room seemed full of men and the only thing he could say with any certainty was that none of them had seen him. They were all moving in on Talan.

'A pity,' said Hirad. 'You should have joined The Raven.'

Isman snorted. 'One young blade in a band of old men. Instead I'm the man who'll be responsible for the end of you all.'

'Yeah?' Hirad's mind cleared as an adrenaline rush hit him. He flexed the muscles of his arms. 'You died the same moment as Sirendor Larn, and The Raven will see this castle burn.'

He sprang forwards, sword before him, aiming a cut at Isman's midriff. The Black Wing blocked it, moving sharply right and coming to a ready stance. Hirad searched his eyes for fear and found none. The two men circled each other. Hirad looked for a flaw in Isman's posture and was impressed to find nothing. Both men used the long sword, both were finely balanced but only one had the enormous combat experience and the knowledge of countless one-to-one victories. It was he who launched a ferocious attack.

Initially stabbing forwards, Hirad used the momentum given him by Isman's anticipated defence to follow up with a powered swing, bringing his blade through an arc from shoulder to hip. Isman couldn't hope to be ready in time but his body reaction was pure instinct. He leaped backwards, Hirad's strike missing him by less than an inch.

Out of position, the barbarian straightened in time to field Isman's return before slashing horizontally in riposte. This time, Isman evaded with room to spare.

Hirad came back to ready, his muscles suddenly aching. He shook himself and the ache dimmed. Isman smiled and drove forwards, delivering four cross-strikes in fluid succession, driving Hirad up the room beyond where the two mages lay in helpless audience. Hirad heaved a breath and arrowed in a return, beating Isman's guard and nicking the swordsman's leather jerkin.

The Black Wing's eyes narrowed and he squared again, wary now. Hirad switched his sword between his hands twice. His legs were leaden and dragged in his next attack, all but exposing his chest to Isman's defensive swipe. Something was badly wrong. Hirad could feel his stamina flooding away but knew he couldn't afford to tire in front of Isman.

The younger man lunged again; his disguised flick left tore a section of padding on Hirad's left shoulder armour and his follow-up to the neck was blocked, but only just. Hirad was sweating hard and a cramping nausea gripped his stomach.

Isman's smile widened, leaving his eyes hard. He strode forwards, his overhead strike knocking Hirad from his feet though his sword caught the force of the blow. The barbarian scrabbled backwards into a half-crouch and Isman slashed at his head. He blocked, ducked and even managed to stand but was ill prepared for the uppercut which knocked the sword from his hands. The blade clattered away over the stone-flagged floor and Hirad, his body shaking its pain and its fear, looked into Isman's face.

'I told you to go home, but you wouldn't listen,' he said, and plunged his sword into Hirad's defenceless stomach. The Raven man's legs gave way and he fell, not feeling the blade as Isman pulled it clear. In fact, he couldn't feel anything. Or see anything. He could sense himself falling. It was a long way down.

Thraun had run into a large, plush room, dimly lit by the embers of a fire and two guttering braziers. It was all the light he needed. Standing in front of a door near the far left-hand corner of the room were two swordsmen. Thraun ran at them, uttering a roar that made one flinch visibly. He leapt a table and sofa in one bound and, two paces later, struck the sword arm from the first man.

Blood was everywhere. The man, too shocked to cry out, stared at the stump, gasping, his eyes wide and filled with tears of purest torment. The other faltered and Thraun took him through the chest, pushing his half-hearted block aside with contemptuous ease. The one-armed man had collapsed, whimpering, barely moving. Thraun pulled a dagger from his belt and opened his throat.

Pulling the bodies aside, he opened the door and ascended the stairs he found. At the top, another door was bolted shut. He slid the bolts back then paused in the act of turning the handle.

'Erienne?' he ventured. He heard a movement. 'Erienne?' he repeated. Nothing this time. He continued. 'It's Thraun. Can you hear me? Don't prepare or cast. I am here to help.' He took a deep breath and pushed the door open.

For a second time, Talan slithered on the blood-slick floor and took a pace back from the three bodies already at his feet. Another trio were advancing, albeit without much conviction, having seen the short work Talan had made of their comrades.

But The Raven man was damaged. A cut on his right thigh was bleeding well and beginning to ache, and a slash across his chest made him very conscious of his breathing. And worse, he felt a heaviness in his limbs as if he'd been fighting all day. It was growing steadily and he wasn't entirely sure he could fend off the next attack for too long. Still, there was one more ace up his sleeve. None of them had seen Will. The little man was behind them now and Talan didn't think he was the kind of man to ask them to face him before he struck.

The three Black Wings closed. Talan breathed deep and squared up. He shook himself to relieve his tiredness, feinted right and struck left. His intended target blocked the blow, forcing his blade downwards as he jumped up and back. He was in no position to defend a second attack but Talan couldn't risk exposing his right flank. He turned, fielded a clumsy overhead, and drove his blade deep into his assailant's neck. One down.

He shuddered as he stepped back, ready for the attack he knew would come. The muscles of his back felt as if they were about to lock and his next breath was constricted and shallow. His eyes lost focus for a second and he slipped as he put his foot down. Seeing him off-balance, both men moved in. Talan braced himself, cleared his vision and roared to try to clear his mind.

From his left came a stab to the stomach which he blocked with a cross-sweep, left to right. Even so, blade on the right side of his face, he only half blocked the strike from the other man, deflecting the blade aside but allowing the fist to crash into his jaw. He staggered backwards, tripped and fell, the base of his skull connecting sharply with a pillar—

Will speared a short sword into the nearest man's kidney, knowing that even if he lived through it, the wound would cripple him for enough time to allow an escape. He glanced up as Talan fell like a bundle of rags, surely dead. His killer made the mistake of stopping to survey his handiwork, unaware for a fatal second that someone was behind him.

Will wiped his blades on the body of the second man and stopped to listen. Outside, he thought he could hear voices, though he wasn't sure he recognised them. He decided to lie low for a while and take in the atmosphere. No sense in them all dying after all.

Courtesy demanded that he be sure Talan was dead, though it seemed a mere formality; the warrior hadn't moved. Will took a place towards him and heard a door open behind. He spun round, blades ready, and for the second time in a matter of minutes, his eyes widened. Even as he backed away, the excuse was forming on his lips.

Alun had reached the big open room. It was cold and dark but he could see a shattered chair and the door was open at the other end. There was fighting and he could hear shouting. He could hear it all around him. His sword hung limp from his hand. He had absolutely no idea what to do. At least he understood the look that Hirad had given him when he talked about the Rage. Not contempt, but worry. And a lack of confidence in him. He sat in a plush chair and shook all over.

Travers didn't wait for the outcome. He shambled back down the narrow passage and opened the door to the main corridor on the upper level. He had walked out and shut it behind him when he was attacked. From the stairs dead ahead it flew like an arrow and with a flurry of leathery wings, spiked tail and fangs it hit him. Its claws tangled in his hair, its tail coiled around his left arm and its face appeared, upside down, in front of his own. It was no larger than a market monkey.

He recoiled but the face came right back with him. He would have sworn it was smiling but it couldn't be human. Indeed, he knew it was not human and the stench of its breath chilled his spine. Yet he could not take his eyes off it.

It was completely hairless, its scalp taut and shining, its brain pulsing in its skull, sending rivulets of movement through the veins in its face. It cocked its head slightly to one side and then it did smile, revealing upper and lower sets of needle teeth that knitted as its mouth closed, but not before its pointed tongue had darted out to lick Travers' mouth.

He thought he would vomit but its eyes held him in thrall. They were black and sunk into hard ovals of bone. And deep. Deep enough to fall into and drown in the depths of his terror. Travers could feel his heart pounding as he stared at the thing, its flat slits of nostrils sucking in air, its tiny ears pricking at the slightest sound.

And then its hands came down and gripped his cheeks, its claws digging deep, bringing blood to his face. It leaned in closer, firing its stinking breath into his eyes. He blinked and tried to lean away.

'Come,' it said. Its voice rattled in his throat, soft like an old man's yet brimful of malice. Travers shivered and squirmed, hanging on desperately to his bowels. 'Walk with me.'

'Where?' he managed. Again it smiled – a hideous movement. Travers closed his eyes but it was still there, etched in his mind.

'My Master demands your presence. It is not far. Walk.' The face disappeared but the talons tightened in his hair. Its tail constricted his right arm, which was held up and away from his scabbard so that his forearm dangled parallel to his face.

Travers began to walk, knowing with complete certainty that it was the last one he would ever take.

Alun came to his senses with a start that made his head spin. He could hear fighting above him, the sounds of men dying. And some of them were fighting and dying for him. His boys were in here. His wife was in here.

He stood up, an anger as pure as a virgin's kiss flooding his body. He wanted to make someone pay for the anguish and loss they'd put him through. The days like months, the months like years. But today it would end and his sword would spill blood for the first time.

They'd be held upstairs, of this much he was certain. He ran to the open door and took the stairs at a sprint, pausing when he reached the top. Someone was at the other end of the corridor and walking towards him, something on his head. He ran towards them, the man never once focusing on him. He stopped again and raised his sword to strike but then locked eyes with the cat he'd seen Hirad carrying. Something in those eyes stopped him cutting the man down and instead they turned him to look at the door at the end of the corridor.

Alun nodded and ran on again, dimly aware of fighting to his right and the flap of wings behind him. His trophy was close. He could feel them. Gods, he could almost smell them! They were his boys and he would rescue them.

He stormed through the door and up the narrow passageway, bursting into the guardroom and all but knocking the solitary guard from his seat. Before he could react, Alun opened his throat with a furious swing and, not daring to think about what he had just done, clattered up the spiral staircase.

She came at him, a rage of blonde hair in a shabby and torn dark nightshirt, her arms outstretched, hands gripping at his shoulders.

'My boys?' she shouted, eyes darting all over his face. 'Have you got my boys?'

Thraun shook his head. 'No . . .' he began, but she was past him, screaming.

'Fools. They'll kill them. They said they'd kill them!' She flew down the stairs, across the room and out into the corridor, Thraun right behind her. She tore left and through a door into a narrow passageway. There was a cry from up ahead, then a clash of swords. Erienne increased her pace.

'Come on, Selik, killing me would serve no purpose. I mean, I still owe you.' Will backed up further, knowing there was a door a few paces behind him. He sent a prayer that it was not locked.

'Yes you do. Once it was just money, and now it's your life.' Selik ducked under the doorframe. Will swallowed hard. The equation was simple: if the door behind him was locked, he would die. He slid back another step.

Selik was Will's greatest mistake. He'd seen a farmer's boy who'd be an easy take and he'd never been more wrong. He'd owed the gifted swordsman ever since.

'I've got a lot of money coming, Selik. All I need is a little more time.'

'You have never fooled me, Begman, and you never will, because time is something you just don't have any more.' Selik advanced, drawing his sword. 'Try and offer some resistance.'

'I don't think so,' said Will. He turned and ran for the door, yanked it open and headed for the stairs, his relief turning to dismay as Selik barred his way, appearing from the door Talan had used earlier. The Black Wing shook his head. Will skidded to a stop and fled in the other direction, racing through the first door he found. It let into a narrow passageway and he heard voices ahead. One was female. He ran on. It was too late to turn anyway, and company was about the only chance he had.

Alun hauled open the door at the top of the spiral staircase, rushing in to live his dream but discovering his waking nightmare.

A man stood with his back to him, leaning over a double bed on which two children lay, the blood and their stillness telling its own story. Alun's breath caught in his throat, his legs weakened and his sword point struck the floor as his arm lost the strength to hold it aloft.

He'd contemplated no other scene but his boys rushing into his arms, their faces alight, their mouths chattering identical delightful gibberish, their bodies warm against his face. But they would be silent for ever. He couldn't move, not in or out, until the man turned, talking as he came.

'I was just making sure they were de—'

Alun mouthed the word 'you' and attacked with his sword, his feet his hands, his teeth – a frenzy of raw fury. The guard fell back, fielding blow after blow on stained dagger blade and armoured forearm, taking cuts, bruises and scrapes all over his body. But Alun's frenzy had no clear purpose and one wild sweep of his blade left him hopelessly exposed. The guard simply swayed inside and stabbed him through the heart.

Relief flooded Alun's dying mind, his children called him and he thought he heard the man say sorry.

Isman's face loomed in Ilkar's field of vision and once more the mage found himself wishing it was all over. The sounds of combat were distant yet intrusive in Ilkar's ears and he wanted them to stop.

'And now you, Ilkar of The Raven.' Ilkar merely raised his eyebrows and waited for the blow which never came. Instead, with a startled grunt, Isman fell to his knees, then on to his back, an arrow puncturing his right eye.

There was the sound of footsteps coming towards, past and then back to him and finally Ilkar saw another face, this one a stranger. An elf.

'Who are you?'

'Jandyr. No time for talking. Hirad needs help. You are a mage, I take it.'

'Hirad is dead,' said Ilkar, a cold dread filling his heart as he uttered the words.

'No, he is not. Not yet.'

It wasn't until he sat bolt upright that a searing pain reminded Ilkar his lung was torn by his broken ribs. It was going to be a flip of a coin who died first.

Thraun barged past Erienne as they entered the guardroom and was first on to the spiral stairs. At the top, he found Alun's body and a man staring at him, confusion all over his face.

'Oh no,' said the man.

'Oh yes,' said Thraun and swept his blade through the man's ribs, where it lodged in his spine, sending new blood spraying over the corpses of the boys. He wrenched his sword clear and took in the charnel house the moment before Erienne reached the door to see her slaughtered family.

'I—' began Thraun, but the look in her eyes silenced him as surely as a blow. She stepped over Alun, not sparing him a glance as she moved to the bed, Thraun edging aside to guard the door.

Erienne said nothing. She reached a steady hand to each of her children, smoothed matted hair from their faces, stroked their cheeks and brushed her fingers over their lips.

Thraun gazed at her, pity clashing with admiration at her bearing. But then she turned and if fury had been light, he would have been blinded by it. The air around her seemed to crackle, almost bend as her eyes sucked it in. Her mouth, a thin line below her nose, was still, but beneath, the skin of her cheeks moved as her jaws pressed together over and over.

The sound of running footsteps brought Thraun to himself and he swung to face the door, sword ready.

'Stand aside.' Erienne's voice, like the sounding of a death bell, brooked no argument, and Thraun took a pace backwards. He turned to her, saw her hands, palms together in front of her face, felt the room chill and smelt frost.

The power was frightening and his pulse quickened. He tore his eyes away and focused again on the doorway. Feet clattered on the spiral staircase, then another set, the sound of laboured breathing, a shadow and then a figure, small, wiry and scared. Talan's heart missed a beat.

'Erienne, wait!' But her hands were outstretched and the spell was ready. Her eyes snapped open, her mouth framed the command word and the room temperature plummeted.

'Will, duck! Get down!' Thraun threw himself at Will's legs, bringing him down in a confused heap. Erienne's IceWind roared over both their heads, catching Selik square in the chest as he reached the door. The warrior staggered back a pace, dropped his weapon then collapsed, lips blue, eyes glass, hands white, shattering to a thousand fragments as he hit the ground.

Thraun clambered to his feet, hauling Will with him. Erienne brushed past them and started down the stairway.

'Erienne, wait,' said Thraun, but she shook her head, not pausing in her stride.

'Travers is next.'

Chapter 16

Ilkar wept. He didn't know how, but Hirad was still alive. The wound in his stomach was deep and surely fatal, yet he wasn't dead. And now Ilkar would have to sit and watch him fade into the grave because Travers had taken away his capacity to save him.

Even if he and Denser had uninterrupted sleep for a dozen hours, it was debatable whether they would have the combined strength to heal him, such was the damage to all three of them.

And so he knelt by Hirad, his hands on that awful wound, ignoring his own pain as he fed mana directly into his friend's broken, mercifully unconscious body while his tears dampened his cheeks and dripped to the cold stone floor. It would keep him alive for now, but Ilkar was so weak himself he knew it was ultimately hopeless.

He felt a hand on his shoulder.

'Ilkar, I share your pain.' He hadn't heard Denser move. He'd assumed him already deep in restoring sleep.

'I can't save him, Denser,' said Ilkar. His voice, cracked by his sobs, was rendered unsteady from sheer fatigue. 'He's going and I can't save him.'

'There might be a way.' Denser's voice too was barely recognisable. His battered face stopped him framing his words with anything close to accuracy.

'And what would you suggest, Xetesk man? There's no magic wand we can wave!' Ilkar jabbed the words out, coughed and spat blood.

'But there is another mage in this castle.'

'Erienne,' said Jandyr.

'The bitch that betrayed us,' said Ilkar.

'No,' said Jandyr firmly. 'She was forced. Travers took her sons too. We came to get them all.'

'Erienne Malanvai?' asked Denser. 'Dordovan Lore Scribe?'

'Yes.'

'That could prove a very useful piece of fortune.' He frowned. 'What the hell did he want with her?' He shook his head and turned his attention to the elf. 'How long before you die?' Ilkar looked up at Denser and shook his head. 'How long, Ilkar?'

The elf shrugged. 'Three hours, perhaps a little more.'

Denser grunted and immediately sat behind Ilkar, his legs straddling the Julatsan.

'Lean into me,' he ordered. Ilkar lay back. Denser turned them so they were both facing the same way as Hirad, Ilkar having to reach to his right to touch the barbarian's wound.

'Now stretch out your legs,' said Denser and, with wincing stiffness, Ilkar did.

Jandyr gazed on, confused. There sat Denser, his hands now on Ilkar's shoulders, while Ilkar himself lay propped in Denser's lap, his hands probing Hirad's stomach ceaselessly.

'What's going on?' he asked.

'I'll explain later,' said Denser. 'Bring a chair. Place it supporting my back. Now, Ilkar, exactly what is it that's going to kill you?'

'A combination. My right lung is punctured, it's filling with blood and may collapse. My kidneys are too bruised to function correctly and I believe my liver is also bleeding.'

'Very well.' Denser adjusted his hand positions, moving one to the base of Ilkar's skull and placing the other over the right side of the elf's chest. 'Release control to me. Feed your mana into Hirad.'

'And you?' Ilkar's wave of gratitude was tinted by a virgin worry over the Xeteskian's condition.

Denser managed a chuckle. 'They beat every inch, but little is broken except toes and fingers. I am in no danger.'

'Thank you.' Ilkar's voice shook.

'There is a wider purpose.'

'Thank you anyway.'

Denser said nothing, merely squeezed Ilkar's neck a moment before turning to Jandyr. 'We need the other mage. Every second is critical.'

Jandyr nodded. 'They'll have her by now. I'll bring them in.' He made to move, but the far doors opened and in walked Travers, the cat perched on his head. The Captain's eyes were glazed, his stance bent and stooped as if he had aged twenty years in the few minutes he was out of the room.

Denser smiled. 'I see you found my pet.'

Travers came to his senses as the cat jumped to the ground and trotted to Denser. He took in the scene, his eyes travelling over Isman's body and the strange tableau presented by The Raven trio. He frowned.

'I thought—'

'You are no longer important, Travers, you are nothing. The chain you are wearing, however, is everything.' Travers groped inside his shirt, his frown deepening. Denser caught Jandyr's eye. 'I think you should stand outside, you don't want to see this.' Jandyr paused, a dubious look on his face, then walked from the room, another arrow ready in his bow.

'Please . . .' Travers took a pace towards Denser, who ignored him, locking eyes with the cat.

'Kill him.' The cat changed, and Travers' pleas turned to a blubbering fear. Denser looked at him a last time.

'You thought to tame The Raven. So did I. But it can't be done. At least I will be alive to atone for my error.' There was a slavering sound next to him. 'Thank the Gods we beat you. At least Balaia still has a chance to save itself.'

Denser's demon streaked across the space between him and Travers.

'Close your eyes, Ilkar,' said Denser.

The Captain screamed.

Jandyr fought the desire to open the door. Travers' cries sourced from a fear deeper than any man should touch but, thankfully, were cut off quickly. The elf heard a sound akin to a melon hitting the floor. He fought equally hard not to vomit.

He turned at the sound of hurrying footsteps descending the stairs opposite. He stretched his bow but relaxed it as he saw a woman, Erienne surely, moving towards him flanked by Thraun and Will.

'Get out of my way,' said Erienne, trying to push past him. Jandyr grabbed her by the upper arms and restrained her.

'You can't go in there. Not yet.' He looked past her at Thraun. 'Stop her while I check what's happening.' Thraun took Erienne, who made just one attempt to break his grip.

'You can't protect Travers for ever.' She grated the words out, the fire in her eyes bright and hard.

'I can assure you we are not protecting him,' said Jandyr.

'What's going on, Jan?' asked Will.

'The Raven are in there, three of them at any rate. So was Travers, but I think he's dead now.'

'Think?' hissed Erienne.

'They wouldn't let me remain to see.' He paused. 'Hirad's hurt. He's dying. The Raven mages want you to help.' He nodded at Erienne, then turned to the door. 'Wait a moment.'

He peered inside. All was still save the pool of blood expanding slowly from beneath the blanket that covered Travers' head and upper body. Denser and Ilkar hadn't moved from Hirad's side and the cat lay curled on the chair supporting Denser's back, cleaning its paws and whiskers.

The elf walked back into the room, holding the door for the others. As one, they stopped to take in what they were seeing. Only Erienne understood, and she walked slowly towards Denser. She paused, sampling the movement in the mana.

'Well, well, well. A Julatsan and a Xeteskian joined in a mana drip for a dying man. I've surely seen everything now.' Her voice was cold but the dampness on her face gave away a fraction of what she felt inside.

'I wish we could have met under easier circumstances,' said Denser.

'*Easier!*' she screamed. 'My children are dead, you bastard! Dead. I should bleed the lot of you where you sit.'

Denser looked up and around, catching Thraun's eye. The man nodded.

'It's true,' he said. 'One of the guards cut their throats.'

'And all because your people wanted to save you,' managed Erienne, sobs now racking her body. 'My life has been taken and there was nothing I could do.' She sagged into Thraun's strong grasp. He supported her to a chair. 'I wasn't even there . . . they died alone.'

'Take your time, Erienne,' said Thraun. 'Take your time.' He smoothed her hair.

'Please,' said Denser. 'We don't have long. Hirad is dying.' Erienne dragged her hands from her face, her eyes, red and swelling, driving into his.

'And you think I should care?' She stood and walked over to him, looking down in disgust. 'You know why I was taken? Because Xetesk started a search for Dawnthief and Travers thought I could help him control it. My boys are dead because of you and your College. Well, Denser the great Dawnthief mage, I might just sit and watch your friend die. At least that's a choice I can make, unlike the one to save my children.' Her chin wobbled again and fresh tears sprang into her eyes. She turned away.

Denser framed an apology but anything he came up with would have been woefully inadequate. Instead he said, 'Xetesk doesn't want Dawnthief for itself.'

'Drop dead, Denser, I don't believe you.' Erienne walked back to her chair and sat.

Denser breathed deep, beaten muscles protesting. 'You have to believe me. The Wytch Lords have escaped the mana prison and are back in Parve. Dawnthief is the only way to destroy them and stop eighty thousand Wesmen tearing our land apart.' She looked at him again, brow creased. 'Please, Erienne. No one can touch the suffering you must be experiencing, but you can save Hirad. If we are to defeat the Wytch Lords, we must have him.'

'Why?'

'Because he leads The Raven and they are recovering the spell. Without him, we won't be strong enough.' Denser coughed, a line of blood dribbling from the corner of his mouth.

Erienne half laughed. 'That's one hell of a story,' she said. 'And what do you say, Ilkar? Or I presume you are Ilkar, the Raven mage?'

'I believe him,' said Ilkar, his voice soft and weak.

Erienne raised her eyebrows. 'Really? Well, that is impressive.' She walked stiffly to the doors, not bothering to wipe her cheeks. 'You know I didn't have the power of life over my children, but I have it over you. Or death,' said Erienne. 'My children need me.'

'Think hard, Erienne,' said Denser to her back. 'And get rest. Replenish yourself. Right now, the fate of Balaia is in your hands.'

Erienne paused and turned to Denser. He managed to catch her eye and hold it. 'I mean it,' he said.

She left the room, Thraun shadowing her all the way.

'It's going to be a long night,' said Denser.

Ilkar stirred, wincing. He opened his eyes and looked around blearily.

'Where are the others?' he asked.

'Who?' Will walked towards him.

'Talan and Richmond.'

Will's gaze flicked to Denser and he bit his lip. Denser felt a new weight settle on his heart.

'I saw Talan fall. I don't know about Richmond but, well, he's not here. I'm sorry.' Will shrugged.

Ilkar shook his head slowly and refocused on Hirad. The barbarian's breathing was shallow but he was stable for now. Ilkar only hoped there was a point to it all. Denser could keep him alive and he could keep Hirad alive for perhaps another twelve hours, but that was all they could do. The efficiency of the beatings administered by Travers' men had seen to that. Then, the mana, the last drops that even Travers couldn't take from them, would be gone. And when the support went, the final nails would be in place and The Raven would be lost for ever.

Denser squeezed his shoulder. 'She will help us. Just hang on.'

'There's nothing else I can do,' said Ilkar. 'He's all I've got.' He looked at Hirad's face, still and calm. 'Just you and me now, old friend. Don't even think of dying without me.'

He would have lapsed back into his semi-trance, his mind roving in Hirad's ruined stomach to feel where his trickle of life-sustaining mana could do most good, but the bottom doors opened and in walked joy and sorrow in equal measure.

A little unsteady on his feet but very much alive, Talan entered the room. Will and Jandyr relaxed their stances; Will smiled. So did Ilkar for a moment. But his euphoria was quashed as easily as it had arisen. In Talan's arms, his legs limp from the supported knees, head lolling and arms hanging, was Richmond. The fact of his lifeless body was etched in Talan's grim face. The warrior laid his friend on the nearest table.

'This is one Vigil too far,' he said. 'It must . . .' His eyes, so far locked on Ilkar, moved to capture Hirad. A look of pure panic swamped his grief. 'Oh no,' he said, his voice leaden. 'Please God, no.' He started to move but Denser's voice stopped him and the relief he felt at the mage's words robbed his legs of their remaining strength and he sat heavily.

'He is still alive,' said the Xeteskian. 'And we can keep him that way for the time being.'

'And then what?' Talan felt disquiet at Denser's tone.

'Erienne, I hope. She represents Hirad's only chance.'

'What do you mean, "I hope"?' Talan probed the back of his head, felt the swelling, the crusted blood, the matted hair.

'Her sons are dead, her life, she believes, is over and she holds The Raven to blame.'

'And if she doesn't help?' Talan's face suggested he knew the answer. Ilkar merely confirmed his fears. And worse.

'Hirad will die,' he said. 'And so, I am afraid, will I.' The Julatsan offered Talan a bleak raising of the eyebrows, then his mind once more was lost to Hirad's desperate cause.

Talan put a hand to his mouth and massaged his bottom lip, the thudding at the back of his skull forgotten as he contemplated a far grimmer reality. It was laid in front of him yet he still refused to completely believe. And at the same time he knew there was no doubt. Ilkar always called things as he saw them and he'd just called the end. Possibly. The key was Erienne. She had to be made to understand. He stood up.

'Where are you going?' asked Denser.

'Where's Erienne?' demanded Talan.

'You can't help by confronting her,' said Denser.

'And what would you know?' shouted Talan. 'Is it your friends dying in front of your eyes? I don't think so. The Raven has been taken down for the first time and it could get even worse. She has to understand the consequences—'

'She knows.' Ilkar's voice was dark with fatigue. 'We have to trust that her mage instincts will override her grief before it is too late. We've done all we can.' He breathed in, a ragged sound full of pain. 'Please, no more noise. This is hard enough already.'

'We could all do with some food, I'm sure,' said Denser. 'The kitchen's—'

'I know where it is.' Jandyr went in search of sustenance, partly in response to Denser's request but mainly to get out of the room. The intensity of hurt, of grief and of loss was all but tangible. He found it oppressive. Closing the door on it, he could breathe freely again. He stepped past two bodies and made his way to the range.

Ilkar probed with his mind and fingers, allowing the mana to ease from him in life-sustaining pulses. Isman's sword had driven deep, lacerating and severing Hirad's intestines in half a dozen places. Its point had nicked his spine but there was no other damage to his back. The main worry stemmed from the upward trajectory of the thrust, taking the blade through the barbarian's stomach. His digestive system was in total collapse, his multiple internal cuts needed constant attention and Ilkar was just waiting for his kidneys to fail.

A WarmHeal wouldn't be enough – two or three, carefully targeted, might do the job but he wasn't sure Hirad had that much time. The simple fact was that Hirad needed a BodyCast and Ilkar knew of only three mages who could cast it in reasonable safety. None of them was in this castle.

With Hirad tended for the moment, Ilkar turned his mind on himself. He could feel the mana pulse and drip from Denser's hands. Over his chest, the gentle flow had stopped the bleeding in his lung, relieving his breathing, while from the base of his neck, pulse after pulse of mana fled down his veins to caress his most damaged internal organs.

Ilkar sent a prayer of thanks that in this one way at least, the Colleges would forever be united – every mage had the ability to use tiny amounts of mana to maintain a body in whatever condition it was found and indeed were morally bound to do so. Nevertheless,

Ilkar had still found Denser's actions surprising. Perhaps he shouldn't have.

Time crawled. Ilkar was dimly aware of strong daylight edging around the heavy drapes, and of being fed soup. But as the hours wore on, Hirad required more and more of his concentration and the world beyond faded.

He was tiring, he knew that. It was evident in the return of pain in his back, arms and legs. Denser couldn't cover it all. His mana remained where it would keep Ilkar alive. But the Julatsan's mana reserves were stretched, and as they became ever more so, he demanded yet greater input from Denser.

There would come a point when neither of them could suppress the pain in their own bodies as their mana was all directed elsewhere. Then, the end would be near. Then, Erienne would have to help, or he and Hirad would die.

Styliann relaxed, smiling to himself as he recovered from the communion. He pictured Selyn in his mind, saw her body arching with pleasure, all but felt the caress of her lips and the gentle touch of her hands. Her return would signal a change. He needed a son.

But for now, she travelled deep in Wesmen-held lands towards Parve and the almost certain confirmation of the fear the four Colleges had harboured ever since the Wytch Lords' banishment. A return. And a return to a power greater than before, harder to stop and impossible to vanquish. That is, without Dawnthief. Because the Colleges were no longer as strong and their armies no longer as big. Without the spell, everything would be lost.

Concealing herself during the daytime and flying on ShadowWings for parts of the night, Selyn was making swift and safe progress towards the edge of the Torn Wastes. She would reach its boundaries in three days, Parve itself in four. He could expect his next communion with her in five. It was going to be a hard time. This was danger like she had never faced before. And he would see to it that she never had to face it again.

His mind wandered and he glanced out of his study window, tracing the outlines of Nyer's and Laryon's Towers. Nyer's man had breached Septern's workshop but had not held communion with his Master since then. Apparently. Styliann felt he was not being fed all the information. That irritated him a great deal.

He smiled again. Everyone trusted Laryon. The worker, the genius, the friend. Perhaps it was time to take the new member of the circle a little closer in. Styliann couldn't track Nyer's moves or question him further without arousing suspicion. Laryon, on the other hand, would have no such problem. Styliann reached out his hand and pulled the bell chain by the fire. The wine he ordered would come with two glasses.

Time had become an irrelevant quantity for Ilkar long before Hirad's kidneys finally failed. They went one after the other in quick succession, forcing the Julatsan to abandon all remaining sedation of his own body as his fight to save Hirad reached its last desperate stage.

'Denser,' he mumbled.

'I know,' said Denser.

'Where is she?'

'She's coming. Hang on.' Denser pulsed mana through Ilkar's bruised back, the sense of relief serving only to heighten his awareness of his pain.

And so it had come to this. Hirad was dying, fading fast. Ilkar took everything he had and fed it into the barbarian's failing body. He was forced to ignore one kidney, letting it bleed and drain as he concentrated on the other. And all the time, his own cracked, bruised and aching body yelled for relief. His broken right arm sent waves of nausea through his head, his lower back seared as if it were atop a fire and his legs felt as though hammers pounded them up and down their length.

But it was a relief he was unable to grant himself – unless he let Hirad die. Nor could he ask it of Denser. The Xeteskian was already keeping him alive with almost his entire mana stream. Ilkar couldn't fail to note the gasping breaths Denser was taking with increasing regularity. It was clear he had been less than honest with his assessment of his own injuries.

'How long, Ilkar?'

'Me or him?' Ilkar gritted.

'Isn't it one and the same thing?' Denser's voice was appallingly tired.

'Not quite. He's got less than an hour. It's his kidneys.' And then, so suddenly that Ilkar had to think to maintain his flow to the barbarian, a new, strong anaesthetising warmth moved through him and he knew she had come. The warmth travelled on into Hirad, following his mana trails.

'You're being generous.' A woman's voice sounded very close to his ear. 'He has little more than half an hour. You are unaware of the gravity of your own state.'

As suddenly as it had come, the warmth was gone and pain engulfed Ilkar once more.

'Well?' asked Denser.

'It can be done.' The woman's voice again.

'Both of them?'

'If you can hold on to the Julatsan. If that's what you want.'

'That's what I want.'

'There will be a price.'

'I understand.'

'I hope that you do.'

Ilkar shook his head. A price between a Dordovan and a Xeteskian. Still. As Denser had said earlier, there was a wider purpose. The warmth returned, tracing into Hirad's body.

'Release him to me, Ilkar,' said Erienne.

'I—'

'You must,' she urged. 'Or Denser may not be able to save you.'

Ilkar knew she was right. With one last pulse, he withdrew from Hirad, taking his hands from the barbarian's stomach and focusing inside at the ruins of his own body.

He shut off the pain, feeling Denser put a hand on his forehead. Slowly, the world dimmed to peace and he was adrift.

Erienne scanned Hirad's body and sighed. She should let the man die. In front of her was one of the reasons her sons were dead. The leader of The Raven. It would be fitting for him to die too. It would redress the balance just a little.

But Denser had seen into her when he had asked for her help. Knew she would be too fascinated by the prospect of Dawnthief to refuse him. And knew she could not refuse her calling. But her healer's code did not stop her striking bargains for the lives of those she was asked to save. And this time, the bargain might just give her a reason to carry on herself. Same goal, new subject, and Denser's seed would be ideal. It would, of course, be all for nothing should Hirad and Ilkar die. She bent her mind to the immediate problem. For Hirad, a BodyCast was his only hope. It would take more than twenty minutes to prepare. As she began, she prayed he would last that long.

From the well of his agony, Hirad fought to rise. Somewhere, far above, the heat was calling him. He didn't realise he'd fallen so deep and he didn't think he could climb back. *Try, Hirad, try.* A voice penetrated his unconscious. A woman. He tried.

Chapter 17

The next thing that assaulted Ilkar's senses was a smell, cloying, with a sweet after-taste. Pipe smoke.

He was lying down, still in the big room, and the view afforded him when he opened his eyes revealed nothing but a ceiling lit by bright sunlight. It was a fuzzy view and he lay listening to the quiet while his eyes found their focus. Erienne had saved him. He was tired, dull aches flagging his more serious injuries, but he knew he was no longer in any danger. It was a good feeling.

He pushed himself up on his elbows and there was Denser. The Xeteskian sat on a chair with his feet on a table, legs outstretched. His face, what Ilkar could see of it, still bore the scars of his beating but, dressed in his familiar black and with skull cap in his lap, he looked pretty much like the old Denser. His pipe smoked gently in his mouth, a steaming mug sat on the table by him and the cat lay on his thighs, curled and asleep.

'Never in my wildest dreams did I think I'd be pleased to see a Xeteskian.'

Denser laughed, and his movement woke the cat, who yawned, stretched and leapt to the ground. The mage took his feet from the table and ambled over to Ilkar.

'And good morning to you, Ilkar. Or should I say good mornings?'

'I don't know, should you?'

'There have been two so far.'

'Hirad?'

Denser smiled. 'See for yourself.' He indicated to Ilkar's left before returning to the table to swap his pipe for his mug.

Ilkar looked where Denser indicated and for a brief, dreadful moment knew that Hirad was dead. But then his chest rose and fell, gently and smoothly. It was a quite wonderful sight. Hirad was lying, like Ilkar, on firm bedding, his head propped on a pillow and his body covered to his bare chest with blankets. A mound around his midriff told of heavy bandaging beneath. He looked pale, but that hardly mattered. Ilkar's heart flared with joy and tears came unbidden to his eyes. He wiped them away.

'Uh—' he began.

'You are allowed to get up,' said Denser. 'Come and have a mug of coffee.'

Ilkar nodded and moved slowly to a sitting position, holding himself as the blood rush hit his head, threatening to knock him down.

'Are you all right?' asked Denser.

'I think,' said Ilkar, 'that I'll take that drink sitting here.'

Denser chuckled and ambled over to the kitchen door. He leaned through it.

'Talan? Stop chopping and bring a coffee through. There's someone you'd like to talk to.'

There was the clatter of a knife on a hard surface, a few footsteps and then Talan loped in, spilling coffee as he came.

'Ilkar!' He practically threw the mug into the elf's hands. 'You don't know how good you look!'

'Steady,' grinned Ilkar. 'Thanks for this. How's everything?'

Talan became solemn. 'I conducted Richmond's Vigil alone. He's buried in the garden near the stables.'

Ilkar nodded, sipped from his mug. 'I'm sorry.'

'So am I.'

'And what about him?' Ilkar inclined his head in Hirad's direction.

Talan sat on the bed next to him. 'I've got to tell you, it was amazing,' he said, brightening a little. 'The woman, Erienne, she's sleeping I think. Denser said she used a BodyCast, is it?' Ilkar nodded. 'All over him. I could *feel* it, a deep warmth. It shifted as she moved her hands, it went in his mouth, his ears, his nose . . . she was with him for hours.'

Ilkar nodded again, glanced up at Denser.

'BodyCast, eh?'

'Textbook preparation. She's good, Ilkar. Powerful. From what Thraun said, she used an IceWind too.' Denser raised his eyebrows, drained his mug and wandered into the kitchen for a refill.

Talan leaned in closer. 'And he now commands my complete admiration.'

'Oh?' Ilkar bridled in spite of himself; an inbred reaction.

'Erienne rested after the BodyCast. Then she used another spell to finish the job and make Hirad sleep. Then she rested again before seeing to Denser. Two days in all. He just sat there and kept you alive. Said hardly anything. Just ate a little, drank a little.'

'I appreciate the sacrifice he had to make,' said Ilkar, yet he had been unaware of the extent of Denser's effort and was reeling inside.

'They'd broken his jaw, fractured his cheeks, smashed his nose, broken most of his fingers and toes and cracked half a dozen ribs. He must have been in total agony the whole time. You owe him.' Talan shook his head. Ilkar gaped. The door opened and Denser walked back in. He smiled, and it was then that Ilkar noticed the cat at his feet.

'It is a debt I will never call in,' said Denser. 'It is merely what had to be done.'

'Whatever you say,' said Ilkar. 'I'm lost for words of thanks.'

'You are alive and talking, Julatsan, that is thanks enough.' Embarrassed, Denser stalked to the other doors, heading for the hallway, his cat in close attendance..

Later that day, standing one to either side of him, Ilkar and Talan helped Hirad to his feet. The barbarian was ready for the pain and nausea that swept his body as the newly knit muscles of his stomach strained and protested. Another WarmHeal, Erienne said, and he'd be fit to ride tomorrow – three days after he'd entered the castle on the crest of a Rage.

He gazed down at Richmond's grave. The Raven symbol still scorched proud on the packed earth. His feelings were mixed but dominated by one of inevitability. Ras, Sirendor, The Unknown, Richmond. Had The Raven died with them? Only he, Talan and Ilkar were left and he questioned whether that was enough. He decided that while any of the founder members lived, it was. They had always expected to evolve as men died, or left, and others joined. It was an insult to the memories of those who had gone to let The Raven pass into history.

But who would be next to die? Clearly, it should have been him, and the stories of his salvation by the three mages had turned his view of their whole order in general and Denser in particular. He still didn't trust the man further than he could spit, but he had to admire his fortitude and sheer determination. Denser also had his gratitude – so did Erienne, but she wouldn't catch his eye, far less speak to him.

He looked across at her, kneeling, as through almost her every waking hour since their burials, at the graves of her family. That of Alun, Erienne ignored, but those of her sons commanded her unswerving attention. He felt for her but knew he could never articulate how, because she would not listen.

And here, standing by him, was the man for whom no level of

admiration could ever be enough. Ilkar would have died with him – indeed, had chosen to do so, had Erienne not healed them both. Loyalty in battle he could readily understand but this was something more. He felt a lump in his throat, swallowed it away and crushed Ilkar to him with the arm slung round the mage's shoulder for support.

'We all set?'

Ilkar nodded. 'We've enough fit horses, including all of our own, the bodies are all destroyed and Will has rigged the castle. He's a clever bastard, I'll give him that.'

'Very effective,' agreed Talan.

Will, in response to Hirad's desire to see the castle razed to the ground, had devised a way of doing so while allowing them to be half a day's ride away when it happened.

'Better your enemies are attracted to the beacon when you're not there,' he'd said.

And now, all but the kitchens and banqueting room, where they'd spent so much time, were no-go areas. Oil soaked drapes, rugs, furnishings, books and timbers. Lines of oil criss-crossed the castle from top to bottom, piles of wood and kindling were placed in strategic areas and, where Will wanted flash flame – in the towers and the entrance hall – mountains of dry flour sat awaiting ignition.

All but Hirad and Erienne had worked to his direction while he had either patrolled the castle, ensuring all was laid to his exact specification, or sat laboriously testing myriad styles of long-burn fuse. Rope, oil and tar were mixed in minutely changing quantities then set alight to be timed for their burn by the beating of Will's heart. At last, satisfied, he had manufactured yards of a material about as thick as his thumb and placed one upstairs and one down.

'All that's left is to saddle up and pack the horses and prime the last couple of rooms tomorrow morning. Will and Thraun will light the fuses and then we're away.'

'Good. I know Denser's anxious about the time we've lost,' said Hirad.

'He's not the only one,' returned Ilkar.

'And how's she reacted to us travelling to Dordover to plunder one of her ancient's tombs?'

Ilkar smiled. 'Good question. All I can say is that whatever deal it was they struck, it's important enough to her not to betray us.' He paused, reflecting. 'I don't know. She knows a good deal about Dawnthief and she certainly believes Denser.'

'And the others?' said Hirad.

Ilkar shrugged. 'They are good-quality people, Hirad. Thraun is a born swordsman. Erienne is a well-known magical talent, Jandyr gives us the bowman we've always wanted, and Will, well, he's quick and clever. They balance the team, Talan and I swore them into the Code and, in your absence, accepted them into The Raven. I know it's not how we really do things but we haven't the time to assess them in any more action and we need to know that they'll follow you without question. I'm confident they will. Talan?'

'I agree.' Talan nodded, though his eyes were distant. 'Your only doubt is Will, but I think Thraun can keep him under control. Erienne's grief might make her unpredictable, too. Watch out for that.'

'They've signed the current job contract and they know what they're getting thennselves into,' continued Ilkar. 'Denser has told them the whole gory story and they didn't find it too hard to accept. It's the choice we were never allowed to make, isn't it? They survive, they're rich, if not, well, the money's not important then, is it?'

Hirad raised his eyebrows. 'True enough.' He felt tired. 'I think I'd better amble back inside, lie down for a while.'

The Raven trio walked slowly back to the courtyard at the front of the house. At the door, which faced the open gates, Talan stopped them.

'Look,' he said. 'There's no easy way to say this, but I can't go any further. I'm leaving The Raven.'

Ilkar and Hirad weighed his words in silence. He carried on.

'We were very close, me, Ras and Richmond. Joining and fighting for The Raven was the pinnacle for us. But two corners of the triangle are gone now and next time, it'll be me. It hit me when I found Richmond . . . he died alone.' He sighed and scratched his head. 'I'm sorry, I'm not explaining this very well. I don't know . . . inside me the desire isn't there suddenly. The fire has gone out. Richmond's was a Vigil too far and I'm not prepared to bury another member of The Raven.'

Hirad said nothing, only nodded. Ilkar's face clouded, his eyes narrowing as his frown deepened.

'Do you understand?' Talan asked. 'Say something, one of you.'

'Yes, I do,' said Hirad. 'When I was alone with Sirendor, just looking at his dead face, I was ready to break my blade. I chose not to and I'm only sorry you can't do the same.' Hirad lowered himself to the steps, Ilkar reflexively offering a helping hand.

'Is that all you're going to say?' demanded the Julatsan.

Hirad shrugged. 'What else is there? If his heart isn't with us then he's a liability and we're better off without him. He knows it, I know it and so do you, Ilkar.'

'Under normal circumstances, yes, but in case it's slipped your attention, we are not involved in just any old job. And I have to say that he will be much more of a liability away from us than with us.'

'I hardly think so—' began Talan.

'They know you!' snapped Ilkar. 'They know what you look like, where you come from and they'll be after what you know. Gods, Talan you have information any Wytch Lord servant would die for. Not only do you know what the Dawnthief catalysts are, you know where to find them. And if you walk away now, we'll never know if you're safe or whether you are telling them everything.'

'I would die first, you know that.'

'Yes, but you can only do it if you have the choice.' Ilkar paused, saw the anger in Talan's face. 'Look, I am not questioning your loyalty or your faith. I'm just saying that choosing to die may not be possible. You're not a mage. You can't just stop your own heart.'

Talan nodded slowly. 'Nevertheless. How will they find me if they don't know I've even left you? If they don't know where I've gone?'

Ilkar gave a short laugh. 'There's only one safe place for you, Talan, and that's the Mount of Xetesk; and somehow I don't think they'd welcome you with open arms.' Ilkar sighed. 'You must change your mind. Or at least think it through.'

'What do you think I've been doing these last few days, working on my life story?'

'You are walking out on the fight for Balaia.'

Talan leaned forward and jabbed a finger at Ilkar. 'Let me tell you something, Ilkar. I don't need you to tell me what I'm doing. I know, and I feel bad enough without you pushing my face in it.' Talan threw his arms in the air. 'I want your understanding, not your consent. I'm leaving. It's over.' He stalked off towards the gate.

'We can't let him go,' said Ilkar.

'Neither can we stop him,' said Hirad.

'Denser won't like this.'

'Well, Denser knows what he can do with it. This is Raven business.'

'Hirad, I really think . . .'

'It's Raven business.'

'Oh, I give up!' Ilkar turned a small circle in frustration. 'Haven't either of you grasped what's going on here? This is bigger than The

Raven. It's bigger than everything. We can't afford to fail this job and we need all the help we can get.'

'Nothing is bigger than The Raven,' said Hirad evenly. 'The Raven is the only reason we got this far in the first place and The Raven is the only reason we'll win. And that's because we always do.'

Ilkar stared at Hirad, his hard, open-mouthed expression slowly softening.

'There just is no answer to that, is there?'

'No.'

'Blind faith is a wonderful thing.'

'It's not blind faith, my dear elf, it's fact. You name me a job we've failed.'

'You know I can't.'

Hirad shrugged.

'Ilkar?' Talan called.

'What do you want?'

'Your eyes. Over here.'

Something in Talan's tone stayed Ilkar's next remark and instead he hurried over. Hirad levered himself painfully to his feet, hugged the wall for support until the nausea passed, then walked after him.

'What is it?' said Ilkar at Talan's shoulder.

Talan pointed. 'Straight ahead. I thought I saw movement.'

Ilkar nodded. 'Yes. A rider. Coming this way and at a tan gallop by the looks. He's a big bastard too.'

'Jandyr! Thraun! Front gate!' shouted Talan. 'If there's trouble, Hirad,' he continued, hearing the barbarian shuffle up behind him, 'you keep out of it.'

'Sod off.'

'Thought you might say that.'

'Why did you say it then?'

'Old time's sake?' He caught Hirad's eye and the two men smiled.

'Come back any time,' said Hirad.

'You never know.' Talan fixed his gaze out of the front gate once again.

By the time Jandyr and Thraun had joined them, they could hear the hoofbeats and see the rider in the distance.

Dark cloak billowing behind him, he came on astride a huge grey. As he neared, they drew their blades, Ilkar readying to cast. But perhaps thirty yards away he reined in and trotted to the gates, one hand out in a gesture of peaceful intent. He was wearing a full face mask but no helmet.

'That's far enough,' growled Talan. 'What's your business?'

'You can put up your swords,' said Denser, walking to the cluster around the gate. 'He's on our side.'

'Oh yeah? And who is he?' asked Hirad. Ilkar already knew the answer.

'His name is Sol. He's a Protector. And let's face it,' Denser stood squarely in front of Talan, 'as I overheard someone say just now, we need all the help we can get.'

'You don't think you might have at least mentioned you'd requested a Protector?' asked Ilkar. He had kept his silence on the subject throughout a rather tense afternoon, preferring to let Hirad believe it was part of a plan agreed while the barbarian was still comatose. But now Hirad was asleep, resting under Erienne's final WarmHeal, and the sun had disappeared behind night.

Ilkar and Denser were sitting alone on the front steps of the castle, taking in the warm late evening air. The Xeteskian's pipe was, as ever, between his teeth. The cat was nowhere to be seen.

'Would it have made any difference?'

'Courtesy is such a simple thing to observe,' said Ilkar testily.

'Then I apologise. But I did not request the Protector. Xetesk believes he is necessary to my security.'

'I bet.'

'Why must you always take the negative view?' Denser refilled the bowl of his pipe and tamped down the tobacco. 'This has nothing to do with the ultimate return of Dawnthief to Xetesk.' He lit the pipe, blew a smoke ring. 'It would be easier for us all if it was.'

'And how do you come by that conclusion?'

'Well, things are getting more complex out in the big wide world we seem to have left behind.'

'Complex.' Ilkar was immediately worried. Denser had a habit for understatement. 'Things' were possibly very bad.

'There's something you have to know. I've had a report on the Triverne Lake meeting. There is a four-College agreement which deals with the raising of an army to defend Understone Pass and Triverne Inlet. Apparently, they are trusting Blackthorne and Gresse with the defence of the Bay of Gyernath.

'Unfortunately, the rest of the KTA have chosen to ignore the warnings and it's leaving the country largely undefended should the Wesmen break through our lines.'

'Sounds about right. And how did they react to the news that we were after Dawnthief?' asked Ilkar, imagining the sparks flying. Denser said nothing. 'Well?' His smile faltered.

'There was no news. We didn't tell them.'

'I beg your pardon?'

'The other Colleges have no idea that we are looking for Dawnthief.' Denser looked away.

Ilkar's ears pricked and his eyes narrowed to slits, blood boiling in his head. He stood up, unable to sit beside the Xeteskian.

'How stupid of me to think that Xetesk might consider a Wytch Lord-backed Wesmen invasion more important than their own advancement.' Ilkar breathed deeply. 'You know, I was beginning to believe that Xetesk had really turned the corner. And now it seems that their prime objective isn't to see our country out of this crisis, it's to be sure they are dominant should we win.'

'But it isn't the way I think,' said Denser.

'No?'

'No!' Denser's face coloured. 'Why do you think I told you in the first place?'

'Because it would have been pretty bloody obvious when we got to Dordover and didn't find them standing at the gates with the ring gift-wrapped for us, that's why!'

'I understand you must be angry,' said Denser.

'I don't think you understand anything at all!' stormed Ilkar. 'Your College is expecting us to go on fighting and dying and not for the greater good of Balaia. I will not be a pawn of Xetesk and neither will The Raven.'

'So what do you want to do?' asked Denser into the vacuum.

'Well, that's the worst of it, isn't it?' said Ilkar. 'I don't have much choice but to continue, because I believe Balaia is under threat. But let me tell you this. Now Erienne and I are both with you, Dawnthief belongs to the Colleges, not just Xetesk.'

'You're going to find this hard to believe, but I agree with you, and I do feel for your position,' said Denser. 'But I also agree with the position of Xetesk and you're wrong if you think that Xetesk wants dominion. But if we had announced the search for Dawnthief at Triverne Lake, the interference would, we believe, have jeopardised the entire job, and with it Balaia.'

'Convenient,' muttered Ilkar. 'If you really believe that, then you've swallowed too much of your own doctrine. Whatever, we now have to go into Dordover under cover because your Masters have not learnt the power of co-operation. None of us had better get hurt.'

Sol walked in through the front gate and disappeared around the side of the house. Ilkar felt somehow that he was under close scrutiny. He shivered inwardly. Something about the Protector made him uneasy. At least this time he could put a finger on it almost straight away. The mask. It was simple, plain and black – carved, Denser said, from ebony. It was moulded to his face but would not, the Xeteskian assured, be a good likeness.

To Ilkar it looked like no one living, and that was certainly apt. He shivered again, as the reason for the mask rose unbidden in his mind. Protectors were effectively living dead, men promised to the Mount of Xetesk from birth and called should they die. So long as the soul could be taken, the body could be re-created. It was a hideous hangover from centuries of Xeteskian misuse of the living and the dead. It should have been banned but the Dark College refused to give up one of its most powerful callings.

And what the reanimated body and soul went through, Ilkar could only guess at. None would ever tell, as they were bound to silence except in the course of duty. To break the binds was, said Xeteskian lore, 'to bring down an eternity of torment in the Mount such that Hell itself would seem release, peace and tranquillity for the soul in thrall'. That same lore stated of Protectors that 'never again shall light or the eyes of the living gaze upon their faces. Neither shall they speak unless the life of their Given should suffer risk if they did not do so.'

Singularly, Protectors were utterly loyal bodyguards, knowing dissension would bring down torment, but the real reason for their creation was that an army of Protectors would move and fight with a power and synchronicity that would be practically unstoppable by all but magic. And even that wasn't certain. Protectors were gifted an innate magical defence when they were created. They were truly terrifying adversaries.

Sol would be Denser's mute shadow everywhere the mage went, and the shadow he cast would be large indeed. He was a huge man. Bigger than Thraun, perhaps even bigger than The Unknown. Crossed on his back were a double-handed and bladed axe and two-handed sword. Ilkar fancied that he could wield one in either hand and made a mental note to be out of the way when he did. He dragged his thoughts back to Denser.

'Sorry, I was distracted. That makes his appearance rather easier to understand, doesn't it? You were going to say something.'

Denser relit his pipe, flame as always from the tip of his right thumb. 'I noticed. He will not harm you. He has been closely informed of the who and the what of our situation.'

'Who by? I haven't seen you say more than a dozen words to him since he arrived.'

'He has been walking with my Familiar.'

'Enough said. Go on.'

Denser shifted his position slightly and brushed some grit from beneath him.

'Well, our decision not to talk about Dawnthief at this stage, and we will announce it when the time is right, has given us another problem.'

'Why are The Raven working for Xetesk?' Ilkar framed the question.

'Exactly. And this gives us a big problem where we're going next.'

'Dordover.'

Ilkar pursed his lips.

'If you, Hirad or I are seen in the City it will trigger untold problems with the Dordovan College. We can't afford a split because if we don't stand together, the Wytch Lords will trample us underfoot.'

'We're going to have to be incredibly lucky in there not to be spotted.' Ilkar shook his head, wondering how the Colleges would ever stop bickering long enough to stand together. He tried to believe Denser a liar but somehow, given that he was as much at risk as The Raven, he couldn't. The actions of Xetesk, though, were despicable.

'We aren't going in at all. Will, Thraun and Jandyr will have to do this alone.'

'And Erienne?' Ilkar was uncomfortable with trusting the theft of the Lore Master's ring to untried and unknown people. Yet he knew Denser's solution made sense.

'We can certainly trust her not to betray us.' Denser's eye had a twinkle. 'But that's not the problem. She's not exactly Dordover's favourite daughter and if we have to send her in, well . . .'

'I don't like the feel of this at all,' said Ilkar. 'I need to think. I'm going to check on Hirad.'

Selyn awoke with a start, the sound of running feet jerking her to instant wakefulness. It was late afternoon and she would have normally remained asleep for another two or three hours before casting her ShadowWings for the journey to Parve. She lay concealed in a dense area of shrub midway up a crag that overlooked the road from the Torn Wastes to Terenetsa. She was still four days from Parve.

Moving carefully to avoid rustling the foliage all over her, she edged her head above a rock formation and looked down on the road. Wesmen were jogging past, thousands of them, punctuated by Shamen on horseback. She watched for five minutes, trying to gauge the strength of the unbroken line of armed and fur-clad men running towards Understone Pass.

By the time the last riders were through, she estimated she'd watched the passage of around seven thousand. And at that speed, they would reach the pass in approximately six days.

'Gods, it's happening,' she breathed. She wasn't due to make another communion until reaching Parve but she couldn't let that many men surprise the Understone Pass defence. And assuming more were taking the southern trails from the Heartlands, they meant to throw a massive force at eastern Balaia. Shaking her head, she lay down and probed the mana for Styliann.

Chapter 18

The morning began calm. Dawn broke to the sound of people checking horses, stowing equipment and preparing food. The weather was fine and cool, ideal conditions for riding. Nonetheless, there was a storm about to break.

With horses saddled and castle rigged, most of The Raven, old and new, had gathered in the courtyard. Talan was astride his horse.

'Second thoughts?' probed Hirad. He was feeling good, strong. A few practice moves with Talan had revealed a dull ache and nothing more. Erienne said the ache would be with him for ever.

'With every breath I take,' said Talan.

'And?'

'I'm still right to go.' He shrugged.

'Where?'

'Never you mind, barbarian. Least said, least knows, never does find.'

'What?'

'My mother used to say it. God knows why, but it sounds right.'

Hirad raised his eyebrows and offered Talan a hand which the other shook. 'You'll always be Raven,' he said. 'Don't forget.'

'Thank you. Gods, Hirad, I—'

'It's done, Talan. We wish each other life and luck. It's all we can do now.' He smiled. 'See you in Korina when it's all over.'

'Depend on it.' Talan turned his horse and trotted towards the gates. As he neared the walls, Sol stepped squarely into his path.

'I think you'd better stop, Talan,' said Denser, emerging from the house, cat in his arms.

'What's up?' Hirad turned to the Xeteskian.

'I didn't really believe he'd go. I was trusting you to change his mind.'

Hirad felt a chill through the warmth of the morning.

'This is Raven business. It's his choice,' he said. 'It's his right.'

'No, it is not,' said Denser, his voice calm and cold. 'We cannot take the risk of his capture. He cannot be allowed to leave.'

'Don't do this, Denser,' urged Ilkar.

Denser ignored Ilkar. 'Reconsider.'

Talon shook his head. 'No.'

At a signal from his Given, Sol snapped the axe from his back to the ready.

'Reconsider,' Denser repeated.

Another shake of the head.

'You'd kill him?' Hirad's face darkened.

Denser shrugged. 'It's what Sol does best.'

Hirad didn't even think about it. He covered the ground to Denser, locked an arm around his neck and pushed a dagger under his chin.

'Reconsider,' he grated.

Sol broke towards them, his movement measured, implacable.

'Not another step, maskman, or this whole thing ends right now.'

The point of Hirad's dagger drew blood. Sol stopped dead. 'And don't even think about a spell. You aren't quick enough to beat me,' said Hirad into Denser's ear. He looked over at Talan. 'Get out of here.' Talan nodded his thanks, spurred his horse and galloped away. 'Like I said, it's Raven business.' He released Denser and sheathed his dagger. 'Now you can either kill me or we can get on with our job.'

'No purpose would be served by killing you,' said Denser, rubbing his neck.

'I thought not. Let's go then.'

Ilkar let out his breath, paused long enough to glare at Hirad and walked back towards the stables. Thraun and Will disappeared into the house. Erienne was still at the grave of her sons.

Sol moved to stand at Denser's side, the cat now on the Protector's shoulder. All three stared at him.

'What is it? Surprised I care that much?' Hirad's anger had not entirely left him. 'You still don't understand us, do you, Denser? The few of us that are still alive. And though you are sworn to the Code, until you do, you will never be truly Raven.'

'No,' said Denser. 'I don't and I'm not, although I'm getting a better picture every day.' He paused. 'You would really have killed me?'

'It's what I do best.' Hirad smiled.

'And handed Balaia and Dawnthief to the Wytch Lords.'

'I will not let you use that as a weapon to dominate us. You had no right to stop Talan—'

'I had every r—'

'It was Raven business!' snapped Hirad. 'I won't repeat myself again. Now I know you're important and I know we need to keep you alive. But if you pull another trick like that, I will stop you any way I can. And if that means we both die and Balaia with us, so be it.'

Eventually, Denser nodded. 'But you understand my fears.'

'Of course. Ilkar shares them. But you should have spoken to us about them. Did you really think we were going to stand by and let your shadow chop down a member of The Raven?'

Denser was silent for a time. He breathed in deeply.

'In hindsight, no. Look, I wasn't thinking straight. We're in a lot of trouble—'

'Ilkar's told me.'

'—and I just saw it as one risk too many.' He paused. 'I panicked. I'm sorry.'

'Then it's forgotten.' Hirad accepted Denser's hand. 'As long as he realises it was nothing personal.' He switched his gaze to Sol. Behind the mask, the eyes stared back, betraying no reaction.

'He will not attempt to harm you unless you threaten my life,' said Denser.

'I think we both know how to avoid that, don't we?' Hirad turned at a sound from the castle. Will and Thraun trotted out.

'Fuses are lit,' said Will. 'They'll burn for around four hours. I hope we can find a convenient hill to watch from.'

'We'll see what we can do.' Hirad drew breath. 'Raven! Mount up, let's go. The sun won't stop moving!' He paused to grab Denser's arm. 'You'll see to Erienne?' Then ran to his horse. Minutes later, the hiss and crackle of fuses was the only sound echoing around the stone walls of the Black Wings' castle.

The Raven rode along the trail from the castle for ten minutes before cutting away up a gentle incline into woodland. The ground was easy but rocks here and there dictated a measure of caution. It was three days' ride to Dordover; an injury to a horse would add delay and time was something The Raven simply didn't have to waste.

The first stop, earlier than Denser would have preferred, saw them on the slope of a hillside over three hours from the castle. Though not an ideal viewing point – the castle was partially obscured by both trees and distance – it was the best they could hope for and Will for one was not moving.

'Something wrong, old friend?' asked Ilkar.

Hirad looked away from the castle. 'I was just working out how long it was since I had a drink and I'm not happy with the answer.'

'It was in the ruins of Septern's house, wasn't it?'

Hirad nodded.

'Travers had a stock,' said Ilkar.

'I'd rather drink the contents of my own bladder,' replied Hirad.

'Very wise. It made a good antiseptic, though, so Talan said.'

Hirad raised his eyebrows. 'He'd better be all right,' he said. 'I'm going to miss him, I think.'

'Yes,' agreed Ilkar.

'Are you surprised he's gone?'

'Surprised and very disappointed. I really thought . . . you know, after four years . . .'

'Yes, I know. And talking of being disappointed, I'm beginning to lose faith in this great firework display of Will's.' He turned to where Will was standing, hands on hips, a few yards away. 'Hey, Will, any danger of this event of yours actually happening?'

Will tensed and shot him a sharp glance. 'Patience,' he said.

'Smoke!' said Jandyr immediately, pointing and standing up.

'Where?' asked Ilkar.

'Front door, all around the cracks.'

'Got it,' said Ilkar.

'Where?' And as Hirad strained to see what was visible only to elven eyes, the front door and surrounding walls blew out. A huge tongue of flame lashed into the courtyard, bringing with it a cloud of debris and smoke, causing him to shudder at the unwelcome reminder of his escape from Sha-Kaan.

The muffled thump of the first detonation reached them seconds later, moments before the two towers exploded in perfect synchronisation. One tore itself apart, collapsing inwards. The other's force was concentrated upwards, its ornately pointed top section spinning lazily into the air atop a plume of powdered masonry. Will shouted, delighted. Erienne burst into tears. Denser moved to her, held her and wiped dry her damp cheeks. She looked up at him and smiled.

And then, with the castle wreathed in flames and smoke, Hirad patted Will on the back and hurried them on their way under Denser's anxious gaze.

Understone.

Once the focal point of trade and travel both east and west of the pass, the town had fallen first to disuse, then to disrepair following the surrender of the pass to the Wesmen. All that remained was a poorly provisioned garrison of first-tour career soldiers paid for by the

Korina Trade Alliance, though the parlous state of that organisation scarcely warranted the name, such was its fading reputation.

Seventy-five men made up the total defence against incursion from the west, an incursion that none in the KTA believed would happen after the first five years of quiet.

How times change. In the aftermath of Travers' extraordinarily brave but ultimately doomed defence of the pass, Understone was fortified and garrisoned with three thousand men. With the entire eastern part of Balaia deemed under threat, no cost was too much in ensuring the Wesmen got no further than daylight the other side of the pass. Temporary accommodation was built, and traders, prostitutes, entertainers and innkeepers saw their best-ever years. But it didn't last. The Wesmen never attacked again. It seemed, after five years, that control of the pass and the tolls Tessaya could exact was the limit of their ambition.

Why they took the pass was a question left unanswered at the time. In the years before the series of battles that led to Travers' defeat, an uneasy peace had been maintained, allowing trade from the richer east to flow west, opening up new markets and developing new industries. But now nine years after the fall of the pass, the situation was unfortunately clear. The Wesmen had taken the pass as a precursor to the eventual return of the Wytch Lords.

The town of Understone stood no more than four hundred yards from the thirty-feet-high by twenty-five-feet-wide open black arch that was the entrance to Understone Pass. To either side, the mountains spread up and away, rolling into hills and scrubland which stretched as far as the eye could see, north, east and south. It was a bleak but beautiful sight, the town standing squarely in the middle of a carved wagon trail, its tumbledown houses littering neighbouring hills or jostling for position on the inadequate flatter spaces away from the main street.

It was bleaker still when the rains came, as they often did, cloud sweeping over the mountains on the prevailing wind to disgorge their contents on the hapless inhabitants below.

Flooding, mudslides, subsidence, all had left their scars on the town, whose solution to the rains was a lattice of drainage trenches probing in all downhill directions. They had worked well but disrepair now limited their effectiveness and the floods had returned. The main street was ankle deep in a thick, clogging mud, its stench rising with the sun.

The unannounced arrival of more than five hundred men and elves from the four Colleges caused panic in the small garrison. While a few stood in the way of the mounted force, most disappeared into buildings or ran shouting for their commanding officer. By the time he had dragged his way from an old inn, buttoning his tunic over his ample belly as he came thrashing through the mud, only twelve conscripts remained. It was pitiable.

The garrison commander looked past General Ry Darrick at the long line of horsemen who filled his town's main street almost end to end. He looked at those of his men who had chosen to stand their ground and nodded his thanks before facing Darrick, who leaned forward in his saddle, not even honouring the man by dismounting.

'And this is how you would face those who would take our lands,' said Darrick.

The commander smiled. 'No,' he replied. 'Because those who would take our lands would hardly draw breath while slaughtering so small a garrison. Whom do I address?'

'I am Darrick, General, Lystern cavalry. And you are Kerus, commander of the garrison standing at the gates of hell.'

For a second time, Kerus frowned, gauging the meaning both of Darrick's words and of the weight of numbers behind him. Choosing to keep the rest of the conversation private, he walked through the mud to stand by Darrick's chestnut-brown mare.

'General Darrick. What I have here are seventy-five men, none of whom is above nineteen. They have been sent here to patrol the area outside the pass and to deal with any raiders who might come through. They were never expected to repel an invading army because no army will ever come through the pass. And now, I must ask you, what is your business in Understone?'

'Preparing to repel the invading army that you say doesn't exist. I have five thousand foot two days behind me.'

'Perhaps we had better talk in my quarters,' said Kerus.

'Perhaps we had.'

Chapter 19

It was late afternoon. Will had the wood burner firing and a pot of water bubbled on top of it. No light could be seen.

'I'm astonished, frankly,' said Denser. 'We didn't meet another soul. How likely is that?' He, Ilkar and Hirad had walked away a few yards to talk. Jandyr and Thraun were seeing to the horses and Erienne had already put her head down to sleep.

'He's a good tracker, I'll give him that,' said Hirad.

'*Good!* It's hardly desolate out here. We didn't even hear anyone. It's extraordinary.'

'Not only that, half the time we didn't hear him ourselves,' agreed Ilkar.

'All right. Meeting of the Thraun appreciation society closed,' said Hirad. 'What about Dordover?'

Denser gestured for Ilkar to speak.

'It's the largest of the College Cities. It is more closely linked to Xetesk than Julatsa and has a history of allegiance with Denser's lot, although they now barely talk. It wouldn't make our job any easier if they did. One thing you have to understand is that the colleges guard their lore more jealously than any other possession. What we are about to steal is part of Dordover's lore.'

'So it'll be protected.'

'Yes, but not by people. Spells,' said Ilkar. 'That's our problem. Wards, alarms, traps, all coded. If the wrong person moves in their sphere, they'll be triggered.'

'So how?' asked Hirad.

'Our only choice, unfortunately, is Erienne,' said Denser.

'Why unfortunately?'

'Because we shouldn't be asking her to take such a direct part in this theft. She's already torn apart by losing her sons. I wonder whether this might not be one thing too many for her to take.'

'I know,' said Hirad. 'But if she's only telling us what to do . . .'

'You misunderstand,' said Denser. 'She'll have to go in.'

'So we're talking of sending Will and Thraun into this place in the company of a woman who's out of her mind with grief and was schooled just around the corner, to steal a ring which is central to her beliefs.'

'That is a very accurate summary,' said Denser.

'Do they know she's coming?' asked Hirad.

'Yes, of course,' said Denser. 'Just one more thing. There's to be no killing. Erienne will not stand for it.'

'Want me to lop their hands off too?'

'Sorry, Hirad.'

'Let's hope we're not all sorry before tomorrow.' He moved away and called to Thraun before turning back. 'So before we met Erienne, what was the plan?'

Ilkar and Denser exchanged a glance and the cat raised its head.

'It is possible to subvert weaker minds remotely, given time,' replied Denser.

'Believe me, you don't want to know the details,' said Ilkar.

Hirad nodded and walked over to the stove.

Styliann rattled his glass back on to the table, his eyes blazing, his face colouring red in the lanternlight of his study.

'The Protectors are under *my* direct control. No one assigns a Protector without my prior authorisation. Not even you.'

'But the situation, my Lord . . .' began Nyer.

'Should have been discussed with me,' said Styliann. 'I do not like the flouting of my authority. And I particularly do not like your choice of Protector.'

'Sol is extremely capable.'

'You know precisely what I am talking about,' snapped Styliann. 'You will recall him at once.'

Nyer dropped his eyes to the floor and nodded his head. 'Naturally, my Lord. If that is your wish.'

'Damn you, Nyer, I don't know!' said Styliann. He poured the older man a drink. 'What has got into you? You always discuss such matters with me. Always.'

'You were in conference at Triverne Lake. I felt a decision had to be made.'

Styliann considered and nodded. 'Very well. Let the Protector stay. At least until after Dordover. But keep me closely informed of progress. I want a full account of all communions and I would hate to have to employ TruthTell to be sure you were telling me everything.'

Nyer recoiled as if slapped, but recovered to smile. 'I suppose I deserved that,' he said. 'Selyn is well?'

'Considering the invading armies of the Wesmen trampled her toes on the way to Understone, yes.' Styliann sucked his lip nervously.

'She'll make it, you know.'

'Thank you for your thoughts.' The Lord of the Mount rang the bell by the fire. 'I need to rest. Please don't work behind my back again.' His expression was bleak. Nyer left in response to the opening of the door. Styliann sighed. He wouldn't have believed it of Nyer, he really wouldn't.

Erienne, with a few brief words to Denser and a squeeze of his hand, left the camp well before sundown alongside Thraun and Will. Unlike Xetesk, Dordover was not a closed city and the trio rode through the gates under the disinterested gaze of the west gate guards two hours later.

'I couldn't bear to go back to the house,' said Erienne when they were seated at a table downstairs from the rooms they had taken for the night at a quiet inn near the College.

'I understand,' said Thraun. 'When this is over, we'll sort the place out for you.'

Erienne nodded her thanks, tears again threatening behind the sunken, dark-ringed eyes in her pale face. 'So many memories, so much happiness. And now . . .' She shook her head and dropped her gaze to the table, pushing her hair back over her ears.

'We'll help you through this,' said Will. 'We'll always be here for you.'

Erienne reached out a hand and squeezed Will's arm. She breathed in and composed herself. 'Now listen,' she said. 'Although Dordover is far more open than somewhere like Xetesk, the College has strict rules concerning visitors. You're not allowed in the College grounds after full dark, so please, take my lead and try not to say too much.'

'Will you be recognised?' asked Thraun.

'I expect so, near the College anyway. I spent a lot of years here, after all.'

Food and drink arrived at the table.

'Let's eat,' said Erienne. 'Then we need to get out to the College. We won't gain entry after dark.'

The College itself consisted of a group of ten or so buildings arranged in a rough circle around the 'Tower'. That the Tower looked nothing like its name suggested it should was something Will was quick to point out.

The trio were walking up to the single gate of the walled-in college, and the Tower, in actuality a twin-winged four-storey mansion house, lay directly ahead of them.

'There used to be a tower before the College was formalised as a centre of excellence in magic,' explained Erienne. 'It was the done thing about four hundred years ago, I think, but completely impractical. When the College developed around it, the Tower was eventually demolished to make way for the house. Only Xetesk retains towers. They've got seven, and that's a reflection of the College hierarchy's thinking.' She couldn't quite keep the sneer from her voice. 'Everyone else has moved with the times.'

'So what was the point of a Tower, if you'll excuse the pun?' asked Thraun.

'They were a symbol of power and authority.' Erienne shrugged. 'Phallic symbols for men whose mana ability was less than their egos demanded. Pathetic, really.'

At the gate they were stopped by a single guard who, after a moment's reflection, recognised the mage in front of him.

'Erienne,' he said kindly. 'It's been a few years since you came here.'

'We all have to fly the coop sometime, Geran, but it's good to see you.' The guard smiled, then looked at Will and Thraun. 'Friends of my husband,' said Erienne. 'I've had a little trouble, I'm afraid.' Her voice caught and she stopped.

'And now you're here for some help.'

'Something like that.'

Geran stepped aside. 'You know the rules on visitors,' he said.

Erienne nodded and walked past him. 'I'll see they don't encroach.'

'How is Alun, by the way?' asked Geran.

Erienne stiffened but carried on walking, not turning. Thraun came to Geran's shoulder.

'That's the trouble. He's dead. And the boys.'

Geran's face fell. 'I'm—'

'I know. Best left.'

It was close on two hundred yards to the Tower from the gate. To their left, a line of stubby wooden windowed huts – classrooms – arced away, and to their right a long, shuttered building, metalled and black.

'It's where range spells are practised and new spells live-tested. It has to be strong,' said Erienne, stopping to look. 'Did you know that across the Colleges one in fifty mages die in their long rooms and test chambers? No, of course you didn't. You thought we all just wake up one morning able to cast. There never has been enough respect for the dangers we face in training and research. You think it's a gift, but to us it's a calling we have no choice but to obey. We don't walk in here, they find us and bring us.'

'Take it easy, Erienne.' Thraun, taken aback by her sudden anger, put a hand on her shoulder. She shook it off and began walking again.

'Behind the Tower is another place to dread. The Mana Bowl. That's where mages learn to accept, build and control mana. Next door is the ward where the ones who opened their minds too far too soon lie gibbering and drooling until death takes them. Mercifully, that isn't usually too long.'

She marched up a short flight of stone steps, across a paved relief and hammered on the massive oak doors that fronted the Tower. The left-hand one swung open silently and a man stepped out. He was old beyond anything they had seen or even dreamed. White hair cascaded below his shoulders and his mouth was obscured by a grey-flecked beard. While his body was bent with age and he supported himself on two sticks, his eyes were a clear blue, flashing from a face wrinkled and rolled into a grotesque caricature of the man he once was. But the eyes gave him strength and Erienne bowed to him.

'Master of the Tower, I am Erienne. I seek knowledge in the library.'

He considered her for a moment before nodding.

'Indeed,' he said in a voice brittle and quiet. 'And your companions?' He gestured vaguely with one stick.

'They guard me.'

'They may enter the hall but go no further.'

'I know, Tower Master.' Erienne wrung her hands.

'You are impatient, Erienne Malanvai. It was always your weakness.' He chuckled. 'Go and seek your knowledge. You have been absent from the library for too long. Perhaps age is finally bringing you wisdom.' He took a pace towards Thraun and Will, squinting at them in the failing afternoon light. The thief received only a cursory glance, but Thraun's face he held with his eyes for some time, a frown deepening the wrinkles of his forehead still further.

'Hmm,' he said eventually. 'Do not trespass. The penalties are swift and severe.' He shuffled back into the Tower, leaving the door open for them to enter.

Erienne came down towards her companions. 'What was all that about?' she asked.

'I must have a scary face.' Thraun smiled, but it was less than convincing.

'We could ask you the same question,' said Will.

'The Tower Master, you mean? Just do as he says. He runs the house for the Lore Masters. No one goes against his word and it worries me that he didn't like you.'

Thraun shrugged. 'What now?' he asked.

'I'm going into the library to check up on the defences around Arteche's ring. The heavy door you'll see to the right of the library leads to the crypts. Take a good look at the lock but I'd advise against turning the handle.'

She turned on her heel and walked into the Tower. She headed left and opened a wood-panelled door, then stopped and turned. 'Don't – are you two all right?'

Thraun and Will had only taken one pace into the Tower before stopping. Both men had paled, eyes widening more in fear than in reaction to the half-light inside.

Will felt a weight settle on his body like a metal shroud. Oppressive and cloying, it squeezed his lungs and chilled his heart, breath catching in his throat. His eyes swept around the hall. Directly in front of him, a flight of stone stairs led upwards into darkness, and to the right of them, a single closed iron-bound door.

Erienne stood by another door, and to her left, the one that led to the crypts sat next to the stairs. The half-light inside was spread by dim lanterns high on the walls, and from every panel a portrait glowered down – staring, enquiring, demanding. Beneath Will's feet, the stone-flagged floor was covered by a dark rug, and from every pore leaked power.

'Would you rather stay outside?' asked Erienne.

Thraun shook his head weakly. 'No, we'll be all right.' Will was alert enough to shoot him a sharp glance. 'What is it?'

'Mana,' said Erienne simply. 'The legacy of ages. Lore Masters and mages. The living in the rooms above your head and the dead below. It's something you'll never be able to understand, but you can feel it, can't you? A dead weight for you and the purest form of life energy for me. I will draw strength while you merely endure.' She almost smiled. 'I won't be long.' She turned and disappeared into the library, the door thudding home.

Behind Thraun and Will, the light was fading fast and the lanterns on the wall lightened in response. Will sank into a chair near the library while Thraun closed the main door.

'I wonder what she means by not being long?' he said.

'Hmm.' Thraun leaned against the lintel the other side of the library entrance. 'I don't know. Whatever, it's going to seem an age in here.'

'Better make ourselves useful, then. Let's see about that lock.'

Denser dozed fitfully. In his half-dreams, the Familiar struggled to free itself from a cage too strong to break. Its form swam from cat to true, its claws scrabbled, talons flashed, teeth rent, voice howled . . . Denser awoke, uneasy. He sent his thoughts through the gloom and relief flooded in as he felt the calm beat of the Familiar's force. He bade it be cautious.

In the street outside the College of Dordover, a black cat withdrew further into shadow, its eyes never shifting from the gate and its solitary guard, who sat smoking at his post.

'You must be seen to leave.' Erienne's search had been brief and she stood in the hall with Will and Thraun once more. Their wait had seemed interminable. Not a sound had registered in the Tower the entire time she was gone.

'And then?' asked Will.

'Wait until full dark, then come back. I'm staying to do a little more research.'

'Is the gate well guarded after dark?'

'No, same as daytime. Either way, I suggest you come over the wall behind the long room.'

'Isn't it spell-guarded, the wall?' Thraun shifted his stance; something wasn't quite right and it irritated in his subconscious.

'No.' Erienne shrugged. 'Who'd want to break into a College grounds?'

'Who indeed?' Will smiled ruefully.

'Your problems start when you try to get back in here.'

'Why leave then?'

'You aren't allowed in the College after dark. They'll kill you if they find you. Meet me in the library.'

Will nodded and led the way outside, gasping in the air as he stepped out into the dusk, the weight lifting from his body as quickly as it had settled. He glanced over his shoulder to see the door shut behind them, and he and Thraun hurried down the path, past the guard and out into the street.

Erienne stopped short of the door to the library, hand outstretched to the handle, at the sound of movement behind her.

'Erienne, Erienne,' said the Tower Master. 'You of all people should know that the walls of the Tower have ears.'

In the shadows outside the College gate, the cat pricked its ears, feeling its hackles rise. It shifted, looked behind it, but there was nothing. From nowhere a hand clamped around its neck, pinning it to the ground. It could feel the mana shape which mimicked the shape of the hand, and fear swamped its senses.

'Don't think to change, little one. Your bones are thin beneath my fingers.'

The cat was lifted up to a face, dark, with long black hair tied back. The eyes, brown and narrow, bored into its skull. The man spoke again.

'I could smell you from within the walls,' he sneered, tightening the mana hand a little. 'Let's see if we can't draw your master from his hiding place.' A bag, heavy with invested mana, covered the cat's head, cutting off its sub-vocal howl.

Denser's scream of pain shattered the peace of the woodland hiding place. Hirad jerked violently from his doze then sprang to his feet, hand already on the hilt of his sword. He ran the short distance to the stricken mage and took in Sol, who was standing near by looking on in what appeared to be disinterest, if anything could be gained from the eyes behind the mask. Denser was hunched on his knees, hands clasped to the sides of his head, nose scraping the leaf mould. A dark trickle ran from a nostril.

'Denser?' He could see no wound, no reason for the mage's sudden cry. That scared him. He felt Ilkar and Jandyr at his shoulder. Ilkar went past and knelt by the Xeteskian, an arm about his shoulders.

'Denser?' asked Ilkar. 'Can you speak?'

Denser gurgled and groaned, shuddering the length of his body. He gasped and allowed Ilkar to pull him upright. Even in the gathering gloom they could see his eyes dark with blood against his stark white face. He seemed years aged, and when he opened his mouth to speak, the muscles of his jaws spasmed. Blood ran from his mouth.

'They've taken him,' he managed in a voice thick with phlegm. 'They've taken him to get me.'

'What?' Hirad was confused. 'Taken who?'

'The Familiar,' said Ilkar. 'A Dordovan mage must have captured it.'

'Why a mage?'

'Because no one else would have the power to keep it subdued.' Ilkar scratched his chin. 'Gods, this is serious.'

'I've got to get there,' said Denser, starting to rise.

'No way, Denser.' Ilkar held him down. 'They'll destroy you.' The mages stared at each other.

'They'll hold him till he dies. What then? What then?' Denser's eyes were desperate, his body shivering with the aftershock.

Ilkar shook his head. 'I don't know . . . oh, no.'

'What?' Hirad stopped halfway to resheathing his sword.

'Thraun, Will, Erienne. The College are going to be expecting something, aren't they? And those three are pig in the middle. How much chance do you reckon that gives them?'

'But there's no way they could link them with the cat, is there?' said Jandyr.

'It doesn't matter,' replied Ilkar. 'The College'll be on high alert once the capture of the Familiar is announced. They'll think Xeteskians are about and no one will get in or out, believe me.'

Hirad rammed his blade home the rest of the way.

'Oh, that's just great. Not only will Denser have his brain fried when the cat dies, but we're going to lose half our people without claiming the ring.' He walked away a few paces and kicked at a tree, cursing under his breath. 'Anyone got any bright ideas or do we just serve ourselves up to the Wytch Lords now?'

'I'm going to get him,' said Denser. 'I can't leave him in there. You don't understand.'

'There's only one person who can try to find out what's going on, and that's me,' said Jandyr. 'I'll saddle up and go.'

'Thank you,' said Ilkar. He switched his attention to Denser. 'Remember why we're all here and remember the people who have died so far. If you stamp off into Dordover you'll just be committing suicide and all we've achieved will be wasted.'

He paused and glanced up at Sol. The Protector's eyes were hidden by the gloom but Ilkar knew he was looking at them.

'You understand all this. It's up to you to see he stays put.' He squeezed Denser's shoulder. 'I'm sorry. I know the depth of the bond. I'm sorry for the pain you've suffered and for the pain you still have to face. But Dawnthief is bigger than any of us, you said so yourself. You are hearing me, aren't you?'

Denser nodded and slumped against Ilkar's body. He looked up into the Julatsan's face, tears brimming in his eyes.

Chapter 20

Will and Thraun saw it happen, knew straight away that it wasn't just a man snatching a stray cat, but didn't know what it meant. Crouching deep in shadow outside the College and near the wall by the long room, they reached a decision quickly enough.

'We said we'd go back,' said Thraun. 'She could be in trouble.'

'I know you're right but can we really help in there?' Will jerked a thumb at the College.

'We'd better hope so. We do have one ace up our sleeve.'

'Hmm.' Will eyed Thraun, a frown creasing his brow. 'There's always that, though I didn't like the way that old man stared at you, like he knew something. And to be fair, there's no way they would connect Erienne with the cat, it's a Xeteskian beast. Still . . .' He trailed off and shrugged.

'I know,' said Thraun. He studied the sky. 'We'd better get inside. I'd hate to be late.'

Though smooth, the wall was no challenge. Will swarmed over it in seconds and it was low enough for Thraun to jump and catch the top edge. Within a minute, they were behind the long room.

The building was dread and sinister. The walls were scarcely taller than Thraun and the roof swept down either side, overlapping almost to ground level. Clad in iron, the strength and weight had to be immense, and when Will touched the wall he flinched. It was warm. But there was more; an aura similar to that they had experienced in the Tower, but uncontrolled somehow. Dangerous.

'Can we move from here?' His unease was heightened by a creak in the metal.

'It would be a pleasure.' Thraun started off along the length of the building, heading towards the Tower but shielded from it. His eyes, sharp and clear, picked out every twig and dry leaf. Behind him, Will, through long years of experience, concentrated solely on placing his feet in the imprints left by Thraun, which he could just make out in the darkness.

The two men moved like ghosts through the College, so quiet that someone two paces away could miss them with back turned. They stopped at the corner of the long room and studied the Tower. Light came from three windows and lanterns hung either side of the main doors. The ground floor was completely dark, but between them and more welcoming shadow were thirty yards of open space.

'Any ideas?'

'Just one,' replied Thraun.

Erienne laid the unconscious body of the Tower Master in a far corner of the cavernous library, making him as comfortable as possible.

Her action had been swift and without error, her straight punch catching him square on the jaw. He'd crumpled into her arms and she'd dragged the dead weight into the library, panting at the sudden exertion. With the door closed, she'd shaped a gentle sleeping spell which would keep him under the entire night.

When she stopped moving, the enormity of what she'd done struck her like falling rock. She pulled out a desk chair and slumped into it, hands over her face, elbows on the desk and tears beginning to prick at her eyes.

That the Tower Master had heard her conversation with Thraun and Will was bad – his suspicions would be plenty enough to see her expelled from the College. But to have struck him and then disabled him with magic . . . they'd tear her brain to pieces. Her only hope now was to avoid capture and pray the circumstances of the deception would mitigate future punishment. Either way, she couldn't ever see herself setting foot in Dordover or its College again.

After a few moments to gather herself, she moved to kneel by the Tower Master, and smoothed a strand of hair from his face.

'I am sorry. But underneath it all, you are still just an old, old man. Please forgive me.' She rose. 'It is not a betrayal. I'm trying to save us all.' The Tower Master lay still, his gently moving chest the only indication he was alive at all.

Twitching aside a heavy drape, Erienne checked the sky and frowned in surprise. Full dark had come. She'd had no idea she'd dallied in the library so long and there was one question she hadn't answered. She hurried to a shelf and dragged off a large volume. She leafed through the pages quickly, scanning for the information she knew had to be there.

*

Denser turned the Understone Pass Commander's badge he'd taken from Travers over and over in his hands. It was hard to see in the lessening light and he augmented his sight for a better look.

The badge itself was quite plain, though its importance to the survival of Balaia could not be measured. Formed from an amalgam of gold and steels it was about three-quarters the width of his palm and ringed with an embossed leaf design. In its centre, an intricate engraving of the southern entrance to the pass gleamed at him and on the reverse were etched the names of previous commanders.

It was the first time Denser had studied the badge, and he should have found it fascinating – particularly its constitution. But as he twiddled it absently, his thoughts were dominated by the fate of his Familiar. His mind was shorn of its touch and the loneliness he felt was merely the prelude to the agony of its death. He fancied he could feel its fear, anger and desolation; and the howls of despair ready to be unleashed at its demise. He couldn't let that happen.

Sol stood near by, a statue of controlled power. His eyes, as ever, scanned everywhere, missing nothing that could prove a threat. Nothing until now. His eyes could not penetrate Denser's mind.

'Sol,' said Denser softly. The Protector turned his head. 'Catch.' He tossed the badge and chain to Sol, who enclosed them in one gloved hand. 'Keep it safe.'

Now Sol looked at what he held and his eyes widened. His gaze snapped back to Denser but the mage had already finished his incantation.

'You know I had to do this.' Wings of pure night appeared at Denser's back, and with one lazy flap he shot into the air, orienting himself for Dordover.

'No!' Sol's shout put birds to flight and shocked Hirad out of a doze for the second time. For a moment he was confused by the sound – it was the first word he had heard Sol utter. He sprinted to the Protector and, following the tilt of his head, could just make out a shape dwindling against the starscape.

'What the—?'

'ShadowWings.' Ilkar was at his shoulder.

'That's *Denser*?' Hirad pointed at the smudge in the sky.

''Fraid so,' said Ilkar.

'Well, that's just bloody great!' Hirad hurled his sword to the ground at his feet, fury bringing heat to his cheeks. His hands clenched. 'He threatens to kill Talan because of some imaginary risk to his precious quest and now he's off to commit suicide in Dordover all because someone's stolen his pet bloody cat!' He flapped a hand in the direction Denser had taken, breathing out loudly through his nose. 'I mean, just what does he expect us to do now?'

'Nothing.' Sol flicked the badge and chain to Ilkar, who caught it effortlessly. 'Stay.'

'Talking to me or to your dog, maskman?' Hirad squared up, his blade still lying in the fallen leaves.

'Hirad . . .' began Ilkar.

Sol considered the situation briefly, Hirad half believing he could see the Protector frowning.

'Stay, please,' he said, then turned and sprinted for his horse. Hirad made to follow him, stooping for his sword on the way.

'Don't, Hirad.'

'What?'

'I think he's right. We should stay.'

'You're agreeing with a Xeteskian?'

Ilkar grinned. 'Unusual, I know, but yes.'

'Why? Their recent record for decision-making is very poor.' Another gesture in the direction of Dordover and the departed Denser.

'Because if they all die, someone has to go on who knows the whole story.'

'But without that flying prat no one can cast the spell, isn't that right?' Hirad pushed his sword back into its scabbard.

'He's the only chance right now, admittedly, but without any of us to report back to Xetesk, there's no chance at all.' Ilkar shrugged.

'So we just sit and wait?' Hirad was unused to being unwanted in what looked a certain fight.

'No. We clear the camp and get ready for a quick exit. One way or another, we won't be here long, I think.'

'How will we know if he dies?'

'We'll know. Believe me, we'll know.'

The library door opening shocked Erienne into dropping the book like a guilty child. Her heart hammered then missed a beat in relief as Will and Thraun stepped in and closed it behind them.

'Gods, you scared me! How did you . . .' She pointed vaguely to the outside.

'By looking as if we owned the place,' said Will. 'You'd be surprised how often that works.'

'Yes, but *here*?' Erienne was dumbfounded.

'I have to admit the College was pushing the point, but seeing is believing.' Thraun smiled. 'Our only bit of luck was avoiding your friend the Tower Master. I thought we'd have to deck him.'

'I beat you to it.' Erienne reprised the events of the past hour or so.

'One thing,' said Will. 'Someone here's got Denser's cat.'

'Fool!' spat Erienne, slapping the table next to her. 'I told him they would detect a Familiar. That man's arrogance knows no end.' She breathed in deeply but her eyes betrayed her thoughts. 'The pain he'll be suffering . . . poor man, it'll be terrible.' She paused. 'Come on, we can't stop to worry about that now. All in all, I'd say we've been luckier than we deserve. I've already lost my reputation pursuing this ridiculous folly, I don't want to lose my life too.'

'Reckon we can take the ring?' asked Will.

'I'm not sure,' admitted Erienne. 'There's a ward down there I don't know.'

'So . . .?'

'So until I can plot the mana shape, I don't know what it does or whether I can move it. To do that I need to get near it.' She walked to the door. 'Let's get moving.'

Thraun gave the all clear and they padded quietly to the crypt entrance.

'Will?' asked Erienne.

'It's a standard through-bolt operating a latch on the other side. Heavy but crude,' he whispered. 'I need to know if it's spell-guarded or conventionally trapped.'

'Neither,' said Erienne.

'Good.' Will bent to his task, inserting a metal rod the size of his little finger into the lock. He probed briefly for the latch assembly. 'Very crude.' He withdrew the rod and fished in a belt pouch, taking out a flat piece of metal about one and a half inches wide, welded to a cylinder which slipped over the rod and clicked into place. He pushed the makeshift key into the lock, angling it slightly and manoeuvring it back and forth. Presently he smiled, turned the key and heard the latch slide up on the other side of the door.

'Want to go first?' he asked Erienne.

'I think I'd better.' She stepped past Will as he stowed his tools and opened the door. Inside, the weight of mana was heavier than ever, causing her to pause for breath. It was also pitch dark.

'There's a lot of static mana here, keeping the wards sound. I can navigate by the trails. What about you two?'

'I'll follow him, don't you worry,' said Will.

'No light?' queried Thraun.

'Not until we're down the first steps. There's a light-sensitive ward about halfway down the flight which activates at dusk. It's an alarm.' She began to move carefully down the stairs, Thraun and Will behind her, the latter closing and rebolting the door behind them.

To Will, the darkness was impenetrable, the mana-laden atmosphere cloaked him in anxiety and the air was musty and stale. He hooked the fingers of his right hand into Thraun's belt and traced the near wall with his left, relying on his friend's directions for his every footstep.

He was concentrating so intently, he hardly heard Erienne as she advised them they were passing the first ward, but it registered and he was sure he could feel it: a deeper quality to the level of mana all around and a spike that sent fear into his heart and sent his sightless eyes probing desperately for something to anchor him. He stumbled.

'Easy, Will,' said Thraun, his own voice hushed by the power all around them. 'There are maybe a dozen more steps and then we're down.'

'I'm not enjoying this.'

'Nor me. Just take it steady. Step down now.'

The descent of the thirty steps ended with a right-hand bend in a narrow passage and another door through which Erienne ushered them before closing it and beginning an incantation. Will leant against the door, finding comfort in the wood and iron at his back while somewhere to his left, Erienne murmured on.

'Illuminate,' she said eventually, and light grew steadily. It came from a globe that expanded to a size approaching that of Will's head, and at that moment it was the most beautiful thing he'd ever seen.

He noticed the chamber next. It was long, narrow and cold, stretching away into the darkness beyond the throw of Erienne's LightGlobe. And stacked three high to left and right, separated by shelves, were stone sarcophagi. Here as nowhere else, the mana beat down upon him. The moment's relief he felt as the light flooded the chamber was extinguished by the reality of his position, which forced him back against the door. He gasped, looking vainly for help from Thraun, but he too was suffering; the bow of his shoulders telling a clear story.

'Erienne . . .' Will began. He could feel his face flushing. His legs were trembling with the exertion of keeping his body vertical.

The Dordovan mage nodded. 'I'm sorry, Will, I had no idea it would be so strong. Take a few moments and it will ease enough for you to carry on. We've got a way to go yet.'

Will grimaced and levered himself from the door, forcing himself to concentrate on the darkness that enveloped the chamber a dozen paces ahead.

'It's all in the mind,' he assured himself.

'No, it isn't,' said Erienne. 'Mana is a force that controls and adapts nature. It is physical and, as you are discovering, is tangible in concentration. Some people attract it and the ones who can welcome and harness it are mages, like me.'

'Thanks for your help and support,' muttered Will.

'Just remember that in this state, it is harmless. It's mages who shape it and make it unstable and dangerous. Let's keep it going.' She strode off along the lines of tombs, Lore Masters and Mage Lords, some centuries dead. The LightGlobe followed her, marking a smooth course slightly above and to the right of her head.

Will and Thraun followed as best they could, heads down and slogging as though labouring under heavy packs.

Jandyr thundered into the stables of the inn and slid off his horse. A quick word and a few coins exchanged with the stable lad gave him the information he needed, and a bag of feed for his horse.

Snatching his bow and quiver from their saddle straps, he jogged out into the Dordovan evening, following the directions given him and not having a clue what he'd do when he arrived. Something would suggest itself; it normally did.

To Denser, the mana flowing around the Dordovan College was a beacon of soft orange that swamped the lights of the City. The ShadowWings beat lazily, propelling him at good speed towards his goal. One hand was pressed on his skull cap, the other kept his sword from flapping against his leg, and he squinted through eyes half closed against the wind of his passage.

All thoughts of Dawnthief and the salvation of Balaia had vanished from his mind. Somewhere in the College was his Familiar, an integral part of his mind and consciousness. No one could be allowed to take that away. He pulsed a thought of calm and relief in the hope it might penetrate the mana cage the Familiar had to be in.

He dived towards the College and its centrepiece, the Tower – an ugly squat house not worthy of the name given to the greatest of mage structures. But then, Dordover misunderstood the focusing power that a tower conferred upon its incumbent, just as it misunderstood many things. Like the reaction from the master of a stolen Xetesk Familiar.

Circling the Tower at a height of fifty feet above its highest point, Denser knew that whoever held his Familiar would be waiting, that they could feel his presence but would not know where he was. Experience dictated that man will rarely look up to find other men. Denser had an edge.

He dropped silently towards the roof of the Tower, hovering scant feet from its slates, pulsing the same search message all the time. He moved slowly to all corners of the roof, hoping for some signal, some clue as to the direction he should take. He was close, he could feel it, but a wrong move now would mean disaster.

In its mana cage, the Familiar abruptly stopped struggling and cocked its head. It grasped the bars with its hands and strained forwards, a grin cracking its hairless face.

The mage flinched involuntarily from the sight but managed to smile through his revulsion.

'Excellent. I take it he has arrived,' he said.

'Yes,' said the demon, in a voice like footsteps on wet gravel. 'And you are mine.'

'I don't think so,' said the mage. He turned his chair to face the door, the smug expression on his face hiding the huge effort he was making to ignore the taunts of the beast in the cage behind him.

'Stay back around the corner, I'm at the next ward.'

Erienne's voice brought Will back to himself. He'd been staring at the floor, filling his mind with thoughts of freedom as his body fought the constant pressure of the mana.

He looked up, past Thraun's back, to where Erienne stood at the centre of a cross-passage, the globe bright over her head. Behind her, the passage led on into darkness, and to Will's left and right, the shelves of caskets had given way to blank walls as the passage narrowed.

'Where are we?' he asked.

'Arteche's vault,' said Erienne, indicating to her right. 'The door down here is the entrance. It's guarded. No one is allowed in there bar the present Council of Lore Masters. They are excluded from the ward.'

'But you can get round it?'

'Sort of. It would be more accurate to say I can move it.'

'Then why—?' asked Will.

'They're just a deterrent to Dordovan mages and moving them's not without risk even if you know the structure. People like you, though, ordinary people, you wouldn't stand a chance. What was left of you I could scrape into the palm of my hand.'

'Nice,' muttered Thraun. 'So what is it, exactly?'

'Essentially, it's a bubble of mana which covers the door and inside it is the trap spell. If you're careful, you can make the bubble slide, if not, it will burst . . . I'll call you when I'm ready, but tread slowly.'

'Good luck,' said Thraun.

'Thanks,' she said, and walked away around the corner.

At the ward, she refocused her eyes, tuning in tight to the mana spectrum. It was exactly as she had described, a bubble of mana which bulged out some five feet from the door and was anchored flush with all four edges. It was a gentle orange – the static mana which kept it active didn't have the bright force of focused mana – and inside, the trap spell pulsed blue, cold and deadly.

She reached out her hands to the bubble and pushed very gently against it. The surface gave like a full water skin. It was a good sign. The give afforded her some margin of error which a taut ward did not. It had clearly not been maintained for some considerable time.

Erienne dropped her hands and concentrated, beginning the process of creating a mana shape to completely isolate the ward. She built out from the centre, drawing on the reserves of her body only slightly as the crypts supplied almost all she needed. The shell grew, expanded and reshaped. A circle at first, it soon took on the outline of the target ward, matching its shape utterly in every detail. In form, though, it was entirely rigid.

It took perhaps five minutes, leaving Erienne nervous about possible discovery. She moved her shell over the ward, forcing it home and feeling a satisfying mental thud as the ward accepted and bonded with her creation. She probed for weak points and there were none. Now, she unlocked the rigidity of the shell and used her mind to press against the whole left-hand side. The ward-shell slid gently back into itself, freeing first the handle of the door, then more, until half of it was out of the ward's influence. Satisfied, she stood with her back to the shell and called Will and Thraun.

'Will, there's the lock, it needs picking,' she said as they appeared. 'On no account attempt to move behind me. Only walk in front of me. Do you understand?'

'Yes,' said both men.

The lock was so easy that Will felt vaguely insulted. At Erienne's nod, he turned the handle and pushed the door ajar.

'Go inside and move to the left. Lean against the wall, you'll be safe enough. You too, Thraun, I've got to let the ward back.'

The two men moved inside. By the partial light cast by Erienne's globe, they could make out a dim shape in the centre of the room, long and low. The light brightened as Erienne stepped inside, closing the door behind her. The globe illuminated a simple chamber, panelled in stone with its ceiling at around eight feet.

The shape in the centre was a single stone sarcophagus. It was flat, wide and featureless but for an inscription at one end. On top of it lay a sword, a deep blue and orange robe in a glass case, and an ornamental ring. The atmosphere was easier in the chamber, and Will breathed in deeply, gratefully. He looked around again. The walls were plain and they'd entered by the only door.

'Is this it?' Will was singularly unimpressed.

'What did you expect?' asked Erienne, walking to the sarcophagus, her eyes fixed on the ring, frowning.

'Something a little grander, frankly.'

'A Lore Master may be ostentatious in life, but in death he needs nothing but mana to cloak him. Oh, dear.' She made a slow circuit of the casket, hands deep in her robes.

'What is it?' asked Will.

'The ward surrounding the ring. I . . . hold on.' She breathed deep and looked again at the extraordinary mana shape. It was small, perhaps the size of a human skull, but two factors set it apart. It had three bands of rotating colour – orange, blue and a deep green – and the shape itself was spiked, giving the whole the appearance of an oversized mace.

Erienne had never heard or read of anything like it before, and when she moved her mana-shielded hands towards it, the ward's colours shifted and darkened, threatening to break the shield. She withdrew, arms tingling in the aftermath of the encounter.

'You'd better lock that door, Will,' she said. 'This may take some time.'

'What's the problem?' asked Thraun.

Erienne favoured him with a sympathetic smile. 'I don't think it's something you'd understand.'

'Try me.'

'All right then. The ward shape and construction isn't of purely Dordovan origin. It contains lore from another college and I can't read it. Does that help?'

'Not really,' said Thraun. 'Have you any idea what will trigger it?'

'Someone breaking the shape, I expect,' said Erienne a little petulantly.

'I need you to be more specific,' said Thraun. 'What exactly passing through the shape will break it?'

'I don't follow you.'

'Remind me how a ward works,' said Thraun.

'Why?'

'Humour me, please.' His tone was insistent.

'A ward is a shape of static mana positioned to protect a target,' quoted Erienne. 'The base lore of the shape allows the caster to include or exclude any class of object or being, living or inanimate. So what?' There was an edge to her voice.

'Do you think you can match the mana shape?' asked Thraun.

Erienne sucked her lip and shrugged. 'No,' she said at last. 'Not without considerable risk to us all.'

'In that case, I suggest you concentrate on finding out if there are any exclusions to the ward,' said Thraun quietly.

Erienne stared at Thraun as if he had slapped her, mouth slightly open, eyes wide. '*You suggest?*' She reddened. 'What are you, all of a sudden, some kind of ward constitution specialist? No, I'll tell you what you are, you're a walking slab of muscle who shouldn't presume to speak on subjects you have no knowledge of. How *dare* you try to teach *me*?'

'It was just a suggestion. A simple no would have done.' For all Thraun's voice remained calm and quiet, there was an animal menace in his very slight change of stance.

Will, who had been happy to watch the exchange from the door, now stepped forward, anxious to calm the situation and only too aware of the precarious position they were in.

'Do you have an alternative idea if, indeed, you can't match the ward shape?' he asked.

'With one sweep of my hand I could end all this, how about that?' she said coldly, lifting an arm.

'I mean a sensible one. There's no point in losing everything.'

'Not for you. In case you've forgotten, I already have.' Erienne moved her arm closer to the ring. She sneered. 'Look at you. Big man Thraun and clever little Will. I have the power of life and death over you both. How easy it is to snuff out life.' Abruptly her eyes were full of tears.

Will and Thraun shared a glance. Thraun nodded.

'Erienne, you know how much we grieve for your loss,' said Will, moving towards her. 'We loved your children and we loved Alun and no one can compensate for their deaths. But right now, we need you to help us. We need this ring and we don't have much time before we're caught.' He laid a hand on her arm to draw her to face him. 'Please, Erienne. There is time to cry when we're out of this tomb.'

Erienne stared at Will while tears rolled down either cheek. She shook off his hand and wiped at her face.

'The answer to your question, Thraun, is that, like most Dordovan wards, it excludes people by being triggered by human brain activity, and anything inanimate that passes through it will trigger it too.' Her voice was shaking but she appeared to have regained rationality. 'Not that knowing that does us any good.'

'On the contrary, it means your work is done,' said Thraun.

'Apart from finding and training an animal to take the ring.' The fire was back in Erienne's eyes. 'In case you hadn't noticed, there are none in here.'

'That's not strictly true,' said Thraun.

'What do you mean, not strictly true?'

'Thraun—' Will had tumbled to Thraun's thoughts. He walked over and stood close to the other man. 'You retain a critical part of your sentience. I don't think that qualifies you as an animal,' he hissed.

'We don't have time for anything else,' said Thraun evenly. 'And Erienne can't move the ward. It's our only option.'

'Will you two stop talking riddles? What are you suggesting?'

'Are you sure about this?' asked Will. Thraun nodded. 'Then you can explain.'

'I wish one of you would,' said Erienne, irritation edging her tone.

Thraun took a deep breath. 'It's quite simple.' He shrugged. 'I'm a shapechanger.'

In its cage, the Familiar chittered loudly, like a monkey. It hopped from claw to claw, unfurled its wings as far as the bars allowed, hissed, spat and taunted.

'Close to death, Dordovan, close to death.'

For his part, the mage kept as calm as the situation allowed, never taking his attention from the door, his chosen mana shape part-prepared and quick to complete.

The taunting stopped.

'Now,' hissed the Familiar. It turned its back and covered its head with its wings, actions the mage didn't see. Perhaps if he had, he would have been prepared. Perhaps.

The windows at his back blew in, glass and wood splinters showering the room. Next came Denser, ShadowWings sweeping back as he shot feet first into the middle of the floor.

The mage, disorientated by the sudden explosion behind him, was only halfway up and turned when Denser's fist caught him full on the jaw. He staggered back, concentration broken, spell lost and unable to raise a defence to the next punch to his nose or the boot in his gut. He collapsed on to the floor, sliding down the door by which he'd been so sure Denser would enter.

The Xeteskian stood over him, hauled him to his feet, dark eyes burning into him with uncontrolled hatred.

'More will arrive, you can't beat us all,' said the Dordovan.

Denser's laugh was pure scorn. 'Too late for you.' A headbutt split the Dordovan's lips open, spattering blood. Denser dragged him towards the mana cage.

'You'll never open it,' said the Dordovan defiantly. 'And I'll die before I help you free that thing.'

'So foolish.' Denser, his voice suddenly quiet, held the other's face close to his. 'So very, very blind. One magic, one mage.' He dropped the man back to the floor and simply flipped the latch. The mana cage dissolved and a ball of fury came boiling out.

Chapter 21

Jandyr stared through the gate at the house, which was partially obscured by trees and other buildings. All appeared quiet in the Dordovan College. The street outside had some passing traffic but certainly wasn't busy, and the guard at the gate seemed unconcerned by his attention.

He was at something of a loss. He knew he wouldn't gain entry to the College at this hour but took the lack of activity as a sign that nothing more had gone wrong after the taking of the cat. All he could do was wait and see.

Away behind him, towards the centre of the City, he heard a commotion. The shouting resolved into the sound of hooves getting closer.

Pain flared briefly in Erienne's skull and she staggered, clutching at the sides of her head. She dropped to her knees as the jolt momentarily robbed her of her balance. She felt dazed and squeezed her eyes tight shut. She heard Will rush to her side.

'What is it? Are you all right?'

'Gods, that hurt,' she spluttered, shaking her head as the rattling in her brain subsided. She calmed herself, probing the mana trails that ran the length and breadth of the Tower, looking for the breach. It was in the Tower's top storey, and when she found it, she gasped.

'There's a Xeteskian in the Tower,' she grated, staggered by the audacity of the act.

'Denser?' asked Will.

'Who else?' She pulled herself to her feet. 'He'll have woken every mage in the building.' She looked at Thraun. 'Whatever you're going to do, make it quick. We've just run out of time.' Thraun's revelation of his nature had at once shocked Erienne and made perfect sense. How else could he see like an elf in the dark? How else could he track and trail as silently as a hunting animal? How indeed? She had no idea whether to be afraid, fascinated, disgusted or amazed at him.

Thraun immediately began stripping off his clothes.

'Listen, Erienne, the change is quick but people tend to find it horrible. Feel free to look away if you need to, I won't be offended because I won't know. Will, don't leave my gear, I won't get a chance to re-form until we're away from here.'

Will nodded. 'I hope you know what you're doing. Good luck.'

Once naked, Thraun lay down on the cold stone floor, flinching at its touch. He lay on his side, legs drawn half up and arms straight out in front of him. He closed his eyes and slowed his breathing before tapping into that part of his mind which he feared, loved, loathed and cherished.

In a heartbeat his thought patterns changed. His mind filled with dreams of the pack, the joy of the chase and the glory of the kill. He could scent blood in his nostrils and the myriad odours of the forest. He dreamed of speed and the muscles of his limbs thickened, bones shifting, pads forming. He dreamed of the power in his face and his jaws extended, fangs growing, tongue flattening, nostrils developing. He dreamed he could hear the noises of the world all around him and his ears rose from the top of his skull. He dreamed of strength and his rib cage rounded, lungs expanded and heart pumped faster.

He could feel the sky above him, remember the prey at his feet and hear the sounds of his brethren calling him. He knew he had come home, but deep in his psyche, a voice tolled one word: 'Remember.'

He rose quickly to his feet, growling deep in his chest, strength pouring into his re-formed muscle. He saw the woman-friend move backwards and the man-packbrother raise a hand that all was well. He turned his attention to the lid of the tomb.

Erienne had always prided herself that she could view anything with an objective eye. The horrors she had seen during her training had numbed her to most things, but Thraun's transformation was something completely out of her experience. He was right, it was quick, but it would live with her for ever. And now he was standing, about four feet at the shoulder, massive jaws slightly apart, just staring at her with those same yellow-tinged eyes. His coat was a pale brown, flecked with grey, and down his neck ran a stripe of pure white. Beside her, Will waved, and at that, Thraun leapt on to Arteche's tomb, walked through the ward sweeping up the ring with his tongue, then jumped down again. He dropped the ring at his feet and looked up squarely at Will.

Relief flooded Erienne. Had Thraun triggered the ward, they would have been obliterated, and Will's lack of fear at the sight of the wolf had an instantly calming effect on her nerves. She reached out and Thraun sniffed her hand.

'You'd better move that ward outside again,' said Will. 'I've left my key in the door, just give it half a turn.' He whistled to attract Thraun's attention. 'When we leave, we will be running. You can re-form back in the forest. It will be dangerous. Follow me.' He half crouched and reached out a hand to the ring. Thraun growled and placed a paw on it. 'You keep it then.'

'How much of that did he understand?' asked Erienne. She had the door open and was looking over her shoulder at Will, who shrugged.

'It's hard to say. He gets the gist of most things, I think, and there are certain words I know he understands. Unfortunately, he can't remember how he understands, just that he does.'

Thraun took his paw from the ring and licked it back into his mouth. There would be threat, man-packbrother had said. He would be running. There would be a forest. The calls of the brethren echoed in his ears once more.

Reversing the ward was easy, fortunately. The construction of the mana shape meant the bubble couldn't be burst from the inside. But because the trap spell could still be triggered, Erienne had to move it aside. It was the work of seconds.

'Will he follow us?'

'Yes,' said Will. 'But remember he's completely independent. He won't necessarily listen to anyone, not even me, and that makes him dangerous.'

'To us?'

'No, he knows we're friends. But he's essentially a wild animal and will react to threat as such.'

'Right.' Erienne set off, the globe above her head lighting the way.

'Thraun, let's go,' said Will loudly. He jogged after Erienne, hearing his friend loping along in his wake, padded feet kissing the floor gently.

The demon streaked across the space to the mage and buried the claws of its feet in the man's shoulders. All pretence at bravado gone, he gibbered and whimpered, thrashing his limbs on the floor but unable to strike the beast that drooled on his face.

'Kill him,' said Denser.

'No!' wailed the mage. 'Please.'

The demon cut him off, pushing his mouth closed with one hand. 'Your soul is mine,' it said. It arched its back, spread its arms wide, clenched its fists and brought them back to impact the sides of the mage's head with massive force. His skull crumpled like pottery between stones, his brain exploding into the Familiar's delighted face. It fed, gorged itself on blood and brain while Denser looked on, dispassionate but appeased.

He became aware of people approaching the room. Multiple footsteps hurrying, and an urgent sound of voices.

'Enough,' said Denser. The Familiar looked up, disappointed. 'We have company.' Denser prepared another set of ShadowWings, his reserves of mana stamina falling low.

'Disperse them and find Erienne. Downstairs. Bring them to the gate and be sure she remains unharmed. I'll be watching over you.'

The Familiar smiled, blood dripping from its chin. 'You will always watch over me?' it asked.

'Until the day my soul departs this world,' responded Denser. He turned and flew from the shattered window, rising into the night sky and augmenting his vision to bring the house and its surrounds into bright focus.

The Familiar, content and sated, paused on its way to the doors, deciding to let whoever it was open them. It hovered a few feet above the corpse of the mage, sitting cross-legged on the air, wings beating time.

The doors crashed open and more than half a dozen people spilled in, guards with swords glinting and mages with hands free for casting. They pulled up short at the sight of their brother, head a mass of brain, blood and shards of bone. A beat later, they saw the Familiar. It laughed, a cold sound delighting at the death and mayhem it had created. Then it was among them, talons outstretched, wings beating around heads, saliva flying, tail flashing, roaring with mirth as they ducked and scattered, shouting alarm and fear.

It paused to see its handiwork, took in the bloody faces and the expressions of confusion and disbelief, turned a loop and stormed down the central stairwell, laughter echoing from the portraits hung at every level.

Jandyr stepped back into the street as Sol powered his horse through the protesting Dordovans. He ignored them, reining in by the elf and dismounting.

'Go to the inn,' he said. 'Bring the other horses here.' He handed Jandyr the reins. 'You will be quicker on this,' he said, every word carefully spoken as if his vocal chords were stiff from under-use.

'Please,' he added before running for the gates, hands free, weapons on his back.

'What's going on?' called Jandyr after him.

'Trouble.'

Jandyr shrugged, mounted up and hurried back to the inn stables.

Erienne hit the stairs at a dead run. She'd felt the life force of a mage dissipate violently through the mana, and anger at Denser's assumed action swamped her already frail thoughts of caution.

'The ward, Erienne!' shouted Will. Labouring under the weight of the mana, he was trailing her by a good many paces.

'Too late to worry about it. That idiot's already seen to that.'

'Who?'

'You know who.' There was disappointment in her voice but sympathy in her mind. Her LightGlobe triggered the ward, setting off a clarion call that echoed through the Tower and battered at Will's ears. Behind him, Thraun yelped and accelerated past, bounding up the stairs and overtaking Erienne as she opened the door.

The hallway was empty, but as the alarm faded away, the sounds of angry voices and movement came from all quarters. Thraun chased to the front doors and pawed ineffectually at the handles with Erienne only a few paces behind him. They both missed the descending Familiar but Will, last out of the crypt, was greeted by a sight far beyond his worst nightmare.

He had glanced around to check for enemies and had just seen Erienne open one of the main doors when his vision was filled with the blood-smeared face of Denser's demon. Its skull pulsed and crawled and it laughed wildly, raising a claw to strike before recognising him. It leaned into him and said:

'Come, come. Out. Out to the gate.'

Will opened his mouth and screamed.

Denser saw it all unfold. As Jandyr rode for the city centre, Sol strode up to the guard and felled him with a single punch. He ran into a College which had woken to mayhem.

Erienne emerged from the Tower, followed by a massive wolf, but before Denser could even think how to stop it catching and killing her, it had turned and run back inside.

Erienne faltered too, half turning as she dashed for the gate. She stumbled.

'No, no!' hissed Denser, and dived for the path. Mages, guards and acolytes were coming from everywhere, giving Erienne a shield of chaos. One even helped her to her feet. Denser shot in towards Sol.

'See her out,' he shouted above the rising noise of discovery, anger and organisation. 'And find my Other. I'm going to help Jandyr.' Sol nodded and Denser flitted back into the sky, trailing the elf astride Sol's fast-moving horse.

Erienne smiled at the mage who had helped her up and dashed back towards the Tower.

'What's happening?' asked the mage, making to chase her.

'There's a Xeteskian in the College.' She ran on into the house, sliding to a stop at the scene that greeted her eyes.

Thraun and what she assumed had to be Denser's Familiar circled each other in the centre of the hall, loosely ringed by a group of four disbelieving mages. The winged beast darted left, right, up and down while Thraun lashed claws and bit at empty space. He already sported a deep cut on his nose. She couldn't see Will.

The only thought in Erienne's mind as she shouted at them to stop was that she might get badly hurt. But there was no time for any other action. She ran in front of Thraun, who snarled in frustration as his target was obscured. She put her back to him and shuddered as the Familiar dropped into her view. She felt Thraun tensing behind her.

'Thraun, no!' she ordered over her shoulder. 'Friend.' It was the only word she could think of that he might understand, but one more inappropriate she couldn't imagine.

'And you stop it now!' she spat at the demon. It grinned and chuckled, looked past her at the wolf.

'Leave him, it's Thraun,' she warned.

The demon backed off immediately, grin replaced by an expression of surprise. 'Shapechanger—' it said, expelling breath in a hiss.

'Yes, now get out after your master and never presume to defile the grounds of this College again.'

'Yes, mistress,' said the Familiar, and powered out of the door.

Erienne turned and found herself facing the quartet of mages for whom the spell of incomprehension had been broken.

'You know these . . . things?' one asked. All of them had read the mana trails to identify her as Dordovan.

'Acquainted, certainly,' said Erienne brusquely. 'And soon you'll be free of all contamination, I'm seeing to it personally. Now please excuse me, I'm in a hurry.' She started towards the crypts, then saw she wouldn't have to find an excuse to search them. Will was huddled near the door, shaking. 'Will? What the—?'

A hand was laid on her arm. 'I think you'd better come with us. That was a Xeteskian Familiar you spoke to. It called you mistress.' The man holding her arm was middle-aged. His greying hair was receding and thin but his eyes, dark and brooding, were strong as they bored into her face. Erienne didn't recognise him.

'Yes, and as you can see, I have ordered it from the College. And now I'd like to help my friend.' Her heart was beginning to beat faster again. She had to buy enough time.

'A commoner in the Tower after nightfall,' he said, at once dismissive and threatening.

'Never mind that, he needs help. Look at him,' urged Erienne, casting a glance to where Will hadn't changed his position. What had happened to him?

The mage did not trouble to look. 'It isn't that simple, as you must be aware.'

'Let go of my arm.'

'No.' The grip tightened and the rest of the mages began to close in.

Erienne flicked her head nervously, in her mind cursing Denser's stubbornness in sending in the Familiar to watch her. Thraun growled deep in his throat and moved towards her. The mages looked as one.

'Do it,' she said. 'Please. I can't control him.'

'We can take them both,' said another of the mages. 'You know what to do.'

'Gods,' said Erienne, knowing instinctively which spell they would cast. 'Thraun, run!'

The wolf didn't hear her. Man-packbrother was hurt and the woman-friend was under threat. He removed the source of the threat.

The mage's shout of alarm was cut off abruptly, Thraun's jaws clamping around his neck, bearing him to the ground hard. Erienne stumbled as the grip on her arm was wrenched off and the hall dissolved into a few moments of total confusion.

Erienne shouted for Thraun not to kill the mage as Sol charged through the main doors, scattering the mages and swatting one with a punch to the back of the neck as he ran. Their concentration broken, the mages ran into the library, slamming the door behind them.

'Thraun, leave him!' yelled Erienne, rushing to the wolf's head, expecting to see nothing but blood. Instead, Thraun looked around and she could see, under his paws, the terrified mage, pressure marks in his neck but otherwise very much alive. Sol saw him into unconsciousness and Erienne turned her attention to Will.

The little man had curled into a ball and was rocking slowly to and fro. He was silent but tremors racked his body, pushing breath through his clenched teeth in a juddering hiss.

'Will?' Erienne touched his arm and he flinched violently. 'We've got to go.'

Thraun padded to her side and nuzzled him, licking his face. There was no reaction but a movement in the mana had Erienne jerking upright.

'Casting!' she said. She yanked at Will's sleeve. 'Come on! Get up!' He wouldn't move. And then Sol was at her shoulder. He stooped and swept Will into his arms.

'Run,' he said. They ran.

Jandyr galloped into the stableyard wondering how he was going to saddle and bring four horses to the College in the short time he had, only to find Denser already there. He was barking orders at the stable lad, whose fear was all too apparent. Denser had what appeared to be wings folded at his back.

'You took your time,' he said.

Jandyr didn't reply. He dismounted and ran to the lad. 'Which one next?' he asked.

The lad pointed at Thraun's horse. 'T-tack and saddled inside on the left, first h-hook,' he said. And then to the elf's back, 'He just flew down. He flew. He shouldn't . . .'

'All right, son.' Jandyr reappeared with saddle and bridle. 'He won't harm you.' He caught Denser's gaze briefly. His blasted cat poked its head from his cloak and Jandyr swore it was smiling.

The mage pulled a girth strap tight and buckled it. 'You lead, I'll be above you,' he said. 'I'll make sure the other horses follow you, don't worry about them.'

'Whatever you say,' said Jandyr.

'Hurry.'

'Shut up.'

Erienne had no idea what spell was being cast from the library, but she was sure it would be an entrapment of some kind. And as she sprinted down the steps on to the path, she heard the door fly shut behind her, crackling and fizzing. WardLock. They had been very lucky.

Sol forged on ahead, carrying Will like a sack over one shoulder. Thraun loped easily by Erienne, who was pushing hard. The grounds of the College were still wreathed in confusion but too many people were paying them attention, Thraun saw to that.

Even so, Erienne thought they'd escape the gates unchallenged, but felt her heart sink as she heard a single voice shout: 'Stop them.'

Jandyr would have preferred to smooth his passage with apology but he'd never have left the stableyard. Pausing only to flick some coins to the lad, he climbed on to his horse, kicked its flanks and charged out into the streets of Dordover. Above him, Denser kept pace at a height of about one hundred feet, and behind him, the quartet of riderless horses kept close form.

The streets were busy with early evening traffic and walkers. Jandyr kept up a barrage of shouted warnings, conscious of the attention he was undoubtedly drawing to his headlong dash in the direction of the College. Most cleared the way but the odd one, he knew, would take a kick or be trampled by the barely controlled stampede.

Thundering away from the centre of the City, Jandyr was approaching a residential and parkland area when Denser abruptly swooped to his side.

'Trouble ahead,' he shouted above the clatter of hooves on cobbles. 'Take the next left, carry on to a large warehouse and go right. Keep going down there and I'll catch you.' He disappeared back into the sky.

Jandyr had no desire to find out what the trouble was and swung his horse left as indicated. The others followed, though not without some pause, Denser's influence diminishing with distance.

Two things saved Erienne in her chase for the relative safety of the streets outside the College. The reluctance of any mage to cast a spell with so many innocents in the way was one, and the dual threat posed by Sol and Thraun the other. The Protector threw Will over one shoulder, snatched his axe from his scabbard and simply roared his way to the gates, while the howling maw of Thraun kept any blade from their rear.

And so it was that they rushed out of the gate and on into the bedlam that was overtaking Dordover.

Denser flew fast for the College. The mana over the buildings was again a solid orange and he refocused to search for Erienne and the shapechanger.

Between them and the horses, Denser knew, was a cordon of City Guards. More would follow. To the north, the College Guard was coming together, some already on horseback. And there, running blind along the main street and pursued by at least ten College Dordovans, were Erienne, Sol and the wolf. It was a moment before Denser saw Will carried like a sack over Sol's left shoulder, one massive arm clamped around his midriff. They were going to be trapped.

Jandyr turned along the side of the warehouse and continued his gallop. His eyes pierced the dark of night and the blank of shadow, while at his back, the four horses were getting skittish. Denser had strayed too far. A few strides further on, Jandyr halted to tie the horses off and fix the reins to his saddle. In the midst of the mêlée of flank and fetlock, he grabbed at bits and bridles, snapping out orders that were half obeyed.

He linked pairs of reins then looped the master set over the rear of his saddle, tied in a slip knot. Halfway back on to his horse once more, he was stopped by a voice.

'Want to sell those horses? They look a little much for one man – I beg your pardon, one elf.'

Denser dropped to Sol's shoulder.

'You're running into trouble. Go right and follow me.' The mage led the fleeing trio off the main street. He rose to get his bearings on Jandyr and saw him backing away from a ring of torchlight.

'Damn it.' He melded minds with his Familiar. 'Follow my eyes and bring Sol to me.' The demon flew from his cloak.

There were five of them, one for each horse, noted Jandyr drily. Three carried torches, all carried blades. He had snatched his ready-strung bow from its ties, quiver already over one shoulder. With one arrow nocked, he backed off, keeping the horses behind him. He knew he had to buy time, he just wasn't sure how much.

'Move away from the rides,' repeated one. Their faces harsh in the torchlight, the men moved forward.

'I can't do that.'

'Then we'll be forced to kill you.'

'One of you goes first. Which will it be?' Jandyr swung his bow in an arc, encompassing them all. 'You,' he said, targeting one with unease in his eyes. 'One more pace and you're a dead man.'

His intended target stopped walking, but the others moved on, quicker now as they closed.

'You can't stop us all that way.'

Jandyr glanced at the sky in the direction of the College and saw Denser descending like an eagle on its prey. He smiled.

'I won't have to.'

Denser, knees raised, cannoned into the head of one man, sending him crashing into another. Both hit the ground hard. Jandyr released his arrow and took his target in the chest. He nocked another, stretched his arm and aimed at the two still standing.

'If you want to run, run now.' They needed no further invitation.

Ignoring the men he had felled, Denser untied the horses and climbed on to one, his ShadowWings gone. Jandyr paused to cut the arrow from his lifeless victim.

'Let's go, come on.' Denser urged his horse to move, the others following mutely. Jandyr hauled himself into his saddle and the race was on.

Erienne felt her lungs were about to explode. Her heart slammed painfully in her chest, her legs were tree trunks and her head thudded. She was slowing them down, she knew, and behind her, the pursuit was closing. An arrow missed her by inches, plunging off into the street where an innocent was equally lucky. Shouts of recrimination reached her ears and that threat at least was removed.

Beside her, Thraun still ran easily, and half a dozen paces ahead, Sol, with the Familiar standing on his right shoulder, one hand pointing the way, the other arm around his head, cleared a path with his presence alone.

They were running up a wide street towards the centre of Dordover. It led straight into the central marketplace, taking them past the old grain store which was now the headquarters of the City Guard. While the roads around the College were quiet following nightfall, Dordover was a lively city after dark, and the City Guard were plentiful, policing the street theatre crowds, the food stalls and the alleys where whores plied their trade and the dagger was as much currency as was coin.

As she thought to shout a warning, Sol veered right, taking a narrow passage leading directly away from the main street. Here, the life ahead was replaced by the quiet menace of the industrial quarter. Footpads haunted the shade and every corner was a trap for the unwary. With no lamplight, the shadows extended their dark fingers across the ground. Erienne stumbled but remained on her feet, while behind her, Thraun howled. The sound bounced from the walls and echoed into the sky like a cry from hell. Erienne found herself wondering who was chasing them and whether the noise would stop them. It would have stopped her, she was sure of that.

Running on, she followed Sol round a left-and-right combination into a wider alley. Tall buildings rose to either side, their walls glaring down, deeper black than the night. Thraun was again at her side and she could hear the mob behind. Their shouts were mixed with the unmistakable sound of hooves clattering across stone and slapping through mud.

And then she could see them approaching through the gloom, reining to a halt in front of them. Sol ploughed on, the Familiar back in cat form, and Erienne realised the two horsemen had to be Denser and Jandyr. She staggered into the group.

'Are you hurt?' asked Denser.

'Don't talk to me,' she managed between gasps. 'They're close. We need to rush.'

As if to add weight to her words, the chasing pack of around twenty men burst into the alley. Arrows rattled and skipped off the walls and the Dordovans charged. Sol threw Will across his saddle and all but picked Erienne up and dumped her in hers. Mounting up, he wheeled his horse in a tight arc and galloped off. In a cacophony of whinnies, flashing hooves and ducking heads, the others followed.

Thraun turned and ran at the enemy.

Leading the way, Sol pushed his horse back past the warehouse and left into the main street. Denser was close behind, with Erienne, her strength gone, clinging grimly to her saddle and flanked by Jandyr, who held the reins of Thraun's riderless mount.

Arrows flew over his head towards the horses as Thraun crashed into the front of the mob, his bulk bearing him straight over one man to bury his jaws in the neck of another. A swing of his head and the victim's throat was torn out, his cries lost in blood. In ten seconds of claw and fang, Thraun had scattered the bewildered pursuers. Some had run, some backed off. Others lay still and one or two would never move again.

His job done, he broke off and stretched his limbs for the long run into the forest, howling his delight as he went.

Chapter 22

'It's exciting being in The Raven, isn't it?' said Hirad leaning back against his tree and stretching his legs in front of him.

'Feeling more comfortable about it now, are you?' asked Ilkar.

'No, I'm feeling surplus to requirements.'

'Well, you're not.'

'You know what I mean.'

The campsite was clear. All equipment was stowed and tied to the saddles, and the three horses, which included Denser's, were tethered just a few yards away.

Hirad smiled, remembering his friend's urgent words as they scurried around the camp to clear it. And now they'd been sitting with their backs to trees for getting on for an hour. He thought he ought to be worried about what was going on in Dordover, but for some reason, apart from his remaining anger at Denser, he felt oddly calm. Maybe it was just that none of them was original Raven so he didn't care that much. Actually, that was certainly part of it, but there was more – there were some of them, Thraun and Jandyr in particular, in whom he found he had great confidence. Almost the sort of confidence he had had in The Unknown and Sirendor. Almost.

Sadness fell on him with the force of night, and the memories swept through his mind, images of death and loss overwhelming the good times he recalled so fleetingly. Ras dying as they fought around him; Richmond trying to defend a man he didn't even know and paying with his life; The Unknown, his blood soaking the earth outside the low barn; and Sirendor . . . Sirendor, his life draining away while all Hirad could do was watch. For all his great words, he hadn't been able to protect any of them, and now Talan was gone too, driven away by fear and the knowledge that if he stayed on his death was inevitable.

He wiped at his eyes and looked over at Ilkar. Gods help him if he lost Ilkar, his only link to The Raven he loved and for which he had lived.

His heart began to race and his breathing shallowed. It was all beyond his control. There in Dordover, the fate of the new Raven, and perhaps that of Balaia, was being decided, and he was on the edge. A peripheral figure reduced to saddling horses and clearing campsites. Maybe they'd been right those short weeks ago in another life when they'd joked about his age. It was no joke. He'd slipped from leader to led and he hadn't noticed the change. Denser. Denser had done it. And the one thing he couldn't have was Denser in command of The Raven. Not after what he had caused.

He lifted a shaking hand to wipe across his nose and took a slow, deliberate breath, glancing again at Ilkar, hoping his fears weren't written for all to see. But Ilkar wasn't looking at him. He'd cocked his head to one side and, as Hirad watched, put an ear to the ground, hands either side, and tensed.

Hirad was already halfway up by the time Ilkar said:

'Someone's coming.'

'Let's hope it's them.'

'Well, I'm not standing around waiting to find out.' They ran for the horses but had not covered half the distance when light bloomed behind them, creating a false dawn, sweeping away the night and throwing sharp shadow ahead of it. A heartbeat later, the detonation and a noise like rushing water.

The horses bucked and pulled at their tethers. Hirad clutched at his mount's bridle, dodging a flailing front hoof and coming face against a wild rolling eye.

'I don't like the sound of that!' he shouted, trying in vain to calm his horse as he tugged to release the rein.

'No time,' gasped Ilkar. 'Just get on.' His horse was calmer, and Denser's, after flinching violently at the light, was still.

'On this?' Hirad hauled the rein free and his mount whinnied, front legs pawing the ground. 'We're going, we're going!' He hooked a foot into a stirrup while the mare jumped and snorted, threatening to bolt before he hit the saddle. 'Calm down, damn you!' He swung on to its back and forced some semblance of order on the terrified beast. As he turned it, a wolf streaked into the clearing from the direction of the light and away into the forest the other side. His horse reared again. He couldn't hold it.

Above the rushing sound, hoofbeats, and Denser broke cover.

'Go, go,' he yelled, and plunged off after the wolf. Erienne galloped through, holding an arm in front of her face to ward off branches, and behind her came Jandyr and a riderless horse, followed by Sol with the body of Will across his saddle. None of them paused in their flight.

Hirad fought his horse in desperate circles as it champed and kicked, too scared to run in any direction. And then as it slowed to a stop, quivering before bolting, Hirad looked into the light and saw what the rushing sound was. Fire. Moving towards him, engulfing tree, bush and grass faster than a man could run.

'Oh, dear God!' He hauled on the reins and jabbed his heels in hard. The horse responded. Into the fire was certain death. At least following the wolf gave them a chance.

And as he began to gallop into the forest, Hirad couldn't shake the vision of the wolf from his mind. If they weren't chasing it, there was only one reason why they should be following it, and that reason made Hirad's stomach lurch.

Ilkar drew to Erienne's side as they exited the forest a few hundred yards from the clearing. He'd lost sight of Hirad and could barely hear the other horses he knew were around him, the roar of the FlameOrb was so loud. That it was a type of FlameOrb he had no doubt. How they'd managed to create one so big and powerful was another matter.

'When will it burn out?' he yelled at Erienne.

'The forest is fuelling it, it won't reach far past the borders.'

'How did they do it?'

'ManaStack. It's a co-operative spell casting. I knew they were working on it but I had no idea they'd applied it to the FlameOrb. It's very draining, they'll all be spent who cast it.'

'Then why are we still running?' asked Ilkar.

Erienne began to rein in, and further ahead, could see that Denser had reached the same conclusion. In fifty yards, the dash was over and, horses wheeled, they lined up to see the FlameOrb spend itself at the edge of the forest.

'Where is he?' whispered Ilkar. 'Where is he?' The yellow bloom of the FlameOrb grew as it thrashed towards them. Above it, a thick cloud of woodsmoke cluttered the night sky, obscuring the stars. On the grassland in front of the tree line, the shadows lengthened at a frightening pace as the flames demolished an area of woodland easily seventy yards across. With a great whoosh it broke clear of the confines of the trees and expired in the open air, and as the last flame faded to orange and disappeared, Ilkar saw a single silhouetted figure on horseback, riding hard towards them.

The elf let out a breath he didn't realise he was holding and his face cracked into a grin. He looked across the line of horses, caught Denser's eye and nodded. Denser raised his eyebrows.

'Not easy to lose, is he?' he said.

'No,' agreed Ilkar. His face hardened. 'Right, Erienne, what can we expect now?'

'The casting mages will be spent but there may be others. There were certainly some soldiers in the pack. No doubt they'll be behind the flame.'

'And not far behind it,' said Jandyr. 'Look.' Ilkar followed his hand and saw seven or eight people running out of the forest. And, skimming the trees, a pair of mages.

'Damn,' said Ilkar. 'Can we outrun them?' Erienne shrugged her shoulders. Hirad pulled up, his face red with exertion, his horse shaking all over.

'Too close,' he said. 'Too bloody close.'

'It's not over yet. We've got ten to deal with,' said Ilkar.

Hirad turned his body and stared behind him, squinting slightly into the half-light from the stars and the fires still burning in the forest. He slid off his horse. 'We'll take them here.'

'We've got two mages in the sky,' said Ilkar.

Hirad shrugged. 'So shield us. You're the best there is.' He looked right and left. All but Sol were still on their horses. Gods, he'd have to drill them. The Raven would have been in skirmish formation by now. If they weren't all dead. Sol was already striding forwards, unhitching his sword as he went. At least someone knew what was going on.

'Jandyr, to Sol's left. I'll take the right. Where's Thraun?'

'No time to explain, but—'

'He's a shapechanger. Gods alive!' said Hirad. He pushed the knowledge from his mind. 'We can do it with three swords. How many of them are there?'

'Eight swords, two spells.' Ilkar began readying the shield. 'Either of you two know HardShield?'

'I can't cast,' said Denser, drawing his sword.

'Yes,' said Erienne.

'Good. Get it over our heads, I can sort the magical attacks. Denser, put your sword up and go away with the horses. Send Thraun back if you see him.' Ilkar locked eyes with the Xeteskian for a moment. The latter put up his blade, whistled to his horse and trotted away behind them.

Thirty yards and closing. Hirad felt a double surge as the magical and hard shields went up around them. Jandyr loosed off an arrow, taking down one man. He thought to try another, but they were closing too fast. The enemy mages landed to cast, a spell clattered against the shield, flashing orange as it died.

Hirad breathed deep and roared to clear his head. Just like the old days except they weren't so old. The enemy were splitting, trying to flank them. He glanced over at Sol. The masked man stared straight ahead, taking in the scene, concentration so complete it could almost be felt. Just like . . . Hirad became aware of a sound and looked to the ground in front of Sol. The Protector was tapping the tip of his blade rhythmically against the ground. Hirad almost dropped his, clutching it as the nerves returned to his muscles. Just like the old days.

'Unknown!' he shouted. Sol turned to him, and there, in his eyes, was the unmistakable flicker of recognition.

'Fight,' he said, his voice laden with sorrow.

'But . . .' began Hirad.

'Fight,' said Sol again. From nowhere, Thraun smashed into the enemy's left flank and battle was joined.

Nothing could stop Hirad. No one could stand in his way and he almost felt sorrow for the hapless Dordovan soldiers as they were systematically destroyed. His heart was full of joy, the back of his mind full of confusion, but his fighting brain was irresistible.

As the first man went down under Thraun's jaws, the enemy strategy fell to pieces. Hirad battered the nearest skull, while beside him the big man slaughtered two without even moving his feet. Sensing Jandyr holding his own, Hirad strode forwards, slitting the stomach of one, parrying a blow from a second then slicing his sword through the attacker's hamstrings as he was forced around. The two remaining men turned and fled, their mages close behind them.

'Shield down,' said Ilkar, staring at Sol. 'Come on, let's get out of here.'

'Are you kidding?' asked Hirad, his face alight. He wiped his bloodied blade on one of his victims and resheathed it. 'Ilkar, it's him! I don't know how, I don't care, but it's him!'

'Please, Hirad,' implored Ilkar. 'This isn't the time.'

'What do you mean?' The smile was fading from Hirad's lips.

'Just bear with me. We have to get away from here first, then we can talk.' Ilkar started walking in the direction of Denser. The elf could see the Xeteskian's face and knew at once that he had no idea of Sol's former identity.

'Hang on.' Hirad tugged at Ilkar's shoulder. 'Has this got something to do with him being a Protector?'

Ilkar stopped and faced him. 'Everything.' He held up a hand against Hirad's next utterance. 'And Denser knew nothing. He has no say over the choice. Please, let's go.' He was moving again, leaving Hirad to throw his arms up. Thraun loped by.

'And what about him?' demanded Hirad. 'How are we supposed to deal with him?'

'He won't harm you,' said Jandyr. 'Please let him be.'

'You can't just . . .' began Hirad. Sol strode past him. 'Unknown, please!' Sol didn't falter. 'Will someone tell me what is going on!' Hirad shouted.

'Later,' said Ilkar.

'Now.'

'No, Hirad, we can't stay here. The Dordovans will be back. We've got to find a place to hide.' Ilkar jabbed a finger at Denser. 'This may not be your doing but have you *any* idea what Xetesk has just uncorked? I cannot believe that even they could be so stupid!' He shook his head.

'Neither can I,' said Denser. Hirad saw him look at Sol, close his eyes and rub a hand over his face. 'Neither can I.'

Hirad stood it for half an hour as they rode hard away from Dordover, heading for the Blackthorne Mountains. And when he could take it no more, he drove them off the trail and into some low hills, stopping in the lee of a crag, completely hidden by the road.

He watched in silence as Sol helped the now conscious Will off his horse. The thief sat down, looking at no one, taking in nothing, staring inside of himself. Jandyr walked across and sat next to him, trying to get through, but there was no reaction. Sol walked away a few paces and sat down himself, stroking the Familiar, while Erienne moved to Denser. Thraun trotted away into the gloom and disappeared.

'First things first,' said Hirad. 'The Unknown.'

'Is it him?' asked Denser. He was filling his pipe, standing in between Ilkar and Hirad.

'Shouldn't I be asking you that question?' asked Ilkar.

'I don't know.'

'It's him. Tell me how it's him, how he's not dead and tell me why there's a problem, because you two obviously think there is.' Hirad looked across at Sol again. 'Gods, I don't know why there should be.

The Unknown coming back could make all the difference.' He smiled briefly. 'Well?'

Denser breathed deep. 'I may as well tell you. I knew The Unknown was a Protector. That night after we'd buried him, I was on watch. I heard the demons taking his soul.'

'And you didn't see fit to let us know?' Ilkar was stunned.

'What would have been the point?' snapped Denser. 'You were in bad enough shape as it was. All I'd have done was ruin your memory of him by claiming him as a native Xeteskian who'd denied his lineage. I mean, do you think you would have believed me?'

'No, probably not,' said Hirad after a time. 'But if you knew . . .'

'Never in my wildest dreams did I think he'd be assigned to me. If I'd thought so for one moment I'd never have accepted him.'

'Not good enough, eh?'

'Hirad!' warned Ilkar.

'What does it matter anyway?' asked Hirad, moving away a little and gesturing at Sol. 'Let's get that ridiculous mask off and get on with it.' Silence. 'What?'

'Hirad, I can't take the mask off him,' said Denser.

'Well, I'll do it then.'

'No!' Denser voice rose to a shout. He quietened it instantly. 'No. You don't understand. If the mask comes off, he'll be destroyed. Eternally.' He chewed nervously at his unlit pipe and took it back out of his mouth. 'If you say that The Unknown's mind is in Sol's body, then I believe you. But you must realise that he is no longer The Unknown Warrior. He's changed. He's a Protector, he's Sol. There's nothing I can do.'

'You can change him back, that's what you can do.' Hirad's face was stone.

'He can't, Hirad,' said Ilkar. 'That's not The Unknown, not any more.'

'No? He *recognised* me, Ilkar. Didn't you see?'

'He what?' Ilkar leaned forward.

'He knew me. I called him and he knew me.' Hirad shook his head. 'He tapped his blade before he fought. No one else does that.' Hirad's voice was edged with desperation. 'It's him. It can't be anyone else.'

Ilkar turned on Denser. 'Got an explanation for that? I understood that all life memories were blanked.' Denser stared at the ground. 'Tell me that's true,' demanded the elf. 'Tell me.' Denser looked up and held his gaze, his eyes moist. He shook his head. 'Oh, no,' breathed Ilkar. He fell back a pace and turned to where Sol – The Unknown Warrior – sat, his mask facing them. He could all but taste the big man's desolation. 'God's, Unknown. I am so sorry.'

'Ilkar, please?' Hirad put a hand on his shoulder.

'He remembers everything,' said Ilkar. 'Don't you see? He remembers The Raven, The Rookery, all our fights, all those years. His whole life! And he can't ever speak of it or acknowledge it. Ever.'

'What are you talking about?'

'He's in thrall, Hirad. His soul is held by the Mount of Xetesk. If he steps out of line, they will make what he's going through now seem like a Raven party. He'll be dying for eternity.'

Hirad let what Ilkar had said sink in. He walked slowly over to The Unknown and squatted in front of him, gazing deep into his eyes. And there he could see the lifetime of pain and loneliness that lay ahead. Mapped out in those orbs was all that had gone before. Everything. But it was locked away. Lost behind a mask of Xeteskian domination.

'I'm going to get you out of there, Unknown.' Hirad stood up and stalked back to Denser, not seeing the single shake of the masked head behind him.

'Never mind that it's The Unknown,' spat Ilkar. 'You knew what he was going through by the mere fact that he was a Protector.'

'I know! I can't reverse three thousand years of calling. Do you think I want this?' Denser gestured at The Unknown and searched the faces of Hirad and Ilkar. 'I can't begin to make you understand how sorry I am. Please understand that I never wanted this.'

'You know, I'm tired of your apologies, Denser.' Hirad moved in, menacing. 'Everything bad that's happened to The Raven has happened because of you. And not just all my friends who have died on your behalf. All those times when you' – he prodded Denser in the chest – 'you could have killed the rest of us. It's all down to you, this mess, and I've had it. Until you help The Unknown, I'm no longer with you, can you understand that?'

Denser removed his pipe from his mouth 'I realise this is difficult, but I really . . .'

'But nothing, Denser!' Hirad pushed Denser away, the mage stumbling backwards but keeping his footing. 'Through the rip, you risked everything because you were curious. You were going to kill Talan because he couldn't handle it – make The Unknown kill him. With Sha-Kaan, you risked my life without even blinking, and just now you chanced the lives of four people because your precious cat was in trouble, not to mention mine and Ilkar's in your haste to get away.'

'I don't think you're being quite fair.'

'*Quite fair?* It's all down to your mistakes, your haste and your pig-headed arrogance that we're this deep in trouble. I told you to leave it to The Raven but you always had to do it your own way. I told you we survived by being a team but you wouldn't listen. And now,' Hirad moved in again, his nose right at Denser's, 'now the final insult. Him.' He pointed behind him at The Unknown. 'You're telling us you have to leave him in hell and yet you still expect us to ride with you?'

'There's nothing I can do.' Denser shrugged.

Hirad snapped, grabbed him by the collar and hauled him almost off his feet. 'I'll tell you what you can do, Xetesk man. You can commune with your masters and you can tell them that until they release my friend from thrall it's all over. No Dawnthief, no victory. Reckon you can tell them that?'

'Let me go, Hirad.'

'Reckon you can tell them that?' Hirad repeated, barking his words, spittle flying into Denser's face.

'It'll make no difference. They won't release him.'

Hirad looked over at Sol, sorrow swamping his anger in an instant. 'Try. Please?' His voice, suddenly quiet and imploring, was backed by his eyes, searching Denser's, desperate and pleading. He let the Dark Mage go. 'This is my friend. You have to do something.'

Denser wanted to tell him that this wasn't his friend. That he was a Xeteskian fighting machine, a man with natural magical defence and strength augmented by the weight of all the Protectors whose souls resided in the catacombs of Xetesk. A being with no mind but to defend his master. A man quite without emotion or fear. A man whose ability in a fight was increased the more Protectors were around him. That he was no longer The Unknown Warrior.

Instead, he nodded. He couldn't do anything else. And he needed to find out for himself just why Nyer had sent him this Protector amongst the hundreds in the College. And why Styliann had approved the assignment. Something wasn't quite right, and Nyer needed to understand the strength of feeling that bound The Raven together.

'I will commune in the morning, the moment I have recovered my strength,' he said.

Hirad nodded his thanks. 'I mean it,' said the barbarian. 'I can't go on with him still a Protector. I know Balaia is in danger but it would be a betrayal of everything I have lived for.'

*

It was truly astonishing. But at the same time, it was terrifying.

Selyn had visited Parve once before, perhaps ten years ago. It was part pilgrimage, part orientation, part initiation for a mage spy. That time the City had been deserted and devastated, the dust of centuries blowing over scattered ruins, the wind howling across open spaces where great buildings once stood. Then, her march across the Torn Wastes had been simple. A stroll through cracked earth, harsh bramble and shivered stone to an empty ruined City.

Xetesk's mages and Protectors of three hundred years earlier had certainly been thorough. Within Parve itself, every building had been taken apart in a systematic destruction. Anything of any religious or magical significance had been buried. Roads were dug from their foundations, small dwellings obliterated and marketplaces turned inside out. All because Xetesk felt the desire to warn anyone who stood against the Colleges that their magic was no match.

And in an area roughly seven miles in every direction from the centre of Parve, nothing of any worth would ever grow again. The sheer concentration of mana and, myth had it, anger poured into Parve and its surrounds poisoned the air and the earth, snuffing out vegetation and driving all animal life into the surrounding hills and woodland.

So, as the trees rotted and fell, the crops shrivelled and died and the scrubland roots delved deep to lie dormant, the Torn Wastes were born as eternal testimony to the awful power of offensive magic.

As Selyn approached the periphery of the Wastes, she all but ignored the emptiness, registering only that it would take a superhuman CloakedWalk to reach Parve across so large an open space. Because, with the afternoon fading towards a gloomy dusk, hundreds of lights and fires were burning in the City of the Wytch Lords. And surrounding the city were tented encampments bristling with life. The Torn Wastes were awash with Wesmen.

Her vantage point was the tree line which stretched across the eastern border of the Wastes. To her right, not two hundred yards away, a Wesmen guardpost stood at the head of the main east–west path through the scattered woodland. About fifteen men stood or sat around a fire, watching a stream of Wesmen marching from the Wastes, moving in the direction of Understone Pass.

Her decision was a simple one. Either take communion right where she was and be forced to spend the night recovering outside the City, or move on as darkness fell, making her successful passage to Parve more likely.

She knew she should report in, she was overdue, but her chances of capture were greater in the open than ensconced on the roof of an outhouse in the west of Parve. But should she be caught before she had a chance to communicate the incredible sight before her, Xetesk would be denied critical information.

She wasn't long in making up her mind. With a smile, and her eyes on the main prize of her journey, she waited until full nightfall before checking her camouflage and slipping out of the relative safety of the trees and into the evil of the Torn Wastes.

'How disappointing,' said Nyer after Denser had outlined the discovery of Sol's former identity. 'It is clear that the suppression of memory is not perfected.'

'Why did you send him, Master?'

'There was a need to know the answer to the question of latent knowledge affecting performance.'

Denser paused, mind racing, feeling Nyer's presence in his mind. He wanted to remain calm but found he could not.

'You used us for an experiment*?' He fired the thought, knowing it would cause discomfort. 'Do you know what you have done?'*

'Calm yourself, Denser,' warned Nyer. 'There has been no damage. We will merely recall the Protector.'

'It is too late for that. The Raven are demanding you release Sol from thrall.'

'Really?' Nyer's tone suggested amusement. 'They are an interesting group. And what is the penalty for failing to accede to their request?'

'They have threatened to walk away from the search.'

'And will they carry out this threat?'

'I have no doubt that they will,' said Denser. 'I could only be sure of retaining the Dordovan mage, Erienne.'

'You do know that the release of a Protector is still only a theoretical possibility?'

'Yes.' Denser sent a feeling of irritation at the question. 'But the attempt needs to be made if we are to remain on target for the recovery of Dawnthief.'

'Bring your Protector and bring your friends. But be careful. There is treachery in the College from those who would have Dawnthief for themselves. I will do what I can to release Sol. Trust no one.'

Ilkar looked at Denser, lying still on the grass as dawn broke across the sky behind him. He'd seen the occasional movement of his face as his communion progressed, but it gave no indication of the probable outcome.

Hirad came to his shoulder. 'Ready?' he said. Ilkar nodded. The Unknown stood near by, arms folded, impassive behind his mask. 'Will they see sense?'

Ilkar snorted. 'Sense is not a word often employed when talking about the Xetesk Masters. We just have to hope.'

Denser's eyes snapped open. He took a shuddering breath, dragged himself to his feet and faced Ilkar and Hirad.

'Well?' demanded Hirad.

Denser closed his eyes and sighed, a half-smile touching his lips. He spread his arms wide.

'We'd better get saddled up,' he said, swaying.

'Where are we going?' asked Ilkar.

'Xetesk.'

Chapter 23

It was, Ilkar reflected as The Raven rode towards the City of the Dark College, the only viable route to a solution. Yet somehow he'd convinced himself that the Masters would be able to issue instructions to Denser remotely.

Understandably, Denser looked calm and happy. There was something undeniably comforting about returning to your College. It was like going back to the welcoming arms of your family. But watching the Dark Mage chatting easily to Erienne as they rode ahead of him, he couldn't help but feel there was more to his high spirits than his imminent return home.

Xetesk wasn't far. None of the Colleges was far from each other. When they had set off, they had a little over two days' ride ahead of them. Now they were no more than half a day from the closed City, and so much was still to be straightened out.

At least the Dordovan chase had been called off. Denser, following another communion, had confirmed that a four-College meeting had been called at Triverne Lake. The secret of Dawnthief would soon be out.

But there was going to be trouble at the gates of Xetesk. Plenty of it.

Will had refused point-blank to enter the City and wouldn't even ride near Denser and the Familiar. He was still shaking slightly; his nerves – his lifeline – had not recovered and yet the nightmares with which he was plagued worried him less than the grey which flecked his hair.

And Hirad. Hirad didn't want the two catalysts entering the City but he hadn't informed Denser of this. His view was that they might need some bargaining power, and Ilkar was inclined to agree. As for Denser himself, he was curiously tight-lipped. Brooding on something he'd heard in communion.

Ilkar, for his part, was just plain scared. He'd never visited Xetesk – few Julatsans had – but he knew he'd have to go in. And so would

Erienne. What Jandyr and Thraun – now back in human form but still tired – thought, he couldn't guess. Confusion, probably. And wishing they hadn't bumped into The Raven, certainly. Only Erienne had a smile on her face, and for some reason he couldn't fathom, that worried him. Much of the time they rode in silence, keeping to the main trails now they were free of pursuit, but still wary.

Ahead of Ilkar, Hirad, who had done little but stare at The Unknown and glare at Denser, was finally talking to the latter. Ilkar urged his horse forwards, anxious to hear what was being said.

'. . . I haven't given up on you, Denser. I just want to know where you stand.'

'I'm not sure I follow.'

'I mean do you align with The Raven or with your masters?'

Denser thought for a moment. 'If you'd asked me that a week ago I'd have been firmly with Xetesk, the way I was when I met you. But now there's no definite answer – wait, before you say anything, let me explain.

'What I believe is that Balaia faces disaster if we don't recover Dawnthief and use it to destroy the Wytch Lords. In this, I agree with my master that The Raven was, and still is, the most likely route to success.

'But as regards Sol, they have misled me, betrayed your trust and beliefs and so damaged our chances severely. I cannot forget that, because it was a conscious decision to send him and I'm not sure I buy the story that we were the subject of an experiment.'

'Meaning?' Hirad frowned.

'Meaning someone there has a vested interest in my – our – failure.'

'But—?' Hirad was at a loss. 'But if we fail—'

'Not everyone in Xetesk accepts the threat from the Wytch Lords needs to be met with the casting of the spell, but everyone wants Dawnthief to be found. There is a power struggle going on in the Mount, and ownership of Dawnthief will end it. I'm sure Ilkar would be happy to tell you that in Xetesk, Mount politics cloud every decision.'

'All right.' Hirad tried to sort things out in his mind. He rubbed his nose with thumb and forefinger. 'So who sent you out in the first place?'

'My master, Nyer.'

'Well, that's something I suppose, isn't it?'

'Yes,' agreed Denser. 'And it is he I talk to in communion and who has warned me of potential danger inside the City.'

'So what's the problem? Won't he protect you?'

'Possibly. But it was he who sent Sol to us. Look, I think we'd better all stop and talk before we go any further.'

Hirad nodded. They rode off the trail a short distance and Will set up the stove.

'Xetesk is a very different City to Dordover,' said Denser, once a cup of coffee was in his hands.

'I bloody hope so,' muttered Thraun.

Denser ignored him. 'Not only does my presence not guarantee our safety, in certain circles it will invite trouble. Dawnthief and the Wytch Lords have caused a split of opinion as wide as Understone Pass. We must have a strong bargaining position and this is what I suggest.

'I have to go to the Mount with Sol, and to give us the best chance of fair treatment, Ilkar and Erienne should be with me. As a three-College party and with representatives already in Xetesk, we should be all right. You two?'

'I wouldn't want to be anywhere else,' said Erienne, smiling at him. He smiled back.

'Agreed.' Ilkar was less than enamoured to hear the confirmation of his fear.

'And as for the rest of you, the good news is that I think you should stay well away from Xetesk,' said Denser.

'But the bad news is you want us to guard the catalysts while we're at it,' said Hirad. Denser nodded. 'Good. I wondered whether you'd see sense.'

'So did I,' muttered Ilkar.

'Well, we all harbour misconceptions, don't we, Ilkar?' said Denser shortly.

'If that's what you want to call them,' replied Ilkar with equal cool.

'You know, I thought we were really coming to a meaningful understanding.' Denser sighed.

'On the occasions we have had to work together, the situation has been successfully resolved.' Ilkar chose his words with care.

Denser shook his head and pursed his lips. 'What hurts me is that we have really suffered together. Do all those hours with the Black Wings mean nothing? Or our fight to keep Hirad alive? What else do I have to do to prove that I am different from your image of me?'

'Bring The Unknown out alive. Really alive. Then I'll believe. Until then, I can't forget where you were schooled and what that has meant for countless hundreds of years.'

'Julatsa!' Denser threw up his arms, got up and moved away, spilling what was left of his coffee. 'You look forward with both feet planted firmly in the past. You know something? Around this stove it's you who everyone sees has the closed mind and the chilled heart. I make no secret, Ilkar, that I respect and like you despite your College ancestry. I think I deserve the same treatment from you. Shall we ask what the others think? Shall we?'

Ilkar said nothing, just stared back, impassive.

'This is a fascinating debate I'm sure,' said Thraun. 'But tell me, is it how the Triverne Lake meeting will proceed? If it is, we might as well all fall on our swords now, because you'll still be bickering when the Wytch Lords stroll in and take your precious Cities.'

Denser and Ilkar looked at him as if he'd spat in their dinners.

'It won't be far off the level of debate, I can assure you,' said Erienne before either could reply. 'It's getting us nowhere, and there's something else I think we'd all like to know: what exactly will this meeting achieve?'

'Well, isn't it obvious?' Denser frowned.

'No, it is not,' said Erienne. 'If Xetesk is as split as you suggest, then the message you bring to the table will be confused and likely to cause further division.'

'No.' Denser shook his head. 'It won't be confused. The Lord of the Mount is delivering our message personally. The College delegates already accept the threat, and Dawnthief is the only solution.'

'I hope you're right,' she said.

'So do I. We mustn't lose the four-College co-operation or any force will be too weak and the Wesmen will sweep us into the eastern seas.'

'Cheerful, isn't he?' said Hirad.

'Getting back to the reason we all stopped,' said Jandyr. 'What is the risk to us outside Xetesk?'

'To be honest, I'm not sure,' said Denser. 'I've been away a while and I don't know the strength of those who want Dawnthief for themselves. However many, they'll be dangerous if they discover your location.'

'And you're leaving us without any magical protection,' said Hirad.

'But not out of contact,' replied Denser. 'The Familiar will stay with you much of the time.'

'You are joking,' said Jandyr. He was sitting next to Will, who stared at Denser in mute disbelief.

'I—' began Denser, then saw Will. He sighed. 'It's the only way to cover all the angles.'

'After what he did to me, you can even suggest this?' It was the first time Will had spoken all day.

'I'm sorry for what happened, Will,' said Denser. 'But he didn't actually do anything to you.'

'You call this nothing?' Will's voice rose to a shout. He pointed at his greying hair. 'And this?' He lifted a spread hand, palm downwards. It trembled. 'This is your *nothing*, Denser. Without my nerves, *I* am nothing. Your bastard creation has ruined me.'

Denser regarded Will for some moments.

'I understand your fear, but it will pass. Talk to Erienne, understand its nature. It will not harm you.'

'With you here, I believe it is under control. In your absence – well, I have seen the results.' Will drew up his legs and hugged them to his chest.

'It will not harm you,' repeated Denser.

'Accepting that,' said Jandyr into the silence that followed, 'I understand that it can communicate with you, but how does it do so with us?'

'Someone will have to agree to see Him,' said Denser. 'For whatever reason, He seems to regard Hirad as acceptable company.'

Ilkar sniggered.

'The feeling is barely mutual,' growled Hirad.

'Do you consent?' asked Denser.

Hirad shrugged.

'Don't,' said Will.

'I really don't have too much choice, do I?'

'Good,' said Denser. 'Come with me. Introductions have to be made.'

'One more thing.' Thraun stopped them. 'Where will we hide?'

'I know a place,' said Denser.

The darkness suited her, and with her keen sight picking out pitfalls in front of her feet, Selyn began making her way towards the once dead and now apparently resurgent city of the Wytch Lords.

With night falling on the Torn Wastes, the scale of the Wesmen encampments was hidden, but the firelight and noise of laughter, talking, shouting and fighting; of dogs barking and wind flapping canvas, all served as reminders of her precarious position.

But they were clearly preparing to leave. Before the light had failed completely, she'd made a rough count of the tents she could see, surmised a total to encircle Parve, added the number of Wesmen she'd seen marching away from the Torn Wastes two days before and multiplied it by a likely number of occupants per tent that still remained. Twenty thousand. And that was probably conservative. Call it twenty-five thousand. She'd shivered. That took the total number of Wesmen way past eighty thousand. And they were clearly once again servile to the Wytch Lords.

It was now merely a question of when the Wytch Lords could take significant part in the impending invasion. Too soon, and the Colleges would merely become the wavefront for the tide that would wash eastern Balaia into the Korina estuary. It was a question to which she had to find the answer, quickly.

Selyn dropped to her haunches behind a large lichen-covered boulder. She was a little over halfway to the first buildings of Parve, and already the smell of fear was invading her nostrils.

Low, dark cloud moved slowly overhead, lit by myriad fires, but none burned more brightly than the six beacons that ringed the top of the pyramid housing the shattered remains of the Wytch Lords' bodies.

Now, the folly of her Xeteskian predecessors could be seen for what it had become. Built by Xetesk and sealed by its magic, the pyramid had represented a warning to any who challenged the might of the Dark College. But now, with their mana cage empty, it merely served as a focus for the growing power of the Wytch Lords, and the massing of their acolytes and soldiers. She shook her head. Overconfidence and ultimate arrogance. Not traits shared to such a degree by the current Lord of the Mount, but he would surely suffer for their presence in those who had gone before him.

She looked over and to either side of the boulder. A stand of seven tents, lit inside and out, was directly in front of her, no further than three hundred yards away and ringing a large fire. Wesmen stood, sat, crouched or lay in the light of the flames, making silhouettes of bulking shoulders, powerful frames and bull heads that filled her vision.

To her left, a similar encampment, this one hosted by a Shaman. She could not risk running into the mind-sight of one of them. Right, the tents stretched into the dark, the noise of thousands filling the air with a restless energy.

Looking away towards Parve, she assessed her options and found she had none. Her principal problem was that the mana drain for a CloakedWalk of such distance might not leave enough for communion. But considering the sprawl of enemies in her path, she knew it was a chance she simply had to take.

She gathered herself, formed the simple mana shape, spoke the single command word and started running.

Hirad studied the cat lying curled asleep in his lap, breathing fast and shallow. With eyes and mouth closed, the black was so complete you could lose yourself in its depths. Hirad shuddered. How different to the beast Denser had shown him. Even prepared, he had found it hard to keep looking as the demon's eyes bored into his face from inside its pulsating skull. And, try as he might, he had flinched when it had placed a clawed hand on his arm and spoken his name.

Will's terror had been so easy to understand, then. Already scared half-witless by his journey through the Dordovan crypt, to see this thing in all its hideous glory would have been too much for most men.

It wasn't just the look, though. A look you could get used to, however awful. There was something else. In demon form, the Familiar exuded an aura of contempt, as if it was only there on a whim and could break out at any time and do anything.

The sound of a door opening brought Hirad to himself. Jandyr walked in.

'What do you think?' asked Hirad.

'Of this place?'

'Yes.' Denser had brought them to a farm some three hours outside Xetesk before riding immediately for the College City with Ilkar, Erienne and Sol. It was a working property, sprawling across several dozen acres and providing meat and cereal crops for nearby villages.

The house itself stood apart from the collection of barns and outbuildings, but all were clustered in the centre of the farm's land. In every direction, the ground undulated gently away, giving clear vision for a good six hundred paces before a stand of trees or a low hill obscured what was beyond.

Denser and Evanson, the farmer, were clearly on good terms, and though Hirad had initially opted for a barn, the farmer insisted they stay in the house.

'It's more comfortable for one thing, but more important, it keeps you out of sight of my workers. Village locals all of them, and none would keep their mouths shut if they saw you.' Evanson was middle-aged, with a face deep russet brown and wrinkled from long exposure to the elements. He had huge hands and powerful shoulders that bulged inside his loose shirt. His eyes sparkled from beneath his brow and his mouth was set in a smile. There was plenty about him to remind Hirad of Tomas back at The Rookery.

So they had agreed to stay in the house, and it was certainly a cosy option. Two storeys high, the building had beds enough for all of them to enjoy a little privacy. The range in the kitchen maintained a pot of hot water and food on demand, and with enough rest to let the adrenaline levels sink, all of them discovered a deep tiredness. Consequently, there had been little action save for some gentle snoring and a round or two of cards.

'I think several things,' said Jandyr. 'It's easy to defend. We have clear vision, plenty of warning and these beds are sent straight from paradise.'

Hirad smiled and lay back, arms supporting his head. 'My thoughts too. Where are the others?'

'Will's asleep and Thraun is reading one of Evanson's books. He's assembled quite a library.'

'Tell me about Thraun,' said Hirad. To him, shapechangers had been figures of myth. Until now. Now he had seen with his own eyes, and he didn't know whether to be scared, disgusted or amazed.

Jandyr nodded. 'It is something he tries so hard to hide.'

'How did it happen?' asked Hirad.

'It's a hangover from old Dordovan spell research. Thraun is descended from mages who tried to enhance their strength, agility, eyesight, hearing, whatever, by blending themselves with the essence of animals. For Thraun's forebears, it was strength and speed, hence the wolf shape.'

'But . . .'

'I know what you're going to say,' said Jandyr. 'The problem was that they didn't understand what they were doing. So rather than enhance what they already had, they replaced it. Some lived out their lives as the animals they used. Others found they could control it and the knowledge was passed down through the generations.'

'Why won't he talk about it?' Hirad had seen the benefits, the power and the speed.

'Because of how people view him,' replied Jandyr. 'There are enough who think all shapechangers are abominations whose lines should be stopped by death to make him scared to admit what he is.' Jandyr rose. 'Look, you have to understand that Thraun is a man like any of us. But he has another side he would rather not have. He is not to be feared, more to be pitied. Just treat him like a man. It is all he wants.'

'I understand,' said Hirad.

'None of us can ever truly do that,' said Jandyr.

*

Denser opened his door in response to the soft knocking. He didn't consider a threat – with Sol guarding the corridor for all of their rooms, he didn't need to. Anyway, he knew who it was.

So there she stood, and the first thought that rose in his mind was that, cleaned of all the grime of the trail and wearing soft, loose fabric, she was, as he had thought since he had first laid eyes on her, very attractive.

His groin stirred, unbidden, and he suppressed a smile. He wondered if she could read his face. He would enjoy this. He pushed the door wide.

Erienne swept into his room, smiling. 'Tonight I will conceive.' Her face was turned away from him, her voice emotionless.

He chuckled. 'Is that really all it is to you?'

'We made a deal. This is the payoff of that deal. What else could there be?' But her smile betrayed her words.

Denser closed the door and moved towards her, his eyes tracing the shadow of her body beneath her white robe as it flickered in the candlelight.

'It may be that the payoff of the deal could be pleasurable to you,' he said, eyes sparkling, pupils dilated.

'That isn't why I struck the deal,' she said quickly. 'But things do, um, develop.' Denser saw her face colour.

He stood close to her now. She didn't move away.

'I did it because I respect your skill as a mage.'

'And my power,' added Denser.

At last she turned to him. 'That's the main reason I chose you instead of Ilkar.'

'Ilkar, he . . .'

'He is certainly more handsome than you.' She was smiling again.

Denser stood squarely in front of her. 'But Ilkar's an *elf*!'

'Yes, and a Julatsan. Two more reasons I favour your seed.' The smile broadened and softened her face to beauty.

'Well, I'm flattered my College is so much more attractive to you,' said Denser.

'Lucky, more like, or I could be standing in front of Ilkar now.'

'Not short on self-confidence, are you?' He placed a hand on her cheek, cupping her face as she leaned into it.

'It covers the emptiness,' she whispered. She pushed a hand through his hair, smoothing it down his neck.

'Do you still hurt inside?' asked Denser.

'Like a knife is twisting through my heart.'

'Tonight, I want to stop that.' His voice was barely audible as he moved his lips to her ear. 'Together, we can make you whole again.'

She grabbed his face in both hands and looked deep into his eyes, searching for lies. She found none and felt tears well up.

'What's wrong?' Denser asked.

'Nothing.' She kissed him gently and he let his tongue whisper across her lips. Her hands moved to the back of his head and his arms caught her about her waist, crushing them together.

The kiss gained intensity, their tongues meeting, exploring mouths, heads moving, breath drawn in hard. Hands searched. He felt hers trail to his neck, where they kneaded and pressed before moving down to his chest to pick at the buttons of his shirt.

She was wearing a simple white shift, clasped at the shoulder. He found the fastening, fumbled briefly, and snapped it open, hearing her gasp involuntarily as the shift dropped soundlessly to the floor. Beneath it she was naked. Denser's arousal was complete. He walked her to the bed and laid her down, straddling her body on hands and knees and looking down at her face and at her breasts, which were moving in rapid response to her breathing.

He cupped one in his hand, feeling the nipple harden.

'You didn't want to waste any time,' he remarked.

'No. And I still don't.' She grabbed at his belt and the button of his fly, and while she hauled his trousers down over his hips, Denser pulled his shirt over his head. Together, they added his trousers to the pile of discarded clothing.

She took his penis in one hand and guided it towards her, Denser looking down at the hair between her legs, which was as dark as her skin was pale. She moved her legs apart and he responded, moving his inside hers and leaning down to her. His mouth was on her breast as he entered her, and as he began to move inside her, the clamour of the mana swept him away.

Shafts of blue light shattered before his eyes as he pushed himself fully inside her. The trails they left spread away, flickering and dying, absorbed by the warm orange pulsing all around Erienne.

She felt smooth but he barely noticed as, with each gentle thrust, the mana poured around him in ever darker tendrils, catching and mixing with the Dordovan strain. The sight was so beautiful it took his breath away, and as Erienne began to move with him, it took his rhythm too.

'Don't stop,' she whispered, and he picked it up once more.

To Erienne, it was a mana-meld miracle. She could feel his hand on her breast, his lips on her neck and his movement inside her, confident and sensual. She held herself in check, denying herself orgasm as she watched their manas weave while the colours became indistinct, ultimately forming a cocoon of softly pulsating deep mauve.

Now the conditions were ideal. Denser's thrusts were more urgent, his tempo increasing, and she felt him deeply, her legs and back tingling and numbing with pleasure.

She reached a hand down to cup his testicles, his breath hissing out suddenly against her shoulder. She moved her pelvis with him, swift but controlled, bringing herself to the point of orgasm.

Above her, Denser moaned as he approached climax. His penis hardened further, delighting her with its touch, and they came together in an explosion of mana light. The cocoon disintegrated, sending rainbow teardrops splashing around them. Erienne cried out in pleasure and triumph. Denser pushed hard once more then stopped moving, still deep inside her.

She placed a hand low on her stomach and probed down with her mana to warm the semen, to keep them alive and to imbue them with the beginnings of the power her child would possess.

Denser lifted his head and looked down at her. Erienne smiled, put her hands either side of his face and kissed him.

'Now we should sleep,' she said. 'And then next time we can concentrate on pure enjoyment.'

Chapter 24

During her run into Parve, Selyn thanked the Gods for the unusual order of the Wesmen encampments. Although it had seemed from a distance that they were pitched anywhere, the stands of tents were all grouped in half-circles around large fires, giving her the opportunity to skirt the light, people and dogs.

A CloakedWalk spell, although rendering its caster completely invisible, did nothing to deaden noise or scent, and Selyn's principal concern was the Destrana pure-bred war dogs favoured by the Wesmen tribes. Men's eyes deceived the other senses; not so those of the Destrana.

Unable to stop except in deep shadow, Selyn ran, walked, crawled and trotted as circumstances dictated, always with one eye on the ground for a stray twig or loose rock. A thrill was in her heart. This was what she had trained for so long to do. Deep infiltration, awesome odds, a deadly enemy, and Selyn passing through it all like a breeze through the undergrowth.

Where the firelight cast good illumination on the ground, Selyn slowed to examine the encampments more closely. All had the same characteristics. A tribal standard stood proud in front of a blazing wood fire, over which cookpots hung and steamed.

Between six and ten squad tents were pitched in formal order around the fire, and here and there, knots of smaller tents denoted beds for senior ranks and, presumably, Shamen. To these, Selyn gave the widest berth.

Everywhere, there were Wesmen, most lounging in the heat of the fire as the night cooled off. Lanterns lit most tents, and here and there the screams and moans of women punctuated the noises of the night – some in pleasure, others not.

There were no guards, no patrols and no lookouts. Arrogant in their confidence, the Wesmen looked to the renewed might of Parve and wallowed in their safety. And safe they were, though for a mage spy, the shadow, the noise and the eyes forever turned inwards were more than enough to make a secure if cautious passage.

The City itself was quiet on its outer reaches, where the hand of the Wytch Lords and their acolytes had not yet been laid. Here, the legacy of the past, broken stone and splintered wood, served as a reminder of the battle scars of history.

For Selyn, though, it provided stark and terrifying contrast to what lay beyond – a City rebuilt. She moved through the rubble and into an area of low storage buildings. Long, flat-roofed constructions of slate and stone, topped by chimneys, none of which was smoking. Away towards the central square, higher buildings rose into the night, testament to the effort of the Wesmen and the acolytes of the Wytch Lords who in scant months had turned a blasted region of stone and dust into a City with a heart that beat once more.

Selyn walked in a couple of blocks before swarming up the side of one of the store buildings and lying down in its centre to rest, the CloakedWalk slipping from her. Her pulse, which had raced through her journey to Parve, hardly slowed. Her next step was to reach the pyramid itself, and with her mana stamina gone, the dark would now be her only disguise.

Dusk was settling, throwing the Mount into shadow. Puddles of wan light cast from windows grew slowly in intensity, and the sounds of the day began to ebb. Denser, Erienne and Ilkar sat around a table with Laryon, a close associate of Styliann. He had intercepted them at the door to the rooms of Nyer, Denser's mentor, and hurried them back to his chambers, where he spoke of Nyer's recent troubles with the Lord of the Mount. Nyer had subsequently been seen closeted with a splinter group of mages and it had fallen to Laryon alone to assess the chances of releasing The Unknown from thrall.

Sol himself stood silent guard by the door of the study, and Denser pushed his concerns about Nyer's intentions to one side to concentrate on rescuing the search for Dawnthief. At a nod from Laryon, Denser refilled their glasses with wine.

'The risk is great,' said the Xeteskian Master, leaning back in his chair, the lamplight catching his close-cropped grey hair and emphasising his bulbous nose and small mouth.

'But it is possible,' said Ilkar.

'Technically,' Laryon said carefully. 'You must understand the process by which a Protector is created.'

'I think I understand only too well,' said Ilkar shortly.

'No,' said Denser. 'You do not. And please can we leave aside the morals of the situation. What you are about to hear isn't pleasant, but keep in mind that we are all of us trying to help Sol.'

'Really?' Ilkar chuckled mirthlessly. 'I'd like to believe that, but I think we all know that this is purely to stop Hirad running off with Dawnthief.'

'He wouldn't get far,' said Laryon dismissively.

'Want to bet?' Ilkar bridled.

'Can we leave this?' Denser's patience wore a notch thinner. 'Ilkar, this is not productive, and, Master Laryon, I wouldn't take the bet. You have no idea what they are capable of.'

Laryon opened his mouth to reply but chose instead to exhale audibly through his nose.

'A Protector,' he said, 'is a self-supporting resurrection with a body reincarnated from soul memories. The critical point about soul memories is that they are far more accurate than brain memories. As long as the soul is taken within about twelve hours of death, re-creation of mind skills and body will be complete.'

'There's a but in here somewhere.' Ilkar was looking at The Unknown, shaking his head.

'Correct. The soul does not re-enter the body.'

'What?' Erienne jerked upright in her chair.

'Then how—' began Ilkar.

'What started as the only way to forge a bond became the ultimate mode of control,' said Laryon. 'When the spell was in its infancy, the only way to ensure life was to link the body and soul using a DemonChain – this is a spell which enthrals the mass consciousness of a multi-demonic conjuration. It works supremely well. Because the demons are under our command, we can instruct them exactly as we wish. Usually, this involves them in keeping a clear channel between body and soul.'

'Usually,' muttered Ilkar, seeing the bigger picture in all its horror.

'Yes,' said Denser. 'And the Masters can also instruct the demons to do anything to the body or soul. They can even give free rein, and that is where hell for eternity begins. Now you can see why I couldn't take it on myself.'

'It's barbaric,' said Ilkar.

'Worse,' agreed Laryon.

'So where are the souls?' asked Erienne.

'In stasis, here in the Mount. They are all together, and that's what gives the Protectors their true power. Communication and action are instant. An army of them would be unstoppable.' Laryon raised his eyebrows.

'And what's the procedure for releasing The Unknown?' Ilkar indicated the statuesque figure of Sol.

'Ilkar,' said Laryon gravely, 'I told you about the forming of a Protector so you would understand the risks involved – or at least the ones we can guess at. You must be aware that what Denser and I will attempt has never been tried before. I will do everything in my power to keep Sol alive, but I can't guarantee it.'

'It'd be convenient if he died, wouldn't it?'

'Not really. What would I gain?'

'The continuation of the Protectors,' said Ilkar. 'You could prove to the Colleges that you'd tried and failed and could sit back on your "some life is better than none" argument. I personally would question whether being a Protector qualifies as "some life", knowing what I now know.'

'I understand your cynicism,' said Laryon. 'And although you won't believe it, I agree with you. There's a growing faction in the Mount demanding acceleration of reforms to certain antiquated and unpalatable practices. Denser is one such, and I am perhaps the most senior supporter. I want this to succeed, both as a reformer and as a research mage, which is why Denser will assist me. Surely you trust him.'

'As far as I trust any Xeteskian.'

Laryon smiled. 'It is all I can offer.'

'Then it will have to do. But a word of warning. If The Unknown dies and you can't explain why to Hirad in terms he'll understand, you'll find the result the same as if you hadn't helped in the first place.'

'Thanks, Ilkar,' said Denser, sighing. 'More wine anybody?' He refilled their glasses.

'Quantify the risks for me,' said Erienne.

'Quantify, no. Postulate, yes,' replied Laryon. 'Firstly, it is only technically possible to repatriate a soul, and then only by channelling it through the DemonChain. We do not know what damage it might incur. We also have no idea whether the soul will volunteer to return or what harm prolonged suppression of total consciousness will have done. We are merely guessing at the system shock when the DemonChain is broken and the body is once more under its own control. Don't forget, he was dead.'

Ilkar looked across at The Unknown. He was watching them. Or perhaps the DemonChain was listening and watching through him. As always, his eyes, hooded by the mask, gave nothing away.

'A return to death would be preferable to what he has now,' said Ilkar.

'I tend to agree,' said Laryon. 'Denser? We must prepare. But first we must assess the situation with our friend Nyer. Denser, if you would contact your Familiar?'

Denser nodded and closed his eyes.

The cat shifted suddenly in Hirad's lap, waking him from his doze. He sat up in his chair and looked out of the window. It was late afternoon and the sun was losing some of its strength, allowing a breeze to cool the fields. Hirad could see one of the farm hands working a plough away in the distance, and closer to home, the sounds of work echoed to him from the barns and outbuildings.

He glanced back at the cat, starting as he met the eyes of the demon.

'Don't do that!' snapped Hirad. The Familiar smiled and chuckled, a hollow rattling that had nothing to do with humour. 'What is it?'

'They are coming. We must be ready to leave here.'

'Denser?'

The Familiar shook its head. 'Those who would have Dawnthief. We must be ready.'

Styliann gathered his thoughts as he looked around the hostile table. With the Wesmen already close to the Bay of Gyernath and nearing Understone Pass, he couldn't afford to lose the support of the Colleges. And while he was furious with the actions of Nyer's mage, Denser, he was equally livid with the actions of the Dordovan mage who had begun the trouble.

'The unfortunate events' – Vuldaroq snorted. Styliann stared him down before continuing, already biting back the reply his heart demanded – 'in Dordover a few days ago have forced us to reveal to you something we wanted to remain secret for a while longer.'

'You didn't trust us?' asked Heryst, no malice in his tone.

'I felt that certain likely reactions at too early a stage would have jeopardised Balaia,' said Styliann.

'And you expect me to accept that your rape of my crypt was therefore justified?' The voice was quiet but brimming with poison.

Styliann kneaded his brow for a moment before replying, choosing to look the Dordovan in the eye when he did so.

'The answer to your question has to be yes, but permit me to qualify that answer. Under any circumstances other than these, there is no doubt our action would have been different.

'It is also true that before we authorised the action we took, lengthy consideration was made of the potential ramifications as we saw them. The manner of your discovery of our actions is deeply regretted.

'It is also true that we believed that informing you of the impact of our actions would have been unwise and divisive.'

Vuldaroq nodded slowly, his face red, his jaw set. He leaned back in his chair, one of its wings hiding his face.

'Lengthy consideration,' he said. 'Deep regret.' He brought his face back into the light. 'One of my mages *died*.' He let the word hang in the air above the table.

'Hmm.' Styliann settled into his chair. He took a sip of water and read the notes written by his aides. They agreed with his line of argument. 'Tell me, Vuldaroq. Why did he die?'

'Because he tried to stop the rape of our crypts.'

'Is that what he was doing? My understanding is a little different. Perhaps you would like to explain to the meeting how kidnapping and imprisoning a Familiar as bait for its master's trap was supposed to help him achieve this?'

'I am not some child caught doing wrong,' snapped Vuldaroq. 'Do not treat me as such. Our mage was murdered by your bastard Familiar, let us not forget that.'

'Very well. I am prepared to concede that this was the end result. But I think we owe Barras and Heryst a complete view of the events leading to the unfortunate circumstance. I would hate them to feel they could not continue to lend their support to the alliance because of a misunderstanding.'

'What is there to misunderstand?' Vuldaroq was dismissive. 'It is hard to misunderstand murder.'

Styliann's eyes flashed and he made to rise. An aide pressed a hand on his arm and he relaxed.

'What I fear,' said Styliann carefully, 'is that our colleagues might not realise that the Familiar was taken outside the walls of your College—'

'It was still in the City,' growled Vuldaroq.

'Is that a crime?' countered Styliann.

'It was part of a—'

'Is that a crime?' repeated Styliann, his voice rising.

Vuldaroq's scowl deepened. 'No. It is not.'

'Thank you for that clarification. I would also be unhappy unless I told our colleagues that the Familiar was merely an observer, that Denser was placed in woodland some distance from Dordover and that he would never have entered the city but for the kidnap of his Familiar.

'Now I do not expect anyone to condone our theft, but I do expect everyone to understand its necessity and respect that we planned to take the ring quietly, peacefully and without using mages from any College but Dordover. Violence only occurred because of the actions of a maverick mage who suffered the inevitable consequence of caging a Familiar that was subsequently set free.'

There was a furious scribbling of notes all around the table. The delegates huddled and whispered while Styliann looked on.

'Do you disagree with Styliann's description of the events?' asked Barras following his consultation.

'The Familiar was removed from outside the College walls,' conceded Vuldaroq. 'But don't forget that at this time, our grounds had been penetrated by two unauthorised individuals.'

'I'm afraid your timings might be slightly awry.' Styliann's smile was laced with contempt. 'The two members of The Raven you are talking about witnessed the kidnap from their position outside the walls.'

'While they plotted an illegal entrance.'

'Their actions are not disputed,' said Heryst, his gentle voice cutting across the tension. 'The actions of your College are.'

'We are the victims here!' Vuldaroq stood and slammed his fists on the table.

'In that the ring was taken, yes, you are.' Heryst shrugged. 'But you are basing your objection to Xetesk's actions on the death of a mage. A mage who kidnapped a Familiar from outside the College walls.' He leaned into the light, a half-smile playing about his lips. 'The first crime of the evening was committed by Dordover.'

'Your point being?' Red-faced, Vuldaroq wiped sweat from his forehead, his shoulders sagging slightly.

'His point being that we have two separate incidents that you have intertwined. One Styliann has confessed to and given reasons for. The other, regrettable though it was, appears to have been instigated by a Dordovan, brought a Xeteskian and his Familiar to the College where they would otherwise not have been, and resulted in inevitable consequences.'

'Inevitable? When can murder ever be inevitable?'

'Enough!' Styliann rose again. 'You are well aware of the bond between a Xeteskian mage and his Familiar, and so was your foolish student. Another time he might have been successful in trapping both, though why he should wish to is beyond me. His great misfortune was that he chose to steal that belonging to a particularly talented man. Denser was bound to release his Familiar and then your man's life was over. I have little sympathy.

'Now. Two incidents, as Barras correctly deduced. We are talking about the theft. I have explained why it was carried out and why we were secretive. Vuldaroq has since demonstrated to me that our secrecy was entirely justified. We are facing catastrophe if we don't work together. I must have your support and you must believe as I do that Dawnthief is our only realistic chance of success.'

'I agree with you,' said Barras. 'But I, personally, am insulted that you kept such information from me.'

'I see.' Styliann scratched his ear. 'All right, let me put it this way. Let's assume for a moment that I opened up about Dawnthief at the last meeting, and we, as the four-College delegation, went to the Dordovan Council and asked for the Ring of Arteche. What would have been the result? Vuldaroq?'

'You know full well what the result would have been,' muttered Vuldaroq.

'Yes, I do, they would have initially refused.' Styliann threw his arms wide. 'Then, following pressure they might have agreed to release the ring, but they would have demanded a senior mage in attendance at any use of Dawnthief, and to advise on the search as it continued. How long would all this have taken to agree? A month, two months? Gentlemen, I believed that we didn't have that sort of time, and the movement of the Wesmen invasion forces proves me correct.

'I apologise for misleading you all about our ideas for the destruction of the Wytch Lords, but we are now in an advanced enough state to stand a realistic chance of success. Now you all know that your councils would have delayed the recovery of the spell, perhaps critically. And you also know that The Raven as it stands contains members of three Colleges, and that, with Heryst's blessing, is a quorum.' Heryst inclined his head. 'Good. All that we need now is to facilitate The Raven's entry into the west.'

'And how might we do that?' asked Heryst.

'We'll have to take Understone Pass,' said Styliann.

Vuldaroq scoffed. 'Styliann, there are eight thousand Wesmen in that pass. Just how do you suggest we achieve this miracle?'

Styliann smiled.

Denser turned to Ilkar and Erienne, his message finished. 'I've done all I can. He will see them away from the farm and on their way to Triverne Lakes, then return to me.'

'Will they make it?' asked Ilkar, uneasy at leaving The Raven to travel with no magical escort.

Denser nodded. 'And so will you if you leave now. One of Laryon's Protectors will take you to the City boundaries. If you ride through the night you'll be there by dawn. I'll join you as soon as I can.'

'And where exactly is Nyer?' Ilkar's eyes shifted up and down the corridor. He half expected the Master to loom out of nowhere and attack them.

'On his way to the farmhouse,' said Denser. He chewed his bottom lip. 'I can't believe he is betraying me.'

'Denser!' Laryon called from inside the spell chamber.

'I must go.' He kissed Erienne, holding on to the embrace. 'Be careful.'

'I'll bear it in mind.' She smiled and stroked his face.

'Get this right, Denser,' said Ilkar.

'If it is possible, I'll beat you to Triverne Lake and The Unknown will be with me.'

'Now that would be impressive.'

'Then I'll see it is done.' Denser held out his hand. Ilkar hesitated a moment before shaking it.

'Denser!' Urgently.

Denser raised his eyebrows, stepped into the spell chamber and closed the door. Ilkar and Erienne heard solid bolts slide home. No one else was getting in.

'Let's go,' said Ilkar. Erienne paused to stare at the door a moment before leading the way back from the catacombs and the suffocating press of Xeteskian mana.

Inside the armoured spell chamber, deep beneath the Mount, The Unknown, Sol, blinked into the candlelight. Denser and Laryon talked at the foot of the slab on which he lay pillowed, clothed in traditional dark tunic and breeches.

'What I require from you is a mana channel to keep the Demon-Chain under control until the soul is returned.' Laryon flexed his fingers. 'They will resist you, and once the soul moves, they will try to break free. Do you understand?

Denser nodded.

'Then let's begin. I am anxious for the safety of The Raven.'

Laryon moved to Sol's head, placed his hands over the Protector's eyes and muttered a short prayer. Sol's body relaxed, his eyes closed and his head fell to one side. He wasn't breathing.

'Time is short. Denser, prepare the mana channel. Hold it in readiness until the Chain is visible. You'll know what to do instinctively. Trust me.'

Denser breathed deeply and began to construct the shape of the channel. He tuned his consciousness to the mana spectrum, seeing Sol shrouded in a deep blue radiance – the static mana channelled by the DemonChain.

In essence, the shape was simple. It was tubular, with a spiral movement heading away from him. The difficulty was keeping both ends open and firm to accept and contain the DemonChain.

To Denser's left, the mana shifted, sharpened and deepened in colour. Laryon was casting.

Almost immediately, the radiance encasing Sol rippled, pulling towards the shape Laryon was creating. It shimmered and sparkled, coalescing into something Denser couldn't make out at first. But steadily, the form became clearer. The mana formed a conical shape, left Sol's body and settled, one end in the centre of his torso, the other splashed through the floor of the chamber beneath the slab. Energy lines ran up and down its length, and suddenly the DemonChain was there. Faces, limbs, bodies, mouths, fingers, hair. All distilled from the cone. Voices hissed and individuals writhed, but the whole locked together in chaotic form.

One had hands lost in another's chest. Another's head melded to a third's foot. Any combination, but all of them were alive, identical in every physical aspect and very, very angry.

From the centre of the chain, one locked its eyes on Denser and screamed its hate. Denser looked unfazed.

He took in the beast with a body the size of a newborn child's, arms long and wiry, legs stubby and malformed and a face full of evil. Blue drool ran from its lipless mouth, tongue licking at its cheeks, fangs tearing rents in its own being. The eyes, huge and slitted, were orbs of dark malevolence and its ears ran high above the crawling skull to meet in a spire over its head.

'Time, Denser,' said Laryon, his voice distant with effort.

'Envelop,' commanded Denser in response, and his mana channel flashed towards the DemonChain, muffling howls of fury as it opened for the merest moment all along its length and snapped shut around the whole.

'Excellent,' said Laryon.

Denser felt him release control of the DemonChain. They turned their attention to the channel holding them and battered at it with feet, fists, fangs and minds.

'They cannot break through. Keep your concentration steady. They aren't strong enough,' said Laryon. 'Attend to my voice. Now it gets difficult. Only remove the channel on my word.'

Laryon breathed deep and prepared the path for The Unknown's soul.

Chapter 25

The Familiar alighted on Hirad's right shoulder. He winced involuntarily and pressed his lips together in irritation.

'How did they find us?' he asked.

'Someone has betrayed us. Someone powerful.' Anger and surprise edged its tone. 'You must leave for Triverne Lake. Evanson will guide you.'

'I'm not running,' said Hirad stiffly.

The Familiar ignored him. 'I will distract them while you get away.'

'Why don't we just stay and take them out?'

The Familiar regarded him blankly. 'You do not understand. They are too powerful for you. And for me. They will kill me.'

Hirad started, and frowned.

'Good luck, Raven man. Look after my master.' The Familiar flew from the open window, high into the night sky.

The Unknown juddered violently and his soul scorched along the DemonChain into his body. Laryon smiled but was totally unprepared for the backlash. He hadn't seen the possibility at all. The returning soul negated the DemonChain's fastening to The Unknown's being and the result was violent severance.

With howls of triumph, the Chain whipped away from The Unknown's body, slashing in a wide arc at the two mages. Laryon was caught on the side of the head and slammed against a wall, groaning as he slumped, a trickle of blood running from his mouth.

Younger and quicker, Denser ducked the Chain, feeling the mana slice above his head and the unmistakable sensation of a draught through his hair as the demons began to gain corporeal form.

Dragging his concentration to himself, he fought to close the end of the mana channel but knew, as he watched the head of the Chain tearing at the very fabric of the mana, that it was futile.

And, with the Chain coiling like a snake for its next strike, Denser felt something he had never truly felt before. Fear. Fear because he hadn't the power to stop the DemonChain forming a corporeal state, and fear because he couldn't stop it killing him. But mainly fear because he didn't know how, and the gap in his knowledge was going to be fatal.

The Chain writhed, Denser's mana channel was torn apart and the sound of their hate assaulted his ears. They promised him death. They promised him torment for eternity and they laughed at his weakness.

The Chain lunged at him, missing him by a whisker as he hurled himself to one side, landing heavily near the still form of Laryon. The mage was still alive. Denser shook him hard.

'Help me,' he said. Laryon groaned. 'Help me!' shouted Denser. Out of the corner of his eye, he saw the Chain whipping into a frenzy of speed and sound by The Unknown's head. The warrior lay, breathing slowly, oblivious to the horror above him.

Laryon said something. It was a mumble Denser didn't catch.

'What?'

'Lymimra,' said Laryon.

'I don't understand.'

Laryon's eyes opened and he looked past Denser before grabbing the mage's head in both hands and pulling his ear close. 'LightMirror,' he whispered before clutching Denser's head hard to his chest. Above Denser, the DemonChain ploughed into Laryon's face, his cry of pain cut off abruptly, his grip dropping.

Denser looked behind him. The DemonChain writhed, still attached through the floor of the chamber, its laughter echoing off the walls, its triumph all but complete. Scrabbling to his feet, Denser paused briefly to look at Laryon. He shuddered. Though the Master was unmarked, his eyes were open in death, and through them Denser could see into his soul. Only it wasn't there.

He turned back to the DemonChain and formed the mana shape for the LightMirror. It was a simple rectangular structure and he had it in seconds. The Chain began to coil again, winding in on itself like paper in a whirlwind. Then it was still, poised, but the noise of its fury hammered ceaselessly on Denser's ears.

As it moved to strike, he cast. A thin, horizontal beam of light about eight feet wide cut the candlelit room in front of Denser at floor level. The Chain flashed forwards and Denser brought his hands up sharply in front of him. The LightMirror deployed like a blind moving up a window to let in the sun.

A brilliant light flooded the room, gathering the pinpoints from the candles and casting them back a hundredfold brighter. The Demon-

Chain shrieked in terror and tried to swing away, but its blue mana light was victim to the mirror.

Denser shielded his eyes as the light was stripped from the howling demons being dragged ever closer. The light speared into the mirror with increasing intensity and speed, the mana creatures howling as their life-force was ripped away, and then they were gone, leaving silence, the echo of violence and a gentle blue in the mana spectrum.

Denser refocused to normal light and saw The Unknown sitting upright.

They left the lights burning in the farmhouse. Hirad didn't like it but it made sense. Triverne Lake was the only place of sanctuary for both The Raven and, more importantly perhaps, the two catalysts he held. With strong presence from all four Colleges, there should be no threat. And yet he was uneasy. He needed Ilkar. Ilkar would know what to say to smooth the passage of their arrival. Without him and his knowledge, Hirad felt exposed.

As they spurred their horses northward into the gathering gloom of evening, a confused but compliant Evanson leading the way, Hirad scanned the sky for the Familiar. He couldn't see it, knew he wouldn't, and felt a passing regret. It was not something you could ever *like*, but respect was something else. Unlike Ilkar, he couldn't see the Familiar as inherently evil, and its assertion that it would die causing a diversion represented a sacrifice he couldn't ignore.

Presumably Denser knew it too, and the knowledge that the mage was genuine in his determination to see Dawnthief used to save Balaia and not to further Xetesk made Hirad feel guilty he'd ever doubted him. He dug his heels into his horse's flanks and made up the ground to Evanson, wondering what their reception at the lake would be.

They hadn't sensed him and he grinned. They were riding over open ground, still an hour from the farmhouse and keeping away from any trails. Twelve of them in cells of three, one mage and two Protectors, close formed against attack from the ground but completely exposed to anything from the air. High up in the darkening sky, he circled, pulsing his warning cry through the mana to his master as he selected the target that would produce the most mayhem.

There he was, and the sight sent a warm thrill of fear through his body. Nyer, the Xetesk Master. The man with whom his master had communed for so long. A traitor. And about to die.

He flew higher, a silent death about to unleash itself on an oblivious victim, and circled still unnoticed behind his target.

He dived, suppressing the urge to scream his laughter and gurgle his delight. Eyes fixed on the back of Nyer's head, wings swept back, he tore through the air. At the last, he extended wings to brake his descent, swung his taloned feet in front of him and buried them in the Master's unprotected neck.

Nyer grunted and pitched off his horse to tumble and sprawl in the dirt. The Protectors shouted warnings but were way too late. Even as they halted, wheeled and closed, the Familiar arched its back and slammed its fists into Nyer's head, crushing his skull.

Now it laughed and turned for its next quarry. With a beat of its wings it took to the air and shot past a bewildered Protector, who swung his sword hopelessly wide.

Chittering in exultation, the Familiar arced back into the sky, scanning below as the enemy halted and the three remaining mages prepared spells to bring him down. But he knew he would be safe. His master had answered his call and was already on his way. A warmth stole over his heart, which beat faster with new energy, and he turned a lazy somersault.

The spell caught his left leg and seared along his tail.

Pain.

Flashing over the ground, ShadowWings shaped for raw speed, Denser wailed as the jolt from his Familiar's wound thundered in his head. He clung to his concentration, held the wings together, kept flying, tears rolling down his cheeks, vision a blur.

He looked over his left shoulder. The Unknown was close behind him and Denser still had the energy to admire the way he had accepted the use of the ShadowWings. The ability to hold mana placed in his body was a given ability of Protectors and he no longer was one. The trouble would surely start when he had time to think and remember.

'What's wrong?' called The Unknown.

'They've hit him, the bastards. They've hurt him.' Denser took a deep breath and pushed his wings beyond the safe limits of their speed. Behind him, without knowing exactly how, The Unknown did the same.

The Familiar was weakening. Pain forced tears from his eyes and his circling became ever more desperate as the fire ate along his tail and leg. His master was coming but he could not home in on the direction, and the dark shroud that threatened to steal his consciousness drove cogent thought from his head. He circled on, dimly aware that beneath him, a mage prepared another spell. He wept now, knowing death was upon him.

'Master,' he breathed. 'Come for me. Avenge me.'

The spell caught him in the throat. The Familiar crumpled and plummeted to earth.

Nothing could prepare Denser for it. Like having needles pushed into his eyes and his brain crushed by rock, the Familiar's last agonised whisper and the snuffing of its life shattered his mana stamina and took his consciousness. The ShadowWings vanished and he fell from the sky.

The Unknown saw it coming, saw Denser's head snap back and his hands claw at his face as if he was trying to tear his skull apart. He saw the wings flicker, flash bright against the dark sky, then blink out. Already slowing and diving as Denser began to fall, he shot past him once, banked, turned and caught him on the next pass, maybe fifteen feet from the ground.

With the Dark Mage limp in his arms, he hovered, gaining height slowly. Looking down on his face, pale even in the gloom and taut with pain through his consciousness, The Unknown felt protective towards him. He frowned, knowing that he had felt hatred before, but it seemed long ago. Other memories were filtering slowly through the morass of his recently ordered mind, but he quashed them, keeping his attention on the ShadowWings.

He felt anger too. Anger at whoever had damaged Denser. Anger at Xetesk for taking him as a Protector and stealing his death. But desire for revenge was put aside. Right now he had to reunite The Raven. He flew for Triverne Lake.

Selyn appraised her route to the pyramid, her professional dispassion flawed by a shiver down her spine as she gauged her final, troubled half-mile. It wasn't that she was concerned over her chances of making it alive. No. There was something more. An atmosphere hanging around Parve of power, energy, fear and anticipation. It was as though the very stones of the rebuilt City of the Wytch Lords sensed the coming of something.

Xetesk had been quietly aware of the Wesmen threat for months. Latterly, the news of the Wytch Lords' escape had scared them into overt as well as covert action. Now she was here to answer the final question. And the question was no longer 'if'; it was 'when'.

The building she had been resting on for the past hour was

completely encircled by streets. Three chimney stacks ran its length. She kept very close to the centre stack, body still, head moving slowly to gauge her position.

Behind her, the Torn Wastes stretched away into the night, their noise muted inside the City boundaries. To her right, more low buildings, none lit, gave way to ruins after about a hundred yards, but it was left and ahead that held her attention.

One street across was the eastern of four main thoroughfares to Parve's central square and the pyramid which dominated it. The road ran straight and wide for around seven hundred yards before opening out on to the square. If her information was right, a tunnel, sealed and heavy with wards, led into the pyramid itself. And surrounding it, statues depicting scenes from the war. But it had been a long time since a Xeteskian had been to Parve's ruins and the Gods only knew what might have changed. She had to know whether the tunnel was open. If it was, time would be short.

The City was quiet. She could pick out shapes moving in the streets ahead but there was nothing like the bustle even of Xetesk at dusk, let alone Korina or Gyernath. It should be easy to reach the pyramid tunnel but something inside her begged caution. She stayed and watched.

Three hours later, with night at its deepest, she was rewarded for her innate sense of danger. At the periphery of her vision there was movement in the square, where she expected the tunnel entrance to be. Dark shapes shifted against the firelit square, and although she couldn't make out too much from this distance, it appeared the whole square rippled. Surely a trick of the poor light.

The dark shapes split into four groups and began to leave the square in the direction of the Torn Wastes. They were riders, and enough of them clattered along the eastern path for Selyn to know who they were. Shamen.

One link, at least, was proven. The Wytch Lords were directly controlling the Wesmen through the Shamen, and they would have strong magic. When they had left the City, she moved.

Dropping to the ground on the opposite side to the main street, she hugged the silent shadows, moving carefully but quickly towards the central square. Parve was built on a strict grid, interconnecting blocks making navigation very easy for the stranger. But it also made concealment difficult, and Selyn checked closely for openings, alleyways and deep shadow as she passed, logging anything promising for her escape.

Away from the main streets, the City was dark and deserted but strangely secure. No patrols echoed on the tight new pavings and cobbles, no shadows flitted between doorways or waited for the unwary traveller or lost drunk. It was an atmosphere quite without . . . atmosphere. Then it struck her, and she stopped to take the air more closely.

It wasn't the quiet that caused her pause. There was something else, something that hung over the City like a blanket. Parve was dormant, slumbering. But waiting to awaken.

She quickened her pace, hurrying across a wide, large-cobbled street and into the shadows two blocks from the square and pyramid. She pulled up sharply in a let-in doorway, stilled her breathing and slowed her heart rate. She had been seen and followed. She had heard nothing, seen nothing, but that inner sense told her all she needed to know.

The man came slowly and carefully around the corner, his footfalls barely registering. Selyn's body ceased all movement, waiting to pounce or run. From her position, hidden in shadow, she could see him edging along the opposite wall and her heart sank. It was a Shaman, and if his senses were tuned, he would be able to find her. She took short breaths and activated her wrist bolts, a leather trigger running up each palm and ending in a loop which slipped over the middle finger. Now, a sharp snap back of either wrist would be enough.

The Shaman moved on up the wall, his hand brushing the layered stone, passing out of her field of vision. Quiet reigned in the street. Selyn waited on, poised. Five minutes. Ten. As her hearing attuned, she became aware of the noise of people and fire from the direction of the square, the distant clump of a hoof on stone, a door closing. Fifteen.

And then he was in front of her, the stench of his furs heavy in her nose, his dark face and cold eyes close to hers, his arm reaching out.

'Did you think I could not smell you, Xeteskian?' His accent was thick, the words uncomfortable in his throat.

Selyn said nothing. Batting his arm aside with her right, she rammed her left wrist into the Shaman's eye socket and snapped back. The bolt thudded home. He died instantly, dropping like a sack to the floor.

'Damn it,' she breathed. She rolled him over and retrieved the bolt, wiping it clean on his furs. Struggling with his bulk, she hauled him into the shadows of the doorway. What had he been doing so far behind the others and on foot? Now time was at a premium. It wouldn't be long before a Shaman was missed.

She reached the square less than five minutes later and fought to remain calm at what greeted her eyes. The square itself was more than a quarter of a mile each side, paved with white stone and with a glittering quartz-inlaid pathway leading to the pyramid from the east. The tomb of the Wytch Lords reached at least two hundred feet into the night sky, smooth but for the stairway that led to the six beacon fires at its peak. It was a breathtaking structure and one fitting to house the greatest enemy Balaia had ever faced.

And surely they were set to face it again. Because while Selyn's subconscious registered the stunning architecture, her mind struggled to come to terms with the sea of acolytes who kneeled before the open entrance to the tunnel, silent and unmoving.

The space before the pyramid was a carpet of dark-cowled followers who simply stared into the lantern-flanked blackness. They were waiting. Just waiting. The atmosphere lay heavy on her like a weight between her shoulderblades, the air thick and crackling with anticipation. But overwhelming it all was a feeling of onrushing evil she could all but taste. Above the pyramid, clouds gathered, circling in black impenetrability, adding humidity to the menace. Selyn shuddered. The only sound she could hear above her own thumping heart was the breathing of the acolytes, slow and deliberate, as if it too were an integral part of the ceremony that was surely close.

She didn't need to see any more. Re-awakening was mere days, perhaps only hours away. She returned to her rooftop and called her communion with Styliann.

'Fascinating,' said Styliann, walking a complete circle around The Unknown. 'A Protector unmasked.'

The Unknown and Denser stood in the Marquee, now shorn of its trappings of conference. The tables and chairs had gone, packed for transit with the delegations planning to leave for the relative safety of their own cities – there would be no more meetings at the lake until the war was over. In their place was a rough trestle, backless benches and a fire on which boiled a pot of water.

Behind them, sitting at the trestle and just arrived, were Ilkar and Erienne. The Julatsan had been unable to contain his delight at seeing The Unknown and his admiration for Denser. Barras had quietened him, but he still wore a broad smile and the sandwiches at his elbow were untouched. Erienne had immediately run to Denser to comfort him, to try to erase some of his pain, but he hardly registered her presence. The College Elders all stood near by, impressed in spite of themselves at the feat for which Laryon had paid with his life.

The Unknown stared down at Styliann, his massive frame making even the Xeteskian Lord of the Mount less imposing. The big warrior had abandoned the axe Sol had employed, preferring to retain just the double-handed blade that was his trademark.

'I am not a Protector,' he said. 'Neither am I an experimental result for examination by you or any mage. If you want to talk to me, stand in front of me.'

Styliann stopped his circling. 'My apologies, Unknown.' He smiled. 'But you are a landmark in magical research and a major step forward for Xetesk.'

'I am a dead man alive,' countered The Unknown. 'I would have preferred death, but Xetesk thought otherwise. That's the last time you decide my destiny.'

'You sound a little ungracious. After all, we gave you back your life.'

The Unknown's right hand shot out, gloved fingers gripping Styliann's throat, forcing his head back so their eyes met.

'No. You stole my death.' Styliann's hands began to move. 'Don't do it. You aren't fast enough. If you don't believe me, go ahead and try.' The Unknown's hand tightened. Styliann gagged, his hands moving upwards in a supplicating gesture. 'I had chosen my time to die. Not many men get that chance, and you took it from me.'

'You are alive,' gasped Styliann.

'I could go and visit my own corpse.'

'Denser, please.' Styliann clutched at The Unknown's hand.

Denser appeared to notice the scene for the first time. He took in the other College delegates, the Xeteskian swordsmen standing ready, and Ilkar, whose eyes were fixed on Styliann.

'Unknown, please let him go.'

Unknown released him and turned to Denser. 'Sorry,' he said.

Densor shrugged. Styliann waved his men to stand down but maintained a baleful gaze on The Unknown.

'I will not be your exhibit. I am Raven,' said The Unknown.

'Denser, let's talk. Outside.' Styliann walked stiffly from the Marquee by his own exit.

Denser sighed and followed, squeezing The Unknown's arm as he turned. Leaving the Marquee, he caught sight of the wide smile on Vuldaroq's face.

Styliann didn't walk far from the Marquee before shooing away his aides.

'Tell me of your condition.'

Denser rubbed at the eyes he knew must be sunken, red and ringed in black.

'I cannot replenish mana stamina, my concentration won't allow complex recitation and I cannot tune my eyes to the mana spectrum.' It was what Styliann needed to hear, but it expressed nothing about his true condition.

His sense of loss penetrated right into his bones and chilled his body. His mind was at once crowded with images and empty of feeling. That part of his mind which the Familiar had for so long shared was missing and Denser imagined a hole in his head above his right eye and it itched. Only when he put his hand there, the itch was on the inside and he couldn't quiet it.

But the loss of the voice and the pulse, that was what hurt more than the pain he still felt at its death. The voice had given him calm and comfort but the pulse he had taken as a right, something that was of him. Now that pulse was gone, part of him had died.

'Your faculties will soon return. You merely need rest. As for the grief you feel, that will remain, I am afraid.' Styliann's face softened. 'I am sorry it happened but I fail to understand why it attacked Nyer's party. That isn't to say I'm displeased to hear of the traitor's death.'

'He felt he had to distract Nyer. He thought they were too close.' Denser shrugged. 'They might have taken The Raven before they reached here.' He shook his head. 'Might. I didn't think he had to. I think he felt he had to prove his worth.'

'Worth?' Styliann frowned. 'It was a Familiar. It had no concept of worth.'

'Did you ever take a Familiar?' asked Denser. Styliann shook his head. 'Then you can have no idea what concepts they hold. I have felt. I know.'

Styliann chewed his lip reflectively. He looked up at the early morning sky, taking in the light cloud cover. 'Show me the catalysts,' he said at length.

'I don't have them.'

'Then where—?'

'The Raven hold them. I couldn't take them into Xetesk.'

Styliann exhaled through his nose. 'No. No indeed.'

A brief commotion in another part of the camp interrupted further conversation. The sound of hoofs approaching was followed by the sight of The Raven and Evanson rounding a stand of bushes. They pulled up close to the Marquee and dismounted. Hirad strode over to Denser, expectation on his face. But the question he was about to ask was lost as he read Denser's eyes. Instead, he inclined his head in respect and grasped the Dark Mage's right arm just below the shoulder.

'I understand your pain,' he said.

'And I your anger,' said Denser. He paused, managing a weak smile. 'He's inside.'

The Unknown was sitting on a bench behind a trestle table, talking to Ilkar and Erienne as Hirad moved the curtain aside and walked in. A lump rose in his throat as he watched the big man for a short while until he was sure his voice was steady enough for speech.

The animation in the face, the definite movements when he used his hands, and the way he stroked the top of his head and on down the back of his skull to his neck, as if smoothing out a crease. It was all there. Where Sol had been now sat The Unknown. No mask, no emotionless eyes, no double-bladed axe.

'By all the Gods, it *is* you.' His voice cracked and a tear was in his eye. He wiped it away as he strode forwards. The Unknown walked around the table and the two men met and hugged, Hirad clapping the big man's back. 'How do you feel?'

The Unknown stepped back. 'I don't know,' he said. 'I know it's me.' He shrugged. 'I knew it before . . . you recognised me. When I was Sol. But I couldn't speak to you. Something inside me forbade me recognise you in return, though my eyes gave me away. Hirad, I should be dead.'

'But you're not and I don't care how. It's you. Gods, it's you!'

'Would you say the same if you returned to Septern's barn?'

'I—' Hirad paused, confused. 'Yes, why not?'

'Because I'm still beneath the soil too. Where's Denser?' The Unknown looked past him.

'Outside,' said Hirad vaguely. 'What do you mean?'

'I should see to him.' He walked away from Hirad, who made to follow.

'Leave him,' said Ilkar. 'Come and have a drink and something to eat. You must be starving.'

Hirad watched The Unknown until he'd left the Marquee. 'And knackered,' he said. 'What's going on?' He walked to the table. Ilkar poured him a goblet of wine and pushed platters of meat and bread in his direction.

'Sit down,' said Ilkar. 'You've got to understand how difficult this is for him to accept.'

Hirad stared at him, plainly not understanding at all.

'Look, Hirad, to us it's just the same Unknown. The way he looks, acts, talks, everything. The scars on his back and thigh are there, that lump on his knee, and his little toe is missing. It is him, in every way – his soul is there, his mind is there, his memories, all of it. But he has a knowledge none of us can conceive of having. He knows he can go and physically dig up his own corpse. Think about it.'

Hirad did so but briefly. 'So what does it mean, and why is he so bothered about Denser?'

'Right now, I think he's in a state of total confusion. Erienne will agree with me that not everything he says makes much sense.' Erienne nodded. 'And so he's suppressing what he can't handle and that manifests itself in his desire to protect Denser. Don't forget what he was just yesterday, Hirad. He certainly hasn't. He may never be able to. The fact is, we just don't know.'

'So is it him?' asked Hirad.

'Yes. Gods, yes.' Ilkar leant forwards. 'But he's got some unique problems only he can sort out. You'll have to give him time.'

'I knew it was too good to be true.'

'Hirad, calm down. He thought he was dead, awoke as a Protector and then again as himself. Give him time.' Ilkar held Hirad's stare, seeing the disappointment reflected there. 'All right?' Hirad twitched his head in what Ilkar decided was the closest to a nod he was likely to get. 'Good. Now eat. We've much to discuss after you've rested.'

Selyn awoke to the sound of shouts all around her. Startled alert, she lay flat, listening. Dawn had risen perhaps an hour before, not long enough for her reserves of mana stamina, but it gave her some ammunition.

A search was in progress, and with the accents and language she could hear, Wesmen were trawling the streets of Parve. Presumably they had found the body of the Shaman. Selyn frowned and took the cover from her eyes, opening them gently as they watered in response to sudden light.

She considered herself a little unlucky that the dead man had been found quite so soon. Judging by the organisation she could hear about her, the body had been located well before dawn.

Staying prone, she inched her way to the parapet, ears pricking as each gave her more information about the scale of the search. Below her, she knew, there was no one. Behind and towards the square, the shouts were loud and regular, the thuds of doors, the splinter of wood, the clearing of buildings. Very methodical, very. Particularly for Wesmen. Only it wasn't just Wesmen, it was Wytch Lord acolytes, and one thing they were was efficient.

She formed the mana shape for a CloakedWalk, spoke the command word, dropped to the ground and moved back towards the Torn Wastes. She walked quickly but carefully past the last building; there was no pursuit. Breasting a large pile of rubble, her heart missed a beat and she slowed to a crawl. The eastern periphery of Parve was ringed with Wesmen, shoulder to shoulder. She turned and ran back into the City.

Just inside the borders of the buildings, she saw the line. Wesmen and Shamen on every street, covering the cobbles, walking, looking, searching. Inside and out of buildings, basements and roofs. She was in a net, the mesh was fine and the strings were drawing tight.

She trotted left, towards the main street, keeping an eye to her right, watching the Wesmen advancing, just two blocks away and closing. As she neared, the main street was filled with a line of Wesmen, a Shaman in their midst. They knew she was here, they realised she'd likely be invisible and they could sense her mana emanations.

Fear edged into her mind, the tendrils of doubt chipping at her confidence. And Styliann had been so proud of her the night before, talking of her triumphal return to Xetesk, the part she would play in the victory to come, and the place at his side for ever. Her heart surged. She about-turned, never coming to a standstill, and walked quickly back. She was in an area three blocks by two and shrinking, and it seemed the Wesmen had all the ways out covered.

All except one. She looked into the sky. A thousand feet up she would be swallowed by the cloud and lost to sight. Not ideal, but the only option would always be the best one. Moving quickly now, Selyn scanned the rooftops for a launch point, finding it on a building close to the edge of the City.

She climbed the wall of the flat building and ran to the chimney stack at the Parve end, the Wesmen less than one hundred yards from her. Across the street, half a dozen Wesmen clambered on to a roof and spread themselves, arms outstretched. For a moment, she wondered whether she might try to dodge through the thin barrier when they reached her roof. But then she saw the Shaman climb up behind them. It had to be now.

Pressing herself against the lee of the chimneys, she dropped the

CloakedWalk and began to prepare the mana shape for ShadowWings. Almost at once, a shout went up. She opened her eyes. She had been seen from the boundary, and men were running and pointing. She gathered her concentration and re-formed the mana shape. In seconds, it was done.

'Deploy,' she said. At her back, wings formed, shifting in the daylight and barely visible to the naked eye. She took a pace forwards and lifted off, moving quickly out and upwards towards the Wastes. Below her, commands were barked and projectiles whistled into the air. Nothing came close. She smiled. Not the way she wanted to get out, but good enough. She could almost smell the fire in Styliann's tower.

Something slammed into her back, driving the wind from her and sending her tumbling downwards. She barely kept hold of the wings as she fought to right herself and regain lost height, but she felt weighted with lead. She glanced over her shoulder. A thin beam of white light connected her body to a Shaman. Below her, Wesmen were jeering and shouting, faces upturned, teeth bared.

She drove the wings harder, inching away, but a second blow, this time at the base of her neck, sent her crashing side first into a building. She hit the ground, dazed, the ShadowWings gone.

'Damn.' She shook her head, hearing delighted whoops and running feet. She struggled to rise, pushing her back up the wall, head throbbing but vision clearing. From the left and right they came, it seemed like hundreds of them. She drew the sword from her back-mounted scabbard and stood ready. One of them laughed, unhitching an axe. On a signal, the others dropped back a pace to give him room to fight alone.

He was a large man, heavy-set, with an untidy black beard and close eyes. He ran in, swinging his axe through chest high. Selyn simply ducked the blow and came up fast, taking him clean through the stomach. He grunted and fell sideways and backwards, clutching at his wound, blood pouring through his fingers.

A moment's shocked quiet was shattered by a roar as the mass ran forward. She snatched a dagger from her boot. They were on her quickly, a mêlée of furs, steel and fists.

The first Wesmen died with the dagger through his heart. Another took a cut to his thigh, but then they had her hands. The sword was knocked from her grasp as she struggled to free herself. She was pushed back against the wall; swords and daggers were drawn. One of them dragged the hood from her head and face.

Another pause in surprise at what they had uncovered. The sounds of approval chilled her to the bone, but when the grips on her arms loosened instinctively, she reacted on the instant, turning her wrists and releasing the bolts. One man was taken under the chin, the other bolt glanced off a head and away. Both men fell back, but there were so many others.

They dragged her to the ground, yells of animal pleasure filling the air as the clothes were cut and torn from her body. Hands pawed her, scratched and clawed her, blood oozed from a dozen cuts. She squirmed and fought, keeping a determined silence as they pinned her down, spread-eagled naked and terrified.

A single voice shouted a command and the mob quietened and parted, admitting a Shaman. He was middle-aged, clad in heavy cloth and with his greying hair tied in a ponytail at his neck. Selyn's terror stilled, replaced by the calm of certainty, and she gathered herself to stare him square in the eye.

'Well, well, well, my pretty,' said the Shaman, loosening his belt and kneeling between her legs. 'Perhaps death won't come quickly enough for you.'

The rape was brutal. He thrust hard inside her, his hands gouging at her sides and breasts. She winced as he pushed up, a cheer rising from the watching crowd. She closed her mind to the humiliation and the pain and picked her head up to catch his gaze a second time.

'They will have to cut me in half to release you,' she said. She bit down hard on her back tooth and convulsed. 'Goodbye, my love,' she whispered. The nerve toxin from the broken tooth cap acted instantly, every muscle in her body contracting with extraordinary violence. The last sounds she heard as the mana pulse fled eastwards were the screams of the Shaman.

Chapter 26

Styliann's cry of pain and fury could be heard clear across Triverne Lake. Selyn's dying mana pulse struck him like a stake through the eye. It took six men to restrain him and two spells to sedate him, and even as he slept, the tears rolled down his face and the fire burned in his cheeks. When he awoke, the light had gone from his eyes and he strode to the Marquee, time suddenly precious.

The chairs were back, arranged in a shallow crescent on one side of the trestle, which was now clothed, candled and decked with food and wine. Styliann took his place next to Barras in the centre chairs. Vuldaroq to Barras's left, Heryst next to Styliann. And on the other side of the trestle, The Raven. On a bench drawn up to the table sat Denser, Ilkar and Hirad, with The Unknown standing in close attendance of the Dark Mage. Behind them, sitting on cushions and chairs, and invited principally as observers, were Will, Thraun, Jandyr and Erienne.

There was no set agenda. A day ago, this meeting would have been unthinkable. But it was a measure of the deterioration of the situation to the east of the Blackthorne Mountains and Understone Pass that The Raven had agreed to submit to a discussion about their next move.

Hirad sat forward, leaning on his elbows, hands supporting his chin. Denser had adopted a more relaxed posture, while Ilkar sat stiffly upright, in awe of the seniority of the mages opposite him.

Styliann, his eyes dark, his hands constantly wringing, spoke in a monotone as he informed them of the decision to help them through Understone Pass, though he wouldn't be drawn in their company as to the magic that would be employed to retake the pass. Denser looked closely at him, tried to probe the periphery of his emotions with his mind. The Lord of the Mount sensed him, shot him a glance full of anguish.

'They have taken Selyn from me,' he said. 'They will suffer.'

'I am sorry, my Lord.'

Styliann nodded. 'Yes,' he said. 'Now, tell me of your plans when you reach the other side of the pass.'

'No,' said Hirad.

'I beg your pardon?' Vuldaroq spluttered. All the delegates had tensed.

'Some tact, please, Hirad.' Ilkar sounded suddenly strained. 'What he is trying to say is that—'

'We aren't telling you anything because for one, you don't need to know and that makes us all safer, and for another, we don't know ourselves until we get close enough to see what we're up against. Once we get through the pass, we'll head for the Wrethsires, as you know. After that, we'll be on our way to the Torn Wastes.' Hirad poured himself a goblet of wine. 'What can I say? We'll be in touch.'

There was silence around the table. The delegation's was down to sheer disbelief, The Raven's due to trepidation. Only Hirad seemed unaffected.

'What?' He spread his hands and looked at his friends. 'What's the problem?'

'The problem, Hirad Coldheart,' spat Styliann, 'is that you have no conception of what you are dealing with. You blithely speak of taking the most powerful spell ever created into the heart of Balaia's most potent enemy as though it were a stroll through the woods. We can't afford for this to fail.' His final words were accompanied by raps on the table.

'Well, it strikes me you've been doing your level best to screw it up ever since you recruited us.' Hirad leaned right into Styliann, half rising from his seat. 'We know how to deal with this and we'll succeed if you leave us alone. It's been your interference that has caused us most of our trouble.' He sat back down, but pointed a finger at Styliann's eyes. 'And never, ever tell me I don't understand what is going on. The fact that I am still sitting by Denser while so many of my friends are either dead or in hiding should tell you I understand only too well how important this is.'

'Calm down, Hirad,' said Ilkar. 'This isn't helping.'

'I don't care. Look, it's quite simple. You let us do things our way and we'll succeed. Interfere and we'll more than likely fail.'

Styliann looked at Hirad with a mixture of rage and respect. His cheeks were slightly coloured and he refused to take in the expressions of the others in the delegation. 'I am unused to having my authority challenged in this way,' he said quietly.

'I'm not challenging your authority,' said Hirad. 'I'm just telling you how to give yourself the best chance.'

'I think it is about time we moved on,' said Heryst. 'I am sure we all agree that The Raven can best deal with the Wrethsires on their own. But I do think it would be wise if we – that is, the four-College delegation – held the two catalysts found so far until the third is recovered.'

'I'm sure you do.'

'Why are you smiling?'

'Because you must think I'm an idiot, and that's what idiots do all the time.'

'Hirad,' said Ilkar, 'tell me you haven't done what I think you've done.

Denser clapped Hirad on the back and started laughing, though he surely could scarcely feel like doing so. 'Oh, very well done, Hirad, very well done,' he said.

The delegation looked on, Styliann at Denser, Barras at Ilkar.

'Explain,' said Vuldaroq, his face reddening by the second. 'I hate to feel I am being laughed at.'

'Let me assure you I am laughing at nothing but Hirad's capacity to surprise. Tell us all where the catalysts are, Hirad, please.'

Hirad shrugged. 'Somewhere between here and the farm we stayed at. I don't think I'll be any more specific. And before you bluster and shout, let me explain that I am sick and tired of people trying to run my life and so I have given The Raven a little bargaining counter against further betrayal.'

'But surely you know that was a rogue Master from Xetesk!' Vuldaroq thumped the palms of his hands on his chair. 'And now the most valuable pieces in Balaia are unguarded.'

'And untraceable,' said Hirad. 'And I don't care who it was that was coming to kill us. The fact is that there are only three mages in the entire world that I trust and they are all sitting with The Raven. Now we need to get through the pass without wasting any more time. If your intelligence is right, the Wesmen will be at our borders in four days or less and I don't want to meet them in the middle of the Blackthorne Mountains.'

Hirad took in everyone. Denser was smiling, The Unknown was gazing studiously at the back of Denser's neck, Ilkar was staring at him with jaw slack and eyes wide, and the delegation sat in mute fury. All except one. Heryst. He was nodding and was the first to rise.

'Congratulations, Hirad Coldheart. You have out-thought us all.

For now. It's a shame you mistrust us, because we really are on your side, and the side of Balaia,' he said. 'I only hope for your sake that your mind is as alert in the days to come. The game for our land is about to be played out and Dawnthief is the only card we have. It would be criminal to lose it.' He led the delegation from the Marquee.

'Are you absolutely out of your mind?' Ilkar waited until only The Raven remained in the Marquee.

'We got the result we wanted,' said Hirad. 'Why?'

'Why?' Ilkar spluttered. 'Have you any idea how powerful Styliann is? All the delegation for that matter. Yet you have to go rubbing him up the wrong way, and as if that wasn't enough, you've planted Dawnthief in a bloody field somewhere. What, are you thinking it'll grow and bear fruit or something?'

Hirad smiled again. He glanced at Denser, who had returned to his shell and was staring into nowhere.

'Ease up, Ilkar. Listen—' He broke off. 'Will they be listening?' He jerked a thumb.

'I'd expect nothing less,' said Ilkar. Hirad raised his eyebrows. Ilkar sighed, spoke a few words and made an enveloping motion with his arms. The sounds from outside the Marquee faded to nothing. 'Go on,' he said. 'Where exactly between here and the farmhouse have you put the catalysts?'

Hirad held his right thumb and forefinger and inch apart. 'About this far.'

'I beg your pardon?' Ilkar blinked slowly.

Hirad pulled a chain from under his shirt. From it hung the Understone Pass Commander's Badge and the Dordovan Ring of Authority.

'Grow and bear fruit! What do you take me for?'

A transformation had taken place in Understone since the arrival of Darrick. Drainage had been restored and the main street was merely sole deep in mud, aided in its drying by a stiff wind and a hold-off of rain. Around the town itself, a city of tents and corralling had sprung, housing the four-College cavalry, its horses and, latterly, the five thousand foot soldiers who were the advance force detailed to defend the eastern end of Understone Pass from Wesmen incursion.

Defensive positions had been raised out of bowshot of the mouth of the pass, from where there was nothing but silence. The mages he had sent in under CloakedWalks had not returned. The quiet was disconcerting. It was as if they were waiting for something more than just reinforcement before attacking. It made Darrick uneasy, and when Darrick was uneasy, there was usually magic in the air.

The Raven arrived in the company of thirty Xeteskian mages two days after leaving Triverne Lake. Darrick was waiting for them, and in the evening before the attempt was to be made to take the pass, he heard the details of Xetesk's new offensive spell. He and Hirad sparred in the main street later as he tried to shake off the images the mages drew. He had taken an instant like to the Raven man and was envious of his role and the sheer determination he saw in his eyes.

The next morning would see the Wesmen a little over a day from the pass. He found himself irritated that they couldn't wait for the maximum number to be inside when the spell was cast. And it wasn't just to do with the fact that The Raven had to gain quick passage to the other side either. It was to do with the correct alignment of dimensions. He hoped someone would be good enough to explain it to him sometime.

The wind blew from the south, along the Bay of Gyernath. The afternoon skies were clear but cloud was gathering, thick, dark and ominous. Rain was already falling far out in the southern ocean, dark grey reaching from sea to sky. It would hit land by nightfall.

The Barons Blackthorne and Gresse stood on the eastern shore of the bay where the shingle gave way to sand and sloped steeply into the lapping waters of low tide. To their right, the Blackthorne Mountains towered sheer from the water, beginning their six-hundred-mile journey to the Triverne Inlet and Balaia's northern coast. At their backs, and perhaps two hours' ride north-east, was the walled town of Blackthorne and its castle.

The seat of Balaia's most powerful Baron was the principal hurdle in the way of any Wesmen move to Understone to the north and, to a lesser extent, Gyernath to the south-east. Its seven thousand inhabitants were principally from mining or farming backgrounds, giving Blackthorne considerable muscle in addition to his standing militia.

With Gresse's four hundred men and mercenaries, the defence of southern Balaia numbered around one thousand regular and two thousand reserve soldiers, and they would need every one. Word from Understone suggested that as many as six thousand Wesmen would attempt the bay crossing. The battle would be hard and bloody.

Gresse and Blackthorne stood flanked by mages and aides, the former providing EagleSight-augmented information to add to what could be made out in miniature on the other side of the bay. The sand was black with boats and Wesmen.

'There are more than six thousand there, surely,' said Gresse.

One of the mages turned to him. 'It's impossible to say. They are stretched over three miles but that's a function of the number of boats they have assembled. More are arriving from the south-west all the time.'

Gresse squinted and peered across the bay. The shore seemed to be crawling, shifting, moving. Individuals were impossible to make out, but the mass was there for all to see. Beside him, Blackthorne cleared his throat.

In his mid-forties, Baron Blackthorne was tall and slim with an angular face, heavy brows, black hair and beard. He rarely smiled, suffered no fools and carried his worries in his walk, which was head down, shoulders hunched and very fast. Like Gresse, over his breeches, shirt and leather tunic, he wore a heavy cloak, at which the wind picked.

'Is equipment being loaded?' he asked, the weariness in his tone suggesting this wasn't a problem with which he should really be concerned.

'Yes, my Lord,' replied his senior mage.

'Then we can expect them to put to sea quite soon. Under cover of darkness, one suspects.'

'Yes, my Lord.'

'Hmm.' He licked his lips and smoothed the beard along his jawline. 'I want as many of those boats sunk as is humanly possible without overstretching our resources. HotRain, FlameOrbs, BowWave, Ice-Wind, whatever. Take half of our mages and keep one hundred guards. I need wards in the sand, I need the first boats to land set aflame and turned around to obstruct the beach.

'Do not be overrun. Retreat to the castle as soon as the Wesmen come ashore in large numbers. They won't have horses, so you should be able to outrun them. Is that all clear?' The man nodded. 'Then Gresse and I will return to town. We will form our principal defence there. Baron Gresse?'

He turned on his heel and walked back up the gentle grassy slope to his horse, his footman coming to attention and handing him the reins. Behind him, the mage was already issuing orders. Gresse smiled as he walked beside the younger man, hurrying to keep up. The Wesmen would not reach Gyernath or Understone easily.

'And what of the rest of the KTA now?' asked Blackthorne as they rode together towards the castle, bodyguards behind them.

'Too busy squabbling over my lands to help us or too pig-headed to believe the threat is real. Distrust of the Colleges is habitual,' said Gresse.

'And historically wise.' Blackthorne turned to him. 'What have you done with your people?'

'At Taranspike?' Blackthorne nodded. 'They're still at the castle but under instruction not to resist any attack. I've told them it isn't worth it. My sons are there to see them safe, they have my seal of authority and they can stay in Korina at my expense if necessary. He won't hurt them if they surrender.'

'Pontois?'

'Yes.'

'Hmm.' Blackthorne frowned. 'I won't forget this, Gresse.'

'It is for Balaia, not just for you,' Gresse reminded him.

'But you are the only man with the balls to stand beside me,' said Blackthorne. 'It will give me great pleasure to reciprocate when you reclaim Taranspike. It was scum of the calibre of Pontois who killed the KTA and left us with no real defence against what we now face. His greed has shut his mind and he will be called to account. I, personally, will see to it.' He paused, his face softening, much to Gresse's surprise. 'Assuming we survive the coming storm, that is. But for you and me, my friend, it is time to put our feet up in front of a large fire, take the best wine my cellars have to offer and await the sound of the horns.'

The Barons spurred their horses towards Blackthorne Town.

Chapter 27

Understone's fateful morning broke dry, but heavy cloud was blowing over the Blackthorne Mountains towards them. At first light, Darrick's cavalry mounted up and began the move to the pass. In front of the slowly advancing column walked thirty Xeteskian mages, young and old, all wearing the insignia of the Lord of the Mount on red tunic and shoulder – a tower atop a crown, edged in gold, embroidered on black.

The sound of voices had stopped as the cavalry formed up behind the mages, The Raven at its rear. All that could be heard were the sounds of hoofbeats, the nervous whinnies of horses and the flap of five hundred cloaks in the breeze.

Darrick sat tall in his saddle, proud and determined. To be appointed the first general of a four-College force for over three hundred years was an honour he could never have conceived even two months before.

But now, in front of him, thirty Xeteskians awaited his command, and behind him, five hundred horse would charge into the pass at the drop of his sword. The cavalry were split on College lines, each centile having its own defensive mages to cast hard and spell shields and provide the light to see them through the pass. The livery was mixed: green for Lystern, shades of deep blue for Dordover and Xetesk and yellow for Julatsa. Not ordered enough for the trained military mind but imposing for all that.

At the rear of the column lounged The Raven and their horses. Hirad, Ilkar, Erienne and The Unknown stood in loose formation around a still pale but more talkative Denser. Jandyr, Thraun and Will, whose grey hair now covered much of his head, spoke amongst themselves. Hirad allowed a half-smile across his face, seeing parallels with the early days of Richmond, Ras and Talan. They would take more part, of that he was sure, so long as they lived. And of that, he wasn't.

'What are they going to do, exactly?' asked Hirad. 'I mean,

whatever it is, it's going to be impressive, right? There's thirty of them after all.'

Denser shrugged. 'It'll be something to watch.'

'Oh come on, Denser, you can do better than that,' said Ilkar. 'They've been researching for twenty years, you must know something.'

'Ah, Ilkar,' said Denser, moving closer to Erienne, 'there you go assuming our research teams are as forthcoming as yours. Don't forget, in Xetesk, new spell construction and mastery leads to Master status.'

'But if you haven't heard any rumours, you can take your arm from my waist.' Erienne smiled. Denser's arm stayed where it was.

'I just don't want to spoil your surprise, and if I've heard right, it's going to be something like you've never seen.'

'Elucidate,' said The Unknown, who still said little and never strayed far from Denser's side.

Denser pushed out his bottom lip. 'Right. Well, all I'll say is that it's dimensional, it's incredibly difficult to control and, if my hunch is right, it'll be wet.'

'Wet,' said Hirad.

There was a contemplative quiet.

'Wet,' said Hirad again.

Denser smiled. 'Just watch.'

Darrick gave the instruction to cast. Twenty-one mages stepped forwards, forming three sides of a square. The lead mage gave the command to mana-form and at once, all their heads dropped but their hands reached out as if gripping something too heavy to hold. Closed-eyed, they leaned back against the invisible grip. There was a moment's calm. Denser grunted as the mana shape developed.

'This is powerful,' he said.

The mages started walking towards the pass. There was no movement from within.

'HardShield up.' A trio of Julatsan mages raised their defence around the vulnerable Xeteskians.

Twenty yards from the black maw of the pass, the arrows began to fly, bouncing harmlessly from the core-strength Julatsan hard shield. The mages stopped walking, still concentrating, still developing the mana shape.

Denser, who had attuned his eyes to the mana spectrum, marvelled at the shape of the spell. It mapped a pattern at once random but with a perverse sense of rhythm and symmetry. And it was huge, covering a space in the air which totally obscured the pass, the path in front of the casting mages and the hills rising either side.

'I have never . . .' he breathed.

'It's incredible,' agreed Ilkar.

'Unstable,' said Erienne. 'I only hope they can hold it.'

'What does it look like?' asked Will.

It was a deep, pulsating blue, edges shifting and changing, mimicking the outline of the Blackthorne mountain peaks high above, then swarming to depict oceanic power. It was shot through with streaks of orange, which flowed ceaselessly through the whole, joining, spiralling, splitting. To a mage, it was beauty incarnate; to everyone else, an inconceivable mystery.

A rank of archers moved up quickly as the first Wesman appeared at the pass entrance, sword in hand. He disappeared just as quickly. Bows strung, arrows nocked, the archers waited for the inevitable charge.

Perhaps twenty Wesmen ran from the darkness, heavy furs bouncing on their bodies, braided hair flowing backwards, their shouts echoing along the path and their eyes wild beneath steep brows.

The archers fired. The shouting stopped. The survivors turned and fled.

'Deploy,' said the lead Xeteskian immediately afterwards.

It began with a horizontal line of red light suspended above, and ten yards in front of, the entrance to the pass. A heartbeat later, it was joined by three more, forming a perfect square some fifty feet each side, hanging in the air. The lines fizzed and crackled but held rock steady. Behind the square, the mages swayed backwards, arms outstretched, hands gripping mid-air. The angle was crazy, they should all have fallen but the mana shape held them.

'Connect and open,' ordered the lead mage. There was a buzzing in the air and the lines of the square revolved through a dazzling spectrum of colour. Two mages were hurled from the square to lie motionless in the dirt and mud, smoke rising from clothes, skin and hair. Next, a moment's silence so deep it hurt the ears. And finally, the awesome sound of water obliterated the peace.

And a beat after the sound came the sight. With the power of the deep, froth flying, came a force of water the size of the square. It howled out of dimensional space, striking the ground well inside the pass. Out and out it came, ocean from a clouded sky, screaming into the darkness and surely dashing to fragments everything in its path.

Behind, the mages fought to maintain the square as it bucked and twisted in the air, buckling and strengthening as the deluge hammered out into Balaian space. The water lashed against rock, tore vegetation from its roots and smashed the very earth from its bed of ages, spray flying backwards, streams running in every direction from the mouth of the pass. Echoing from the walls of rock inside, a pounding sound rose to join that of the rush from the mouth in the sky. The tumbling of loose stone, the crack of timbers snapped like twigs, and faint, so faint it may have been a trick on the ears, the screams of men could all be heard. The power was extraordinary.

Ilkar swore softly. 'They've tapped an ocean,' he said quietly. 'They've tapped a bloody ocean.' Had he shouted, no one would have heard him as the roar battered at the ears and the sight simply blotted out the capacity for anything else.

The mages held it for what seemed an age, the exertion visible, the effort tangible. The gate was kept open for over two minutes until, as suddenly as it had begun, the stream was shut off.

Another silence that tore at the ears was followed by the rising hubbub of excited voices. The exhausted mages didn't even have the energy to congratulate each other before collapsing to the floor, every mote of mana stamina gone.

Applause rippled the air but was silenced by a shout from Darrick.

'Clear the path!

There was a ripple through the cavalry line as reins were drawn tighter. The metallic sounds of bits and bridles tautening added to the stamp of hoofs and the running of feet as Julatsan and Xeteskian mages came to the aid of their exhausted colleagues, hurrying them off the path and up a gentle slope. The bodies of the two for whom the spell had simply been too much were carried away.

Darrick raised his sword. The Raven mounted up. Five hundred blades swept from scabbards, ringing the air.

'Shield and light!' The teams of mages cast quickly and without error, and 'shield-up' confirmations travelled the column, followed by two dozen LightGlobes.

'Advance!'

Darrick dropped his sword, kicked his heels into the flanks of his horse. Hoofs threw up mud, thrumming on the poor surface of the trail. The shouts of the centile commanders mixed with the clamour of horse, metal and hoof, and the cavalry column moved on, gathering pace.

And, with water still pouring from cracks in the rock above the entrance, the cavalry charged into Understone Pass.

*

As it happened, Gresse and Blackthorne chose to watch the start of the Second Wesmen War from a low hill three hundred yards from the beach where the landings would take place.

The horns had been sounded and beacon fires lit as dawn broke to reveal the Wesmen already in the bay, attempting to steal a march under cover of darkness. It was a move anticipated by Blackthorne, and his beach force had been at readiness three hours before first light.

The stern Baron surveyed the dense fleet of craft, ranging from rowing boats taking only a dozen, to merchantmen with a capacity running into the hundreds. It was a strange and deeply disturbing sight, compounded by the silence broken only by sail and row orders and the noise of oars and timbers through calm waters.

Rain had swept through the bay as night fell, backed by a vicious wind, no doubt hampering the Wesmen's start, and Blackthorne considered them to be behind schedule. He was certain they had planned to land at first light, not still be over three hours distant.

In front of them, forty mages stood, thirty to cause mayhem among the boats, and ten to maintain shields over their colleagues and the centile of swordsmen charged with routing the first wave of boats to hit the shore. Finally, invisible and anchored to the sand, three dozen explosive wards, ready to be activated in retreat, each one capable of killing a dozen men.

Blackthorne announced himself satisfied.

'This should give them something to think about.'

The boats drew closer, prows packed with Wesmen, silent, watching. Gresse didn't know what he expected but it wasn't this silence. The loudest noise in his ears was the flapping of his own cloak in the breeze.

'There must be four hundred boats out there.'

'Not for long,' said Blackthorne. 'Not for long.'

Sails trimmed, oars stroking through the water, the Wesmen fleet approached the shores of eastern Balaia. The calm was eerie but a storm was about to be unleashed over the flat waters of the Bay of Gyernath.

With the fleet four hundred yards from land, the offence mages split into three spell groups with overlapping defensive support, and moved out on to the sand dunes overlooking the shore.

At the same time, the centile of swordsmen, most carrying torches, moved up and gathered around the beacon fires. Shouts of warning echoed around the bay, bouncing off the sheer walls of the mountains.

Oars dug more deeply, sails were pared tighter, the fleet increased its speed.

The senior mage spoke. 'You have your targets. Don't wait around if you lose your spell. Don't wait around when you have completed casting. I need you all back in the castle, fit, well and rested in twelve hours. Cast at will.'

Gresse could hear the hum of voices on the breeze as the mages built mana shapes and linked spells. The process lasted little more than two minutes, and then the fire came down.

In an area covering three hundred yards each side, drops of fire coalesced from clear air and fell like lead among the boats. A thick, driving rain of fire, spatting in the water, smoking into wood, scorching canvas and setting hair and fur ablaze. While the drops flared harmlessly against the magical shields surrounding the larger vessels evidently carrying Shamen, there was instant panic among the smaller craft.

Hundreds of small fires leapt from every exposed plank. Sails smouldered and burned, hands and skulls lit up, fear spread and discipline disappeared. In the midst of the throng, one Captain made an emergency tack to take the direct route out of the HotRain, ploughing across a smaller rowing boat. Rudders went left and right as tillermen ducked and dodged the hail of fire, sending craft in all directions, spilling warriors from port, starboard, prow and stern. The sea boiled, alive with floundering survivors, the wash of oars plunged frantically into water and the myriad fires that snuffed out as they hit, leaving spirals of smoke in their wake.

Over it all, the howls of pain, the screams of the dying, the crackling of fire and the splintering of wood. And through the carnage came the back of the fleet, unable to change course or slow sufficiently, such was the press of boats all around. On and on they came, into the HotRain, scything over abandoned burning craft and running down Wesmen in the water by the score.

The HotRain shut off as quickly as it had started, but relief was momentary. A thick pall of smoke covered a wide area of the bay and fleet, and emerging from it, and undamaged, came many of the larger ships, their occupants roaring with rage and lust for blood.

Now, FlameOrbs lit the sky. Combining the mana of three or more mages at a time and creating great depth and intensity, dozens of yellow and orange orbs, each the size of a man, arced across the sky to fall like rock weights on the spell-defended ships. Some bounced, others did not, and Gresse saw one crack a shield and splatter on the deck, reducing the three-hundred-man transport to a burning shell in an instant.

Gresse turned away. Through all his years of combat, combining magic with muscle, he had never seen carnage on such a scale. The calls of the dying, drowning and ablaze would haunt his every living day. Yes, he'd seen shields crack and magic engulf its victims before. But he had never seen an enemy so unprepared for the quantity or quality of magic thrown at it. And here were only forty mages. At the castle, there were double that number.

Blackthorne watched the events with dispassionate satisfaction.

'Don't forget they have come to kill us, take our lands and drive our memory from Balaia for ever,' he said. 'If their Shamen are not strong enough, it is not for us to weep.'

'Why did you not simply devastate them on the water?' asked Gresse.

'I had no idea we would be this successful,' admitted Blackthorne. He chewed his lip. 'And I couldn't leave my town undefended. What if they chase us all the way to Blackthorne now?'

Still the Wesmen came on, and still Blackthorne's men weren't finished. The sea was ablaze on a half-mile stretch but the undamaged and handicapped sailed through the human and wooden wreckage. Scores, hundreds of boats came on, the first beaching against the shingle only to be met by the swords and fire of Blackthorne's warriors.

A dozen craft hit the beach, disgorging Wesmen into the surf and on to the sand. They came roaring into eastern Balaia, axes and blades flailing. Blackthorne's men just cut them down, given huge advantage by the rise in the ground, ranks of archers on the dunes above the sea and the confidence of seeing their enemies in the water, burning and in disarray.

True to the Baron's orders, the first boats were turned, burning, into the paths of the next. But hundreds more approached on a mile stretch. Spent, the mages ran for their horses and, with the Wesmen press of numbers threatening to overwhelm the small force of swordsmen, Blackthorne ordered full retreat.

With hardly a scratch, Blackthorne's men had won the first skirmish of the war. And those Wesmen who did give chase died in a deluge of magical fire, the sand traps exploding, sending sheets of orange, yellow and blue flame lashing across the sand, igniting everything in their compass. Great gouts of sand shot into the air to sprinkle back down, a rainfall of grit on the dead and wounded.

The survivors, and there were many thousands, began to construct a beach-head. Turning in his saddle to watch, Blackthorne smiled.

'No one takes my castle,' he said to himself. 'No one.'

Gresse caught his words though he had his doubts. A victory it was, but gazing over the shoreline as the smoke cleared and boat after boat reached the shore, he realised their estimate of numbers was way too low. And the Shamen would not be as unprepared another time.

The moment of truth would be at the walls of Blackthorne Castle.

Understone Pass was the result of a monstrous effort to widen a natural fissure that ran on a dog-leg through the Blackthorne Mountains. Ten times as many lives as years were lost in its creation at the behest of a group of Barons who were the forerunners of the Korina Trade Alliance. The result was a secure passage through Balaia's almost impassable mountain range.

Through the carved gateway, the roof of the pass closed in sharply to a height just above that of a covered wagon and didn't begin to open out for over three hundred yards. Always two wagons wide, the pass let out into incredible natural chambers and across chasms the bottom of which were littered with the bones of the unfortunate and the murdered. Elsewhere, the rock roof closed in, and always the sounds of rushing water stole quiet from any journey. A gallop through the pass would take something a little over four hours.

As he entered the pass, Darrick rode in awe of the devastation caused by the Xeteskian dimensional connection. LightGlobes chased the shadows away from the cavalry as they rode past the remnants of the Wesmen's fortified posts. There was precious little left to evidence that a defence had been built along the first part of the pass.

Here and there, wood clung to clefts in the rock wall, tumbles of stone were washed against the sides of the pass and planks and ripped timbers had been speared into crevices by the force of the water. But of the Wesmen, there was no trace.

Darrick increased his pace as the pass opened out both above and on either side, only to slow as the true results of the spell became awesomely obvious. Here, Darrick knew, was the main focus of the Wesmen's defence. Built into the walls were crossbow and catapult positions, archer galleries and oil runs. Deep into the rock, living quarters for anywhere between four and seven thousand men were dug, and the warren of rooms and passageways spread up either side of the pass for at least half a mile.

But the silence punctuated by running water told its own terrible story and of the accuracy of the Xeteskian calculations. The size of the dimensional rip had been larger than that of the first zone of the pass. The ocean, already travelling at incredible speed, had been forced through the smaller pass opening, gathering in pressure and velocity before exploding into the chamber occupied by so many completely unprepared Wesmen.

Nothing besides evacuation would have sufficed. The water would have blasted on and on, crashing through every passage, every room, every position, and simply scouring all signs of the Wesmen and the trappings of their lives from Understone Pass.

Water still ran from some of the upper positions and passages that Darrick could see, and as he moved further up the tight cavern, he could hear behind him the gasps of his men as they too took in their first sight of the sodden former defence of the Wesmen. It sparkled in the light of the Globes, pools of water casting dancing shadows over the walls and the roof as it rose gently into the darkness ahead.

'They had nowhere to run,' whispered Darrick, surprised at the tinge of sorrow he felt for the men who had had no chance of survival. No chance at all.

'Shall we search the barracks, sir?' asked one of his lieutenants.

Darrick shook his head. 'I don't think you want to see what might be left in there.' He looked about him as he trotted forwards, scratching his head. 'How far did the ocean travel?'

'The Xeteskians estimate it would not drain away for perhaps a third the length of the pass, until we reach the first deeps,' said an aide.

'I wonder how far this sort of research should be allowed to go,' said Darrick.

It was a sentiment being echoed by Ilkar as The Raven took their first sight of the obliteration of the Wesmen under the light of Erienne's Globe. 'We just don't know enough about the effects on the relative dimensions of channelling resources from one to another,' he said.

'It's all a question of how often such a spell is used,' replied Denser. 'Today we have seen an amount of water that neither dimension will notice.'

'But it has created an imbalance, however small, don't deny that,' said Ilkar.

'Yes, but a grain of sand moved from one side of the scale to another will make no difference.'

'Except that one day, one grain will tip the scale if the movement is all one way,' countered Ilkar. 'What then?'

'The shame,' said The Unknown, 'is that such a spell is only considered for its offensive capabilities. Think what it could do opened under a freshwater lake and over a land with no rain.'

The debate trailed away to silence, and soon the clatter of hoofs and the sounds of the water far below were dominant once more.

There was twilight in the outside world before the four-College cavalry found the first and only pitiful resistance, right at the far end of the pass. It was clear that the word of the Xeteskian water spell had reached the western end and the fear of a repeat had caused complete panic. Everywhere, abandoned guardposts told their own story, and the Wesmen, with no natural magic of their own, had fled.

The cavalry had not seen its first body for more than an hour, just before the first deeps where surely so much death had, mercifully, been washed. Because what they did see was mangled remains jammed into clefts, whole bodies, single limbs, shattered skulls and blood puddling with the standing water. The power the Xeteskians had unleashed on the pass disgusted Darrick.

And now, six hours later, he was confronted by perhaps twenty Wesmen atop the stockade that blocked the cavalry's path into Wesmen-held territory. All had bows or crossbows and their torchfires burned bright and proud. Darrick halted the cavalry column well within range, but confident that the hard shields still in operation would hold firm.

One of the Wesmen stepped forward on to a parapet and shouted down at them.

'Your spells will not hold us. Behind me are forces that will sweep you from Balaia, and the Lords of the Wastes will walk proud once more. Our magic will be too strong for you. Go back and prepare your graves.'

'Move aside or die,' said Darrick, simply, struggling a little at the scale of death that he had ordered so recently.

'We are protected, you cannot harm us.'

Darrick smiled thinly and turned to the contingent of Xeteskian mages. 'I don't have time for chatter,' he said, holding up three fingers. 'HellFire?' The mages nodded and began to cast. Darrick addressed himself to the Wesmen once more. 'Pray to whatever Gods you worship,' he said and turned his horse away.

'HellFire,' spoke the trio of Xeteskians.

The Wesmen and the stockade below them were shattered and the cavalry rode out into the open air less than half an hour later, once a mage under a CloakedWalk had reported that the trail outside the pass was empty.

'I think it would be fair to say that we caught them completely cold,' said Darrick. The cavalry general and The Raven were sharing a farewell drink in the lee of the western pass entrance.

'I'm sorry you had a wasted journey,' said Hirad, smiling. 'We could have taken the stockade ourselves.'

Darrick laughed. 'I don't doubt it.' He passed around the spirit bottle once more, and each of them replenished their mugs.

'So what's your next move?' asked Thraun.

'We need to keep the pass open for a couple of days until we can fortify at this end. Our best method of holding back the Wesmen will clearly be to stop them retaking it.'

'Not easy,' said Jandyr.

'No,' agreed Darrick. 'But we'll have another five thousand foot here in a few days, and if we can get a good rest tonight, I suspect our mages will be able to do most of the work.' He drank. 'But you. You are the ones with the task ahead of you. It'll be difficult.'

'Yes,' agreed Hirad. 'We could do with another blade. Perhaps you should reconsider my invitation to join The Raven?'

'I think I'll stick to cavalry for now.'

Hirad looked into the sky. It was early afternoon and the cloud that was sweeping towards Understone had cleared this side of the pass, leaving broken blue sky and a gentle breeze. Further west, though, it was darker.

'See anything our way, Ilkar?' he asked, following the elf's gaze.

'Nothing but hills and trees and good wholesome countryside. And it'll continue to look good so long as it's not swarming with Wesmen.'

'We'd best be on our way and find a sensible place to get our heads down,' said The Unknown. 'Staying here too long could be bad for the health.'

'Staying here would be fine,' corrected Darrick. 'Leaving to go west later today or in the morning, I suspect, would not.'

'Either way . . .' The Unknown got to his feet, waiting for Denser to rise before moving to his horse. 'Thraun, are you confident of the route?'

Thraun nodded, swinging into his saddle. 'I've studied the maps long enough.'

Hirad shook Darrick's hand. 'Keep the pass open, will you? We might be needing it in a hurry.'

'Just keep yourself alive. I haven't finished sparring with you yet.'
'Four, two, isn't it?'
'Four, three. Good luck.'
The Raven rode away and were lost to sight.

Chapter 28

The castle town of Blackthorne, its fishing fleet beached and hidden, lay in a shallow valley in the lee of the mountains where the rock joined the sea. Its tactical importance had not been lost on those who built it, controlling as it did trails to Understone northwards and Gyernath in the south-east.

Blackthorne was of the opinion that the Wesmen's principal aim in taking his town was to use it to stage raids on Darrick at the pass, and to a lesser extent, to attack the south-eastern port. He had no doubt that control of the pass was paramount to the Wesmen because it gave them the access they required to mount a meaningful offensive on the College cities, key to the domination of eastern Balaia.

The beach attack party reached the castle well before mid-morning on a cloudy, cool and breezy day, leaving scouts to monitor Wesmen movement inland. The sky was dark to the west, and with the prevailing wind bringing that darkness towards them, rain was surely coming. Organising defence of the castle was a relatively simple task. With most of the non-fighting population of the town already halfway to the more heavily defended Gyernath, or heading for Korina, Blackthorne had chosen a two-stage defence.

The outer walls of the town were sturdy and well maintained but not designed to withstand prolonged assault from the kind of numbers the Wesmen would bring to bear. Blackthorne had stationed three-quarters of his archers and a further fifty offensive mages, both with defensive cover, on the walls. When the first Wesmen breached the walls, they were to retreat. Blackthorne considered that there would be a mound of corpses four deep outside his town before they conceded it to the enemy.

The castle was his focus. Set at the northern edge of the town, it had been built to fend off Wesmen attacks from Understone Pass. Its sheer outer walls rose more than seventy feet above the town, completely encircling the keep, with turrets set at six intervals providing lookout support, battle direction and archer cover.

The castle's north gates, usually open to trade – the marketplace was inside the castle walls – had been shut and reinforced with bands of steel. Surrounding them, the gate towers were built forward and over an open arch, creating a lethal killing ground. The town walls facing the Wesmen were of similar construction.

Outside the north gates, cavalry were stationed to force any Wesmen advance around the castle back towards the beach. Inside the walls, the townsmen waited. On the walls, archers, swordsmen and mages. And in the keep itself, a simple circular building with battlements built out in a square around its top some fifty feet above the outer walls, the Barons, healers, bodyguards, cooks and many of Gresse's mercenaries.

The battlements, nicknamed 'the Crown' because of the way they sat slightly uncomfortably atop the keep, bristled with heavy crossbow positions, oil dumps and Blackthorne's best mages. They had food for three months, and Blackthorne reckoned that if it wasn't over by then, Darrick would have lost Understone, Balaia would be open to pillage and the war lost. All they could do now was wait.

The Wesmen didn't keep them long.

Styliann, mind still clouded with rage and an unquenchable desire for revenge, clattered to a stop at the eastern end of Understone Pass at the head of a column of one hundred Protectors. It was early afternoon. The guards at the pass looked at him fearfully but knew what they had to do. They stood in his path.

'Please state your business,' said one with deferential politeness.

'The slaughter of Wesmen,' said Styliann, his voice matter-of-fact, his face brooking no argument.

'I have orders to hold unauthorised traffic here awaiting clearance from General Darrick.' There was apology in his tone.

'Do you know who I am?' demanded Styliann.

'Yes, my Lord.'

'Then you will also know that it was I who set the orders for your commander to follow. I give myself the clearance to travel the pass. Stand aside.'

The guard looked at him, doubt and anxiety in his mind.

Styliann raised an eyebrow. 'Where is Darrick?' he asked.

'At the far end, my Lord, overseeing construction of the fortifications.'

'Then you have discharged your duties admirably,' said Styliann. 'He can personally clear me to travel when I meet him.'

The guard smiled, comfortable with Styliann's logic. He stood aside. 'Good luck, my Lord.'

Styliann stared down at him. 'Luck is something on which I never rely.' He rode into the pass, his Protectors behind him, silent, masked and disturbing.

Styliann's passage through the pass was swift, his horses bred for stamina. He barely noticed the devastation Xetesk's new spell had caused and certainly had no mind to admire its success. He rode on, reaching the end of the pass as dusk gathered, pulling up to a stop when he saw Darrick.

The two men gazed at each other for a time, Darrick reading his face, Styliann burning with the desire to be at the throats of the men who had raped and murdered Selyn. Darrick said nothing, simply nodding, stepping from his path and waving him through. Styliann and the Protectors galloped into Wesmen lands. For them there would be no halt for a night's rest. Styliann had places he needed to reach and something to prove to an arrogant barbarian.

Hirad awoke glad of the leather-clad bivouac shelters Thraun had insisted they raise over themselves the night before. At the time, it had seemed a pointless exercise in irritation, but now, with the rain thrumming on the material above his head, Hirad smiled.

He sat up, scratching his head. He could smell a fire and, looking out, saw Will crouched over his stove, leather over his shoulders and a wide-brimmed hat pulled forward over his face. Water steamed away on an open pot.

Beside Hirad, Ilkar stirred and awoke, opening one eye on the weather.

'Wake me when it's dry,' he said, and turned over.

'I'd hate to be in Understone with this coming down,' said Hirad. Ilkar grunted.

The camp came slowly to life. Set in an area of lightly wooded land on the downhill side of a lively stream, the four shelters sat in a rough semicircle. Will's wood-burner was at its centre. They were a long way from Understone Pass and the relative security of Darrick's cavalry, and Hirad felt strangely ill at ease.

Surrounded by his closest friends and people he trusted with his life, he couldn't shake the fear of the new from his bones. He had rarely been in the lands west of Understone Pass before, and with only a small inkling of where they were headed, drawn from maps and stories, he was nervous.

They all took breakfast hunched under their shelters, the rain showing no signs of easing as it shouldered its way through leaf and branch to patter and drum on earth and leather. Across the stream, and on the other side of the gentle slope on which they sat, the land quickly turned harder as it tracked northwards, becoming steep climbs, cold peaks and barren plateaux. Their destination lay across easier travel to the south-west.

'How far to the Wrethsires from here?' Hirad asked.

Thraun sat with Will at the far end of the half-circle; next to them were Erienne and Denser, his arm about her shoulders, with The Unknown and Jandyr next to Hirad.

'A day, no more,' replied Thraun through a mouthful of bread. 'That assumes we can steer clear of Wesmen.'

'We're heading away from their major concentrations, and with so many on the move, if we keep off the path we should be safe enough,' said The Unknown. 'Anyway, I've heard you're not bad at keeping hidden.' He smiled.

'Not bad.'

'It's a shock, isn't it, discovering you're something you don't want to be.' The Unknown's voice carried a sorrow so deep that Hirad almost spilled his coffee.

Thraun and the big man locked eyes, every other member of The Raven waiting for the reaction.

But Thraun merely nodded. 'Only someone like you can possibly understand the pain and the fear. I would give anything not to be as I am.'

'But in the crypts, you seemed—' said Erienne.

'Only when there is no other way. And then in terror for everything I know and love.' He got up. 'I'll saddle the horses.' The Unknown followed him from the camp, leaving the rest to a confused silence.

'It's not a blessing,' said Will eventually, killing the flame in the stove and unhooking the pieces to cool them on the wet earth. 'He is terrified that one day he will lose himself in the mind of the wolf and never be able to change back.'

The Raven moved off twenty minutes later, with the rain pounding on leathers and the stream behind them thrashing as it filled. Thraun chose the trail but kept his thoughts to himself.

Hirad and Ilkar dropped back to flank The Unknown, who rode directly behind Denser and Erienne.

'Why did Thraun think you could understand him?' asked Hirad.

'Subtlety never was a strong point of yours, was it, Hirad?' Ilkar sniffed.

The Unknown shook his head. 'At least he never changes,' he said. 'Look, Hirad, it's complex and not very pleasant. Not to me, anyway.' He looked to Denser, but the Dark Mage was at least giving the impression of not listening. 'We were both brought up knowing we were different. You'll have to ask Thraun how he came to know, but the point is, we were both something we didn't want to be yet something we could never escape. Mind you, I believed I could.' The Unknown bit his lip.

'Don't feel you—' began Ilkar.

'No. I might as well. At least this way it's just you two, and Denser already knows. There's nothing random about being chosen as a Protector. I'm a Xeteskian. We – they are bred for strength, stamina and speed from carefully chosen lineage. I was weapons-trained early, and at thirteen discovered my destiny. It's not something you are supposed to find out, for obvious reasons. I thought I was just being schooled for the College Guard.' He shrugged. 'I didn't like the idea that my soul was already sold to the Mount of Xetesk so I ran away. Apparently it happens all the time when people find out, and they let you go. I mean, why not? When you can't escape them even when you die.'

'So you've always known?' Hirad felt at once swept empty with sorrow and distrusted. Here was the secret he'd kept for ten years. 'Is this all linked to your name?'

'Yes. Pathetic, really. I couldn't deny my calling but I refused to admit it to myself. I tried false names but they never fitted, so I ended up just never telling anyone anything. When Ilkar came up with The Unknown Warrior, that did fit. A name that was no name, if you like. I felt at home.' Another biting of the lip. His eyes glistened and his voice was gruff. 'And then, of course, with The Raven, I thought I'd never die. But that's no escape either.' He set his jaw and looked forwards.

'Sorry, I've lost you,' said Ilkar.

'Me too,' said Hirad. 'I mean, if you were so anxious not to die, why did you take on all those dogs by yourself?'

'Because when I realised they'd come for me anyway, I thought at least I could die saving you. All of you. And perhaps that I'd get away, dying so far from Xetesk in a place where the mana was unstable. I thought they wouldn't find me.'

'Hang on, can we backtrack a little? What do you mean, they'd come for you anyway?' Ilkar hoped he wasn't beginning to understand. But The Unknown just shook his head again and bored his eyes into Denser's back.

Denser turned his horse and fell in beside Ilkar. 'He means that the demons would have taken his soul from him eventually, dead or alive. He means he knew his time was running out. After all, what good is a forty-year-old Protector?' Denser's words were hard but his tone was thick with disgust. 'That is why he chose to die, because it was his only chance of saving himself as well as us. But they found him. They stole his death.' He urged his horse to join Erienne once more. 'And now you know it all, and why poor Laryon and I wanted to free them. Too many of them were never dead in the first place.'

Hirad formed words but no sound came for a time. He stared first at Denser and then at The Unknown, stunned by what his friend had been carrying all those years. The lies he had told to hide himself not only from them but from himself too. He had never had any future, or choice, and yet he had never once given them the slightest hint of his true self. What he was meant to be, and what he was for a short time.

The Unknown turned to Hirad, as if sensing the barbarian's train of thought. 'I wanted what we had to be true so badly that most of the time I believed it myself. The retirement, The Rookery, all of it.'

'And now you can!' Hirad felt a sudden, irrational surge of joy. 'When this is over, you can! '

But The Unknown silenced him. 'I should never have been released. Too much is lost.' He stifled a sob. Denser looked back over his shoulder, a look of horror on his face. The Unknown nodded. 'Just like you, Denser, just like you.'

'What are you talking about?' Ilkar was suddenly frantic.

'The souls of the Protectors meld in the Mount. We are as one. When mine was taken back, part of me, that part that the brotherhood of the Protectors gave me, was lost for ever. I live, I breathe, I laugh, I cry, but inside I am empty. The Gods save any of you from knowing how that feels.'

The Wesmen army, angry, depleted and determined to exact revenge, marched on Blackthorne the following morning. They arrived just as the rain ceased its intermittent sprinkling, and stood well out of spell range.

Blackthorne watched from the Crown, gazing out over his town, its walls and on to the Wesmen-covered grasslands beyond. Gresse, once again by his side, flexed his fingers nervously, seeing the force assemble its ranks and lines. For more than three hours, they poured into the open space, striding to the beat of drums, their standards snapping in the fresh breeze, carts rattling behind, the shouts of leaders mixing with the howls and barks of dogs.

Thousands and thousands of Wesmen carpeted the ground, a sea of fur-clad hate and power ready to wash against the walls of Blackthorne. The Baron shook his head, barely believing so many had survived the carnage on the water. But still they came, the standards now numbering over a hundred, all stabbed into the earth on a rise less than a mile away. Ignoring the temptation to encircle the town, the Wesmen massed before the south gates, their numbers sending ripple after ripple of anxiety through the thin line of defenders.

From the centre of the army that Blackthorne estimated to number seven thousand or more, six Shamen walked calmly forwards, flanked by a dozen warriors, furs ruffling in the wind, hard faces taking in the walls, blades sharp and heavy. Immediately, mages on the outer walls began preparing. IceWind, DeathHail, ShieldSheer. The Shamen moved on, and at two hundred yards, Gresse thought they might want to talk. At one hundred and fifty yards, Blackthorne issued fire orders.

Spells crackled across the Shamen's shield, lights flaring over its surface, the DeathHail bouncing and shattering as it met the greater magical force which glowed white in resistance. A storm of arrows arced across the gap, those on target bouncing away as the hard shield held. Still the Shamen walked on. At fifty yards, they stopped to cast.

'You need men inside that shield,' said Gresse. But Blackthorne was ahead of him, the flagmen already giving the orders. There was a flurry of movement by the south gates, a clash of steel and the protestation of wood as the gates began their ponderous opening.

Still the arrows and spells failed to penetrate the Shamen's shield, maintained by two with the remaining four chanting and moving. From the barely open gate, Blackthorne's men squeezed, running full tilt at the casting Shamen. They were too late.

Standing shoulder to shoulder, the Shamen raised their arms above their heads, hands splayed. White fire crackled between their fingers, the strands combining above their heads into four twitching beams which searched for purchase in the air like darting snakes' tongues. The beams combined to form one pole of shimmering white light which sprang at the town walls, forking like lightning and flickering over them, knocking away dust, mould and lichen. For a moment, there was no discernible effect, then the light could be seen inside the walls, a map of pulsating, flaring veins. The Shamen cut off the beam and threw themselves to the earth, ignoring the swordsmen scant paces away. A two-hundred-foot section of the wall exploded outwards, sending stone fragments fizzing through the air at enormous speed. Blackthorne's men never stood a chance, taking the full weight of the explosion.

The Baron's plans dissolved as the wall came down, spilling archers and mages and causing pandemonium along the wall. More arrows flew, this time piercing the bodies of the unprotected Shamen, but the damage was done. Seven thousand Wesmen roared their way towards a breach Blackthorne's men could not hope to fill.

'Dear Gods,' said Blackthorne. He turned to Gresse, his face white. 'We'll have to take them hand to hand through the streets. I—'

A flash lit up the sky. FlameOrbs soared away to the closing Wesmen ranks, exploding on impact, deluging men with mana fire. The screams of the unshielded victims rose above the war cries of the survivors.

White fire flared again as the Wesmen approached the breach. The southern gate house collapsed. Spells flickered across the sky, HardRain poured on to the Wesmen in the centre of the charge, IceWind tore through a flank, a quintet of Shamen were destroyed by the columns of a HellFire, but the Wesmen charge was undaunted.

From the base of the castle, soldiers and mercenaries ran to positions around the town, originally fallbacks, now desperate defence.

'Saddle every horse in the compound,' Blackthorne ordered an aide. 'When the time comes, we'll have to take to guerrilla moves in the foothills and plains trails. We can't let them unleash this at Understone.'

The Wesmen reached the devastated gate and walls of Blackthorne and poured through the gaps into the town, sweeping aside the pitifully thin defence. From the standing walls, mages and archers rained fire, ice and steel on the invaders, but by now the Shamen had grouped for defence, and too often the rain bounced off shields, the arrows were knocked aside. And for every Wesman who died, a dozen more took his place. They surged through the town, firing buildings as they passed and cutting down the defenders who fought them at every street corner.

The wall defenders followed the Wesmen's progress through the flaming town, attacking where they could but too often under attack themselves as the Shamen, unhurried groups of arrogant swagger, launched fine meshes of white fire or great rods of hard flame that fell like wet rope on the ramparts. Blackthorne Town was burning down.

'We've lost this one!' shouted Gresse above the roar of the Wesmen, the fires, the calls of the wounded and the crackle of the Shamen's magic.

The stern Baron nodded, jaw set, eyes rimmed with tears. Less than ten minutes had passed since the Shamen had brought the walls down. He signalled the emergency order. Flagmen and trumpeters announced the loss of Blackthorne, and its defenders and people took to the foothills of the Blackthorne Mountains.

From there, they could track the Wesmen north to Understone Pass, harrying them all the way. But unless the Wytch Lords' magic was taken from the Shamen, Blackthorne feared nothing could stop the rout of eastern Balaia.

And if they were to lose it, he hoped that at least he and Gresse could watch the Wesmen tear Pontois and the rest of the KTA limb from limb. It would be scant satisfaction, but right now it was all that kept him breathing. Everything he had was gone.

Chapter 29

The Arch Temple of the Wrethsires was set in a lush glade fed by hill streams. To the east, a lake sat at the base of the Garan foothills, providing peace. The solitude was completed by steep cliffs climbing two sides, sheer and menacing.

The Temple itself was a low dome, ringed with forty spires and having a diameter of perhaps two hundred feet. A single needle spire rose from the centre of the planked and slated wooden roof, and the walls, marble and stone, shone in the post-rain sunshine.

The Wrethsires were as disparate as the four Colleges were intensely familial. Small temples were scattered all over Balaia, but were sparse in number in the west when compared to the east. The order believed in a death force magic that had nothing to do with mana energy and so drew the unswerving scorn of every mage.

They did harness something, that much was admitted, but whatever it was had proved unstable to control – far more so than mana – and the reports of accident and disaster were well documented throughout the two hundred years or so that the order had been established.

The Raven had arrived late the previous evening after a sodden but otherwise uneventful journey through forested hillsides, steep valleys and swollen streams. Had it been dry, the landscape would have been beautiful.

It had been dawn before the rain stopped, and the silence it brought was blessed relief from the incessant patter and drum. Full dawn was a brilliant sun from a cloudless sky, and quickly the land began to dry, steam rising from leaf, grass and shrub.

Thraun had brought them to a stop in a dense area of woodland three miles from the Temple. Approaching unseen would be close to impossible during the daylight, but Denser had agreed to undertake a CloakedWalk around the dome later that morning. For now, though, the talk was of the Wrethsires themselves.

'They are actually very quiet as an organisation,' said Erienne.

'With plenty to be quiet about,' said Denser.

'But they've got something, isn't that right?' asked Jandyr.

'You could say, I suppose.' Denser shrugged.

'Come on, Denser,' snapped Thraun. 'We've all got to go in there.'

Denser bridled. 'They are a quasi-religious, quasi-magical – though I use the term very loosely – organisation. They pray to some idea of an earth death force, pretend they can harness it and claim some sort of brotherhood with the four Colleges because of it. They are frauds, their magic is flawed and their contention to be the fifth College is nothing short of repellent. Anything else?' Denser fetched his pipe from his cloak, filled the bowl from a bulging tobacco pouch courtesy of Lystern, and lit it from a flame on his thumb.

Hirad flicked absently at a piece of leaf mould, his eyes spearing the Dark Mage.

'In case it had slipped your mind, Denser, incomplete information has already claimed the life of my closest friend. And look at you. In fact look at all three of you mages, choking on the contempt you hold for these Wrethsires.' There was an uncomfortable shifting around the campsite. 'Now I don't know whether this contempt is fair and I don't, frankly, give a damn. What I and my friends without their noses stuck in the air want to know is exactly what we might face in there. What spells do they have, are they weapons users, how many are there, you know. If you can't tell me because you don't know, fine. But don't keep me in the dark because you don't think it's important. Got it?' He shook his head at them. 'Bloody mages on bloody pedestals.'

Denser contemplated Hirad's words, raising his eyebrows at Ilkar who, unaccountably, was trying to suppress a smile.

'I'm sorry, Hirad,' said Denser at length. 'You're right. But they aren't magical and you can't call their castings spells.'

'I don't care what you call them. Tell me what they do before I start getting irritated.'

'Start?' Ilkar's smile surfaced.

'Right.' Denser clapped his hands on his thighs. 'What we know about the Wrethsires' castings is patchy. We know that they are based in prayer utterances and that all their work is done in groups – the more Sires, the stronger the result. Their power, such as it is, is based on violent elemental forces like wind, rain, fire and so on and the death force they are supposed to produce.

'The thing to watch out for is that they don't control it well. It makes all their castings unstable and so unpredictable both to them and, in this case, to us.'

'In what way?' asked Jandyr.

Denser shrugged. 'Duration, power, direction, random result, backfire. You name it. Another belief is that when they die, their death force strengthens the Temple whole and that much of their combined power comes from this death element. It gives them a rather misplaced confidence.'

'And you're saying they don't harness this force?' said Will. Denser nodded. 'Are you sure?' he asked.

'Pretty sure.' The Dark Mage's smile at Ilkar was somewhat embarrassed. Ilkar pursed his lips but said nothing.

'Are they aggressive?' Hirad looked back from Ilkar to Denser.

'No,' he replied. 'Not like Wesmen, although for whatever reason, the Wesmen leave them completely alone. Or so we understand.' He looked round The Raven. 'Anything else?'

'How many of them are there?' Thraun took him up.

'I haven't the faintest idea.'

'I mean in the Arch Temple. Are we talking thirty, three hundred, what?'

'I haven't the faintest idea.'

'Great,' said The Unknown and Hirad together.

'The temple will take several hundred but it was built for worship, don't forget. The Gods only know how many Sires they have down there, or blades for that matter. Hopefully I'll have some idea later.'

But he found nothing. Travelling to the edge of the woodland by the Temple with Thraun to avoid being seen, Denser cast his CloakedWalk and strolled up to the pillared entrance. It was shut and he couldn't risk trying the grand polished brass rings that hung on the oak-striped doors. He moved in a clockwise direction around the Temple, taking in the ornate mosaics and carvings that decorated the walls. Great vistas of mountain and forest, sea and cliff and plain and desert mixed with representations of fire, wind through the sky and one particularly grim mosaic depicting a walk of the dead.

Not a sound came from inside. Vents were shuttered, side and rear doors were closed and the spires, beautifully worked cones of black marble standing twice his height, gave no clue to the whereabouts of the Wrethsires. He returned to Thraun and they made their way back to the campsite.

'Should we be surprised, or not?' asked Will, his eyes bright under his now completely grey hair.

'To be honest, I don't see why,' said Denser. 'Like I said, it's a place of worship. Very few, if any, will actually live there. And it's still only mid-morning. But I don't know . . .'

'What's the problem?' Hirad pulled himself to his feet and stretched. 'Sounds to me as though we could get in and out right now and save ourselves a lot of trouble.'

'The thought had crossed my mind too,' agreed Denser. 'But I can't help thinking that if it was my temple, I'd have it guarded. Particularly with what's going on around here right now.'

'I don't get where you're going with this,' said Hirad. 'If they've screwed up leaving the place unguarded, that's to our advantage.'

'I don't know,' said Denser. 'It just didn't feel right.'

'Sixth sense?' Erienne ran a hand through Denser's hair.

He nodded. 'Something like that. I just think we should be careful.'

'We were always going to be that,' said Ilkar.

'So do we move now or stick by the original plan?' Jandyr looked to Hirad but it was The Unknown who spoke.

'In daylight, we risk Wrethsires coming to the Temple; in the dead of night, we don't. I can see no reason to rush in, we're not in any danger here. Hirad?'

Hirad looked into the chasm's of The Unknown's eyes and wondered if they would ever be full again. But though his soul was empty, his mind was sharp, and his voice carried all of its old authority. While he had been gone, Hirad had missed that.

'I agree. Why rush? Let's rest up, make sure we've got our tactics straight and keep to our timetable. I don't think we're going to have too much spare time after this.' He smiled ruefully. 'Darrick is good but there are a lot of Wesmen in his way.'

Baron Blackthorne stood at the entrance to his most profitable mine, half a mile above his blazing town, and looked down on his fallen world. As night fell, the fires died down but the Wesmen encampments burned bright with lights and the noise of celebration.

He and Gresse had a handful fewer than two thousand men at their disposal. Most of them had horses, taken either from the courtyard or the many tithe farms over which he was Lord. Again, the Wesmen hadn't given chase when he had retreated, demonstrating an awful confidence in their ability to secure victory at their leisure. It was a confidence Blackthorne found it hard not to share.

The death toll in the town had been high and the Baron had decided to send his untrained reservists, those that still lived, to safer areas where they could bolster the standing defences of key population centres: Korina, Gyernath, the College cities, even Baron Corin's lands to the far northeast. Even the farms lay idle, their tenants packed on to wagons and ordered east to wherever would have them.

Blackthorne tapped his fist again and again on the rock by his head, his anger undimmed, his humiliation complete. But beneath it was a wash of pride. As he'd ordered the retreat, the horns, backed by flags, blaring out their message, he'd seen his men in the town redouble their efforts to keep the Wesmen back. Closing ranks, they'd grouped in a tight formation in the market crescent, drawing the Wesmen on and providing stout final resistance. Without their selfless action, Blackthorne wondered whether he would be standing where he was now or lying dead in his own blood.

He stared down at the lights blazing in the castle. Someone else would be sleeping in his bed tonight. An enemy. He seethed. Gresse came to his shoulder.

'There was nothing you could do,' he said. 'At least this way we live to fight on.'

'But for how long?' Blackthorne's voice was bitter. 'We've got no defence against the Shamen magic.'

'But at least we survived to warn Darrick and the Colleges. If mages can effectively shield walls, we can still win.'

'But we leave our men open to magical attack,' said Blackthorne. 'We have no idea how many Shamen there are, and without the scale of magical offence we had been counting on, our soldiers can't fight the odds. There are too many Wesmen. You heard the reports. Eighty-five thousand. Altogether, the east has barely half that number in soldiers worth the name. And the Wesmen are already on their way to Understone and, I expect, Gyernath. We had to hold them for three days to give The Raven a fair chance and we managed ten minutes.

'If Understone Pass goes the same way, The Raven will have nothing to return to. It'll already be too late.'

Gresse put a hand on Blackthorne's shoulder. It was the Baron's darkest hour and his assessment of their situation felt uncomfortably accurate. He had lost his home and his people were spreading over the country. Many would never return and he had not, could not, put up any fight. There was no real consolation, but Gresse tried anyway.

'Even if the Wesmen are drinking wine from the KTA vaults in Korina, if the Wytch Lord magic is taken from them, we can rout them.'

Blackthorne turned to him, shaking his head. 'Gresse, if the Wesmen take Korina there will be no one left to rout them. Gods, if they sack the College Cities we may as well sail south and leave them to it.'

Gresse let his head drop. Blackthorne was right. And if the Wesmen strength at Triverne Inlet was as strong as the one camped in and around Blackthorne, they would be at the gates of Julatsa in four days.

The afternoon and evening passed without incident for The Raven. Thraun and The Unknown spent much of the time watching the Temple and its approach. They saw no one, adding to Denser's unease.

Before moving on to the Temple, The Raven ate in the fading light. The mood was sombre.

'If our failure becomes inevitable, we must ensure that Dawnthief is destroyed before the Wytch Lords get it,' said Denser.

'How?' asked Will.

'Just melt the catalysts, or one of them,' said Denser. 'It's simple.'

'So we could take this spell out of the game right now,' said Will.

'If we wanted to throw away our only chance of beating the Wytch Lords, yes.' Denser shrugged. 'But there's one thing I must make clear. If I am killed and it becomes obvious that none of us is going to live to return the catalysts to Xetesk, one or all of them must be destroyed. Because if the Wytch Lords get hold of it, there is no chance. Not even for the Wesmen.'

The Raven exchanged looks around the stove. Hirad helped himself to some more coffee from the iron pot on its hot plate.

'All right then,' said Jandyr. 'Say we do what we have to do and the Wytch Lords are gone, what then?'

'It won't stop the Wesmen, that's certain, although it will remove their total arrogance and belief in victory,' replied Denser. 'You have to understand that it now seems the Wesmen have been preparing for this for perhaps ten years. They are united, they are strong and they are determined. But what's more important is that they know the east is fragmented. They'll believe they can still take Balaia with or without the Wytch Lords. And if they retake the pass before our armies are ready, they might just do it.'

'Aren't you being a little overdramatic, Denser?' Hirad was smiling. 'Surely your mages can hold the pass indefinitely with that water spell of yours.' Ilkar tutted. Denser shook his head and smiled at Erienne. 'You know something, I really hate it when you mages get smug.'

'Sorry, Hirad, you're not to know,' said Denser. 'But to us, that statement is like us wondering why you can't fight so well with one arm or something.'

'So tell me,' said Hirad.

'You saw the spell and you saw the condition of the mages who walked away. Two didn't.' Denser sucked his lip. 'What you don't know is what went on before, or the long-term aftermath. Those mages spent two weeks in preparation, testing and resting. They were secluded from the rest of the College to maximise their concentration level. Now they've cast, they'll be unable to perform any spell for the best part of three days, and as for the DimensionConnect, not for another two weeks. And that assumes that the dimension with which we want to connect is in alignment with ours.'

'But the Wesmen don't know that,' said Hirad, worried more than he hoped he was showing that this spell was not available every couple of days at the least.

'There will be enough Shamen able to make educated guesses about the spell once they've heard information about it,' said Erienne.

'And consider this,' said Ilkar. 'There's probably only one spell written that is more powerful, and I don't need to tell you its name. Any Shaman worth a damn will know we've originated a dimension spell and used it. That'll tell them all they need about the likely effort required to cast it.'

The night was warm but Hirad felt a chill on his body. The powers they were dealing with, the power they'd already seen and the power they wanted to unleash. He couldn't help but feel it was all spiralling out of control. And if they took the Death's Eye Stone from the Wrethsires, it would make Denser the most powerful man in Balaia.

'Something else has been bothering me.' They all looked at Will. 'Do you think the Wytch Lords know we're here, this side of the pass?'

'The Raven?'

'Yes.'

'No.' The Unknown was certain. 'All they can possibly know now is that the pass has fallen – spectacularly – and they'll be doing their level best to retake it. They – or rather, their agents – know there's a search for Dawnthief because of our appearance at Septern's house but they won't have enough information to target us or our position. Not yet at any rate.'

'To stop any confusion,' said Denser, 'remember the Wytch Lords have not regained corporeal form yet and their power is still limited.

When they are walking, that's when we have to worry, though we don't know when that will be.'

'How many Wytch Lords are there?' asked Will.

'Six,' said Ilkar. 'Embarrassingly enough, I don't know all of their names, although I should. Denser?'

'Seriously?'

'It was never high on my learning list, no.'

'Gods, it was a mantra to us. Pamun, Arumun, Belphamun, Weyamun, Ystormun, Giriamun.'

'Very impressive.' Ilkar smiled.

'Not really,' said Denser. 'Names to terrorise errant mages, generally. It's a shame they are no longer an idle threat, isn't it?'

The conversation broke up. The beasts had been named and each member of The Raven, perhaps for the first time, took on the enormity of what they were trying to achieve. And its potential futility. For while they were guaranteed defeat if they lost Dawnthief to the Wytch Lords, they weren't guaranteed victory if they destroyed them.

Denser lit his pipe, his thoughts drifting inevitably towards his Familiar. He forced himself to push them aside, concentrating instead on images of the single great tomb that dominated Parve and the Torn Wastes. A grand stairway led up to the heart of the pyramid. Ornate mosaics and decorations adorned the walls and floor of a great domed hall at the end of which a single door stood at the entrance to the crypt. Inside, the Keepers tended the six stone sarcophagi, preparing the way for the return of the Ancients. Waiting for the movement within that signalled the reincarnation of essence that would stir the Wytch Lords' bones and bring the regeneration of the flesh. He shuddered and prayed they would be in time.

With full night holding sway, The Raven moved on to the trail leading directly to the Arch Temple of the Wrethsires. Thraun was convinced that no one would pass them in either direction, and Denser. beginning to believe the Temple would be empty, wondered why the thought worried him so profoundly.

They were at the Temple in an hour, its squat dark shape looming into view against the flat black of the cliffs behind as the path opened out beyond the edge of the tree line. The silence was complete but for the lake on their left, whose soft ripples brought an aura of calm to the scene that was not reflected in the minds of The Raven.

They fanned out and walked slowly towards the huge iron-banded oak doors. The Unknown stood at the centre of the chevron, Hirad and Jandyr to his right, Thraun and Will to his left.

Behind them walked the three mages, Ilkar with the command word for a spell shield on his lips, Erienne preparing light and Denser something altogether more destructive.

At the doors, Jandyr moved up and placed an ear to the wood. 'I can't hear anything, but these are very solid. Put it this way, there aren't three hundred screaming worshippers in there.'

'Only one way to find out for sure,' said Hirad.

He trotted up the half-dozen worn stone steps, grasped the handles, turned them and pushed. The stench of death swept out as the doors swung back, hinges protesting. Hirad stepped back a couple of paces, his face turned away.

'Gods, that's bad. We need to give it time to clear a little.'

Hastily drawn swords were resheathed and mana shapes were dismissed. No one was going to attack from within.

The Temple was pitch dark inside. While the rest sat on the steps facing away up the path, Ilkar stood to the right-hand side of the doors, looking in at the carnage but turning his head to draw breath. He told what he saw.

The immediate impressions were of bodies and blood covering the black, white and green tiled marble floor. Looking closer, the elf tried to map out the likely course of the fight that had taken place. Right inside the doors, three armed and armoured men in green cloaks lay in a tangle surrounded by four of what had to be the aggressors. They weren't Wesmen, mercenaries perhaps, but their dark leather and look meant they couldn't have been Temple guards.

But what lay further within presented a confusing picture. At the far end of the Temple were sprawled the bodies of at least half a dozen Wrethsires, identified by their deep green cowls, their blood mingling in puddles that collected in dips on the tiled floor. And scattered about the Temple were perhaps twenty more of them, weaponless, defenceless, slaughtered.

Ilkar's eyes, though, rested longest on the scene right in the centre of the Temple. On a five-foot-high plinth, and set in a metal and glass case, sat the Death's Eye Stone – a black orb shot with striations of carmine red and emerald green that swirled around a disc of piercing blue.

Surrounding the stone were half a dozen bodies, though it was difficult to be exact, such was the state of them. Bent, broken, torn and scattered, the swordsmen had been hacked to pieces, in some cases literally. Blood smeared every surface, hugged every crack and spattered every panel of floor and plinth. But it wasn't the dismembered bodies that worried Ilkar; it was that he couldn't fathom who it was that had done it.

So many factors didn't add up. The bodies around the stone were not Wrethsires or guards, their clothing told him that, yet they appeared to have been defending the area around the plinth. And whoever it was that had massacred them so comprehensively hadn't stopped to take the stone. Not only that, they hadn't lost a single one of their number and had then left without leaving a trace of themselves. It just didn't make sense.

He took a deep breath, held it and moved a couple of paces inside.

'Careful, Ilkar,' said Hirad.

Ilkar turned, exhaling. 'Hirad, they're all dead.'

'How long?'

Ilkar knelt and put his fingers to a puddle of blood. It was dry. Not a trace of stickiness.

'It's impossible to say. It must have been an oven in there today, it's still hot now. They smell four days dead but it could be less than a day.'

'Let's get moving. Is it breathable?' Hirad ambled up the steps to join his friend.

'Just about.'

'Right,' said Hirad. 'Let's get inside, secure the place and start clearing bodies away from the stone. Nobody touch that case just yet.'

Erienne set a standing LightGlobe above the Death's Eye Stone while Thraun took a taper to the braziers set around the walls, at about head height. Will and Jandyr hauled bodies from around the plinth, leaving them against the walls, and The Unknown stood guard at the main doors, scanning the tree line for something he knew could not be there but that gnawed at his insides just the same. Ilkar checked the curtained-off rooms at the rear of the Temple.

Hirad joined Denser, who was studying a series of statues let into alcoves around the walls.

'Interesting, don't you think?' said Denser. Hirad turned a slow circle, taking them in. There were eight of them, floor-standing. Cloaked in green, each statue wore a rich coloured tabard over ceremonial plate and chain armour. Painted masks covered the faces and each carried a double-bladed axe in the crook of its arms. They stood more than eight feet high.

'Completely out of place, aren't they?' asked Hirad.

'Not at all.' Erienne came to his shoulder. 'They have a well-documented warrior past. And those masks represented maps of life or death energy, which is where they believe they draw their magic from.'

Denser looked at her askance. 'Something of an expert are you?'

'No, but it pays to have a little knowledge of your contemporaries,' said Erienne shortly.

Ilkar walked back into the main body of the Temple.

'Any idea what happened here?' asked Hirad.

Ilkar shook his head. 'There are a couple more bodies of guards back there but nothing's been touched. What I don't get is that those dead around the stone had to be mercenaries, and I'm certain they wouldn't be hired by the Wrethsires.'

'So you're saying they weren't defending the stone?' asked Denser.

'Well, no, I mean, it's still here, isn't it?

'Does it matter?' asked Will. 'Let's just grab it and go.' He was standing right over the case.

'Don't touch it!' snapped Denser. 'Sorry, Will. We haven't checked it for traps or wards yet.'

'I thought you said they had nothing to do with mana,' said Will.

'They don't. But you can hire it in if you want to.' Denser took in Erienne and Ilkar with a glance. 'Shall we?'

The mages tuned to the mana spectrum and examined the plinth and its case. It was a brief investigation.

'It's clean of mana traps,' said Erienne.

'And what about the Wrethsires' own magic?' asked The Unknown, taking a pace back into the Temple.

Denser huffed. 'They have no static magic capability.'

'You're sure?' said Hirad.

'There's nothing over the stone,' said Denser deliberately.

'Nothing we can detect, anyway,' said Ilkar.

'All right,' said Hirad. 'Are we secure?'

The Unknown nodded, turning back to the path outside. Will hunched low over the case, examining its edges and panels, barely even letting his breath fall on it. The rest of The Raven stood in loose formation, watching, Thraun smiling to see Will's hands so steady.

'It's sealed, not trapped as far as I can see. Access is through the top, or do you want me to smash it?'

'No,' said Denser. 'We can't risk damaging it in any way. Take your time and lift the lid. If even a shard of glass were to scratch its surface, it would affect Dawnthief.'

Will inclined his head and fished out his tools. He sorted through the intricate pieces and selected a flat-headed wedge of metal, which he inserted gently into the seal of the case lid.

There was a whispering in the Temple. A breeze blew from nowhere, taking the doors and slamming them, the sound reverberating through the building. The Unknown was caught a glancing blow. He staggered but kept his feet. The braziers blew out, leaving only Erienne's globe to light them. Shadows fled up the walls, cutting across the masks of the statues and accentuating their height. They loomed into the Temple, threatening. Beyond the limit of the globe, the darkness closed in and the light seemed weak against it, like a child pushing on a heavy door, never quite able to force it right open.

The whispering gained in intensity, multiple voices swirling in the air, unintelligible, malevolent. The Raven grouped, swords clear of scabbards, the whispers becoming a noise like rushing wind, though the air was still, warm and cloying, the smell of the dead rising to assault the nostrils.

'Ideas, anyone?' asked Hirad. The Unknown pulled at the handles to the main doors. They were stuck fast. 'Try the others. Try the shutters. Thraun, take the opposite route.' Hirad was forced to raise his voice over the clash of hundreds of voices from nowhere threatening to drown him out.

He checked either side of him. The mages were unfocused, preparing spells, but the deep frowns suggested they were struggling. Jandyr, scared and wide-eyed, looked everywhere. Will worked furiously at the stone's case. Hirad was dimly aware of the hammering of Thraun and The Unknown on shutters and doors, the dull thuds merely background to the increasing intensity of the whispering voices.

Erienne had her hands to her head, no longer able to concentrate. Ilkar lost his mana shape too, feeling his grip on the fuel of magic loosen. He glanced at The Raven to see them standing in a rough circle about Will and the plinth. His body went cold.

Abruptly, the whispering ceased. The light from Erienne's globe flickered and died. Darkness was total. There was a tinkle as Will dropped his prising tool. Panic.

Erienne stumbled into Denser, sending both sprawling. From the blackness, The Unknown cursed as his head connected with a wall. Will, swords drawn, pushed his way past Hirad into space, breath rushing in and out of his lungs in huge whoops. He stepped on a body and fell, crying out. Hirad, heart beating hard against his ribs, tried to find the remotest chink of light. There was none.

'Ilkar, Jandyr, Thraun, tell us what you see. Erienne, more light. Denser, what's happening?'

The sound of metal scraping on stone rang around the Temple.

'Anybody?' Hirad asked of the dark. To his right, he felt Denser lifting Erienne. 'We need that light. What was that noise?' He swayed, balance diminished by the totality of the blackness, boot smearing through the dried surface of a pool of blood. The temperature was rising, the stench of death closing in, stinging the eyes. 'Can't someone light a taper, for God's sake?'

'Yes, yes.' Will's tone was edged with desperation. His swords rang back into scabbards; he scrabbled to find light. The scraping sounded again, this time accompanied by a series of heavy thuds that rippled though the floor.

'Oh, no.' Ilkar's voice, laden with dread, cut through the tension.

'What? What?' Hirad was shouting. There was a clang. Then more. Another scraping and metal-shod footsteps.

'The statues are moving. This way,' said Ilkar. 'We've got to form up. Fast. Unknown, Thraun, to the centre.'

'Where the hell's that?' snapped the big man.

Ilkar could see him stumbling in vaguely the right direction. 'Keep coming dead ahead. Thraun, give him a hand.' He watched Thraun guide the big man quickly past the scattered bodies of the Wrethsire guards.

Hirad looked right, seeing nothing but sensing Erienne near. 'Erienne, where's that light?'

'I can't get the mana shape.' Her voice shook.

'Calm.' Denser's voice held steady. 'It's all right.'

'No it isn't,' said Ilkar. 'Something's disrupting the mana flow. I can't shape anything. And we've got less than a minute before they reach us. Will, get back to the circle, we need that stone.'

'Yes,' said Will. 'Jandyr, guide me.' He sounded calmer now.

Soon, The Raven was complete. The Unknown stood next to Hirad, Ilkar next to him. To the right of the barbarian, Jandyr, Denser, Erienne and Thraun. In the middle, Will, patting the floor, searching for and finding his wedge tool. He began to nudge again at the lid of the case.

The clang of metal on marble, the scraping of stone on tile came closer every heartbeat, and Hirad could sense them. Looming presences, huge in their invisibility, terrifying in their quiet. He moved his blade to ready.

'Ilkar . . .'

'Gods, it's the Temple itself.' Ilkar's sudden shout made Hirad jump.

'What?' said Denser.

'We were blind before the lights went out. Denser, think. Circular building, domed roof, sealed absolutely, needle point spires . . .' Ilkar trailed off; he could see realisation cross Denser's face like the knowledge of guilt.

'We're in a Cold Room.'

'Hirad, we've got to get a door or shutter open. Trust me on this. They're on us in twenty seconds.' Ilkar swallowed hard.

A clashing sound signalled eight axes brought to the ready on gauntleted hands. Hirad shook himself, fighting to hang on to his senses. Around him, The Raven stood ready. At least they would die working to save each other. He made his decision.

'Ilkar, Erienne, see what you can do. Everyone else, let's close the circle, try to give them and Will time. Careful underfoot, the blood isn't as dry as it seems. Thraun, Jandyr, keep talking. Gods, that smell is powerful.'

To Hirad's left, The Unknown tapped the point of his sword on the ground. It was time.

'Almost on us,' said Thraun. 'Hirad, you have two, axes raised, upper guard. Denser, you have one, Unknown, two. They're all going to swing in unison, left to right diagonal.'

'Ready, Unknown?' Hirad's voice cut through the fog of his own mind. He breathed and gagged, feeling sweat beading in his forehead and dampening his armpits.

'You can never be ready for this. Angle your blade down to move the blows or they'll knock you over.'

Abruptly, the scraping and clanging stopped. There was a susurration around them. Cloaks rustled in the ghost of a breeze. The quiet sent a shiver through Hirad's body.

'Now,' said Jandyr.

The blows came in. At the final moment, Hirad sensed the shape of the statues and the shadow of their blades. Two hands on the hilt, he deflected one strike, swaying from the other. Sparks leapt from blades all round the circle, lighting up the nightmare masked faces of the statues for a beat before plunging them back to darkness. All that was left was the after-image. It would have been better not to have seen them at all. At least everyone survived the first round.

'They're slow to react,' reported Thraun. 'Weapons still low but moving now, probably for a slash. I don't recommend we attack. Let's see what they've got.'

'Very basic conjuration,' said Denser. 'If the next blow comes in the same, it's all they have.'

Inside the circle, Will worked feverishly, blind, head so close to the case he could smell the metal and glass above the hideous odour of the dead. Around him, The Raven fought to protect him. He focused his mind, driving away the fear. He'd felt enough with his fingers to know the glass was reinforced, that he'd need a hammer to break it and that Denser didn't want to take that risk. But the seal was complete and he had to find the mechanism that opened it. It had to be there, he just didn't know how much time The Raven could give him to find it.

Ilkar had taken Erienne's hand and dodged the tightening net. But even as he ducked and side-stepped, he knew a blow wouldn't come. The statues had their target. Knowing the doors would be too heavy, Ilkar made for the nearest shutter. Erienne, still blind, stepped on to the face of a Wrethsire guard, the neck twisting sickeningly as her weight moved across the head. She stumbled, grabbed Ilkar and shuddered.

'Gods, it's hideous.'

'All right, Erienne, we're at the edge now.' Ilkar's words calmed her.

'What the hell can we do?' Erienne, her hands placed on the wooden shutter, scrabbled at its edges. Searching but with no hope of finding.

'Think. The Unknown tried force, we have to find the lock.'

'And if it's magical?'

'We have to believe we can damage the Wrethsires' castings.' He shrugged, although he knew she couldn't see him. 'We have to.'

'Second strike coming. Midriff slash, right to left. Back and block,' said Jandyr. 'Now.'

A whistle as eight axes missed their targets. Hirad found the experience totally unnerved him. He was not in control of the fight. And under his feet, the crusted surface of blood broke, robbing him of confidence in his balance. But the statues were limited in their scope, as Thraun confirmed.

'All right, they're taking up for the first strike again. None of them has changed position. You know what to do. Now.'

The blows came in much heavier than before. Hirad staggered back a pace, his legs brushing against Will behind him. Again his second assailant missed.

'Denser?'

'Still here, just about.'

'Second strike,' warned Thraun. 'Now.'

Hirad just recovered in time. Beside him, The Unknown grunted under the force of the blows.

'That's too quick.' If speed and weight of blow kept on increasing at the same rate, Hirad knew it would be a short fight, and he didn't want to die without seeing the eyes of his killer.

Will found it. A pinhole tucked under the rim of the lid. It was exquisite workmanship but he didn't pause to appreciate it. He fished in a belt pouch for his filament wire and guided it, quickly and smoothly, into the hole, thanking the Gods his nerves had returned following the death of Denser's Familiar. Somewhere in the pinhole was the lock mechanism. Around him the fight was becoming more urgent, denying him the concentration he needed. Twice now, Hirad had stumbled backwards and his retaliating blows had done nothing but strike terrifying sparks from the silent foe.

Denser was struggling badly. The statues had picked up a rhythm whose pace was increasing, and although he could count it, he was not used to the constant strain the axe strokes produced in the muscles and tendons of his arms. And the fetid stink of rotting flesh clouded his mind and caught in his throat, triggering nausea that weakened his limbs still further. Soon his defence would collapse. He was already imagining the pain.

Ilkar and Erienne felt around the shutter. Nothing. Whatever held it was not mechanical, and without the benefit of any kind of mana flow, Ilkar knew deep down that they couldn't hope to damage the Wrethsires' conjuration. It would be like trying to put out a fire with a feather. Unless they could break the shutter there was no way out, and if The Unknown couldn't make a dent, what hope did he have? He drew his sword and hammered the pommel on the heavy wood. It was all he could think of to do while behind him, his friends were being inexorably worn down.

Thraun found the going relatively straightforward. Able to switch grips at will, he, like Hirad, could effectively rest one arm at a time. Jandyr, though, was wilting. The bowman's light blade was no match for the slugging power of the axe blows and his guard was being forced down inch by inch. Soon, they would cut him.

Will almost shouted with delight when he felt it – a let-in to the long pinhole. All he had to do was direct the filament wire down.

'Got it,' he said.

'Will, do nothing.' The Unknown fielded the next pair of blows, thinking hard. 'They'll go for you when you release the stone, I'm sure of it. We need to be ready. Jandyr?'

'Yes,' the elf gasped.

The heat was becoming stultifying and suffocating, the Temple airless, poisoned by the dead. None of them could last much longer.

'On my word, Will's going to pop the lid and grab the stone. Field your next blow, grab him and run him through the cordon to the end of the Temple. Got that? Will?'

'Yes.'

Another blow, stronger, faster. More grunts of exertion.

'The rest of us, field and dodge, they won't come for us. Thraun, you're the eyes, although I'm sure we all know where our enemies are standing. On my word then.'

'Strike coming,' said Thraun.

'Will, now!'

The thief pushed down on the filament, and as the lid swung up, he grabbed the stone.

'I have it.'

The Unknown caught the blows on his blade, ducked and charged through the gap between his two attackers, sensing Hirad do likewise. Jandyr turned and grabbed Will, pulling him upright and forward.

'Run, Will!' The elf's cry echoed around the Temple, loud in the darkness.

Axes rose and fell, clashing sparks off the tiles as they bit. It was enough to see Will and Jandyr sprinting for the far end of the Temple, picking a path through the corpses. The scraping started again, then the clank of metal on stone. The statues were on the move.

'Jandyr, you're the eyes for Will,' said The Unknown. 'You should be able to dodge them. Don't get trapped '

'Count on it.' Jandyr sounded exhausted.

'Let's get one of those bloody shutters open. Thraun, direct me.'

'Dead ahead of you now. Put your arms out. There.'

'Ilkar, what did you find?' asked The Unknown.

The ominous sounds of the walking statues bounced off the walls, mingling with the occasional wet crunch as they drove stone feet through the bodies of their former masters. Jandyr's voice could be heard, low and comforting, but bone tired.

'There is no mechanical switch,' said Ilkar as The Unknown felt around the shutter's edge. 'It's all part of the same casting, I'm sure of it.'

'Then we're going to have to batter it. Thraun, let's see if we can move that plinth. I suggest you sheath your weapons and stand back to the wall. We don't want any accidents.'

It seemed to Will that at every turn, he was exposed to a new fear. First the Familiar, then his useless hands, next the sudden dark and now this. Eight huge statues coming for him and him alone because he held the Death's Eye Stone. He hadn't even let himself think of the power that animated them, or that could remove The Raven's capacity for victory so effectively.

All that bothered him now was the sound of their feet marking the floor, that he couldn't see them coming and that, despite Jandyr's words and hand on his shoulder, he was certain he was going to perish in this nightmare place that smelt so much of death.

'Will, you're shaking.'

'Are you surprised?'

'Listen to me and you'll be fine. They're closing in, so we have to move in a second to force a change of direction. I'm going to move us left. Grab hold of my arm and keep walking – there's no need to run because they can't cover the whole diameter of the Temple. Do you understand?

'Yes.' The scraping was loud in Will's ears, the clang of metal boots sounding his death knell, his mind full of the images of axes falling from the disguise of night.

'Let's move.'

They hugged the wall, Jandyr gasping with every pace, Will trying to concentrate on merely putting one foot in front of the other. The elf walked quickly, and twice Will all but lost his grip, tripping on the bodies they had so recently dragged to the Temple's edge. But the fear of being left alone to be cut to pieces kept his fingers tight on the flesh of Jandyr's upper arm. An abrupt change of direction and Will stumbled.

'Where?'

'Sorry, Will. We're heading to the other side of the Temple.' Jandyr's breath was tortured. 'It'll give me more space for the next move.'

Thraun swept the case from the plinth and tried to tip the column of carved marble. For a moment he thought it was set into the floor, but with a crack that signified the shifting of the dust of ages, it moved.

'Unknown?'

'Thank the Gods.'

The two big warriors hauled the plinth to an acute angle before wrapping their arms around it and heaving it from the floor, grunting with the effort and breathing heavily.

'Lead away, Thraun,' said The Unknown. 'Quickly.'

Will slipped on a slick of new blood and went sprawling, shouting as his hand was wrenched from Jandyr's arm. He rolled over and came to his haunches, eyes probing desperately at the impenetrable dark, recoiling as they touched cold torn flesh.

'Jandyr,' he wailed. 'Don't let them get me!' Movement by him and a hand on his arm. He flinched then relaxed.

'I've got you, Will. I've got you.' Jandyr's voice was a beacon of calm. 'We're all right. They can't get us. Come on, we need to keep moving.'

Will rose to his feet. 'Which way?'

'Just follow me.'

The Unknown absorbed the recoil of the first blow on the shutter, his massive shoulders shuddering under the reactive force. But the wood had given. Magically sealed it might have been, but it was still just wood.

'Next time,' said Thraun. 'Ready?'

'Go.'

The wood shivered. They heard it splinter but still they weren't through.

'Close,' Thraun said. 'Again.'

'Go.'

The marble plinth crashed through the shutter. Thraun let his end go and The Unknown drove forwards, pushing the makeshift battering ram out on to the path. A jagged hole in the wood let in fresh air, a wan light that shone like a watch beam and, more importantly, a flood of mana as the structure of the Cold Room was broken.

'That'll do,' said Denser.

In moments, the Temple filled with a gentle glow as Erienne tempered her LightGlobe, wary of the danger of a new sort of blindness. Jandyr and Will were still evading. As the globe deployed, they began to run towards the main doors. Jandyr was limping badly.

'See to those doors,' said Hirad.

'I've got them.' Ilkar's ForceCone focused where they met. Its casting blew them clean off their hinges to cartwheel into the glorious warm night air.

'Let's go, let's go!' Hirad led the run from the Temple, gulping in fresh air, unfettered by the taste of death. 'If they follow, we can outrun them. Come on!'

The Raven exploded from the Temple, Jandyr and Will last, crashing into the dirt beyond the steps. The statues stopped at the doors, unable to move beyond the confines of their casting. The Raven stopped at the tree line.

First one masked figure, then another, stepped from the shadows. Eyes so long used to the dark took it all in as plain as if it were day. In moments, ninety Protectors barred their passage, headed by a single rider.

The Raven formed up, The Unknown at its centre, eyes boring into the ranks behind the horseman. All the time, he knew they'd been there.

Will stayed by Jandyr. The elf lay face down in the earth, blood running from a gash that led from shoulder to hip.

'He needs help.'

'So do we,' said Erienne.

Will looked up as Denser spoke.

'Styliann. You're a little late for the rescue.'

'Remarkable,' said Styliann. 'It was imperative you survived. Balaia doesn't have much time.'

Chapter 30

The hordes were coming and Darrick had to make the most critical command decision of his career. He'd seen The Raven safely into the west and, a day later, Styliann and one hundred Protectors had galloped through, bent on vengeance. He hadn't spoken to the Lord of the Mount but he had seen into his eyes. He pitied the Wesmen who encountered that centile of death.

The situation was clear to him. While the defence of the east was his charge, the real battle was about to fought in the west by The Raven and, it seemed, by Styliann. Darrick looked about him. He'd assembled the most capable staff he could think of, any one of whom could marshal the defence forces equally as well as himself.

To the south, while Gresse and Blackthorne's loss of the latter's town was a serious blow, their harrying tactics should delay the Wesmen advance on one flank, and to the north, he had to believe that the Colleges would hold Triverne Inlet. There lay the greatest concentration of magic, and there the Shamen could be effectively countered for now.

In his heart, Darrick knew he couldn't stand at the head of Understone Pass and wait for the result in the Torn Wastes. He wanted his five hundred horse, his fifty mages and his freedom to ride.

He wanted a fight, and by the Gods he was going to have one.

Ilkar walked away, back towards the Temple. He was shaking. Styliann's voice came to him through a haze.

'I really am very sorry.'

Ilkar shrugged and turned. 'When did this all happen? What happened at Triverne Inlet?' He couldn't understand how the situation could possibly be so bad.

'Yesterday. I received communion earlier this evening. They wiped us out. We had thought to hold them there for days but their magic was too strong,' said Styliann. 'They've got something we never saw three hundred years ago. White fire that brings down walls and something altogether darker that can eat the flesh.'

The Raven listened in silence, The Unknown standing with the Protectors, his eyes unfocused. The mage force and warriors at Triverne Inlet had been massacred, overwhelmed by magic-wielding Shamen. The Wesmen were less than three days from Julatsa and there had to be doubts over the Colleges' ability to keep them at bay. Blackthorne and Gresse were losing the battle to keep the Wesmen from flanking the Understone Pass defence, and Darrick had ridden into the west and disappeared. The Gods alone knew what he meant to do. Suddenly, their planned approach to Parve had turned into a headlong rush and they could already be out of time.

'And what are your plans, my Lord?' asked Denser, still stunned that the Lord of the Mount should be in the west.

'You know why I am here,' said Styliann. 'They took Selyn and I will take their lives. You will come with me and so will Dawnthief. The Raven can return to Understone Pass. Their skills are better used in its defence.'

The atmosphere changed in an instant. Hirad shifted to a ready stance, sword still sheathed for the moment. The Unknown moved to stand beside him, as did Thraun. Ilkar and Erienne flanked Denser as he stood in front of the mounted Styliann. Will remained with the fallen Jandyr. There was a ripple through the Protectors.

'I'm not sure I understand,' said Denser, though an awful realisation was flooding his heart.

Styliann raised his eyebrows. 'Denser, the balance must be redressed and we must have dominion. Dawnthief must belong to Xetesk alone. Now, bring the catalysts to me or I will take them from the corpses of your friends.' He signalled, and the Protectors unsheathed their weapons, the sound slicing through the night air.

'You can't let him do this!' hissed Ilkar.

'He has no choice,' said Styliann. 'He always knew this would be the result.'

Denser gaped at Styliann, his head shaking slightly. 'And you . . .?' He gestured behind him at the Temple.

Styliann frowned. 'Yes. And you did what even my Protectors could not. I'm impressed,' he said. 'But now The Raven's work is done.'

'How did you get here before us?' asked Hirad.

'I was never very far behind you, Hirad. You chose to rest on your way here; I did not.' He shrugged. 'A pity I didn't succeed. It would have made all of this so much easier.'

'Yes,' said The Unknown. 'Because we hold the cards, don't we?'

Ilkar fell back from Denser behind The Raven. His incantation was short. 'Shield up,' he murmured. The Raven's swords were drawn.

Styliann laughed. 'Do not think you can stand in my way,' he said, dismissive. 'Denser, do the right thing or I'll be forced to take your life too.'

'You wouldn't do that.' Denser moved back, Erienne with him, feeling Ilkar's shield cover him.

'Any reason why not?'

The Protectors came to ready. The Unknown tensed.

'Because I represent the only realistic chance of casting Dawnthief with any hope of destroying the Wytch Lords while leaving Balaia still habitable.' But Denser's words held little conviction.

'If you really are blind enough to think you are the only Dawnthief mage in Xetesk, I pity you,' said Styliann. 'I am offering you glory. You and I will destroy the Wytch Lords and then you will stand by me on the Mount and oversee our rule of Balaia. There are two Towers in need of new Masters. Come.' He beckoned Denser forward and the Dark Mage moved an involuntary half-pace before Erienne's arm, still locked through his, restrained him.

Denser looked about him at The Raven. At Erienne, who carried his child and to whom he would suffer no harm. At Hirad, who had threatened his life twice but had saved it more often and would undoubtedly do so again, given the chance. At Ilkar, who knew the way forward and tolerated him because of it. The Unknown, who was released but still in thrall to his soul memories. And Will, Thraun and Jandyr, who believed because The Raven believed.

But opposite him, Styliann. The Lord of the Mount of Xetesk. A man who could see him to death or glory with equal ease.

Denser came to Hirad's shoulder, his voice a whisper. 'Do you trust me?' he asked.

Hirad regarded him carefully, Denser watching the thoughts chasing themselves across his eyes. 'You're Raven,' he answered, shrugging. 'You risked yourself to release The Unknown. That is the act of one of us.'

'Give me the chain.' Hirad framed a refusal but Denser stayed him. 'He can take them anyway. We can't stop him.'

'We can't just give in.' Hirad's grip tightened on his sword.

Denser's voice was barely audible. 'No one is giving in. Trust me.'

Hirad switched his attention to Styliann, who studied The Raven with obvious fascination. Behind him, ninety Protectors stood ready to wipe them out. He clacked his tongue and lifted the chain carrying the Understone Pass Commander's Badge and the Dordovan Ring of Authority from his neck. He heard Ilkar's sharply indrawn breath, though the shield did not waver.

'Give Denser the stone, Will,' said Hirad. 'We have nothing to gain by dying.'

Will paused in his tending of Jandyr and passed the Death's Eye Stone to Denser. The Xeteskian smiled but, before walking to Styliann, stopped by Ilkar, his back to his Lord.

'Whatever you do, keep that shield up.' He moved to stand in front of Styliann, hefting the catalysts.

'And to think I have the fate of Balaia in my hands,' he said.

'Dangerous,' said Styliann. He reached out. 'Let's not waste any more time. It is a particularly precious commodity.'

'Indeed it is,' agreed Denser, a smile on his lips. 'And I will now decide Balaia's fate.

The mana shape was formed and the command spoken before Styliann had a chance to react. Denser, ShadowWings deployed, shot up and backwards, finishing behind the Temple, high in the lee of the cliffs. Every face turned to look at him, silhouetted against the star-speckled night sky. No one breathed and Hirad's heart thumped in his chest, sweat freezing on his body. Denser shouted down from his vantage point, well out of Styliann's spell range, ShadowWings beating lazy time.

'I can't let you return to the old ways, Styliann. You're out of date. Dawnthief goes with The Raven. That is the contract and we will honour it or die in the attempt.'

'You are a Xeteskian mage and you are my servant,' said Styliann, his voice cold and terrible. 'You will obey me.'

'No,' said Denser. 'I am Raven.'

Hirad's smile was as wide as Understone Pass. He straightened from his ready stance.

'Oh dear, Styliann,' he said. 'Beaten again. Why not admit it and step aside?'

But Styliann wasn't listening. His eyes ablaze, his mind shaped mana with the speed and efficiency only a Master could command. A trio of FlameOrbs struck Ilkar's shield in successive heartbeats, blue and red light lashing over the invisible barrier. Ilkar gasped under the force of the attack, but though he trembled, the shield did not. Styliann looked on. None of The Raven had so much as flinched.

'Ilkar has never lost a shield to magical attack,' said Hirad. 'And I can assure you that he doesn't intend starting now. It's over, Styliann.'

'I hardly think so,' grated the Lord of the Mount. He turned to his Protectors. 'Kill them. Kill them now.' But the Protectors did not move. 'Kill them!' he screamed, face red in the moonlight, fury blazing in his eyes. Hirad prepared to die.

'Relax, Hirad,' said The Unknown, and the depth of his smile at last touched his eyes. 'I suggest you save your breath, Styliann.'

'I beg your pardon?' The words dragged from Styliann's mouth.

'It's something you can never conceive, let alone understand. They will not attack us while I am here and we aren't threatening your life. And in the same way, I will not let The Raven attack them. But I warn that should I die at your hand, your Protectors will turn on you.'

There was a shifting behind Styliann. He looked around. The Protectors were all staring at him, their masks reflecting the starlight.

'You can choose not to believe me, my Lord.' The Unknown walked forwards, out of the spell shield. 'But you've already lost the spell. Why lose your life too?'

Styliann's face darkened still further. He swung round in his saddle again, studying the Protectors' postures, unable to conceive the potential scale of their defiance. Eventually, he turned back to The Unknown.

'But you have been released. You are no longer one of them.'

'So I thought too. But the bonds forged in the meld of souls are unbreakable. My soul may be my own but it will reach out to the Protectors for ever. I accept that, they understand it. Best you do too.'

A third look behind him and the Lord of the Mount nodded. He had half turned his horse when The Unknown stopped him.

'You can help us save Balaia and gain your revenge,' he suggested. 'If you were to attack Parve from the south or south-east in response to our signal, it might ease our route to the pyramid. At least then you might have a College to return to.'

Styliann's face was blank. 'You might tell Denser that while I am Lord of the Mount, he is most unwelcome in Xetesk. As for The Raven, you will be paid on your return through Understone Pass. Be very certain never to cross me again.'

'I will sign you through the Protectors,' said The Unknown. 'If you are near, they will hear me.'

Styliann said nothing, kicking his horse to a canter and making his way through the ranks of Protectors. They remained still for some moments, meeting souls with The Unknown, before following their Given from the Temple clearing.

For several minutes, The Raven held formation while Denser circled overhead, sight attuned to the mana spectrum, probing for a clue that Styliann was about to launch a new attack. When he landed and dismissed the ShadowWings, they relaxed.

'Shield down,' said Ilkar.

Hirad placed a hand on Denser's shoulder, nodding his gratitude as the Dark Mage looked at him.

'At last, I think I can say I understand,' said Denser.

'Will Styliann help us?' asked Hirad.

The Unknown raised his eyebrows. 'Difficult to say,' he said. 'If he stops to think hard enough, perhaps.'

'Thraun, would you check the path and collect the horses?' asked Hirad. Thraun inclined his head and jogged away out of sight.

Belatedly, the focus of attention fell on Jandyr. The elf was still alive and Erienne had joined Will in ministering to him. But he hadn't moved from where he had fallen. His leather armour had been slit by the falling axe of a statue and the wound beneath it was deep and severe. His clothing and the dirt around him were filmed with blood, although Erienne seemed to have stemmed the flow.

'How bad?' asked Will.

'He's been lucky,' said Erienne. 'The blade hasn't sheared any ribs, so his heart and lungs are undamaged, but I'm very worried about the state of his shoulder and lower back.'

'Can we move him?' asked The Unknown.

'Not until morning, anyway, to give me a chance to repair some of the damage. Put it this way, he won't be using his bow for a while. There's a great deal of tendon and muscle damage in that shoulder.'

'We've haven't got that sort of time,' said Ilkar. 'You heard what Styliann said. The Wesmen will be at Julatsa in three days.'

'Then they must hold them,' said Erienne. 'If we ride now, he will die. Ilkar, I'm only asking we wait until dawn. Five hours.'

'Dawn,' said Ilkar. 'It will give us a chance to verify what Styliann has said.'

Hirad considered the situation. He scanned the tree line, then turned full circle, taking in the lake, mountains and Temple. The painted faces of the statues still crowded the doors. He shuddered.

'So long as you can all stand to be watched by that lot, we might as well stay right here until sun-up. Will, the stove, please. Denser, I need you and Thraun to discuss the route to Parve. With the Wesmen on the march we'll have to stay clear of the roads to Understone. Meanwhile, Ilkar, Unknown, I want to talk to you.'

A brief flurry of activity disrupted the peace of the impromptu campsite. Denser and Will hurried out of the clearing after Thraun, Erienne began preparation of a healing spell and the three surviving original Raven members gathered on the steps of the Temple. Hirad spared the statues one more glance before speaking.

'There's things I don't understand,' he said.

'No change there,' said Ilkar.

Hirad punched him on the shoulder. 'You're funny, Ilkar. But not very funny.' He laughed. 'Explain to me what a Cold Room is and why I've never heard of one before.'

'Well, it's not something the Colleges publicise, for obvious reasons.' Ilkar shot a glance heavenwards. 'How do I explain? Right, look, mana flows everywhere and through everything. It doesn't stop for skin, bones, walls, wood, ocean, not even dimensions, as we discovered. No one knows its rhythm or the pattern to its flow, only how to disrupt it to form shapes for spells. But one thing that can be done is to divert the flow, and particular structures will do that.' He jerked a thumb behind him. 'Mana will take the path of least resistance. This temple has been very carefully constructed, and I mean in extraordinary architectural and material detail. When it was sealed, the mana simply flowed around it and not through it.' He shrugged. 'That's it.'

'It was a well-laid trap for the unwary thief,' agreed The Unknown.

'Or mage,' muttered Ilkar. 'We were close to being snuffed out in there.'

'So those bodies we found in there were Protectors?' asked Hirad.

'Yes,' said The Unknown. 'I knew straight away but it didn't seem possible at the time. They were Protectors, some of Styliann's no doubt.'

'But they had no masks,' said Ilkar.

'No doubt, when the threat is removed, the statues move back and the doors unseal. Protectors always take the masks of their fallen brothers. Styliann wanted to get the Death's Eye Stone for himself and was cautious enough to stay outside while he sent his Protectors in. Getting it would have given him real power over us, after all.'

'So he was waiting for us to succeed,' said Hirad.

'Hoping, certainly,' said The Unknown. 'I'm sure us taking the stone and then him taking the entire spell from us was his fallback plan the whole time.'

Hirad shook his head. 'When I saw them all waiting, I don't mind telling you I expected to be dead and cooling soon after. What happened?'

'He did.' Ilkar indicated Denser, who was walking back into the clearing with Will, Thraun and the horses.

'Would you care to elaborate?' asked Hirad.

'Yes, I'd be glad to. We have just witnessed the biggest single step forward in Xeteskian thinking, probably ever. Denser turned down certain power and glory in his College for the greater good of Balaia. I can still scarcely believe it.'

'But that doesn't explain the Protectors,' said Hirad. He looked out into the camp. Will was setting up the stove near by, intent on ignoring them but no doubt hearing everything they said. Erienne was talking to Jandyr and stroking his hair. The elven bowman, although still lying on his front, was conscious. Denser and Thraun were in deep conversation, poring over a map, Thraun making animated sweeping gestures. Denser, pipe smoking gently, was smiling.

Hirad felt warm inside. The Raven was complete again and working smoothly. He hadn't felt this way since the day Ras died.

'You'll have to ask The Unknown about that,' said Ilkar.

'There's not a lot to say that you'll understand,' said The Unknown. 'I just knew Styliann's power over them was less than that of the bond between them and me. They won't ever attack one of their own unless their Given's life is threatened. We didn't threaten Styliann's life.'

'And would they have killed him if he'd killed you?' asked Ilkar.

'No. He is their Given and they can never hurt him. Who cares? Styliann believed me.'

Hirad laughed again. 'Nice work, Unknown. C'mon, let's take a look at the lake, get Will some water.'

The attack hammered in along the entire length of the Wesmen lines as they marched through flat areas of grassland, flanked by pockets of dense forest. It followed a storm of arrows, HardRain and DeathHail, forcing the Shamen to use valuable stamina raising hard and magical shields.

A thousand riders surged into the exposed enemy, hoofs churning mud, earth and blood, blades flashing in the midday sun. The noise was like heavy rain on a slate roof, growing in intensity. Blackthorne's men wheeled after their first charge, disengaging to re-form. The horns sounded again and Gresse's force levered into the other flank, spreading disarray.

Gresse felt like a young man again as he kicked his horse into the suddenly less smug, tanned faces of the Wesmen. He cut left and right as he drove forwards, splitting the face of one man and slicing through the shoulder of another. Blood filled the air, misting in front of his face and spattering his legs, saddle and chest. Noise, tumultuous, filled his ears.

Around him, his men clattered into the enemy, the shouts of Wesmen trying to gather a defence mingling with the cries of the dying. He urged his mount onwards, pushing one man aside with a blow from his shield and fielding a spear jab on the guard of his sword. The Wesmen were falling back under the onslaught, their line order threatening to break, confidence taken apart by the rampaging horses and the flashing steel of their riders. Gresse began to scent victory.

The horns sounded again and he wheeled his horse through a half-circle and ploughed out of the carnage, trampling the dead and dying under hoof. Looking left and right, he counted only a handful of riderless horses and he shouted his delight as he galloped away to re-form out of Wesmen bow range.

Down came the spells and arrows again on the Wesmen ranks, but this time more of them stopped short, bouncing from shields or flaring darkly on magical contact.

A third time, the horns sounded, signalling the push on the Shamen, so far defended by their warrior guards, and Blackthorne came charging back in, mages in attendance, shielding as many men as they could.

By now, the Wesmen had regrouped and stood ready, drawn into tight defensive cells. Blackthorne's spearmen levelled poles and clattered into the enemy, making less ground but fragmenting the outer defensive lines. The swordsmen followed them in, Gresse seeing Blackthorne's blade rise and fall, spraying blood in all directions.

There was a hum in the air, cutting through the din of battle, assaulting the ears and setting teeth on edge. Horses, skittish and with nostrils flaring, threatened to rear. From the fingers of every Shaman issued whip-like lines of black, flailing the air and burying themselves in horse and rider alike.

Agony. Death in terror and pain unimaginable. Where the spell found an unshielded body or breached magical defence, man and beast died by the score. As Gresse watched, a line of dark caught a rider in the midriff and tore up his body, unpicking his leather, stomach and chest like a tailor's knife through fine cloth. His intestines gushed through the rent in his body, ribs shattered, and his dying cry was silenced as the dark reached his neck.

Elsewhere, holes were punched clear through bodies, flesh was burned or eaten aside and the tide of the battle turned with stunning speed. Blackthorne whirled his sword above his head and the horns sounded full retreat. Gresse barked orders to his men, and the Baronial cavalry kicked away from the scene of devastation, leaving the blood of the east to mix with that of the west, the jeers of the Wesmen ringing in their ears.

Glory was turned to darkness.

Chapter 31

A dry and warm night was followed by a cloudless dawn, the rain of the preceding day a distant memory.

Denser had held a brief communion with the lead mage at Understone and at least they knew that Styliann had not been exaggerating. To the south, and moving at worrying speed, the Wesmen were three days from Understone, and Blackthorne's efforts were yielding little but the blood of his own men. But worse, some thirty thousand Wesmen and Shamen were a day from the western entrance to the pass.

'And you said the Wytch Lords haven't yet regained their full strength?' said Hirad.

Denser nodded. 'When they are walking and fully focused, the Shamen's power will be completely unstoppable.'

'If it isn't already,' said Ilkar.

'How far to the Torn Wastes?' Hirad asked.

'Two and a half days' ride to the borders, perhaps another hour to the pyramid,' replied Thraun.

'That is cutting it very fine indeed,' said Ilkar.

'And it assumes we aren't held up on the way,' added Thraun.

There was a contemplative quiet. Hirad pictured a headlong dash into the maw of sudden death – around any corner, Wesmen could be waiting in great numbers.

'We could do with your cat now, couldn't we?' said Will ruefully.

'I could do with him all the time.' Denser's smile was thin and cold.

'How long can Darrick's men hold Understone Pass?' asked Hirad.

The Unknown shrugged. 'Who can say? We haven't seen the Shamen magic. All that's working in our favour is the narrowness of the entrance. There can't be an attack on a wide front and that gives our mages the chance to shield effectively.'

'Hmmm.' Hirad leaned back against the Temple steps, draining his mug. 'And can Jandyr ride?' The elf was being left to rest.

Erienne nodded. 'Wake him any time, just don't ask him to fight or fire his bow.'

'How long before he can?'

'In an ideal world, a day, no more. But we're riding hard and it'll pull at his wounds. If I don't get the time, you don't get your bowman.'

'Great,' said Hirad. 'Well, I guess we shouldn't hang around here waiting for the end of the world. Let's go and create it for ourselves.' He clapped Ilkar on the shoulder and rose.

Inside half an hour, they were riding for the Torn Wastes.

To Darrick, it was all very simple. Ride the secondary trails to the Wastes and there drive hard into the flanks of the Guardians and Keepers of the Tomb. Kill anything that got in the way and see The Raven back to the pass, victorious.

But two hours after dawn of his third full day in Wesmen lands, a third of his men were dead, another fifty were injured and his mage support was in tatters. Stopping to assess the damage fully, his body shaking with rage and humiliation, he still couldn't see how the Wesmen could have known their route.

Seventy bowmen, concealed from the path, launching waves of death and disorder that cut down horse and man alike. At the first wave, the cavalry broke ranks, charging left and right up the shallow incline into the shrubland behind which the trap had been laid. More lost their lives as arrows hurtled in from close range before, at last amongst them, the cavalry wiped out the Wesmen archers. He considered himself very fortunate not to have run into any Shamen.

Darrick surveyed his forces, reading the shock and dismay in their faces. He dispatched the worst injured back to the pass before consulting the lead mage. The Xeteskian was now in charge of only seventeen.

'Can you hold hard and magical shields on the gallop?'

'What's your plan?'

Darrick shook his head. 'We have to push on. If we decide to leave the trails, we may as well turn back now because we'll be too late. I want to turn this around, drive hard the rest of the day and surprise them with how deep we are into their territory. If we meet another ambush, I don't want to pause in the gallop.'

'That's high risk,' said the Xeteskian.

'I know, but we've got to take the initiative. They should never have been that well set. There is no way they could have known our route. No way.'

The mage raised his eyebrows. 'The Wytch Lords must be closer to waking than we thought.'

'Will you attempt the shield?' asked Darrick.

The Xeteskian nodded. 'Of course, if it's what you wish.'

'It is. Right, I've got to talk to the men, bring them up for this. It's going to be one hell of a chase.' Darrick smiled. 'Two days to save Balaia. Ready?'

The Lord Tessaya stood with his Shamen on the hills outside Understone Pass which he had so recently relinquished but was surely soon to retake. Thirty thousand of his countrymen, some enemies less than a year ago, were camped within a few hours of the pass, while a dozen Shamen under protection from three hundred of Tessaya's pass survivors were moving closer to the pass itself. A further five thousand Wesmen were ready to pour back under the mountains. It would be a sweet moment.

'I want them slaughtered to a man for what they did to me. But bring me Darrick alive. I will personally oversee his very slow death manacled to the stone he thought to take from me.' The Shamen nodded; one issued instructions. 'How long before we are in position?'

'We will be awaiting your instruction as the sun reaches its zenith, Lord.'

Tessaya looked to the sky: two hours. Two hours and then maybe he could erase the sounds of the terrified as the sea from the sky crashed through the pass. The echoes of the water beating off the walls and sweeping away his people, their cries, their shouts and their pleas dying with them as they were driven into the chasms. So many would never be found to rest on pyres of honour. So many never had the chance to fight and die as they had dreamed.

But the towering act of cowardice would be avenged as his people forged into the east to take as they pleased. For the first time in days, Tessaya smiled.

'I will mount up and lead my people back where they belong,' he said. 'We will soon all be drinking the blood of College mages.'

The Raven rode hard through unforgiving countryside as the sun rose into a partly cloudy sky. They hadn't seen or heard any pursuit since leaving the Temple. The Unknown could no longer feel the Protectors and had no idea whether they were heading east or west. But though they were making good progress, the way was difficult, the horses would tire quickly and the risk of accident was ever present.

Their principal concern, though, was Jandyr. The elven bowman was struggling. After a night in which he was kept asleep under Erienne's WarmHeal, he had pronounced himself able to ride, though his white, drawn and sweat-sheened face told The Raven about the pain he was suffering.

For an hour, he seemed to be standing it well, but as the morning wore on, he slowed more and more, spending much of his time flanked by Denser and Erienne, or Ilkar and Erienne. The mages, all with well-tuned healing ability, watched anxiously as the wound in his shoulder and back pulled and strained, blood soaking into his leather and shirt and dripping down his left arm, which hung strapped to his side.

At the first rest stop, and with the horses being checked, fed and watered by Thraun and Will, the rest of The Raven gathered around a gasping Jandyr as he lay propped against a moss-covered boulder. They had come to a stop at the head of a valley. Below them, the hills, windblown and stark, rolled away north and west towards Parve, while behind, the forest land they'd ridden through and which had provided such good cover lay like a coarse green blanket covering steep incline and shallow slope alike.

Perhaps a thousand feet below them, the principal trail from Parve to Understone cut along the base of the Baravale Valley, which bored one hundred miles between the west's two principal ranges of hills and mountains. Now and again on the prevailing wind, the sounds of marching Wesmen reached them while they, out of sight, sat and considered their position.

'Is there anything you can do to ease the pain?' asked Hirad. Denser paused from warming Erienne's hands and looked at her.

'Hold on,' she said. She withdrew her hands and helped Jandyr turn on to his side, giving her access to his wound. She unpicked the crude stitching of his leather and, with Ilkar's help, eased the bloody jacket's parts aside, cursing at the ruination of her work of the previous night. 'The wound is pulling from the riding, there's little I can do about that. What I can do is take the pain away, but he'll not be aware of any further damage he's doing. That could be dangerous.'

'Jandyr?' asked Hirad.

The elf breathed deeply, the sound a little ragged. 'I can't ride on like this,' he said. 'The pain is getting too much and I'll hold you up. There's a choice. Either you leave me here and come back when it's over, or Erienne casts the spell.'

'You can't stay here alone,' said Erienne. 'Without treatment you won't survive.'

'Then the decision's made,' said Hirad.

'He'll need supporting some of the time. He won't always be able to hold himself upright,' said Erienne.

'What are you planning on casting?' asked Denser.

'SenseNumb.'

'That's a little strong, isn't it?' said Ilkar.

Erienne hesitated.

'What is it?' Jandyr frowned. 'It's worse than you thought, isn't it?'

She nodded. 'The bleeding is worse than it should be. The flesh hasn't knitted at all. I know you've been straining it in the ride but it should be better than it is. I need to cast SenseNumb to keep you going at all. I should be able to do more tonight.'

'Will I still be alive tonight?' asked the elf.

'I don't know,' she said. 'I haven't got a good record at keeping people alive, have I?' Tears were suddenly in her eyes and running down her cheeks. Denser put an arm around her shoulder. He looked to Hirad.

'I think we'd better get on,' he said.

Approaching the village there was magic in the air. Styliann slowed his advance and moved to the rear of the column of Protectors. Still mounted, they walked their horses in close formation, the innate magical shields of the Protectors overlapping to produce something the Shamen would have to work hard to penetrate.

After leaving the Temple clearing, Styliann had turned south, his fury undimmed following a second humiliation at the hands of The Raven. And while he saw the sense of The Unknown's words, he had already made up his mind that his route to Parve would not be at The Raven's choice of pace. If he arrived in time to distract attention from them, so be it.

He had chosen as his first target a village just inside the Heartlands which would have staged marches towards Understone Pass and, possibly, the Bay of Gyernath. The village lay less than two days from the Torn Wastes. It would be a fitting message to the Wytch Lords about where the power really lay.

'Advance,' he ordered. 'There are no innocents. Spare no one.' It was the only voice that was heard as the Protectors pushed their horses to a gallop, making an arrow formation with Styliann at its rear, already forming the mana shape for his favourite destructive spell. He smiled at the very thought of what he had just ordered.

With only the sound of their horses to reveal their presence, the

Xeteskian Protectors swept into the unprepared Wesmen village. Built on classic Wesmen lines, the village was arranged in a circle around the central tribal totem and fire. It contained about thirty buildings, fencing for animals and open-sided, roofed structures for crop storage.

The ninety-strong force divided into two around the circle, swords drawn and hammering down on the villagers, who scattered screaming in every direction. Men, women, children, no one in the way was spared the blade. And behind them, Styliann rode into the centre of the circle, spell prepared.

'HellFire,' he said.

A dozen columns of fire crashed through the roofs of occupied dwellings, deluging victims and devastating buildings. Wood and flame filled the air. Burning figures ran from buildings, noise pounded the ears.

At the end of their sweep, the Protectors dismounted in almost balletic synchronicity and jogged back through the carnage, axes now drawn in spare hands. The village was in chaos. The dozen buildings hit by Styliann's soul-searching HellFire burnt fiercely, sending palls of black smoke into the sky. Survivors of the flames and the first Protector charge ran, some for the trees, some for their weapons. One marched towards the unprotected Styliann.

The Lord of the Mount slid from his horse, his magical shield formed and deployed immediately following the HellFire, sword drawn. The Shaman cast, ten black tendrils coursing at Styliann, playing over the shield and sending lines of force around his body. The shield should have breached under the pressure. Styliann could see that in the Shaman's eyes.

'Oh dear,' said Styliann. He walked forward and punched the Shaman with the pommel of his sword. Around him, the Protectors, silent, fast, ruthlessly efficient, were firing the remaining buildings and slaughtering everyone they found, young or old, suffering hardly a scratch as they advanced. The Shaman fell back, stumbling to his knees. Styliann's kick into his face hurled him clear on to his back, where he sprawled, blood covering his nose and cheeks. The Lord of the Mount crouched by him, the terrified man unable to do anything but stare into his face.

'You will be a message to your masters, your village will be a shrine to all who follow me, its buildings left to blacken, its people carrion, rotting as they lie unburied in the sun.'

'Who are you?'

Styliann smiled. 'Dare not challenge the power of Xetesk.' He slapped the Shaman's hand from his nose and placed his own hand over the man's mouth, holding it there while casting a FlamePalm directly into his throat. The Shaman died, writhing in agony, fire from his eyes and nostrils, hair smouldering and cracking. Styliann rose, dusted himself down and re-mounted his horse.

'Disengage!' he ordered. He looked about him satisfied, wondering if Parve would burn as well.

'Close up!' yelled Darrick. 'Deploy shields.'

The four-college cavalry was ploughing along the main trail between Understone and Parve before turning north to come at Parve from what Darrick assumed would be right angles to The Raven. They tore down the trail and hammered into the front of the Wesmen force, stopped along the trail and barely armed and ready by the time they were hit.

'Shields up!' called a mage as the spearmen at the front of the column scythed the first Wesmen aside. The cavalry galloped through, swords slicing left and right, shields flaring as Shamen magic hit but couldn't penetrate the overlapping College spells. They didn't pause, didn't turn and didn't look back, and in their wake, seventy Wesmen would never make Understone Pass.

Leaving the main trail shortly afterwards for the northern marches, two days from the Torn Wastes, Darrick drew his cavalry to a halt and a well-earned rest stop.

'Was that really necessary?' asked one of his mages.

'No,' said Darrick. 'But I'll tell you something, it was bloody good fun.'

And all about them, the smiles returned to the faces of his warriors.

Barras stood in the watchtower, unable to drag himself away as light faded on the penultimate day of peace in Julatsa. Behind the old elf mage, his College City prepared for a war they couldn't hope to win following the slaughter at Triverne Inlet only three days before. So many men, so many mages had gone, and while relief had been promised, none of it had arrived. Xetesk had even reported Styliann on his way with a hundred Protectors, but Barras knew in his heart where Styliann had gone.

And so he stood, watching the dark mass of Wesmen advancing. They would be within range of spells early the next morning, and Barras shivered at the thought of the white and black fire that the Shamen used, gouging the heart of Julatsa.

The City and College Guards were ready, the College's mages were briefed and positioned, but Barras knew that, failing a miracle, Julatsa would be in Wesmen hands by nightfall the day after tomorrow. They simply had no winning answer to the Shamen magic. Yes, they could shield effectively against it, but the drain on mana and mage resources was so great, it left too few to cast offensively. And with Julatsan swordsmen outnumbered better than four to one, and with no walls around the City, the outcome of the battle was inevitable because the Shamen never seemed to tire.

Barras felt his eyes filling with tears as he recalled the stories of his great-grandfather, who, as a young mage, had witnessed the first Wytch Lord-backed Wesmen invasion. Towns and cities on fire, crops torched, bodies scattered, children fatherless. Refugees clustered in shelter where they could, marauding bands of Wesmen murdering everyone they found and the Shamen, nowhere near as powerful as this time, performing rites and sacrifices as they claimed eastern lands for their own.

It was all going to happen again and there was nothing anyone could do to stop it. And this time there was no mage force capable of defeating the Wytch Lords, there was no army capable of routing the Wesmen. The only hope was The Raven, but Barras had so many doubts about their chances of success. His last prayer as he made his weary way down from the tower was that they would destroy Dawnthief if they couldn't cast it.

A shudder went through his body, then a moment of calm. At least if the spell fell into Wytch Lord hands, the suffering of the peoples of the east would be short.

Safe for now, with night falling to cloak their hiding place in the hills, Blackthorne, Gresse and the remnants of the Bay of Gyernath force sat in cold contemplation of their fate. Already, many of the mercenaries had left to prepare for the fights for their own families, or simply to run, meaning that little over four hundred swordsmen and mages remained to slow the relentless progress of the Wesmen towards Understone.

Gresse, his left arm bandaged and good for little but lifting his fork to his mouth, bit into his bread, speaking after he had washed it down with water.

'They'll be at Understone in less than three days if we don't delay them again. We have to try.'

'It's suicide,' said Blackthorne, his face smeared with dirt and lined by the constant attrition of his forces. Five times they had attacked the Wesmen and five times they had been driven away by a combination of the Shamen magic and the increasing ferocity of the Wesmen themselves. They had two horses for every three men, and taking away the wounded and exhausted, around three hundred and fifty men fit to fight on.

'We can't let them take Understone,' said Gresse. 'Not without – what was it you said? – giving them something to think about. If they do, they'll control all the entry points to the east and the Colleges will be open from both flanks.'

'So what do you suggest?' asked Blackthorne wearily.

'First light tomorrow, we hit them from the front. The Shamen are far enough to the rear of the lines to give us a few seconds' killing time before we have to put the shields up, and at least it'll stop them moving.'

'They'll slaughter us.'

Gresse nodded. 'I know. But a battle lasting an hour will delay them most of the day once they have re-formed, burned their dead and made sure we are gone for good.'

Blackthorne looked long at his friend, the older man's eyes still twinkling in his head, his energy seemingly boundless. He had a better idea, but the result would be no less final.

'We'll take them at the Varhawk Crags,' said Blackthorne. 'There, we can station archers and mages to cause trouble to the centre of the column while we make a double-shielded charge into the front.'

'How far?'

'We need to leave now or the mages will not get enough rest. And we need to leave quietly or the Wesmen will hear us.' Blackthorne felt himself coming alive. They were going to die but they were going to go down in a river of blood and mana fire.

'We can be set by an hour after dawn.' Gresse put out his right hand, which Blackthorne shook heartily.

'The Gods will see us to paradise,' said the old Baron.

'And the Wesmen and Pontois to hell.'

It was late evening and The Raven had arrived on the borders of the Torn Wastes. Dark cloud dominated the sky and a chill wind picked at branches, loose vegetation, cloak and hair. Like Selyn before them, they were to the left of the west trail guard post on the edge of the forest, looking out seven miles to Parve, the beacon fires atop the pyramid burning bright in the night sky. But unlike the Xeteskian mage spy who had provided crucial intelligence concerning Wytch Lord power, The Raven were not looking through a sea of Wesmen tents.

Thraun had brought them through the woodland surrounding the Torn Wastes without error, and they lay a quarter of a mile from the trail, their horses quietened under a command from Denser and marshalled by his mount. The Wastes themselves stood largely empty. Here and there, camp fires ate into the night, but they were sparse. The vast majority of the Wesmen force was now outside Understone Pass, or nearing it.

But the atmosphere this close to the City of the Wytch Lords was charged with dread triumph. It oozed from the ground and carried on the air, pervading every sense and choking the heart. Standing and staring at the beacon fires, hearing the noise of Parve on the wind and feeling the cold against his cheeks, Hirad couldn't shake the feeling that they had arrived too late. But he couldn't afford to believe that. Not while people fought and died to save the lands he loved, not while the Wesmen marched to destroy his cities and not while The Raven still stood tall.

A day and a half's hard riding had brought them within sight of their goal, and while the ride had taken its toll on all of them, Jandyr's condition was giving Erienne cause for great concern.

'Well, here we are,' said Denser. 'It's seven miles to the pyramid from here. One gallop and we're there.'

Hirad, standing next to him and leaning on a tree, couldn't help but smile. 'I wish it was so simple,' he said. 'Wesmen perimeter defence, Shamen attack, a square full of Acolytes and a tomb full of Guardians.'

'Well, you can always dream,' said Denser. 'Seriously, how do you assess the defence?'

'Just as I described,' replied Hirad.

'And too much for The Raven alone,' said The Unknown. 'Even if Jandyr were fit, our chances of reaching the pyramid and casting the spell are negligible.'

'How is he?' Denser addressed himself to Erienne. The Dordovan mage looked up and held out a hand. Denser helped her up and the two stood, arms around each other's waists. The Raven gathered around Jandyr, who was lying unconscious under Erienne's latest desperate WarmHeal. Thraun stood by his head, with Will crouched by his friend, keeping his brow cool with a water-soaked cloth. Even in the sparse light of early night, the elf's pallor was plain and unhealthy, great dark ovals were around his eyes and his lips had lost their colour.

'Not good,' said Erienne. 'Not good at all. I've cleaned and re-dressed the wound. Thraun and I bound it very tight this time including his left arm, so he'll have very restricted movement. The spell has knitted the muscle in his shoulder and is speeding the skin regeneration, but the riding has really hurt him. I'm afraid the SenseNumb stopped him realising the wound was becoming infected and he has a light fever. I can try a SurfaceMeld, but after that, I'm spent.'

'But he'll live?' asked Hirad.

'So long as he's not made to gallop seven miles to a nearby city and then rushed into a pyramid to face the waking dead, yes.' Erienne's lips turned up at the corners.

Hirad thought briefly. 'How tired are you, Denser?'

'Very,' replied the mage. 'As are we all.'

Hirad looked to Ilkar and The Unknown. Both nodded.

'That settles it, then,' said the barbarian. 'The salvation of Balaia will have to wait until morning.'

'And what then?' asked Will. 'How can we do it alone? You heard what The Unknown said, we can't fight them all.'

'We'll do what The Raven have always done.' Hirad moved to stand with Ilkar and The Unknown. 'We'll walk careful, fight clever and run wise.'

'What the hell does that mean?'

The Unknown replied this time. 'It means, Will, unless I've gone badly astray, that we'll walk our horses into the Torn Wastes perhaps two hours before dawn. If we're lucky, we'll make the City unchallenged and the odds will begin to swing. If not, we'll fight where we have to and run where we don't.'

'But Darrick and Styliann?' Will was frowning.

'We can't wait for them,' said Hirad. 'We don't even know if they're coming. And you heard what Styliann told us. Understone and Julatsa will fall unless we can break the Wytch Lords. We've got to try or the battle will be lost.' He walked over to the smaller man and crouched by him, boring the look into his eyes that had fired The Raven so often.

'This is it. It's down to us and we're going to do it, I can feel it.' He stood and spread his arms wide. 'We've got this far and we've all lost those we loved. We can't, I can't, let that go. It's payback time.'

Chapter 32

Dawn on Balaia's day of judgement broke with fire in the sky. White fire.

It scorched along Understone Pass's hastily erected stone and wood defences, which rose half the height of the pass entrance. They had been built to repulse catapult, sword and spear, the pathways running behind them packed with archers. But there was no defence against the white fire. It picked and chewed at the stone, while defenders, having shot their arrows, scrambled for safety.

Twenty Shamen, magically and hard-shielded, stood silent and tore the walls down. But this time the defenders were ready for them, and as the walls came down, two thousand foot soldiers raced from the breach, protective mages keeping pace behind them.

Caught admiring the handiwork of his Shamen, Tessaya could only stand and watch as they and their bodyguards were cut to pieces before Wesmen warriors could get anywhere near them. He ordered battle joined and blood and noise filled the air.

Their initial mission accomplished, the pass defenders fell back in orderly formation, forming a tight half-circle around the entrance to the pass. From within, and beyond the range of the Shamen who walked behind the sea of warriors, bolts and stone from low-trajectory catapults and heavy crossbows thrummed overhead, dealing devastation to the rear of the Wesmen lines. FlameOrbs and HotRain lashed into the invaders, either flaring over shield or, where it broke through, spewing flame across the ground and over defenceless bodies. The stench of flesh and the pall of smoke stung the eyes.

The defenders' lines were holding. The generals of the pass kept a heavy presence of defensive mages covering the swordsmen outside, and they fought hard, knowing the line could not be flanked. They fought from wall to wall and nothing could get behind them. In front of them, better than thirty thousand Wesmen waited to take their chance. For the defenders it wasn't a question of winning; it was about buying time.

Tessaya watched from his vantage point, admiring the fighting spirit of the defenders and seeing his people die from sword, spell and missile in numbers he had not expected. But, unlike the massacre caused by the water spell, this sight held no fury for him. This was true battle and his men fought and lived or died bravely. He turned to his generals and Shamen.

'Comments?'

'They can hold us until their reserves of mana stamina run low,' said a Shaman, an old man happy to observe and advise. 'Their overlapping magical shields are effective but draining. If we are patient, we will break through.'

'But look at the numbers we are losing,' said another. 'They are killing us five to one because we can't see to cast into the pass and their heavy offence is coming from there.'

'And we cannot afford to give them rest,' said Tessaya. 'We can win by wearing them down man by man, but that is unacceptable.' He gazed at the entrance to the pass, his eye tracing the arch which rose some thirty feet above the battle ground, its rock hewn back so long ago when it was believed the two peoples could genuinely live in peace. He smiled as the solution presented itself. 'I think it's time we widened that arch. Raised the roof a little, don't you think?'

'Five Shamen could do it,' said the old man, catching Tessaya's train of thought.

'See that it is done,' said Tessaya.

The message was passed swiftly to the front lines and the quintet of casters gathered in the centre of the battlefield, a zone of calm in the swarming mass of warriors. Shields were raised over them and, with the noise of battle deafening in their ears and with boulders and bolts slicing the air above their heads, they cast the spell to change the course of the fight for Understone Pass.

The white fire lashed out, catching the top of the arch. It fizzed and crackled away, licking the rock either side and well into the pass itself. The rock glowed and shone, the Wytch Lord spell sourcing every crack, fissure and weakness. It poured down the side walls. dislodging chips and dust as it went, and raced here and there along the roof twenty paces in. The Shamen shut off the spell, the horns sounded a retreat and the Wesmen disengaged, shouting their hate and leaving their dead.

It began with a rumble that seemed to come from deep within the mountains. The arch shook, the walls shivered, the roof undulated and then the whole collapsed. Great boulders of rock fell from left, right and above, spreading panic through the defenders. Some ran inside, others for the slopes either side of the pass entrance, but most just stood as the ground juddered under the pounding rock that collapsed along a fifteen-yard stretch, destroying everything beneath it. Men, defences, catapults, all fell victim to the deluge.

In front of the pass, the Wesmen scented victory and yelled new battle cries of triumph at the floundering defenders. Dust filled the air, shards of stone lashed away into the gloom, cutting down those who had escaped the initial collapse, and then, as violently as it had begun, the fall ceased and all that was left was an echo, rumbling away into the heart of the Blackthorne Mountains.

When the dust began to clear, the sight that greeted Tessaya warmed his heart. The defenders' lines were broken. Hundreds lay dead or dying and those that survived blinked into the new light, leaderless and vulnerable. Because behind them, the pass had gone. Blocked almost from floor to roof by the rock. Nobody was going back, nobody else was coming out.

Tessaya smiled, knowing that his Shamen and warriors could remove the fall as simply as they had caused it in the first place.

'Sound the attack,' he said. 'We've a lot of work to do.' With a roar to cool the heart, the Wesmen set to work.

Selyn had died in Parve and Styliann would see the City returned to dust in revenge. He had stopped to gather his strength and to let his Protectors rest and bind the few wounds they had suffered, and now, with dawn broken, they were riding the Torn Wastes. His commands had been simple. Reach the city as fast as the horses would take them, and once there, kill everything western that moved and burn everything that didn't.

He rode in the centre of his Protectors, knowing they would shield him and feeling the thrill of mana energy coursing through his body. As the sun rose, he saw the pyramid, its fires dulled by natural light but burning all the same, saw the miles of the Torn Wastes and saw a stand of Wesmen tents about three miles in to the right and in front of him. They would be first.

Ten Protectors moved ahead to take the encampment, wheeling their horses out of line with complete precision and forming two lines of five as they raced away to the right. The rest galloped on.

Reaching the tents, the Protectors reined in, dismounted and took the canvas apart, piece by piece. Wesmen hurried to defend themselves as the Protectors moved in a single line through the encampment, silent, masked, deadly. At its centre, they stopped in the ashes of the long-dead fire, waiting. In front of them, the Wesmen, around thirty of them, formed up, nervous, hefting blades and axes in unsure hands.

Ten Protector sword tips tapped the ground. Once, twice, three times. On the fourth, in response to unspoken command, they switched their swords to their right hands and swept the axes from their backs into their left and joined battle in a whirl of blurring steel.

The Wesmen had no defence. Where one thrust forwards, the gap he thought he'd worked was stopped by the blade of a different opponent. Axe followed sword, delivering death and dismemberment. The Protectors marched forwards, each one swatting one strike aside before delivering the next themselves, their wall of strokes complementing each other and giving the Wesmen no chance at all.

The shouts of the Wesmen as they fought and died were met with the eerie silence of the Protectors, who barely even breathed heavily as they advanced, slicing at torso, hacking at neck and stabbing at heart and head. It was all over in a couple of minutes, and without pausing to view their efforts, the Protectors left the Wesmen blood to soak into the earth of the Torn Wastes and rejoined their brethren and Given.

Styliann rode on, slowing only as the buildings of Parve neared through the rubble of the City's outskirts. Half a mile from the first, he saw Parve's defenders lined up against him. Wesmen by the hundred, Shamen by the dozen and, here and there, red-cloaked Guardians and Acolytes.

He nodded, satisfied. He could take them all. And every skull crushed and heart ripped out was another he would offer to Selyn and another The Raven would not have to face. A quarter of a mile from the defensive lines, he brought the Protectors to a halt, dismounted them and marched to the attack of Parve, FlameOrbs already forming in his mind.

Under the cover of pre-dawn night, The Raven made slow and steady progress through the Torn Wastes, elven and shapechanger eyes directing every hoof fall. The horses were walking, no need for a gallop until or unless they were challenged. They would arrive at the City as light broke the darkness.

'Are they here?' asked Hirad. He was riding with The Unknown at the head of The Raven. Behind them rode Ilkar and Thraun, eyes piercing the darkness, low voices warning of any potential threat, although in truth there was little unless they were seen. The Wesmen who had been camped there were marching on Julatsa or pounding the defences of Understone Pass.

Jandyr, his face pale and slick with pain, rode between Denser and Erienne with Will bringing up the rear. The elf had made good progress during the hours of rest. His wound had stopped bleeding and Erienne's WarmHeal had been targeted carefully and successfully on the worst-affected muscles in his shoulder and back. His fever had broken and, although weak, he had elected to ride without sedation, determined to keep his mind clear in case of attack. Although, with barely enough strength to draw his sword, let alone wield it, he wasn't sure he'd be of any use.

'I can't feel them,' said The Unknown. 'But that doesn't mean they aren't there. If they are under instruction from Styliann, they won't be open to me. Don't forget, I'm not in the soul tank any longer and my ties are weak.' He reached out again, not with his mind but with what he felt to be the centre of his being, yearning for the time of warmth he had spent with his brothers. He still felt an emptiness inside him, though his return to The Raven and their unconditional acceptance of him had eased his transition. But he didn't think he would ever truly be free of the Protectors. He didn't think he wanted to be. And so, he would forever class himself as an outsider.

He could feel nothing in return. He anticipated the weight and warmth of the crowd around him, hearing him and believing in him as he believed in them. But so far, he was alone.

The Raven rode on, and an hour later, with dawn throwing a half-light across the Torn Wastes and their pace increased to a canter as they neared Parve, The Unknown felt it. A surge within him as his brothers mounted an attack. He could feel their togetherness, their combined strength and unswerving belief. He could feel their pleasure that he was there. He asked of them one small thing and they obliged. He turned to Hirad, his smile touching his eyes.

'They are here,' he said.

'Where?' asked the barbarian, automatically looking about him.

'South and east of the City. They have come to help.'

'Well, they need to get here fast,' said Ilkar from behind them. 'Look, dead ahead.'

The Raven reined in. The borders of the City were ringed with Wesmen. Not numerous, but enough.

'Any ideas?' asked Hirad.

But any answers were left unspoken as from the north, faint at first but gathering in volume, could be heard the sound of hoofs. Hundreds of them.

Baron Blackthorne stood on the top of a flat stone, Gresse beside him, and addressed his people. They had gathered at the head of Varhawk Crags, the Wesmen perhaps an hour's march behind them. He gazed out into the early dawn light and nodded at what he saw. Scared, tired and hungry men and women but with the desire to save their land still burning fiercely in their hearts.

'I'm not going to lie to you. What we are about to do could well see the death of us all, but I know that you are aware of the magnitude of the task we are performing. We have already set the Wesmen invasion back by two days. I want to make it a third before I die.

'I want to thank each and every one of you for the unfailing effort you have made on behalf of Gresse, myself and Balaia, and I would consider no one a coward if they were to leave now, because this next fight is one in which I will not sound a retreat because we have nowhere left to go. I am proud to have ridden and fought with you and, should we win this war, you will all know my generosity for the rest of your days.

'But I must say this. If we don't hold the Wesmen here for another few hours at least, they will flank Understone. With the pass soon to be under attack, and Julatsa on the brink of war, that flanking could destroy the core of our defences. And if they go, Balaia goes with them.

'For those of you who have heard of what The Raven are trying to do, then yes, every further minute we can give them to achieve their goal and destroy the Wytch Lords in Parve is one they will thank us for. I want them to have a country to return to. I want you all to have a place to live and bring up your families that is free of torment and terror. And if I can't do that, I will die in the trying.' He raised his hand to stop the cheering before it started.

'I know you may want to shout, but the enemy are not far behind and we need the element of surprise. That and a miracle. Remember the faces of those either side of you. One of them could be your saviour this morning just as you might be theirs. Look out for them and they will look out for you.

'You all know what you are being asked to do. You know the signals. All I ask you to do is fight hard, keep believing in Balaia and take as many of those bastards down with you as you can!

'To your positions, and be ready.'

Chapter 33

The Protectors surged into the Wesmen warriors at the edge of the rubble that marked the boundary of Parve, a weapon in each hand. Styliann kept a cordon of ten around him as he walked behind the line, both to protect him from flank attack and for shielding. But so far the Shamen had ignored him, focusing their energy on the Protectors who sought to batter their way through the ferocious but thin lines of Wesmen warriors.

The Lord of the Mount of Xetesk formed his mana shape with care as he arrived in range. Shamen cut three Protectors to pieces, eight of them concentrating black fire, slicing through shields and ripping into armour, flesh and mask. They died without a sound, the remaining closing ranks and fighting harder.

'HellFire,' snarled Styliann.

Eight columns of fire scorched from the clear sky, exploding on the casting Shamen, who, choosing to ignore the threat, were unshielded. The fire simply blew them apart, spattering burning flesh and clothing over the lines of warriors in front of them.

Next, Styliann cast a trio of FlameOrbs into the midst of the Wesmen, his honed, efficient use of mana maintaining his stamina level high. He was beginning to enjoy himself, watching Shamen and Wesmen alike burn and die. In front of him, the Protectors had formed a wedge as the Wesmen attempted to flank them, driving hard into the front of the line and forcing it back. To Styliann, the next move was obvious.

He moved up behind the wedge, the bludgeoning power of his Protectors halting the Wesmen advance. At a glance, they seemed to be no more than normal sword and axe men, but looking for more than a few seconds revealed so much more. There was a fluidity about each individual strike that allowed for no errors in an opponent's defence, but on top of that, the strikes chosen by each Protector exactly counterpointed those of the one either side. Never did they tangle axes, never was one blow blocked by another, and the steel rained down unremitting on the Wesmen.

As he watched, the back of his mind preparing the spell to break the line at the rear, Styliann saw so many Wesmen fall for the loss of so few Protectors. To the right, one died as his block of a sword thrust left his neck open to the following axe blade and his head was struck from his body, which collapsed showering blood over his comrades. In the centre, a Wesmen warrior was driven back by the point of a blade square in the sternum. The Protector dragged the blade clear, blocked a strike to his head with the flat of his axe without seeming to look and opened the throat of the next man before he could raise his sword.

They were breaking through, but not quickly enough. The Shamen, scattered by the violent deaths of eight of their number, had regrouped, and with two clearly shielding seven others had begun casting the black fire again, success limited by the close form of the Protectors.

The core mana shape formed, Styliann stopped moving and concentrated hard, his echelon of Protectors moving close, completely surrounding him. The battle faded in Styliann's ears as the edges of the shape formed, the slow rotation started, the colours, vibrant blue and orange, flashed across its surface and the final additions and adjustments were made. He fed in strength and concentration, opened his eyes and cast, knowing his Protectors would do exactly the right thing in response.

Piles of rubble around the Wesmen lines began shaking, dislodging loose stone to roll down to ground level. The vibrations passed into the ground, rippling the top soil under their feet, unbalancing many and scaring many more. Then they moved deeper, and the earth grumbled. The Protectors, knowing the spell, fought on.

When Styliann was satisfied the mana had reached the right depth, he completed the casting.

'Hammer,' he said, jerking his fists close into his chest.

There was a thud, deep and resounding. At its sound, the Protectors broke formation and scattered, leaving the Wesmen cleaving fresh air, confusion rife.

The ground beneath the Wesmen lines heaved on a square about twenty yards each side. The earth cracked and parted. Huge slabs of stone rocketed from beneath, sending Wesmen in all directions. A dozen and more slabs thrust upwards, carrying dust and earth with them which skittered on the surface and fell as they came to a stop, quivering, tasting the air for the first time. Wesmen and Shamen ran for the security of steady ground, shields and black fire lost as the target of Styliann's spell bucked and heaved, sending up gouts of trapped air.

And even before it had stopped and the Wesmen had time to understand the situation, Styliann and the Protectors were through the broken lines, hacking down unbalanced enemies. It was only a half-mile to the pyramid and, Styliann conceded to himself, time to lend The Raven a hand.

Darrick thundered across the Torn Wastes at the head of his cavalry. He had no idea what he would find. For all he knew, The Raven were already there, or two days behind, or dead. If it was either of the latter two, Balaia was finished. So his relief when one of his elf scouts riding beside him reported seeing The Raven to the south-east of them was great indeed. He signalled the change in direction and headed straight for them.

Hirad smiled broadly as Ilkar confirmed it was the four-College cavalry heading their way.

'Now that,' said Thraun, 'is what is known as a happy coincidence.'

'About time we had some luck,' said Hirad. 'And it's not that much of a coincidence. We all knew the target time to get here, he's just running a little late, that's all.'

The Raven hadn't moved on since seeing the Wesmen on the borders of Parve. Hirad had been ready to attempt the ride through their lines but the arrival of the cavalry gave them the luxury of a far better option. To the left, fire lit up the sky and a heavy explosion sounded. It was followed by two more flashes and a second dull detonation.

'Styliann's busy, I see,' said Ilkar.

'He's a brilliant mage,' said Denser.

'He's got a temper on him, I'll give him that.' Ilkar watched the afterglow of the HellFire and FlameOrbs fading against the light of the new day. 'I wouldn't like to be in the middle of all that.'

Darrick rode up, the cavalry reining to a halt behind him. He leapt from his horse to greet The Raven, clasping Hirad's shoulders as the barbarian slid from his horse, a smile splitting his face.

'This is where it ends,' the General said. 'The sight of you tells me we will be victorious. Thank the Gods you are alive.'

'What did you expect?' said Hirad, grasping the back of Darrick's neck with one hand and shaking the General's head, laughing. 'I knew you'd make it and I'm glad to see your confidence is unbowed, but we've still got to breach the perimeter.'

'What's your view, General?' asked The Unknown. 'Styliann and the Protectors are at the south-eastern border and fighting, as you can see. They'll be through to the square and the pyramid within half an hour.'

'How do you know that?' asked Darrick, frowning.

'Just trust him, he'll be right,' said Hirad.

'Very well. I need to punch a hole through the lines to let you through. That shouldn't be much of a problem. Once you're in, I'll take on any pursuers but you'll be largely on your own for the rest of the ride to the pyramid. Selyn reported it full of Acolytes when she saw it, so take care. I'll get to the square as quickly as possible, but I think I'm better used mopping up Wesmen. All right?'

'Just tell us where you want us.'

'Ride at the rear of the column. When it breaks, keep to the centre of the charge line. I don't expect you to wait if you see a gap.'

In response to Darrick's orders, the cavalry began moving off towards Parve at a gentle trot, four abreast, The Raven attached to its rear.

Darrick breathed in, feeling the cool air in his chest. This was the fight he really wanted. He signalled an increase in tempo and the three-hundred-strong cavalry accelerated to a canter. At a quarter of a mile he ordered the break. From the four-wide column, the cavalry formed a line three deep and a hundred wide, mages riding along behind the sword and spear men, shields deployed and, where possible, overlapping.

'Charge!' yelled Darrick, and the four-College cavalry sprang to the gallop, riding straight at the Wesmen lines. The two forces met head on, the first line of Wesmen going down hard under the hoofs of the cavalry horses, its spears and its blades. In the centre, Darrick half wheeled his mount, striking his enemy through the chest and ripping his blade clear as the man crashed to the ground. All around him, the clash of metal on metal, the neighing of horses, the calls and orders, the grunting and the shouting, the screaming and the crying. Behind the lines, the Shamen cast their black fire, tearing holes in his men and horses where the shields could not hold them. The Wytch Lord magic users would have to go, and quickly.

Beside him, a man was dragged from his horse by two Wesmen. Immediately, Darrick reared his horse, the animal's front hoofs catching one a fatal blow on the side of his head. The other turned in surprise, only to feel the cavalryman's sword in his back. Darrick swung his sword again, missing but forcing an enemy back far enough to allow his man the chance to remount. There was no time for thanks.

Behind the fight, The Raven looked for the weak point in the Wesmen lines. Hirad was fidgeting, knowing he'd rather be there in the thick of the mayhem, lending his blade to the mêlée. The Unknown spurred his horse and trotted right.

'This'll be it,' he said. 'Be ready.' He was indicating a point some twenty yards to the right of where Darrick was fighting. There, the Wesmen were falling back under the weight of assault and the Shamen had run for cover, their spells having foundered on the shields of the eastern Balaians.

As they watched, the cavalry surged forwards and Hirad could see daylight in front of them.

'Shield up,' said Ilkar.

'Raven!' called Hirad. 'Raven with me!'

At a single blast of a horn, the air above Varhawk Crags was filled with arrows and HotRain. Scything through unprotected and unwary Wesmen, steel-tip and fire caused awful damage and brought the march to a halt. Immediately, Wesmen broke ranks left and right and began climbing and scrambling after their attackers while below them, Shamen prepared shields and their nightmare magics.

A second blast of the horn. Blackthorne and Gresse charged around the northern edge of the crags and slammed into the front ranks of the Wesmen, carving a channel seven men deep before they were halted. With all the mages in the crags left and right casting attack spells, there was no shield on any man and the Shamen, if they couldn't be stopped, would kill whoever they liked.

Up in the crags, more fire was cast down upon the milling lines of Wesmen, caught in a steep-sided gully only thirty yards wide. After the first volley of arrows, the archers concentrated fire on the Shamen, picking off as many as they could before the shields went up. Others shot down the scrambling Wesmen.

At the head of the crags, the fighting was intense. The Wesmen had regrouped and pressed hard. Blackthorne, a wound in his leg, turned his horse and shouldered his way left and away, still slicing down at the enemy as he went. Gresse had been overtaken by younger men and horses, and for now was merely a spectator. He decided to press backwards and wait for his breath. Then the fire struck.

Left and right, white bolts arced into the walls of the crags while forwards, black lines of death leapt from Shamen fingertips, seeking bodies to rip and tear. Beside Gresse, a man's eyes exploded outwards as the black fire caught him square in the centre of the forehead. He went down thrashing and twitching. All around now, men and beasts were being slaughtered, but the Wesmen lines were backing off. Gresse changed his mind, dug his heels into the flanks of his horse, yelled men to his side and went after the Shamen.

Crags exploded, sending boulders, mages and archers tumbling. But while the western magic stopped, the Shamen had caused their own disaster as rock avalanched down, sweeping away men and crushing them against each other and the ground.

At the front of the lines, Blackthorne's men redoubled their efforts, hacking their way through Wesmen. Gresse and his men were almost on a knot of Shamen busy preparing new spells and not seeing the danger they were in. Gresse swatted one man aside with an overhead to the chest. Beside him, one was cut from his horse and died under a welter of blows. The old Baron spurred his horse, trampled the last man aside and rode for the Shamen. As he raised his sword to strike, they opened their eyes and their fingers crackled with black fire.

The Raven hit the streets of Parve and galloped for the square. Behind them, Darrick and his cavalry were grinding the Wesmen down but taking heavy casualties themselves.

Hirad and The Unknown headed the gallop with Denser right behind them. At the rear, Thraun kept station, with the rest in the middle. Down empty streets they raced, towards the beacon fires that crested the pyramid, breaking into the square from the north. It was full of Acolytes.

Ignoring the battles behind them, hundreds of red cloaks swayed and intoned, the hum of their voices loud in the sound bowl that was the centre of Parve. There had to be five hundred of them, sitting in ordered rows, the first of which was a good hundred yards distant of the tunnel entrance.

'Go! Go!' yelled Hirad as The Raven threatened to slow. He ploughed on around the side of the square, turning left for the pyramid as the first Acolyte sounded the note of warning. The humming stopped, to be replaced by shouts of anger. The Raven rode on, Hirad slipping from his horse by the tunnel entrance and sweeping his sword through the stomach of one of the guards that flanked it. The second made it no further than The Unknown's blade.

Behind them, the rest of The Raven dismounted, the horses cantering away with Denser's at their head. For a time, the crowd simply stood and watched the invasion of their temple, but as The Raven looked to disappear into the gloom, the Acolytes mobbed and ran at them. Like a wave rushing at the shore, the red tide surged towards them, yelling their fury, their numbers simply overwhelming, the intent clear in a thousand eyes.

'Great Gods in the sky,' breathed Hirad. 'What now?'

'You and Denser, get to the tomb. We'll hold them as long as we can and pray Darrick and Styliann arrive before they tear us limb from limb.'

'No, Unknown,' began Hirad, 'I'm not lea—'

'This is for Balaia now, Hirad. The one thing bigger than The Raven. Go!' He turned to face the Acolytes, Thraun one side of him, Jandyr and Will to the right. Erienne and Ilkar stood behind.

'You come back to me, Denser,' warned Erienne. They clasped hands briefly before the Dawnthief mage and his bodyguard sprinted away along the tunnel, The Unknown's orders in their ears and the sound of his sword point tapping on his stone echoing away before them into the torchlit gloom.

The black fire drilled into Gresse's horse just below the breast plate. The animal screamed and collapsed, an awful keening sound of pain not comprehended. Gresse was pitched hard to the floor, his head connecting with stone.

Behind him, Blackthorne, his wound stemmed with bright red cloth, saw the fall of his friend. Calling men to him, he drove back into the battle while all around him the black fire scorched through bodies and tore flesh and armour apart. The mêlée was confused now, with loose horses causing danger to everyone. The Wesmen lines were buckled and broken by boulder and sword alike but Blackthorne's men had no magic and the Shamen were slowly changing the odds. The Baron kicked on, promising himself that if he couldn't save Gresse, he'd complete the job the older man had started. The Shamen had to die.

Hirad and Denser ran along the tunnel. It was lit by braziers along the walls and carved in runes over the whole of its length. Behind him, the barbarian heard the sound of battle being joined by The Raven and he prayed he'd find them all alive again. The tunnel was two hundred yards long, and at the end of it, double doors stood closed. They were plain and heavy, with great brass handles either side at chest height.

As he approached, Hirad's limbs took on a heaviness he hadn't experienced since his fight with Isman in the Black Wings' castle. Evil weighed on his muscles, pawed at his heart and dragged at his courage, enticing him to turn and run. The power of the Wytch Lords ran from the walls, fuelled the braziers and seeped into the air he breathed. The barbarian felt as if some giant hand was pressed on his forehead, pushing him back. It was Denser who broke the spell, the sound of his breath in Hirad's ear as they reached the doors, the pulsating of his aura as he neared his ultimate goal blowing the evil aside.

Revitalised, Hirad pushed the left-hand door open and ran inside, Denser right behind him. They were in the pyramid; the architecture was different. Either side of a long flight of stone stairs, great slabs of mixed marble and stone rose into the gloom above their heads. The stairs were a good twenty feet wide and lit by pairs of torches resting in free-standing three-legged iron posts. The torch posts stood on every other of the forty steps. Two Guardians stood at the top, dressed in red cloaks and chain mail, each with a long curved blade – ceremonial but effective.

'Stay behind me, Denser.'

'I have no intention of doing otherwise.'

The Guardians moved to the top of the steps and stopped.

'You are too late. The Masters are awakening. Kneel or be destroyed.'

'Save your breath for your prayers,' snarled Hirad. He launched a vicious attack on the right-hand man, sweeping his blade low and leaning in to drag the point across his thighs. Expecting a higher strike, the Guardian dropped his sword too late and Hirad's blade bit deep, sweeping out just above the knee. As the leg collapsed, and the man with it, Hirad hurdled him and faced the other square on. He laughed.

'Want to try?' He didn't wait for a reply. Feinting a lunge, he side-stepped and swung double-handed at the Guardian's chest. The blow was blocked but the man stumbled back under its force. Overheaded, Hirad struck again and again, beating the Guardian's blade down until, face exposed, he caught the point of his jaw. The enemy dropped without a sound. He turned to see Denser pull his dagger from the first man's heart.

The stairs led up to a corridor of marble, perhaps thirty feet long.

Fires lit the way, let into the walls, their flickering glows illuminating the intricate mosaics depicting lines of people in red, bowing before six tall figures with light cradling their heads. Hirad ignored the picture, skating over its slippery surface with eyes locked on the single open door ahead. It was small, like the entrance to any house, but there was movement coming from within. He slid into the wall next to it and peered inside, his breath sweeping from his body as the shock hit him.

Six sarcophagi arranged as the spokes of a wheel, heads pointing inwards, dominated the large chamber. Each was well over nine feet long. And praying in the candlelit room were the Keepers. Twelve of them, two for each casket, heads bowed, speaking incantations in a language Hirad could not understand. Even from where he stood, Hirad could feel the chill inside the Chamber, like midwinter in the Blackthorne Mountains. The Keepers' breath clouded as they spoke and a dull thudding reverberated around the walls.

'Denser, we're here,' he hissed.

The Dark Mage came to his side. 'I'll need several minutes to cast.'

'Well, get on with it.'

Denser moved back a dozen paces, laid the catalysts on the marble in front of him, dropped his head and began to form the shape of the most powerful spell ever created.

The Shamen destroyed the barrier they had created and Tessaya's men stormed back into Understone Pass, running over, round and through the bodies of the defenders who had been trapped when the rocks came down.

Inside the pass, the devastation was startling. Men lay crushed beneath thousands of tons of stone, their catapults and heavy crossbows shattered and useless, defences beaten to splinters. For fifteen yards it was the same. The rockfalls must have claimed the lives of hundreds.

Darrick's generals had retreated with any survivors, their next best defensive position being Understone itself and the sturdier structures, the building of which Darrick had overseen before his ride into the Wesmen lands. Crossbow towers, catapult emplacements, spiked stockades and camouflaged archer positions. None of it would stand up to the magic of the Shamen, but this time the defenders would be far more numerous.

The men of the east had only held the pass for three days, and now tens of thousands of Wesmen were running through it. Pouring over its drying stone, the Wesmen boiled along the pass, a swarm threatening to devour the east, its cities and its people. A howling mass of triumphant warriors dreaming of the eastern sun on their faces and more eastern blood on their swords. And this time, with the Shaman magic backing their every move, there was no one in front of them with the power to stop them for long.

'Shield up,' said Ilkar as The Unknown continued to tap his blade on the stone of the tunnel, watching the Acolytes running towards them, red clothing flapping as they came. Some had weapons but not all, and those at the head of the chase gained hesitancy as they approached.

'We need a fast start,' said The Unknown. 'If we don't scare them quickly, they'll overwhelm us. Erienne, I need a hard shield in case they bring up archers.'

'I hear you.'

'Jandyr, fall back,' ordered The Unknown.

'I'm not moving.'

'Jandyr.'

'Save it, Unknown.'

The first Acolytes ran into the tunnel. The Unknown ceased his tapping and battle was joined. He moved forward a half-pace to give himself room to swing and shattered the chest of the first man at him. The Acolyte was flung right, cannoning into those next to him, dead before he hit the ground.

Ilkar watched the line. To The Unknown's left, Thraun snapped his blade up to deflect the strike of the man in front of him, moved and punched out his left hand with extraordinary speed. He caught the man in the mouth, rammed the hilt of his blade into his midriff, head-butted him, then plunged his blade into the Acolyte's gut. He roared and looked for his next man.

For Jandyr, though, the situation was more difficult. Despite his ability, having only one hand and a weakened body left him very wary. For now, he satisfied himself with defence, the sweat starting to form on his forehead. Will, his dual short swords whirling in front of him, laced cut after cut at the men in front of him, fielding blows and countering with speed and dexterity.

'Shield up,' said Erienne.

Across the corridor, Thraun was destroying his attackers, the speed of his fist and blade too much for the Acolytes, who lacked the experience and determination of The Raven.

After The Unknown had carved open the face of another, the Acolytes fell back in response to shouted commands. Guardians rushed to fill the breach, curved blades flashing in the sunlight then dulling as they reached the tunnel's shade.

'Let's go again, Raven,' shouted The Unknown. 'We can take them.'

An explosion sounded to the right of the square. Blue light flashed briefly. The Acolytes outside froze briefly in surprise and ran left. Styliann had arrived in the square.

Darrick roared his men on as he dashed the skull of a Shaman with his blade, the Shaman's magic shutting off as his lifeless body flopped to the floor. On seven fronts the Wesmen lines were breached and the surviving defenders were weakening.

'Close ranks!' he yelled. 'Pressure the right. We're moving for the square.' He urged his mount forwards, bludgeoning another Wesmen warrior as he picked up pace, his men tightening their grip behind him. With the Shamen threat almost removed, some of his mages turned their attention to the offence, and HardRain fell on the right-hand end of the Wesmen lines. It was too much for the defenders. All along the battle front Wesmen broke ranks and ran, some into the Wastes, others back into Parve.

'Cavalry, to me!' Darrick's shout was picked up by his lieutenants, and the four-College cavalry surged through the remnants of Wesmen resistance and raced for the pyramid, a detonation from the square ringing in their ears.

Styliann's second EarthHammer had torn great holes in Parve's central square and triggered the panic he wanted. The Protectors had fanned into a single skirmish line ninety men wide and were sweeping towards the pyramid, swords and axes rising, falling and slicing, thundering through the Acolytes, whose pitiful defences were ripped apart.

The Lord of the Mount wasn't finished, and his latest FlameOrb fell in the centre of the scattering, milling Acolytes, exploding and sending flame lashing in all directions. Men and women were destroyed, others catching tongues of mana fire, which scorched faces and lit up cloaks.

The Acolytes began to pour out of the western and northern sides of the square but changed direction again, herding and running back towards the pyramid. Styliann's frowns turned to smiles as he saw the first of the four-College cavalry galloping in. Parve was almost theirs.

*

The Keepers felt the beginnings of Denser's casting and surged to their feet, snatching daggers from belts.

'Infidel,' hissed one as Hirad barred their way, his frame large in the doorway. He beckoned them on while behind him Denser closed his eyes and entered another world.

So unlike the test shapes he had made, preparing Dawnthief with the catalysts in front of his kneeling body added a new dimension. Before, the shape had been two-dimensional, and grey in colour. Now, blood red, it modulated in the air, sending shivers through the mana flow around Denser's head. He fought to contain it, willing it to mould into the shape he needed.

But it was as if it had life of its own, and at every turn, more sides joined the complex polygon. He couldn't allow that. To cast with any more sides would be to cast with enough power to destroy everything to the east of the mountains, and deep within him burned the desire to get out alive.

Denser added the catalyst commands to the mix, and the mana shape pulsed with myriad colours. Finally, he had exerted control, but the measurements had to be so utterly precise. He had to be sure of strength, of direction, of distance. He dropped back into himself and checked every line, every colour and every pulse. And as he did so, Dawnthief fought to break free.

Hirad surveyed the slaughter in progress. While he was barring the door, only one at a time could come at him with any freedom, and he just cut them down as they did so. Six-inch daggers could never hope to beat a long sword, and because they would not stop coming, he did not stop killing them. Once six were down, his biggest problem lay in not slipping on the blood-slick floor.

Hirad clambered over the bodies to take the last two. Never uttering a word, he swatted them down and then looked in disgust at what he had done. They might as well have been unarmed, so futile was their defence, and he felt sick to his stomach. Never mind that they had been Acolytes of the Wytch Lords, it was the ease with which he had turned off and massacred them that was the cause of his nausea.

He'd put up his sword and turned to leave the room when he heard the grating of stone on stone. His blood chilled, the temperature of the room dived again and his body began to shake. He forced himself to turn, gorge rising, fighting the urge to scream. One of the sarcophagus lids had moved. Just a little. But it had moved. He backed away. It moved again. He stepped on a body and fell sliding in the gore, slipping forwards and coming to rest right underneath one of the stone caskets. Its lid moved. Then they all did, grating together and sending tremors through Hirad's body that left him heaving for air.

He scrabbled backwards, trying to get his feet under him, but the floor was so wet. He dragged himself to his haunches, turned and pulled bodies out of his way, the only thought in his mind that he had to close the door. He didn't know why, he just had to. The first clang drew a cry from his lips and he felt his heart lurch. The pain in his chest was brief and intense.

'Oh, Gods,' he breathed. 'Come on, Denser. Come on, Denser.' But through the door he could see the Dark Mage still preparing. He dared not look behind him. Another clang. And another. He hauled the last body from the doorway, leapt outside, grabbed the handle and slammed it shut. His eyes caught the scene in the chamber. Long-fingered bone hands were clutching the sides of the caskets, white digits clacking on the stone as they sought for purchase.

Nausea swept through his body. The evil of centuries flooded the chamber, forcing the air from his lungs and the strength from his legs, which sagged beneath him as he clutched and pushed at the door handle, trying desperately to believe that he had been mistaken in what he had seen. But he knew he wasn't. He had seen the end of Balaia rising from the grave, the animation of a horror so black it defied reason and struck at the very core of sanity. A power great enough to cast down mountains, tear holes in the sky and make rivers of blood from the bodies of the peoples of the east.

Hirad gasped, his fingers losing sensation as he struggled to maintain a consciousness that seeped from him with every laboured heartbeat. He held the door against Balaia's greatest enemy, a pitiful wretch trying to stop night from falling.

The Wytch Lords were awake.

The Guardians were skilled and fierce, driven by fury at the desecration of their masters' tomb. In The Raven line, The Unknown and Thraun defended and killed with power and pace. But at the right-hand end, the going was less sure. Jandyr was struggling in front of a clever swordsman who had immediately recognised his opponent's problem and hacked overhead, driving the elf's blade close to his face. Will, although defending stoutly enough, was making little headway, breaking through the guard of his enemy just the once to mark his cheek with a long, ugly cut.

Erienne watched on, maintaining the hard shield but beginning to feel it was pointless. Ilkar was no doubt thinking much the same. As she watched, Jandyr's arm buckled under another heavy blow, and before he could recover, the Guardian had skewered his heart, the elf crying out as he fell.

'No!' The Unknown surged as he heard Jandyr die, crashing his blade through a Guardian's skull and reversing his swing to smash another's hip. A beat later, Darrick ran in at the head of a centile of cavalry and mages. Caught between twin meshes of flashing steel, the remaining Guardians were quickly slaughtered. Darrick nodded at The Unknown, taking in the lifeless body of Jandyr as Will crouched over the elf.

'Damn it,' said the General. He turned to a lieutenant. 'You. I want guard on this tunnel, I want cavalry sweeping the City and I want this square clear of enemies. Do it now.' He swung back to The Unknown. 'Where's Hirad?'

'In the pyramid with Denser.' The Unknown was breathing hard.

'Get after them. I'll hold things here. Styliann's outside, there should be no danger.'

The Unknown nodded his thanks.

'Raven! Raven with me!'

Styliann surveyed the square with great satisfaction. Acolyte bodies covered it, their blood and cloaks making a carpet of red. Here and there, pockets of Wesmen attacked the cavalry and his Protectors, but their resistance was broken. He sighed. As they took Parve by surprise, making a mockery of the wholly insufficient defence, so the weight of the Wesmen armies were surely marching in the east, driving all before them.

He rode towards the entrance to the tunnel and dismounted, leaning against its right-hand pillar, suddenly tired. The last battle was taking place inside, but he found he had no desire to join it.

His mana stamina was low, his desire for vengeance appeased. He could wait for Dawnthief to walk back out and straight into his possession. He sat and rested his head in his hands, a wind ruffling his hair.

Hirad's knuckles whitened on the handle, the sounds from within the room dragging whimpers from his body and sweat from his pores. He felt cold. Hot. So very hot. Cold. His muscles felt they were about to seize and his legs shook so much their juddering unsteadied him. His eyes swam, his head fogged. And then he felt pressure on the handle from the other side. Gentle at first, but quickly more urgent.

'Denser, please.' His whispers choked in his throat. His hands tightened on the door handle. It turned underneath them, just slightly. Fists thudded against the door, jarring his body as he leant all his weight against it. A heavy blow and the door all but opened. From behind, the sounds of exultation, of rising, of power. Hirad felt the breath stick in his lungs.

'Denser!' he screamed. 'Now!' Behind him, Denser moaned and chanted, his short breathing jabbing anxiety into Hirad's mind. He wasn't sure but the Xeteskian sounded as if he was struggling badly. And the spell remained uncast.

The second blow shattered the door timbers. Hirad was thrown skittering across the marble, wrist aflame with agony.

'Denser!' The silhouette of a Wytch Lord stood in the doorway, tattered burial robe hanging, flesh creeping over exposed bones. Hirad saw eyeless sockets in a wedge-shaped head as the towering figure stooped under the lintel. It breathed.

'Heretic.' Its voice like a body dragged over gravel.

As Hirad watched, the flesh began to form and grow on its body. Slowly at first, then with greater and greater pace, enveloping its hands, rushing up its legs and stretching over its ribs, covering the organs which grew and writhed and beat from nothing.

The Wytch Lord, tall and terrible, looked down on him as its body re-formed, empty sockets alive with new life, eyes sucking into being, dark, cold and murderous. Other figures crowded behind it. It took a pace forward, the rags of its clothing growing into robes of pure white, ruffling in the breeze of their creation, its bare feet gaining bulk and muscle, toes straightening.

Hirad glanced at Denser. The Dark Mage, sweat beading and running from his forehead, fought with the spell. His arms, now stretched in front of him, juddered wildly; his voice, low and hoarse, gabbled words the barbarian would never understand.

'Hurry, Denser,' said Hirad, drawing his sword. 'Hurry.' He moved to the ready. The Wytch Lords stood in the doorway to the burial chamber, looming over him, each one well in excess of eight feet in height.

'Come on then,' he said. 'See if you can take me.' He raised his sword and prepared to move. So did the Wytch Lords, the first stepping into the antechamber, its brothers moving to either side. Hirad licked his lips. He was about to die but it wouldn't be alone. Because behind him he heard the pacing of feet and the tapping of steel on stone, rhythmic, echoing, beautiful. A euphoric sensation ran up his spine, the blood surged in his veins and new belief flooded his mind. It was all he needed to give Denser the time to complete Dawnthief.

'Raven!' he called. 'Raven to me!'

Detached though he was from the danger surrounding him, Denser was dimly aware of the clamour of voices, of running footsteps and the urgency in Hirad's every utterance. Dawnthief's mana shape was as rich as it was difficult to control and deep within his subconscious, Denser thanked the Master for not leaving out any detail or nuance from his long years of teaching.

Never before had a spell fought to control him, use him to develop its potential and drain him as it sought more power. It wasn't that the spell was sentient but that the shape his words, gestures, and thoughts generated only really had one end: total consummation of the caster and, with him, Balaia.

Only now did he realise the true nature of Septern's most awful research. And the truth was that now the basic shape was created, he could simply surrender to a chain reaction that would lead to the destruction of everything. The stealing of light. The theft of dawn.

And so he fought its every effort, cut out every flare of the complex shape, halted every counter-axial spin, every attempt to stop motion and every pull on his rigidly controlled mana reserve. Still it drained him and he was not ready to cast. In front of him, mana joined the catalysts, burning in a triangle that lifted them from the ground and fused them into the core of the spell. The power increased, tempting and probing.

Yet the focus wasn't there, the power too randomised. To cast now would take The Raven into oblivion along with the Wytch Lords. And though sense told him that was a price that should be paid, he was not prepared to give up. He wanted a channel for Dawnthief's energy, and in theory he could make one. But with the sounds of fighting filtering into his mind, he was aware he had little time left in which to put his theory into practice.

Hirad's sword clattered into the undefended side of the Wytch Lord, Arumun. He knew its name, and those of the other five, because the clarion call of fear they had launched at his mind was empowered by the use of the six terrifying identifiers. When Denser had spoken the names, that was all they had seemed. Now, confronting the ancient evil, those names lodged deep in his gut and threatened to take the strength from his limbs.

Arumun howled and fell back, wound gaping, dark fluid oozing. Hirad's shout of triumph cut off abruptly. The wound healed in moments and Arumun straightened and was pushed upright by those behind him, shaking his head.

'Gods,' breathed Hirad. The Wytch Lord stepped forward and whipped out its hand with a speed that almost beat Hirad's guard. He staggered under its weight.

'We can't fight them,' he said.

'Yes we can,' said The Unknown. 'All we have to do is keep them back.' He swung his blade through waist high, connecting with flesh and splintering bone. Belphamun collapsed to the floor. 'They're still weak. Let's keep them that way.'

'Shield up,' said Ilkar.

Hirad half froze and looked behind the three Wytch Lords who confronted them. The other three, Ystormun, Pamun and Weyamun, were casting.

'Let's take it to them, Raven!' Standing half a pace behind and to the right of The Unknown Warrior, Hirad blocked another sweep of the hand from Arumun and buried his blade in the Wytch Lord's chest. The wound was healing before he dragged his sword clear. He glanced along the line.

Belphamun had risen quickly, The Unknown ducked a haymaking punch and chopped at its legs, cracking bone, causing it to stumble. Seizing his chance, he reversed his guard into its face and slashed halfway through its neck. This time, the fall was heavier, the cry of pain more hideous.

'Shield up. Denser is covered,' said Erienne.

Giriamun swatted at Will, catching the frightened man on the top of his shoulder. He shouted briefly and crumpled. Thraun bellowed anger and hacked at the flailing arm, shattering the elbow. Giriamun simply came back with the other, fist connecting sharply with the top of Thraun's skull. The young warrior spun and fell senseless.

'Damn it,' rasped The Unknown.

'Come on, Denser,' whispered Hirad.

The Wytch Lords' spells came sudden and violent, pulses of raw light, dark and malevolent, punching into the shields around Denser and the fighting Raven, flaring over their surfaces, fizzing and cracking. They held just long enough. Belphamun rose, his eyes clear evil.

'Shield down,' said Ilkar, gasping for breath.

The Unknown and Hirad locked gazes for a heartbeat, the barbarian tired to the base of his being, muscles crying for respite, lungs heaving, heart slamming. He didn't know how much more he had in him.

'Do it,' he said.

The Unknown launched a crazed attack, first dropping to his haunches to hack at Belphamun's legs, next springing up to chop at the exposed neck, the Wytch Lord following his movements too slowly. To his right, Hirad switched grip, slicing up and left and catching Arumun in the lower jaw, snapping its head back and forcing it off balance. He followed with a reverse sweep which crashed into the following Lord's face. But the blow from Weyamun came from nowhere.

Belphamun fell but Ystormun and Pamun closed on The Unknown. He swivelled and raised a guard, but as Hirad pitched to the mosaic, he saw the blows fall on the big man. And though he stayed on his feet, it wasn't enough. The Wytch Lords would cast again.

Hirad scrabbled for his sword and started to get up, pain from his shoulder spiking every movement, his vision clouded, aware he couldn't leave The Unknown to fight them alone. He half rose but Weyamun punched him down again. The Unknown fell next to him, blood running from his face.

'Get up, Unknown.'

'I'm here.'

The two friends sought purchase on each other, pain blossoming where the fall of Wytch Lord fists had bruised muscle and bone. Hirad's body protested, exhaustion threatening to defeat the drive to stand, legs shaking, feet aching, sword arm on fire. From behind them, Ilkar launched FlameOrbs which struck the centre of the Lords, spilling fire and light, incinerating robes and charring new flesh, which sprouted again and again through the flame. They didn't pause to damp it down.

Hirad looked up. Six faces wreathed in smoke and firelight loomed over him. Triumphant, exultant, victorious.

'We live,' breathed Arumun.

'Dawnthief.'

The word shattered the moment's pause.

'Down! Down!' yelled Ilkar. Hirad reflexively attempted to rise but The Unknown took his legs from under him and he fell back.

'NO!' yelled Arumun, the roar joined by his brothers.

A column of pure dark coursed above his head, wide enough to encapsulate the Wytch Lords crowded in the space outside their burial chamber. It seared into them, punching them from their feet and blasting them into walls, tearing limbs from bodies and ripping flesh from bones which cracked under the extraordinary force. With high-pitched screams and squeals, Belphamun, Arumun and Giriamun were flung back into Pamun, Ystormun and Weyamun, the sextet hammered against the far wall of the burial chamber to hang like huge rag dolls, limbs flailing, heads rolling, eyes ablaze.

A howl like wind driven through a gully grew in volume, hurting ears and setting teeth on edge. Above Hirad, the column of Dawnthief, black, sleek and pure night, whipped his hair across his face. With an effort, he rolled aside, taking a glance at Denser.

The Dark Mage was on his knees, straight-backed, arms outstretched, Dawnthief emanating from the space between his hands. His whole body juddered violently, his arms vibrating, face taut and quivering, mouth wide, hair flying. His eyes were wide open but saw only the dark in front of him. And he was enclosed in a darkening mist which obscured him more with every passing moment. The mist roiled and swirled, feeding into the Dawnthief tract, adding to its energy. Erienne stood at his shoulder, not daring to touch him, the terror on her face matched by the awe in her eyes.

'Move!' shouted The Unknown. 'The black is widening.'

Hirad could barely hear him but caught the import of his gesture and yielded to the tug on his sleeve. The two men scrambled clear and turned to watch the destruction of the Wytch Lords, and it was then that Hirad saw the prone forms of Thraun and Will. Both men were stirring.

'Stay down!' roared Hirad, flapping his arms in front of him. 'Down!' But they couldn't hear him above the howl of the spell and the screams of the Wytch Lords who beat at their torment with splintered fists. Thraun picked his head from the floor and shook it, groggily unaware of the death scant inches away.

'Oh, hell,' muttered Hirad. He ran forward and dived under the widening diameter of Dawnthief.

Denser's body was consumed with beautiful power. He could feel it driving through his veins, swelling his muscles and sparking his sinews and tendons, forcing the breath from his lungs. But he had no need of breath. Dawnthief sustained him.

In front of him, the Wytch Lords suffered under the tumult of his casting and he laughed at their pitiful attempts to break its bonds.

Trapped like rodents under a monstrous thumb, they struggled, but Dawnthief held them as it always would, driving through their tattered bodies and beating the life out of their new flesh and bones.

And Denser hadn't played the endgame yet. Hadn't chosen where he would send the enemy. Hadn't decided whether or not to let Dawnthief end the world. It would be so easy. In front of him, his arms barely contained the forces of Septern's spell as it fought to free itself from his control. All he had to do was let his arms open and circle and the blackness would encompass them all.

Dawnthief battled him to do just that, but deep inside the recesses of his mind, something stood firm. The knowledge that at last he had found a true place to exist beyond the grasp of Xetesk. A place where he had true respect, was loved and looked after. One where he was free to choose his own destiny. The Raven.

It was time to open the gate to oblivion. To tear the dimensions aside and deposit the diminishing remnants of the Wytch Lords to be consumed in the vortex beyond. But he wanted it to be spectacular, to leave no one in any doubt that the Wytch Lords had been destroyed. He needed to make their last journey through Balaian space as public as it could be in this forsaken city. He smiled and canted his head upwards. He knew just the place.

The roaring of Dawnthief and the wind of living mana howled in Hirad's ears. He lay half on and half off Thraun, pushing the shapechanger's head to the ground. Still dazed by the fist of a Wytch Lord, Thraun struggled against survival, threatening to buck Hirad into the black until Will, seeing the danger as he came to, placed a hand on Thraun's face and calmed him with a long, probing look.

Hirad stared back at Denser, who was wincing as Dawnthief dragged at his body, ripples of tension flowing across his face, the mist building and deepening around him. Abruptly, Denser's expression changed, relaxed and cleared. The Dark Mage smiled, mouthed a further incantation and began moving his arms slowly inwards and upwards.

The Dawnthief column retracted, dragging the Wytch Lords with it. Their struggles were weak now, their bodies tangled in an awful parody of humanoid form, heads twisted on necks, legs and arms at impossible angles to bodies, backs broken. Only the light in their eyes remained to remind Hirad of the souls within.

A mist like that enveloping Denser swam from the end of the column, causing fitful resistance as it netted the Wytch Lords, reducing their spasmodic jerkings to a syrup-like slowness. It hemmed them in, trussing their bodies in a globe of flowing night. In a few moments, they were lost to sight but for a feeble probing at the opaque mesh that imprisoned them. Their howls, now of anguish and fear, were louder than Dawnthief itself.

Denser drew the column and its cargo towards him, angling it upwards until he stood directly beneath it and under the apex of the pyramid. The net shivered, and then, with a sharp jab upwards, Denser released the column, which screamed towards the apex, driving the opaque orb directly at the stone above.

'Gods in the ground,' breathed Hirad. 'Run! Run!' He began to sprint from beneath the apex, The Unknown right behind him, Thraun and Will close by. But neither Ilkar nor Erienne moved. Before Hirad could open his mouth to shift them, Dawnthief obliterated the cap of the Wytch Lords' tomb.

Great slabs of stone blasted skywards carrying with them the dust of ages, material accompaniment to the howl of Dawnthief tearing through the sky. Light shone through the gaping rent in the tomb, pooling around Denser, his arms pointing to the heavens, his eyes wide, a maniacal smile on his face.

But while Dawnthief and its cargo tore through the fabric of the Balaian dimension and into the interdimensional space beyond, the stone did not. Spiralling back to the ground, huge chunks thumped into the pyramid. The ragged edges of the hole Denser had created, already weak, collapsed inwards, showering down on The Raven.

Hirad could see the end and knew he could do nothing. The Dawnthief column shut off, and Denser, still gazing into the light, pirouetted slowly and collapsed. Hirad turned away, unable to watch the rock hit home.

"HardShield up,' said Ilkar and Erienne together. 'Nobody move.'

For Denser, it was the completion of a life's dream. The casting of Dawnthief and all its multi-layered complexities had been every bit as thrilling as he'd dared hope. At one with mana, truly a part of its random life, he had struggled with temptation, overcome energies the power of which he could not have conceived, and triumphed. But more, he'd opened a gate to oblivion and deposited the broken bodies of the Wytch Lords there, souls destroyed by the hunger of Septern's spell as he'd withdrawn from its influence. And now he had nothing left to give. The residue of Dawnthief clung to his mind and encased his body, caressing him, offering him peace, promising him rest. What more could Balaia's saviour desire? Was it not what he truly craved? Denser closed his eyes and gave himself up to its glories.

Mosaic splintered and crumbled under the weight of stone crashing down from above. Shards of rock flew and ricocheted. Hirad flung himself to the ground, covering his head, only to roll over and sit up immediately. The HardShields covering them all repulsed chip and boulder alike. He looked on as a slab fully five feet long and two thick tumbled end over end through the air, impacting the shield directly above the unmoving body of Denser. It slid over the invisible surface to the mosaic with a heavy thud. Elsewhere, stones the size of fists and skulls rained down, the noise of multiple collision drumming hard on the ears and rattling the floor underfoot. And all was washed by a dust-filled light, shining through the blasted pyramid apex.

The tumbling of rock and the cracking of tile and slab subsided. Hirad climbed wearily to his feet, frowning as he caught sight of Erienne's face. The Dordovan had tears streaming down her face, her body quivering, clearly struggling to maintain control of her spell as she stood a few paces from Denser, her eyes fixed on the Dark Mage. The fall stopped, a quiet ringing replacing the boom and thump.

'It's over,' said Hirad.

Across the battle, the mood changed. From a hundred fingers, the black fire shut off abruptly, magical shields dropped and the Shamen's faces of victory turned to uncertainty and then fear.

Blackthorne saw it happen. Knew the change in the air meant The Raven had won, and yelled his delight. His men surged, the Baron himself galloping through leaderless Wesmen lines to his fallen friend. He slid from his horse, slashed his blade across the neck of an attacker and knelt down. Gresse, blood covering his head, was still breathing. Blackthorne called a man over and the two of them carried the unconscious Baron from the battlefield, the cries of the east ringing loud in their ears.

Behind them, the Wesmen were broken. Without the Wytch Lord magic, the Shamen were helpless, and without the Shamen, the warriors had no focus. Individually ferocious they might be, but the tide had turned and Blackthorne's men were alive once more.

Blackthorne opened his mouth and roared in jubilation. Today was going to be wonderful.

*

'Shield down,' whispered Ilkar into the silence.

'Shield down.' Erienne's voice broke and she ran to Denser, dropping to her knees and picking up his head to cradle it, burying her face in his shoulder, rocking back and forth, crying and murmuring soft words.

'What is it?' Hirad started forwards.

Erienne's tear-stained face turned to him. 'He's dead,' she wailed. 'He's not breathing.'

'No.' Hirad slid down beside her. 'Ilkar, come on, do something.'

'There's not a spell for everything, Hirad,' said Ilkar racing to join them. 'He has no wounds. There's nothing to heal.'

Hirad gazed up and down Denser's body. There was not a mark on him, though his lips were blue.

'Right. Lay him down, Erienne. Unknown, get over here and angle his head. Clear his throat.'

'Got it.'

Hirad focused on Denser's face. 'Don't even think about it, Denser,' he said, and started thumping the mage's chest above his heart with the base of his fists. 'Don't you dare die. Come on.'

Erienne stroked Denser's hair. 'Please, Denser,' she sobbed. 'I have your child within me. Don't leave me alone.'

Hirad paused. 'You've got what? Gods in the sky.' He pushed harder. 'Did you hear that, Denser? You've got responsibility now, damn you. Breathe! Breathe!' Hirad slapped his face to either side, hard. The Unknown massaged his neck and worked his jaw.

'Breathe!'

Denser's mouth opened, his lungs seized air, his body heaved and he sat bolt upright knocking Hirad aside. His hands clutched his chest and his throat gulped air. Erienne burst into fresh tears. Denser turned to her but fell back, and she cushioned his head from the fall. She ruffled his hair.

'I thought you'd died, you bastard. I thought you'd died,' she said, a tear falling on to his cheek.

Denser smiled and shook his head. 'I tried my best though,' he said. 'My chest hurts.'

'Well, we had to do something,' said Hirad.

'It feels like you shook hands with my heart.'

'No, no. Just persuaded it to beat.'

'Thank you.'

Hirad shrugged. 'You're Raven. I can't let you die when you've just destroyed the Wytch Lords. No glory in that.' He followed Denser's gaze up through the dust-clouded air into Balaia's mainly blue sky. A rolling grey-flecked brown patch hung there.

'Oh dear,' said Denser. 'I'm not sure that was supposed to happen.'

Hirad looked a little longer at the new rip before settling his gaze on Denser.

'We'll live with it,' he said. He stood up and brushed dust off his tunic and leggings. The rip ate at the sky. 'How're you feeling?'

'Tired. And sore.'

'Well, this is a place of rest,' said Ilkar, not able to take his eyes from the rip for too long.

'It'll do for now.' Denser closed his eyes. 'Wake me in a few days.'

'Could you give us a little space?' asked Erienne, her hand again idly stroking Denser's hair.

'Of course,' replied The Unknown. 'Gentlemen . . .' He sheathed his sword, slung it across his back and made a shovelling motion with his hands.

'What's up, Ilkar?' asked Hirad, coming to the elf's shoulder.

'That,' said Ilkar, pointing at the rip. 'I wonder where it leads. Somewhere harmless, I hope.' He clacked his tongue and sighed. 'What have we done, eh?'

Hirad put an arm round his shoulder and squeezed him.

'We won. Come on, you'll be able to see it better from outside,' he said. He turned Ilkar from the rip to face The Unknown, Will and Thraun. 'We won.'

'At least we can collect on the contract,' said Ilkar.

'I thought you wouldn't touch Xetesk's filthy money,' said Denser from his prone position.

Ilkar laughed. 'It doesn't do to be too proud where money's concerned,' he replied.

'Spoken like a true mercenary,' said Hirad. Erienne cleared her throat noisily. 'Sorry, Erienne.' He indicated the way to the sunlight.

'Raven,' he said quietly, crooking his finger. 'Raven with me.'